D0482118

Mrs. Darcy
and the
Blue-Eyed Stranger

Mrs. Darcy

and the

Blue-Eyed Stranger

New and Selected Stories

LEE SMITH

A Shannon Ravenel Book

ALGONQUIN BOOKS OF CHAPEL HILL   2010

ℝ

A SHANNON RAVENEL BOOK

Published by
ALGONQUIN BOOKS OF CHAPEL HILL
Post Office Box 2225, Chapel Hill, North Carolina 27515-2225

a division of
WORKMAN PUBLISHING
225 Varick Street, New York, New York 10014

Grateful acknowledgment is made to the magazines where these stories were first published: to *American Way* for an early version of "Folk Art" (originally titled "Art Is My Life"); to *Appalachian Heritage* for the opening section of "Big Girl"; to *The Atlantic Monthly* for "Happy Memories Club"; to *Blackbird* for "Fried Chicken"; to *Carolina Quarterly* for "Mrs. Darcy and the Blue-Eyed Stranger" (originally titled "Mrs. Darcy Meets the Blue-Eyed Stranger at the Beach") and "Between the Lines"; to Mud Puppy Press for "Bob, a Dog"; to *Oxford American* for "The Southern Cross" (originally titled "Native Daughter"); to *Narrative* for "Toastmaster"; to *Shenandoah* for "House Tour"; to *The Southern Review* for "Ultima Thule"; and to *Special Report: Fiction 1991* for "Intensive Care."

Grateful acknowledgment is made to G.P. Putnam's Sons for permission to reprint the stories "Mrs. Darcy and the Blue-Eyed Stranger" (originally published as "Mrs. Darcy Meets the Blue-Eyed Stranger at the Beach") and "Between the Lines," from *Cakewalk,* © 1970 by Lee Smith; "Bob, a Dog," "Intensive Care," and "Tongues of Fire," from *Me and My Baby View the Eclipse,* © 1990 by Lee Smith; "The Happy Memories Club" and "Southern Cross," from *News of the Spirit,* © 1997 by Lee Smith. Reprinted by permission of Penguin Group (USA) Inc.

The red-hat ladies of "House Tour" are inspired by Jenny Joseph's poem "Warning" ("When I Am an Old Woman I Shall Wear Purple").

"Heartbreak Hotel," © 1956 Sony/ATV Songs LLC. All rights administered by Sony/ATV Music Publishing, 8 Music Square West, Nashville, TN 37203.

LIBRARY OF CONGRESS CATALOGING-IN-PUBLICATION DATA
   Smith, Lee, 1944–
   Mrs. Darcy and the blue-eyed stranger : new and selected stories /
by Lee Smith. — 1st ed.
      p. cm.
   ISBN 978-1-56512-915-3
   I. Title.
   PS3569.M5376M77 2010
   813'.54 — dc22   2009027915

10 9 8 7 6 5 4 3 2 1
First Edition

For Hal, my dear companion

CONTENTS

The events in our lives happen in a sequence in time, but in their significance to ourselves they find their own order, a timetable not necessarily — perhaps not possibly — chronological. The time as we know it subjectively is often the chronology that stories and novels follow: it is the continuous thread of revelation.

—EUDORA WELTY

Mrs. Darcy
and the
Blue-Eyed Stranger

Bob, a Dog

It was early May, two days after his thirty-ninth birthday, when David left her forever. "Forever"—that's what he said. He stood in the downstairs hallway turning an old brown hat around and around in his hands. Cheryl had never seen the hat before. She stood on the stairs above him, coming down, carrying towels. David said he needed a different life. Behind him, the door was wide open. It was sunny and windy outside. She had made him a carrot cake for his birthday, she was thinking—now what would she do with the rest? Nobody liked carrot cake except David and Angela, who was dieting. Angela was always dieting. David continued to talk in his calm, clipped way, but it was hard to hear what he said. He sounded like background noise, like somebody on the TV that Cheryl's mother kept going all the time in the TV room now since she had retired from her job at the liquor store. David wore cutoff jeans and an old plaid shirt he'd had ever since she'd met him, nearly twenty years before. She must have washed that shirt a hundred times. Two hundred times. His knees were thin and square. He was losing his hair. At his back, the yard was a blaze of sun.

Cheryl could remember the first time she ever saw him like it was yesterday, David standing so stiff and straight in the next-to-back pew of the Methodist church, wearing a navy blue suit, and everybody whispering about him and wondering who he was, him so prim and neat it never occurred to any of them he might be from the Peace Corps, which he was. He didn't look like a northern hippie at all. He was real neat. Cheryl and her sister Lisa and her brother Tom were sitting right behind him, and after a while of looking at the careful part in his hair and his shoulder blades like wings beneath his navy suit, Cheryl leaned forward and gave him her program so he would know what was going on. He acted like somebody who had never been in a church before, which turned out to be almost true, while Cheryl's own family was there of course every time they cracked the door.

But oh, it seemed like yesterday! He was dignified. And he sat so straight. He might have been a statue in a navy blue suit, a figurine like all those in Mamaw's collection. Cheryl had sucked in her breath and bitten her lip and thought, before she fell head over heels in love right then, that she ought to be careful. Because she had always been the kind of big, bouncy girl who jumps right in and breaks things without ever meaning to, a generous, sweet, well-meaning girl who was the apple of everybody's eye.

Cheryl handed him the program, and touched his hand too long. After the recessional she took him into the fellowship hall for a cup of Kool-Aid and wrote her telephone number down on a paper napkin before he even asked for it. "He's just my type," she said to her mother, Netta, later. "Ha!" Netta said. Netta thought he looked nervous. But Cheryl liked that about him, because everybody else she knew was exactly like their parents were, exactly like everyone else. David was older, a college graduate. Cheryl, who had finished high school two years before, was working then at Fabric World. She thought David was like a young man in a book, or a movie. Whatever he said seemed important, as if it had been written down and he was reading it aloud.

Later, when she got to know him, she'd go to the room that he rented over Mrs. Bailey's garage and lie with him on the mattress on the floor, where he slept — the mattress pulled over to the window where you could look right out on Thompson's Esso and the back road and the river winding by — and sometimes afterward she'd open her eyes to find him looking out this window, over the river, and she couldn't tell what he was thinking. She never knew what he thought. Then, Cheryl found this romantic.

But probably she should have gotten herself a big old man who could stand up to things, not that she didn't have offers. Look at Jerry Jarvis, who had always loved her, or Kenny Purdue, who she was dating at the time. When she told Kenny she didn't want to go out with him anymore because she was in love with David Stone from Baltimore, Maryland, Kenny went out and cried and rolled in the snow. That's what his mother told Netta on the telephone: she said Kenny rolled in the snow. But David Stone had a kind of reserve about him, a sort of hollow in him, which just drove Cheryl wild. It was like she was always trying to make up to him for something, to make something be okay, or go away, but she never knew what it was.

David came from a small, quiet family, one sister and a shy divorced mother with her hair in a little gray bun on the top of her head, and a father who was not mentioned. At the time she met David, Cheryl didn't know anybody who was divorced. Now everybody was. Including her, it looked like. With David leaving forever, Cheryl would be divorced too. Should she put up her hair in a bun? Cheryl would be a divorcée. Like her sister Lisa, like her best friend, Marie, like everyone on television.

This seemed totally crazy with all the towels she held in her arms, with how fresh and sweet they smelled. With the bedrooms upstairs behind her so full of all the children, of their shared life. Now Netta would say, "I told you so." She'd swear up and down that she wasn't a bit surprised. And even Cheryl knew — had known when she married him — that David wasn't exactly a family man. She'd had four children knowing it, thinking that he would change. Because she loved him, and love conquers all. You can't decide who you're going to love.

And even though David didn't really believe in God and made fun of their cousin, Purcell, an evangelist, and taught at the community college all these years instead of getting a real job, and refused to help Louis make a car out of wood that time for the Pinewood Derby in Cub Scouts, even so, there were other things — good things — as well. He liked to cook, he read books to her out loud, he'd been the one who got up with the babies in the night. It was weird to find these traits in a man, although they were more common now since women's lib than they had been when David and Cheryl got married, all those years ago.

Cheryl looked down the stairs at David, memorizing him.

"Please don't blame yourself," he said formally. "I feel terrible about doing this."

"Oh, that's okay," Cheryl said without thinking, because she had gone for so long pleasing men.

David started to say something else, and didn't. He turned sharp on his heel like a soldier and plunged out into the shiny day, right through Louis and his friends playing catch in the yard, and got in the Toyota and drove away. Cheryl stood in the doorway and watched him go and couldn't imagine a different life. She wondered if David would wear the hat.

NETTA DID NOT SAY "I told you so." Instead she cried and cried, sitting in her pink robe on the sofa in the TV room surrounded by blue clouds of Tareyton smoke. You would have thought that David Stone had left *her,* instead of her daughter Cheryl. But Netta, now sixty-two, had always been a dramatic woman. When her own husband, Cheryl's father, George, died suddenly of a heart attack at forty-nine, Netta had almost died too. She referred to that time now as "when George was tragically taken from us," but the truth was, it *was* tragic. Cheryl's father had been a kindly, jovial man, a hard worker.

Not like David Stone, who was, as Cheryl's friend Marie put it, an enigma. Marie came over a lot after David left, to help Cheryl cope. Marie was divorced too. She went to group therapy. "He was just an enigma," she said. That seemed to settle it as far as Marie was concerned, only of course it didn't.

For one thing, although David had left forever, he didn't go very far, just about four miles out the Greensboro highway, where he rented an apartment in the Swiss Chalet Apartments, which looked like a row of gingerbread houses. At first the kids liked going over there, especially because of the pool, but then they didn't because their daddy wouldn't get a TV or buy soft drinks or meat. According to Angela, he said he was going to simplify his life.

"Isn't it a little bit *late* for that?" Lisa asked when she heard this news. Lisa, who ran the La Coiffure salon in the mall, had had one so-so marriage and one big disaster and always took a dim view of men anyway. She disagreed with Marie and felt that David was an asshole instead of an enigma.

Cheryl sat among these women — Lisa, Marie, and Netta — in her own velvet armchair in her own TV room, feeling like she wasn't even there. What Angela said about David simplifying his life reminded Cheryl of the old days, the really old days, when she lay with him on that mattress pulled over to the window in the room over Mrs. Bailey's garage, when the sun fell through the uncurtained windows in long yellow blocks of light, warming their bodies. She remembered the way the leaves looked, yellow and red and gold, floating on the river that October. David had loved her so much then. Whatever weird stuff he might be saying or doing now, David had loved her then.

"Good riddance, I say," said Netta, lighting up. David had made no bones about how much he hated cigarettes. If they hadn't been living in Netta's own house, he'd have made her go out in the yard to smoke.

"It might just be the male menopause," Marie offered. Marie was thin and pretty, with long pale legs and a brand-new perm, which Lisa had just given her. Marie and Cheryl had been best friends since grade school. "He might turn right around and try to come back," said Marie.

"Ha!" said Netta. "Never!"

But Cheryl seized on this, thinking, *He might come back.*

Marie's other insight, seconded by their cousin Purcell, was that David's sister's dying of cancer so recently had a lot to do with this whole thing. Louise had died that January, before he left. She was forty-seven, a sweet shadowy English teacher who had never married. She was so shy. Yet it was surprising how many people had showed up at her funeral, ex-students, friends, people from their neighborhood in Baltimore. Cheryl, who never could find much to say to Louise, had been amazed. Louise had lived with David's mother, and now David's mother lived alone. David used to call them up every Sunday night. Now he probably called his mother. Cheryl bit her lip. David leaving was like him dying, was exactly like a death.

The first week, for instance, everybody in the neighborhood brought food. Mrs. Tindall brought her famous homemade vegetable soup, and Mr. and Mrs. Wright, across the street, sent a twenty-six-dollar platter of cold cuts from the Piggly Wiggly, where he was the manager. Helen Brown brought chicken and biscuits, Betsy Curry brought enough chili to feed a crowd. Other people brought other things. Then Johnnie Sue Elderberry came in bringing a carrot cake, and Cheryl sat right down on the floor and burst into tears.

"Mama, *get up*," Angela said. Since her daddy left, Angela had gone off her diet and started smoking, and nobody had the heart to tell her to quit. Angela was sixteen.

"Sometimes God provides us with these hidden opportunities for growth and change," remarked Mr. Dodson Black, their minister. But Purcell, their cousin the evangelist, disagreed. "I'd like to get ahold of him," Purcell said. "I'd like to wring his neck." Purcell was a big blond man with a bright green tie. Lisa and Marie were putting all the extra food they couldn't eat right then into white plastic containers and freezing it. They put labels on the tops of the containers. Finally Cheryl got up from the floor. "Don't make any big decisions for the first year," warned their cousin Inez Pate, who had come on the bus from Raleigh to see how they were holding up. "Try some of this meat loaf," said Marie. "You've got to keep up your strength."

But Cheryl couldn't eat a thing. She was losing weight fast. She was wearing some nice gray pants that hadn't fit her for the last two years. She pushed the meat loaf away and said something to Marie and something to Purcell and went out the back door, under the porch light which wasn't working because Louis had shot it out with his BB gun. He was shooting everything these days. Cheryl couldn't keep up with him. "It's *okay.* He's expressing his *anger,*" Marie had said. But Cheryl wouldn't have a light fixture or a breakable thing left in the whole house, at this rate.

She sighed and wiped her forehead. It was hot. Every summer, her whole family had rented the same beach house out from Morehead City for two weeks. This year what would they do? *What would they ever do?* It was almost dark. Shadows crept up from the base of the trees, from the hedge, from the snowball bush, from the nandina alongside the house. Cheryl had grown up in this very house, she'd played in this backyard. Her daddy used to bring her packing boxes from the store and help her cut windows and doors in them for playhouses.

Cheryl walked out in the yard and stood by the clothesline, looking back at the house which was black now against the paling sky, all its windows lighted, for all the world like one of those packing-box playhouses that she hadn't thought about in years. It was *her* family, *her* house, she had opened all these doors and windows for David, had given it all to him like a present. It was crazy that he had left. *He'll come back,* she thought.

But in the meantime she was going to have to go back to work, because even though David had simplified his life so much and even though Netta had a pension and they got some money all along from the rent of Daddy's coal land, anyway, things were getting tight all around. Luckily Johnnie Sue was pregnant again, so Cheryl could fill in for her over at Fabric World while she thought about her options. One thing she was considering was starting up her own slipcover business. Slipcovers had come back in style, slipcovers were big now. Cheryl wished her mother would go out and get a job too. Her mother was driving Angela crazy. "Don't make any big decisions," Inez Pate had said. Poor Inez was aging so fast, she put a blue rinse on her hair now, it looked just awful. Cheryl held on to the clothesline and wept. But she didn't have to make any real big decisions, because of course he'd come back. It was just the male menopause, he'd come back. How could a man leave so many children?

And Cheryl thought of them now, of Angela too grown up for her age, too big breasted and smart mouth, smoking, suddenly too much like Lisa; of Louis, who'd always been edgy, getting in fights at school; of Mary Duke, only six, and whiny, who didn't really understand; and of Sandy, who was most like his father, so sober and quiet his nickname had always been too sporty for him.

Right after David left, Sandy had run away for four or five hours, and when Purcell finally found him down by the river he said he was sorry he was so bad, he knew his daddy had left because he was so bad. Purcell had brought him home in the rain coughing, and Sandy was still coughing, although Dr. Banks couldn't find any reason for it. Dr. Banks said the cough was just nerves.

Suddenly Cheryl heard a funny, scraping noise. And speaking of Sandy, here he came up the driveway, dragging a box along the gravel, walking backward, coming slow.

"Mama?" he said.

Then suddenly Cheryl felt like she hadn't actually seen Sandy, or any of her other children, for years and years, even though they had been right here. She had been too wrought up to pay them any mind. "What are you doing, honey?" she said.

Sandy pulled the box more easily across the grass and stopped when he reached her. "Lookie here," he said, leaning over, reaching down. Netta opened the back door just then and hollered, "Cheryl?" Cheryl looked down in the darkness, down in the box. Sandy coughed. His hair caught the light for a minute, a blur of gold. Netta slammed the door. Sandy straightened up with something in his arms that made a sniffling, slurping noise.

"Mama, this is Bob," he said.

"There's been something wrong with that dog from the word go," Netta said later. "You never should have said yes in the first place. Yes was always your big mistake."

But by then, by the time Netta got around to "I told you so," it was too late. Sandy just loved Bob to death. The first thing Sandy did after school every day was throw down his books on the hall floor and run into the TV room to see how Bob was doing. Every day Bob was doing the same. He lay between the sofa and the wall, hiding. When he heard Sandy coming, he thumped his tail. But he refused to stay outside. When they put him outside, he sank against the wall of the house and wailed, the longest wail, the most pitiful thing you ever heard. He sounded like Cheryl felt.

The kids thought that this was because he had been abused, and abandoned — Sandy had found him in the weeds along the interstate, near the overpass. Lisa said Bob wouldn't go out because he was stupid. She said he'd never learn anything and said they should take him straight to the pound before they got too attached to him.

But by then it was clear that the kids, especially Sandy, were already too attached.

And if they took Bob to the pound, he'd never find another home. People want a watchdog, a hunting dog. Nobody wants a dog that won't even go outside. Especially not one of this size. Because Bob was growing. It was clear he was getting big. Everybody had an opinion about what kind of dog he was, and although nobody knew for sure, Purcell felt certain he was at least half hound. He had that pretty red freckling, those long ears, and that kind of head. But he hung his head and walked sideways, getting behind the couch. He put his tail down between his legs. Bob looked ashamed, like he didn't have any pride. And the TV room smelled awful, as Netta pointed out.

"It's him or me," she said.

"It's him, then," said Angela, who was tired of having her grandmother at home all the time.

But then Lisa offered Netta a job at La Coiffure, making appointments and keeping the books, so she was gone nine to five anyway. Bob had the TV room to himself. He used a newspaper, but he wouldn't go outside. As he got older, his messes got bigger. This was supposed to be the children's job, cleaning up after Bob, but before long Cheryl noticed she was doing it all by herself. She did it in the mornings before she left and again when she came back home from Fabric World. She sprayed the den with Pine-Sol all the time. She got a stakeout chain so the kids could put Bob out in the yard in the afternoon, so they could get in the den to watch TV. It was clear then that Purcell was right, that Bob had some hound in him for sure, because of the way he howled.

The neighbors, who had been nice about Louis shooting out all the streetlights and nice about Angela's new boyfriend's motorcycle, complained.

"He'll get used to it," Cheryl told them. "He'll quit."

But she didn't believe it either. One problem was that Bob was so dumb he kept tangling himself in his stakeout chain. He'd tangle his chain around the lawn chair, or the barbeque grill, or the snowball bush.

"I guess I need to build him a pen," Cheryl said.

"I think you need to get rid of him," said Marie.

"Well . . ." Cheryl said in that slow, thinking way she had. She stared off into the purple dusk beyond the backyard, beyond Bob on his chain and Marie in a lawn chair, drinking a gin and tonic. Somehow it had gotten to be June. Now Marie was having dates with Len Fogle, a local realtor. She came by every day after work for a gin and tonic and described these dates in detail: where they went, what she wore. When Cheryl sat back in the lawn chair and closed her eyes, listening, it was almost like *she* was the one on the date, and she could imagine herself back with David again. "Then he kissed me in the car," Marie said. "He's got this little Honda? Then he asked if he could come up for a nightcap and I said yes." *Nightcap* was a dating word, a word Cheryl hadn't heard for years and years. She imagined herself and David having a nightcap in Marie's apartment, she imagined David putting his hand on her knee. "I was so glad I'd changed the sheets," said Marie. Cheryl sighed.

The real David was dating somebody else, a frizzy-headed math teacher at the community college who didn't even wear any makeup or shave her legs. Her name was Margaret Fine-Manning. She had been married before. But she was young. Last weekend her yellow Datsun had been parked at David's Swiss Chalet apartment from eleven in the morning until nine or ten that night; Cheryl just happened to know this because she had formed the habit of driving past the Swiss Chalets on her way to work, and then maybe if she ran out on the highway to pick up a burger or what she usually got, a fish sandwich, on her lunch hour, and then maybe also on her way home.

David was growing a beard. He looked skinny and picturesque, like a scientist in a documentary, like Jacques Cousteau. He was also getting a tan, from sitting by the apartment pool with Margaret Fine-Manning.

And furthermore, David, who used to be so quiet and considerate, was turning mean. He asked Cheryl not to drive by so much, for instance, and he was sarcastic about her making slipcovers. "That's a perfect job for you," David said. "Just making pretty new covers to cover up old rotten furniture. Just covering it all up, that's all. Avoiding the issue."

Cheryl had stared at him — this conversation took place in broad daylight in the parking lot of the Swiss Chalet Apartments, in early June. "You must be thinking about upholstery," Cheryl had said. "I don't do that."

"Now listen to me," said Marie. "I'm trying to tell you something." She stood up and got more gin. "It's so satisfying to have a relationship with all the cards out on the table. *You don't have to be in love,* Cheryl, is what I'm trying to tell you. It's much better to have a relationship based on give-and-take, on honesty. No big promises, no big regrets. Pay as you go, cash 'n' carry, as Lenny says."

"I think that's awful," Cheryl said.

"Just *think* about it," insisted Marie. "His needs are met, your needs are met. A mature, *adult* relationship. You've got to shed this high school attitude and get out in the real world, Cheryl."

Cheryl sighed, stirring her drink with her fingers. She smiled to herself in the dark.

Because, speaking of high school, there was something that even Marie didn't know. Cheryl's mind went back to three days earlier at the hardware store, where she had gone to buy a new stakeout chain for Bob, he'd torn the old one up completely, you couldn't even imagine how. Anyway, Cheryl had stepped up to the counter with Mary Duke in tow, and who should just happen to be there but Jerry Jarvis, the owner. Jerry Jarvis owned four stores now, he traveled from place to place. You rarely ever ran into him in town anymore.

"Hel-lo there!" Jerry had said. He ran his eyes over Cheryl and then slowly back over her again. Cheryl was feeling spacey and insubstantial — she wore shorts that day.

"You're looking wonderful as always," Jerry Jarvis said. He probably hadn't realized how fat she'd been. Cheryl hadn't realized this either. "So how are things going?" he asked.

"Just fine," Cheryl said.

"Daddy left us and went to live in the Swiss Chalets," said Mary Duke.

Later, Cheryl could not figure out what had possessed the child. Normally Mary Duke was *too* quiet, and held too tight to your hand.

"I'm sorry to hear that," said Jerry Jarvis. But it was plain as day from the way his eyes lit up that he wasn't sorry at all. He'd always loved her — so he was glad! In fact, that very night he had called her on the phone and asked Cheryl if she'd meet him at the bar at the Ramada Inn on Wednesday for a cocktail, he'd like to help her out in any way he could.

"Thanks but no thanks," Cheryl said then. "You're *married*."

While this was of course *true,* Jerry Jarvis admitted, there were a lot of factors involved. He'd like to talk to her sometime, he'd like to explain these factors, that was all, he'd always thought so highly of Cheryl's opinion. Finally Cheryl had agreed to meet him at the Deli Box for lunch, sometime when she felt up to it. The Deli

Box was right in the middle of town, it proved his good intentions, Cheryl guessed. She couldn't decide if she'd go or not.

Meanwhile a big truck had arrived the next day, from Jarvis Hardware and Building Supply, bringing a four-by-four wood frame and a load of sand to go in it. "For Mary Duke," he had written on his business card. "See you soon? Your friend, Jerry Jarvis," as if she didn't know his last name! Cheryl had told the men to unload it in the corner of the backyard, where it sat right now, in fact, looming up whitely at them from the darkness beyond Bob on his stakeout chain.

"You need to meet some men," Marie was saying. "You ought to sign up for a course."

"Listen — " Cheryl said suddenly. "Listen here — " And she started at the beginning and told Marie all about Jerry Jarvis and the Deli Box and his sending the sand. "Isn't that *weird*?" she asked at the end.

"Why, no," Marie said. "I think it's romantic."

"But he's *married*," Cheryl said.

"So what?" asked Marie. "He might be on the verge of a divorce, you never know. We call those 'men in transition' in my group," she said. "Anyway, you don't have to be in love with him. You can't marry anybody anyway, you haven't even got a divorce. Plus you've got all these children. It sounds to me like he's a real safe bet for you right now. I think you ought to go out with him."

"What?" Cheryl couldn't believe it.

"You know that old song?" said Marie.

"What old song?"

"Oh, you know the one I mean. It goes something about if you can't have the one you love, then love the one you're with."

"I think that's awful," said Cheryl. But she sat out in the lawn chair for a while longer, thinking about it and missing David, after Marie left in her Buick, bound for romance. Lenny was coming by later for a nightcap, so she said. Cheryl wondered what David was doing right now.

And then, in that way he had of anticipating you, of knowing just how you felt, Bob started to howl, low at first like a howl in her own head, and then louder until she took him off the chain and put him in the TV room.

This made Netta furious. "I work all day and what thanks do I get?" Netta said. "I can't even watch my program." Netta's program was *Dynasty,* which was on now. Netta had gotten bitchier and bitchier since she had started working for Lisa, who was real hard to work for. Cheryl sighed. She knew her mother was difficult too. Lisa said Netta insisted on sweeping up hair all the time instead of waiting until the girls were through for the day. It made both the girls and the customers nervous. But Netta said she couldn't stand to see that hair just laying all over the floor, she had to get it up. Then Lisa would yell at her, and then Netta would cry. It was really bad for business, Lisa said, to have your own mother in your shop crying and sweeping up hair. Now Netta was crying again. "Don't bring that dog in here," Netta begged. "Just let me watch my program in peace."

"I can't leave him out on the chain anymore, Mama," Cheryl said. "You can hear how he's started that howling. I guess I'll have to go ahead and hire Gary Majors to build him a pen."

Bob hung his head and scuttled sideways toward the sofa, panting.

"Well," Netta said. "Just do what you want to, then, you always do anyway, both you and your sister Lisa."

"Mama," Cheryl said. It wasn't fair. They were driving her crazy. All of them, her mother and Lisa and Bob and the kids too, oh *especially* the kids, summer was awful with them out of school. Except for Louis, who had flunked ninth-grade math and Spanish — he'd almost flunked everything — and now had to take summer school. Meanwhile David just sat by the pool at the Swiss Chalet Apartments getting browner and younger looking, with Margaret Fine-Manning. Cheryl didn't see how Margaret could get any sun at all on her legs, she had so much hair on them. It wasn't fair. Joan Collins got out of a car on TV, Bob thumped his tail on the floor. "Good night, Mother," Cheryl said.

JULY WAS A BUSY month with a lot of things happening. The first one was that Louis passed math but flunked Spanish and had to take it again in the second semester of summer school. The second thing was that Cheryl took Bob to obedience training at Triangle Vet, where he pitched a fit and tried to chew up his leash instead of walking around in a circle with the others. "Now, now, now!" said the instructor, a Mrs. Livers, pulling the leash out of Bob's mouth and squeezing his muzzle shut with both hands. "We don't love with our teeth!" she exclaimed. After the second class, she kicked Bob out. Then Mr. and Mrs. Wright across the street, who had always acted so nice, showed their true colors at last. They started calling up on the telephone every time Bob howled and then they started calling the police. They swore out a warrant calling Bob a pernicious nuisance, which wasn't true at all, and enjoined him from howling. But Bob refused to be enjoined. If he stayed inside too long, he messed on the floor, but if he stayed outside on the chain too long, he howled. Cheryl was at her wits' end. So she called Gary Majors and asked him to build her a dog pen, and Gary Majors said okay, but she'd have to go to Jarvis Supply and sign for the materials.

As soon as Cheryl walked in the door she saw him, Jerry Jarvis, behind a big computer. He stood up right away and stared at Cheryl, hard, across the store. Their eyes locked. Then he came hurrying over and asked her what he could do for her today. Somehow what he said sounded dirty, and Cheryl blushed. "Oh, I didn't mean anything like *that,* honest, swear to God," Jerry said. Jerry had thinning red hair and beautiful big brown eyes.

Cheryl believed him. She believed that the reason he was still so crazy about her was that in all their years of dating they'd never actually done it. Cheryl had been so religious in high school, plus they all wore panty girdles in those days.

Now, Jerry was trying hard to make conversation. He asked her about playing tennis and Cheryl told him that no, she did not play tennis, and she needed to sign a note for whatever Gary Majors might require to build a pen for Bob.

"Gary Majors?" Jerry Jarvis acted amazed. He said he'd come over and build the pen himself, how about that?

Cheryl looked at his seersucker suit, his nice white shirt, his bright red tie. "No, Jerry, I don't think so," was all she said.

But later that same week, when the stuff from Jarvis Supply arrived, there was a new ornamental gate with wrought-iron flowers on it, and his business card saying, "Pastrami on rye? Chicken on white? Your friend, Jerry Jarvis."

Then Gary Majors, a high school dropout about Cheryl's age, came by and started Bob's pen. Luckily this kept Mary Duke and Bob both happy, someone in the backyard to talk to them. Cheryl was having trouble getting Angela to stay at home and babysit with Mary Duke — Angela kept hanging out at the mall where her boyfriend worked. Sandy was at day camp at the Y, thank God, but Louis was flunking Spanish in summer school.

Finally Cheryl, who didn't know any Spanish at all, went to see Louis's teacher in late July, to ask him if there was any way she could help Louis, anything they could do at home to improve his grade. His teacher turned out to be a short, stocky man with big liquid eyes and so much hair on his body that it curled out over his shirt collar. His name was Amerigo Ramirez, which sounded like a country. Cheryl met him in his office at 5 p.m. on July 21, before a whirring fan. For a while they talked about Louis and Louis's attitude, which was a problem, Cheryl had to admit. Cheryl felt so hot she felt like she was bursting through her clothes. The fan went on and on. Mr. Ramirez gave her a list of verbs for Louis to learn. He gave her a record for Louis to listen to. Cheryl was hot, hot. It was hard to pay attention at all in this heat, surprising that the school had no air-conditioning. "Are there any problems at home?" asked Mr. Ramirez. Cheryl started crying. "Mrs. Stone, you are a very attractive woman in my view," said Mr. Ramirez. His eyes were large and moist; he took off his shirt, Cheryl had never seen so much hair. Mr. Ramirez locked the door and redirected the fan to blow toward the green chenille-covered cot in his office. Cheryl went to bed with him there, that afternoon, while the football team drilled out on the field in that terrible heat. Cheryl could hear them grunting— "Ooh! Oof! Aah!" —like figures in a cartoon. She could hear the coach shout numbers at them through the hot, still air.

The following day, Mr. Ramirez sent her some roses from Jo's Florist, but she wouldn't go out to dinner with him. She didn't think she'd see him again, because, as she told Marie, she just didn't feel a thing. Nothing. Zero. Nothing like it had always been with David, from the word go.

David meanwhile had bought a Nissan station wagon and announced to them all that he and Margaret Fine-Manning were going to Colorado, for their vacation. He gave Cheryl his itinerary, typed out. Bed-and-breakfasts, country inns.

"La di dah," Netta said. "I'd sue his pants off if I was you."

BUT CHERYL AND THE KIDS went with Netta to the beach for a week, which is what they had always done every summer that Cheryl could remember, renting the very same house that they had rented for so many years. Before Cheryl's father died, before the children were born, before David left.

This year, the people who owned the house had installed a new outside shower and bought new redwood furniture for the porch. And even though the boys had a great time and Angela fell in love with a freshman from UNC, even though Purcell joined them for four days, the house seemed twice as large as it used to, way too big. The seashell wind chimes sounded so sad that Cheryl took them down. Netta ate shrimp every night. When Purcell was there, he caught crabs every day by dangling chicken necks on string from the end of the pier. While Louis and Sandy played endlessly in the endless surf, Cheryl lay on the beach and wept with her face hidden under a *People* magazine.

But she tanned easily, and the weather was perfect, and she looked terrific in her new bathing suit, cut up high on the sides of her legs. She had lost seventeen pounds. Netta had started to say something about the bathing suit, but didn't. You could tell. Netta was being nice to Cheryl now since she wasn't speaking to Lisa, who had fired her from La Coiffure. Lisa said that Netta's crying and sweeping was ruining her business, her mother just had to go. Then when Netta refused to quit, Lisa fired her. So Lisa and Netta were mad, and Lisa didn't come to the beach with them this year, but Marie did. Marie came down for a weekend while Lenny went to the National Guard camp.

Marie said everybody back home was talking about Netta and Lisa's big fight, some of them holding that Lisa had been wrong to fire her mother, and others that Lisa had been wronged by a mother who wouldn't act right. Everybody in town had an opinion. Cheryl and Marie rubbed coconut suntan lotion on their legs and talked about it. Cheryl couldn't decide what she thought. It seemed to her that Lisa had a point, but Netta had a point too. People must have stopped talking about her own separation by now, her separation must be old hat. This gave Cheryl a pang. She missed David. She did not miss Lisa, or Bob. With Bob in the kennel, Cheryl was getting a lot of rest.

Then Marie said that Angela had asked her to get her some birth control pills and she had said she'd do it, but she just thought Cheryl ought to know. So Cheryl had *that* to think about too. She and Marie lay back on the sand, smelling like big sweet tropical drinks.

Netta came out of the house then, wearing a flowered robe and a big-brimmed hat, smoking a cigarette, picking her way toward them through the sand. It took her a while to get there. For the first time it struck Cheryl how old her mother looked, and how crazy. Netta was starting to look like Mamaw, who had been dead for years and years. Netta said she was going to take Mary Duke over to the water slide, which she had been doing every day. For some reason Mary Duke had decided on this trip that she didn't like the ocean, and she wouldn't go near it with a ten-foot pole. So Mary Duke was staying mostly in the house watching TV and driving everybody crazy.

"I don't see how she can be afraid of the ocean and not afraid of the water slide," Marie said.

"She thinks there's things in the ocean," Cheryl said. "You know — jaws."

Netta leaned across Cheryl and tapped Marie on the knee. "Did you hear how my own daughter Lisa did me?" she asked, and Marie said yes, she had heard it all right. Then Netta grabbed Cheryl's knee so hard Cheryl sat up. Netta's face beneath the huge hat brim was pale and trembly. "You wouldn't do that, would you, honey?" she asked.

"Do what Mama?" Cheryl said.

"Get rid of me like that, you know, for no reason."

"No," Cheryl said. "Of course not." It was true.

"Grammy, Grammy," Mary Duke called from the house. Netta straightened up and started across the sand.

"My whole body feels different since I've been having this relationship with Lenny," Marie began. "It's hard to explain."

Cheryl lay flat on her back in the warm sand, smelling sweet and staring straight up at the hot white sun.

"*GREAT TAN,*" JERRY JARVIS SAID. The way he said it sounded suggestive, but then when she thought about it later, Cheryl was not so sure. Maybe he didn't mean to sound that way, maybe he was just being nice after all. Certainly it was nice of him to stop by like this after work to check out the dog pen and see how things were going. Not so well, was the truth, which she didn't say. Bob had grown bigger and stronger at the kennel while they were away, and now he kept digging out of his pen despite the pretty ornamental gate that Jerry had sent over, despite the rocks and boards and things that Cheryl and the kids kept piling around the bottom of the fence to keep him in. The week before, Cheryl had bought a whole truckload of cinder blocks, and every time he got out, she'd put a cinder block where he did it, or a big rock she lugged up from the creek. It went on and on. Last Thursday when Bob got out, he went two streets over and stole a three-by-five Oriental rug from the Lucases, who had just moved down here from Fairfax, Virginia. Another time he knocked over Mr. Ellman's brother, who had a pacemaker.

Now Bob bounced against the fence, in high spirits. Cheryl sighed. She knew he could get out anytime he wanted to, until she got something along every inch of that pen. Every inch. Bob was such a hassle, but Cheryl couldn't bring herself to consider getting rid of him, she couldn't have told you why. And now Margaret Fine-Manning had moved in with David and they jogged together every morning. They ran from the Swiss Chalet all the way to Burger King, along the highway. Cheryl, driving to work, saw them every day. Margaret wore ankle weights.

"Cheryl?" Jerry Jarvis was saying. "Listen to me."

Cheryl looked at him. His hair was red, his face was flushed, his eyes were brown and sincere. He was a big impressive man. "I can have a boy over here tomorrow to run you a little old electric wire right around the bottom of this fence and then you won't have no more trouble. It won't hurt him a bit. Just a little jolt is all, he won't hardly feel it, but I guarantee you he'll stay in this pen."

"Well, thanks, Jerry," Cheryl said, "but I think that's awful. Shocking him."

"Wouldn't hurt him a bit, now," Jerry said. He grinned at her. He had big white even teeth, and Cheryl found herself grinning back.

"No," she said. "I know you think it's stupid, but I won't do that. I'll just keep on doing what I'm doing. We'll just put more stuff around until he can't get out, that's all. Sandy would have a fit if Bob got electric shock."

"It's not *electric shock,* Cheryl." Jerry was laughing. "It's really nothing, just a little whammy, that's it."

"No," Cheryl said.

She stood by the fancy gate as Jerry Jarvis walked over to his hardware truck. Sometimes he drove the truck, and sometimes he drove his BMW. It was September now, almost time for school to start. The leaves on the hickory tree looked papery against the sky, yellowing. Cheryl felt cold suddenly, although it wasn't cold. She couldn't think why she was being so silly about this pen.

Jerry Jarvis reached his truck and opened the door and then suddenly slammed it. He turned and walked back to her, fast. He grabbed her and pulled her to him and crushed her up against his yellow shirt. "Cheryl, Cheryl," he said. "I've got to have you, it's only a matter of time."

"Let go of me this minute, Jerry Jarvis," Cheryl said.

"You're driving me crazy," said Jerry Jarvis.

Then he kissed Cheryl slow and hard, a kiss that left her breathless, leaning against Bob's pen. Jerry rubbed her cheek and smiled into her eyes, it was clear he didn't even care who might be looking. "You know where to call me if you want me," he said.

THEN JERRY JARVIS SENT her twelve free cinder blocks, but he didn't come back again. School started. Cheryl was swamped with orders for slipcovers — fall was very big in the slipcover business. Angela cut off all her hair except for one long piece down the back, which she dyed pink. Lisa almost died when she saw how Angela looked. But Angela liked it. Cheryl didn't know what to think about Angela's hair — at least Angela's old boyfriend, Scott Eubanks, had gotten busted for marijuana over the summer and had been sent to live with his father in Georgia, so that was something. Cheryl guessed she could stand Angela's hair. And Louis started off better in school this year. He liked English. Of course he had passed Spanish, after all. Sandy was doing better — he'd stopped coughing, for one thing, and his Cub Scout troop had a new leader who was young and energetic. Sandy had earned merit badges in knot tying, carpentry, and letter writing. For his letter-writing badge, Sandy had to write a hundred letters. He had a Cub Scout pen pal in England who wrote to him on thin crinkly see-through paper. Sandy had also written several letters to his father, which just killed Cheryl. She couldn't imagine what in the world he said. Also, Sandy had a new friend named Olan Barker who had moved in with his family up the street. So Sandy was doing better, all in all, and his interest in Bob had waned. Oh, Sandy still patted him and fed him sometimes, but he never took Bob walking — and in all fairness to Sandy, he almost *couldn't*. For Bob had grown and grown. Sandy couldn't control him. Bob had become Cheryl's dog, finally, totally, after all. And sometimes he still got out of his pen: he'd move a cinder block, tunnel out, and run wild until somebody called the police, who came and got him and put him in the pound.

THIS HAPPENED IN LATE SEPTEMBER. When Cheryl went down to the police station to get him, the officer in charge was very friendly. At first he said there'd be a forty-two-dollar fine and then when Cheryl looked stunned to hear that — it was the end of the month, she wouldn't get paid till the first, and David had paid only half his child support for reasons he hadn't explained — when she looked so depressed, the officer in charge said, well, nobody was there but them, and why didn't he just tear up the ticket like this? — he tore it up before her eyes and dropped it in the basket by his desk — and he'd issue Bob a warning instead. He filled out the warning on a green card and handed it to her.

This officer was young, blond, and plump, with a big wide smile. He said that actually he didn't give a damn, that he didn't think the police ought to have to deal with dogs anyway, that every other town he'd ever heard of had a dogcatcher. He said this was a one-horse town in his opinion, with no nightlife. He said he was from Gainesville, Florida. He wore a badge that said "M. Herron," so Cheryl guessed this was his name. She looked around the police station, and he was right. Nobody else was there at all.

The police station used to be the agriculture extension office. She'd had 4-H in here. The gray painted concrete floor was exactly the same. Almost the only way you could tell it was a police station was by the messiness of it — cigarette butts jabbed down in sand-filled containers, paper cups on the floor. The county extension agent, Betty Gore, would never have allowed this disorder. Cheryl remembered Miss Gore's tight yellow curls and how particular she was about buttonholes. It was right here, all those years ago, that Cheryl had started sewing. She'd made an apron, an overblouse, a Christmas-tree skirt with felt appliqués. Now, wanted posters hung on the wall, full face and profile: one man, bearded, looked like David. Or she thought he did.

Cheryl, daydreaming, was so confused that when M. Herron offered to pick up Bob at the dog pound and bring him home after he got off duty, she said yes. Later she realized she should have said no. But by then it was too late. And when M. Herron showed up just at dark in his police car, it was real exciting. Clearly, Bob was glad to be home. He barked and lunged at them all and rolled on the grass. It took Cheryl, M. Herron, and Louis all working together to catch him and put him back on the stakeout chain, where he'd have to stay until Cheryl could get his pen fixed.

Then M. Herron let Mary Duke and Sandy get in the police car and showed them how everything worked. They even got to talk to headquarters on the radio, and M. Herron drove them around the block with the blue light flashing. He told Netta he loved children. When he finally left, Angela said he was cute. "Ha!" Netta said.

M. Herron came back on Tuesday, Cheryl's morning off, to give them some free burglar-prevention advice, which he said they needed. By coincidence, Netta was not at home, having gone to the outlet mall. M. Herron was not wearing his uniform. He walked through every inch of their house checking doors and windows and then advised Cheryl to go right out and buy dead-bolt locks. "You can't be too careful," he said.

Cheryl went to bed with him in her own bed, and after it was over, she got up and went in the bathroom and took a shower and then came back and saw M. Herron still there in her bed, against the yellow sheets. She thought he'd be dressed, but he wasn't. All he wore was a gold neck chain. He held out his arms to Cheryl and said he wanted to give her a big kiss. Then he said he hated to brag, but he was a pretty good cook, and would she like to come over for dinner on Saturday? He said he lived at the Swiss Chalets. "Well, thanks," Cheryl said without batting an eye — she was proud of herself, later on — "but actually I have a long-term relationship with a dentist in Raleigh and I can't do this anymore. I guess you swept me right off my feet," she said.

BY LATE OCTOBER, Lisa and Netta were reconciled. Purcell, who had a lot of influence in community affairs, had helped Netta get a job at the new Council on Aging, which had just opened its office downtown in the courthouse. This job suited Netta to a tee. It was as good as the liquor store had been for seeing people, but nothing about it made her nervous, the way watching the hair pile up around the chairs and not sweeping it up did. Netta had a list of practical nurses, maids, and companions for the elderly, and she matched them up with names of older people who needed help. Also, she organized craft classes, gourmet cooking classes, genealogy classes, and so forth. Netta loved her job. She said it made her feel young again.

David told the kids that Margaret was pregnant and that he and Margaret were "delighted" by this news. But they did not plan to marry, he said. He said marriage was an outmoded concept in his and Margaret's opinion.

"I bet she doesn't *want* to marry him," Marie said. "She just wants to have a baby with a smart father. A lot of women get like that, they hear the biological clock just ticking away."

Cheryl was astonished. This idea — that Margaret might not want to marry David — had not occurred to her. She thought that David didn't want to marry Margaret, or he would. Or he would do it when the divorce became final, next spring.

"You better watch out now, honey," Purcell said. "He's liable to come traipsing back here with his tail between his legs, any day now. You'd better get yourself a game plan," Purcell said.

But Cheryl didn't have one.

All she did was go to work and come home again, glad to have a permanent job now since Johnnie Sue had had her baby and it was colicky so she had decided not to return to Fabric World after all. Cheryl made $160 a week, plus whatever extra she got for slipcovers, which would be unlimited if she had the time and the energy. She had more orders than she could ever fill; it looked like the sky was the limit in the slipcover business. Lisa had suggested that Cheryl ought to hire some other women to sew them, say three or four women, and then Cheryl could just take the measurements and order the cloth and pay the women by the hour and make a big profit. "You can start your own business," Lisa said. "You can quit working at Fabric World and make a mint." This was a great idea and Cheryl knew it. But for some reason she was dragging her feet, losing orders. Maybe she didn't want to have her own business. Maybe she didn't want to be like Lisa. Maybe . . . oh, who knows?

Anyway, Cheryl had her hands full, what with the children, and Netta, and the slipcovers she'd promised, and Bob. She was stitching a mauve sofa cover for Mr. and Mrs. Holden Bench on Saturday night in early November, just after Halloween, when Bob got out again. She couldn't believe it. But she should have known. First, he'd howled and howled, and then he had fallen suddenly, mysteriously silent, and now here he was barking and jumping against the front door. Cheryl stopped stitching and turned off the light on her machine. She stood up. "Louis, Sandy — " she yelled, and then stopped. Her voice echoed through the empty rooms of this house that she had lived in all her life. Too late she remembered that she was here all by herself tonight. Everybody was gone — everybody in the whole world, it suddenly seemed. Angela was off on a date, Netta was out playing rook with the New Generation card group, Sandy had gone on a Cub Scout camping trip, Louis was at the movies seeing *Rambo* for the fourth time, and Mary Duke was spending the night with her friend Catherine. Cheryl was home alone. She remembered M. Herron and what he had said about nightlife, and burglars.

Cheryl opened the kitchen door and Bob bounded in, wagging his tail so hard that it crashed him into the refrigerator, then into the kitchen table, where her sewing machine was set up. "Now you just come right along here," she said firmly, grasping his collar, dragging him through the kitchen away from the mauve sailcloth all over the kitchen floor, toward the TV room. Bob reared back on his haunches and allowed himself to be scooted along. Cheryl gritted her teeth, dragging Bob. She would fix that pen right now, right this minute, by herself. And he'd stay in it. She shut Bob in the TV room and turned on *The Love Boat* to keep him quiet.

Cheryl put on a dark flannel shirt and a woolen cap. She felt like a burglar herself. She took off her loafers and put on some of Angela's boots. She got the flashlight out of the laundry room and went out the back door. Lord, it was cold! A chilly, gusty wind came whipping along, kicking up all the leaves. You could smell wood smoke in the air, and something else. Cheryl couldn't quite place what it was. Something cold, something sharp, it reminded her of winter. Winter was on the way. The almost bare limbs of the hickory tree showed against the full yellow moon and then disappeared when the moon popped in and out of the puffy dark clouds that ran across it. Cheryl's own backyard seemed unfamiliar, a scary but enchanted place — full of moving light and darkness, wind — and she remembered M. Herron saying a lady can't be too careful. But that was ridiculous. She could do it. Of course if she had let Jerry Jarvis send a man over here, this pen would have been foolproof months ago. But Cheryl could do it herself, and she would.

With the flashlight, she walked the fence until she found the spot where Bob had tunneled under. Then she walked back to the garage and got the last cinder block and carried it balanced against her stomach and placed it carefully in the hole. There now. And that ought to do it too, she thought, flashing the light around the bottom of the fence. There, now.

Cheryl went into the house and got Bob and dragged him across the kitchen and pulled him across the yard to his pen and pushed him inside, latching the ornamental gate securely. She felt flushed, and strong, and ready for anything, the cold night air so pleasant on her cheeks that she couldn't bear the idea of going back in and working on the Benches' slipcover. Instead, Cheryl went to the kitchen and got three California Coolers out of the refrigerator and opened one of them and turned off the kitchen light and went back out and sat down in a lawn chair.

The wind and the shadows moved all around her, she felt like she glowed in the dark. The dry leaves rustled at her feet, red and brown and gold, but she couldn't see their colors, only feel them in the dark. It was true she was artistic, she did have a sense of color, maybe she'd open up a business after all. Bob barked, then rattled the leaves, then made a snuffling, scuffling noise. Cheryl opened another California Cooler, she knew he was digging out. She imagined David and Margaret Fine-Manning entertaining M. Herron right now at a gourmet dinner in their apartment at the Swiss Chalets, she saw the candlelight gleaming in David's eyes, and the gleam of M. Herron's gold neck chain. The moon went in and out, in and out of the tumbling clouds. Cheryl imagined Jerry Jarvis unhappily at home with his fat wife, Darlene. She imagined Marie and Lenny embracing in a motel in Gatlinburg,

Tennessee, where they went this weekend to look at the leaves. Cheryl leaned back in her chair and opened the third California Cooler and laughed out loud finally as Bob scraped out and shook himself off and lurched over to stand for a minute there by her chair before he took off running free across the darkened yards, beneath the yellow moon.

Toastmaster

Jeffrey immediately likes the restaurant, Salute, which is nothing but an old porch built right out on the beach, open to the ocean and the huge pink sky which goes on and on and on, Jeffrey has never seen so much sky. "*Very* Key West!" his mother announces, as a personage in a kind of robe (Jeffrey can't tell if it is a boy or a girl) shows them to their table by the rail. *Personage* is a word from Jeffrey's vocabulary book. He follows his mother and her friend, slipping between the tables, the Invisible Boy. Each table has a different kind of cloth on it, and different chairs. Some people are barefoot and some are dressed up. A girl at the table behind them wears a string halter. A man at the table next to theirs has a big bird just sitting on his shoulder. The bird swivels its head almost all the way around to watch them take their seats, Jeffrey and his mother, Dar, and her friend from the conference, Lindsay.

"Two mojitos," his mother tells the personage, though Lindsay demurs, another word from the vocabulary book. "Not a chance," his mother says. "Ignore her," she tells the personage. "You'll love it, it's very tropical," she tells Lindsay. Dar always gets her way. Lindsay is a nice serious lady in a big navy blue pantsuit. But Dar looks like Rapunzel with her scary red hair puffed out all around her head and halfway down her back. She wears long glittery earrings and a long dress with big flowers on it, she looks like she has lived in Key West all her life. Dar is a professor at the School of Social Work at American University, a specialist in empowerment. She has deep brown eyes and round white muscular arms and legs, from years of yoga. She "goes to yoga" almost every day, like she is going to a foreign country. Dar is a *mother by choice,* as she tells everyone. This means that it was entirely her decision to have Jeffrey, his dad never even knew about him. Jeffrey often imagines his dad walking around some cold northern city with his coat collar turned up, not knowing about him.

Dar and Lindsay sip their drinks and discuss their conference, which is all about community action, how to involve the poor and the marginal and the non-English-speaking in the process. Meanwhile the sun hangs like a Day-Glo red yo-yo on a string above the horizon, dropping fast. Jeffrey watches it intently. It seems to be gathering speed now, plummeting toward the ocean. How can this be? Can gravity *speed up*? The women consult their menus and order Italian seafood dishes. Jeffrey orders a steak, well done, and a baked potato.

"No potatoes," the personage says. It wears makeup all the way around its eyes, like a raccoon. "How about some pasta?"

"Plain?" Jeffrey asks. "Can it be plain?" He hates it when people put stuff all over his food without asking.

"Sure," the personage says.

"*Honey,* this is an *Italian restaurant*!" his mother breaks off her conversation to point out. "In *Key West,* for Christ's sake! Lighten up!" Then she leans over to give him a kiss. "Okay. Sorry. Two more mojitos," she tells the personage. "And a Coke for the kid." This is a special treat.

Jeffrey stares at the sun which seems to be flattening out now that the bottom part of it has touched the horizon. It looks like a flaming beehive, going, going, going, gone! Applause ripples through the restaurant, making him blush. He didn't realize that he was a part of something, that other people were watching the sunset too. Jeffrey goes back to being invisible. Pink jet streams crisscross the sky. A chicken walks by on the sandy floor. A cruise ship heads out to sea, it looks like a floating building. Three tables away, a man and a lady with long blonde hair start kissing each other amorously (word). They have moved their chairs to the same side of the table. But the boy and the girl at the table behind them are arguing. Jeffrey almost but can't quite hear their irate (word) voices. He knows it would not be cool to turn around and look at them. Another chicken walks past.

Darkness falls suddenly, like a blanket dropped over the beach. Little twinkle lights appear everywhere, looped around the poles that support the tin roof and all along the awning above them and the rail beside their table. *This is enchanting,* Jeffrey thinks. Like fairyland. Or like that cookbook Dar uses, *The Enchanted Broccoli Forest.* He likes that title even though he would rather die than eat broccoli. Dar is always trying to get him to eat healthy things because he is small for his age, eleven, though he has been mistaken for eight. He has been taken to doctors about it. He weighed only four pounds two ounces at birth. He knows this for sure because he found his birth certificate and read it, then put it back carefully just where it was, in Dar's file marked "Jeffrey — Imp." So maybe he had a twin brother who died. Jeffrey has asked Dar about this again and again, but she always denies it. "You were just premature," she swears. In many ways, Jeffrey feels, he is still premature. And he still sort of believes he had a twin brother who died, sometimes in fact he feels very close to this brother, whose name is Rick. He feels that Rick is somewhere out there right now, in the enormous sky, where stars are beginning to appear one by one, like those enchanting little twinkle lights.

Their food comes, including a salad that Jeffrey didn't even order. At least it's plain. Jeffrey eats it, then his pasta. He eats only one thing at a time. Now the personage and two other waiters are pushing several tables together to make one big table on their side of the room. The girl behind them sounds like she is crying. "I didn't think it would be like this," she says. Jeffrey can't stand it, he turns around to look, and she *is* crying. Her breasts are slightly blue.

"Eat your steak," his mother says. She notices everything, pouncing like a cat. His mother does everything too much. She is a mother like a battery cable, a mother like a laser (similes). Jeffrey knows that she loves him, but this is almost, he feels, the problem. There must be *some* problem, because he is excused from school one hour early every Thursday to spend the afternoon with Dennis Levering, a cool spiky-haired young man who is actually some kind of counselor. He asks Jeffrey too many questions and tries to take him out to do things like shoot baskets (no), ride bikes (no), kick a soccer ball around (no), take a walk (no), go to a museum (yes!). Next week they are going to walk around the Tidal Basin with a metal detector, Jeffrey is really looking forward to that.

He used to go to the afterschool program at his school, but there were these two bullies in that program, Sean Robertson and Max Gruenwald, who did something really bad to him and even though they had to come to his house with their parents to apologize, Jeffrey hates them now with implacable (word) force and will never speak to them again or be in any cluster group with them or even discuss it with his teacher, the very sweet and voluptuous (word) Miss Hanratty.

So now he goes to Club Creative at the library. He is the top-scoring member of the Club Creative Team, which meets with Mrs. Rogers, he is a Shining Star because he read fifteen books in two weeks. He loves to read books, especially fantasy books and books about disasters such as the *Titanic* and the Chicago Fire. He feels that if he reads enough of these books, he will not be in a disaster. He also loves the Rice Krispies snacks they have at Club Creative. Every day, on his way home, he stops to hang by his knees from the monkey bars in the empty playground next to the library, to make himself stretch out and grow taller. Sometimes he hangs by his hands from the steel rod at the top of the garage door at home too, before Dar gets back.

This is a part of Jeffrey's Invisible Life, which also includes his visits to this old couple who live on the corner, the Hampdens (Jeffrey calls them the Hamsters in his mind). The Hamsters are very old and very diminutive (word) and also very bent over, so that they are not much bigger than Jeffrey himself. He met them one time when he was walking past their house and Mrs. Hamster had fallen down beside their mailbox, and he helped her get up and walk back inside. "Come back!" they said. "Drop in!" Every time he drops in, the Hamsters are always doing the very same thing. Mr. Hamster is sitting in his big blue chair watching baseball on TV, and Mrs. Hamster is sitting in her big blue chair reading magazines that Dar will not allow in the house, such as the *National Enquirer* and *Midnight Star*. Jeffrey likes to sit in Mrs. Hamster's chair with her (there's plenty of room) and read these magazines and eat nonpareils, a flat kind of chocolate candy with hard little white balls all over it. The Hamsters keep the non-pareils right there in a glass dish just for him.

Now Jeffrey eats every bite of his steak while Dar and Lindsay talk about their relationships. Dar has had a lot of relationships because she is so enchanting and intense, but the men tend to blur somewhat in Jeffrey's mind, all kind, earnest doctors and professors, most of them wiry with dark hair and pointy little beards. Many of them have been hikers (no, thank you) and bikers (no, thank you). Jeffrey watches with interest as two girls in very tiny bathing suits run onto the beach and start twirling luminescent (word) hoops out on the dark sand, throwing them high up into the air, then catching them with professional expertise (word). Maybe they are practicing to be on television. Dar orders key lime pie for herself and Lindsay, tiramisu for Jeffrey. "It's kind of like a chocolate sundae, you'll love it," she tells him. She orders Rusty Nails for herself and Lindsay, over Lindsay's expostulations (word).

A big group of big men barge into the restaurant all at once, seeming to fill it up entirely. There's a lot of hugging and shaking hands and clapping each other on the back. They seat themselves at the pushed-together tables and start ordering in loud voices. Dripping pitchers of beer and huge bowls of "u-peel-'em" shrimp arrive.

Dar and Lindsay roll their eyes and lean closer so that they can hear each other. The man with the bird leaves. The kissing couple leaves. Jeffrey watches the girls with the luminescent hoops out on the beach. These girls are very curvaceous (word). He knows that the women are talking about him.

"Why don't you send him to the Friends School, then?" Lindsay asks.

"What?" Dar says.

These are the largest, noisiest men Jeffrey has ever seen.

"The *Friends School,*" Lindsay says. "Don't they have a really good Friends School in Washington?"

"I can't afford it." Dar drinks her Rusty Nail. "Also, if I did that, then I'd have to pay for all the special ed, which he's getting for free now. It's sort of a Catch-22 situation."

The personage puts the tiramisu down in front of Jeffrey; it is nothing at all like a sundae. It's like pudding, which he hates. The girl at the table behind them suddenly runs out by herself, creating a little breeze; the boy follows more slowly, looking harassed and disconsolate (words). Now there is a wide margin of empty tables around the loud men, no more regular diners except for Jeffrey and Dar and Lindsay.

Jeffrey is interested in these men. He has never seen any men like them. They radiate a kind of vitality (word) that he finds enchanting. Though some appear to be a little younger, mostly they are great big middle-aged men with their hair still on. *Men in the prime of life,* Jeffrey thinks. This phrase just comes to him. They wear huge Hawaaian shirts in outrageous (word) colors and patterns. These shirts hang loosely over but don't really hide their big tight bellies. They have baggy Bermuda shorts. They have white veiny muscled legs which end up in shiny loafers or maybe athletic shoes, new looking, as if they have just bought them for this trip.

But it is their manner that Jeffrey especially likes. These are brash (word), confident, public men, *happy* men. Their cheeks are red, their eyes snap and sparkle, they throw back their heads to laugh, they laugh so hard they have to wipe their eyes with their big white napkins.

Then the guy on the end jumps up and announces, "Okay!

Showtime! Horse walks into a bar — " All the other men groan in unison (word), drowning him out. This does not seem to bother the man one bit. "*So a horse walks into a bar,*" he shouts, striding back and forth, "and the bartender says, 'Hey buddy, why the long face?'" When the other men whistle and boo and throw their napkins at him, he does a funny skedaddle walk, like a clown, back to his chair.

"Oh, for Christ's sake!" Dar rolls her eyes.

"I don't get it," Lindsay says.

"*Horse,*" Jeffrey explains. "Horses have long faces."

"Oh!" Lindsay starts giggling.

A tall guy with curly blond hair and thick glasses takes the floor. His yellow shirt has red lobsters on it. "So a three-legged dog walks into a bar and climbs up on a stool and orders a beer, then another, then another, looking all around. Finally a cowboy says, 'Okay, dog, what are you doing in this town?' Dog says, 'I'm looking for the fellow that shot my paw.'"

Everybody groans, but Jeffrey laughs so hard he starts choking. "*Paw,*" he explains to Lindsay. "See, it's a dog . . ."

"I got it," she says, laughing too.

Dar is not laughing. She does not like jokes and has only told one of them in her whole life, so far as Jeffrey can remember. He picks up a spoon and starts eating his tiramisu very slowly, so they won't have to leave.

"All right!" The fattest man hops up and does a funny duck waddle over to the open area which has now become a stage. The bar has emptied out, people moving their chairs into the dining area to watch. The fat man wipes his glistening face and puts his handkerchief back in his pocket. He has round blue eyes, like marbles, and fat hands with fingers like hot dogs.

"It's been a very busy morning at the police station," he begins. "Two cops have gone out on a robbery call, two cops have gone out on a murder call, and another cop has just radioed in for additional help at a wreck when the phone rings again and the guy at the desk picks it up. 'Hello?' he says.

"'Help! Help!' a woman screams into the receiver.

"'Whatsa matter, lady?' the policeman asks.

"'Oh, please, you've got to help me!' the woman cries. 'I've got an elephant in my backyard.'

"'Oh, for Pete's sake!' the policeman says. 'Look, lady, I've got a wreck, a robbery, and a murder to deal with this morning. Whaddya expect me to do about an elephant? Take him to the zoo!' He slams down the phone.

"But the next morning he's feeling guilty about this, so he calls the woman back and says, 'Okay, lady, what happened to the elephant?'

"'Oh, hi there,' she says. 'Thanks so much for the tip. He loved the zoo, so this afternoon, I'm going to take him to the movies!'"

The fat man duck-waddles back to the table, to great laughter and applause.

"I think it's time for us to go back to the hotel," Dar says. "We've got another long day tomorrow."

"Just a minute, Mom," says Jeffrey. He has almost finished his tiramisu.

A trim little white-haired guy, maybe the oldest, steps up smartly. He salutes the table of men, then bows to Dar and Lindsay, which seems to disconcert (word) them, though it does not disconcert Jeffrey, who waves his spoon and grins right back at him.

"Military," Lindsay whispers to Dar.

Sure enough, "You guys may not know I was once in the army," the little man begins. "The first day, they gave me a comb. Then they cut off all my hair. The second day, they gave me a toothbrush. Then they pulled seven of my teeth. The third day, they gave me a jockstrap . . . and now they've been looking for me for forty-seven years!" He marches back to his place.

Even Dar laughs at this one. But she picks up her purse just as the personage arrives with a tray of fresh drinks, two Rusty Nails and another Coke. "We didn't order these," she says in her professor voice. "In fact, I'd like the check now, please."

"The check has already been taken care of by those gentlemen over there. They send you their compliments, and hope very much that they haven't spoiled your dinner."

Dar looks over at the men, who raise their glasses as one. "To the ladies!" they shout. Dar blushes, smiles, and raises her own glass in their direction. "Thank you," she calls.

A younger guy with a buzz cut gets up next, he looks like he's about dad age, though Jeffrey cannot imagine any dad at his school ever acting like this.

"Waal, old Farmer Jones raises pigs," the dad-type guy begins in a fake country accent, "and one time he had this special baby pig he just fell in love with, see, that had a wonderful personality. So he was just spoiling this little pig to death. The little pig especially loved apples, see, so every day old Farmer Jones would pick him up and hold him up in the apple tree, so he could eat an apple. But then the little pig started getting big, and then he started getting bigger and bigger, and it was all that old Farmer Jones could do to hold him up there while he ate his apple. So his friend comes along, and he says, 'Wouldn't it be a lot quicker if you just picked an apple off the tree, and put it down on the ground for the pig?' Waal, old Farmer Jones stared at his friend for a while, and then he said, 'Lester, time don't mean nothing to a pig.'"

Though the men laugh and pound on the table, ordering more beer, Jeffrey thinks this is a stupid joke. In fact, it's the worst joke he's ever heard in his life. But then suddenly, Jeffrey thinks of a joke himself. This joke simply *comes to him,* just like that. Before he has time to think about it, before he even knows what he's doing, he's on his feet, he's dodging his mother's outstretched hand, he's in the center of the floor. Everybody is looking at him.

"Okay! Showtime! Dyslexic horse walks into a bra!" Silence. Jeffrey looks around the restaurant at all their still white faces, like so many moons. *What were they thinking?* he will wonder years later. What in the world were they thinking, to see this skinny knock-kneed child, this pale, unlikely little boy come forward in such a place to tell his joke? Jeffrey swallows hard. *"Okay! I said, dyslexic horse walks into a bra . . ."* The laughter rises with a roar like a freight train, as the men at the table leap to their feet and everybody in the restaurant claps and whistles and cheers for him. *For him,* Jeffrey, the formerly Invisible Boy.

More jokes follow, many more jokes, doctor jokes and psychiatrist jokes and yo' mama jokes and sex jokes about Bill Clinton. *They took a poll of American women, and they asked, "Would you have an affair with Bill Clinton?" and 70 percent said, "Never again."* More drinks follow too. Dar and Lindsay and Jeffrey stay until the very end of the evening, Dar firmly refusing all offers of a ride back to their hotel with the large men, who finally give up and pile into their rented vans.

"Hey!" Jeffrey yells as the last van pulls out of the parking lot. "Hey! Who are you guys, anyway?"

"Toastmasters!" the fat man, driving, yells back. "From Cincinnati!"

"What are toastmasters?" Lindsay asks.

"Some kind of a club, I think. Oh God, I feel terrible." Dar sinks down on the curb, her long skirt dragging in the sand.

"*Mom,*" Jeffrey says. "What are you doing? You've got to drive us back."

"Oh, I couldn't possibly drive," Dar says. "Lindsay?"

"Are you kidding? I'm not even sure I can walk." Lindsay grabs Jeffrey's shoulder for support.

Jeffrey looks around. Their rental car, a white Ford Escort, is the last one left in the parking lot. Somebody has already turned off the pink neon SALUTE sign and all those little twinkling lights. The restaurant sits like a dark square box on the beach with the glistening sea stretched out beyond it, *as far as the eye can see.* This phrase just comes to Jeffrey. A little breeze comes up. And there they are, Jeffrey and Dar and Lindsay, all alone in the Salute parking lot, out in the breezy, starry night.

"Well, come on, then," he says, pulling his mother's hand.

In the middle, Jeffrey escorts the women back to the hotel, walking them all the way down Duval Street where he sees more sights than you can possibly imagine, weirder people than he has seen in the *National Enquirer* or the *Midnight Sun,* while sitting in the chair with Mrs. Hamster. Men dressed as women and women dressed as men and one woman wearing almost nothing at all except black boots and a studded dog collar around her neck with the leash trailing down along the sidewalk behind her. "Hi honey," this one says. "Hi there," says Jeffrey. An old man wearing a name tag throws up in an alley where six-toed cats forage (word) among the garbage cans.

Finally they reach their hotel and take the elevator up together, dropping Lindsay off at her room on the third floor. Luckily Jeffrey remembers their own room number, which Dar has forgotten. "I'm going to rest for just a minute," she says, lying down on her double bed without even brushing her teeth. She falls asleep instantly, mouth open. She is heavily intoxicated (word), Jeffrey knows.

But he has never felt more awake in his life. He slides open the door of the balcony and goes outside to lean over the rail and look out over the shining water. The warm wind makes a clattering sound in the palm trees. It caresses Jeffrey's face. He stands out there for a long time, he's not even tired. A little curved moon like a comma (simile) rides in the sky among all those stars. "Hey Rick," Jeffrey says, looking up.

"Hey Jeff," Rick answers. His voice comes from nowhere and everywhere all at once, it fills the entire enchanted evening. *Knock, knock. — Who's there? — Sam 'n' Janet. — Sam 'n' Janet who? — Sam 'n' Janet Evening.* Jeffrey will learn this joke later, from a book.

As soon as he gets back to Washington, he will go to the library and check out three joke books, and then three more, as many as they will loan him at a time. He will learn them all: knock-knock jokes, chicken jokes, lightbulb jokes, yo' mama jokes. He practices telling them in front of the full-length mirror in the bathroom. He gets so he can tell them real fast, rat-a-tat-tat. He practices walking in funny ways. Dar begs him to stop, but he won't. He signs up for the Moriarty Middle School Talent Show. He works up routines, trying them out on Dennis Levering, who cracks up, and the Hamsters, who titter and shake uncontrollably. But Dar can't even watch. "Honey, this makes me so nervous," she says. He makes her buy him a shiny black suit and a red bow tie, which he will wear in the talent show, with his old Keds and his shirttails hanging out. Dar talks to his teacher. "You don't have to do this," she tells him right before the show. But just then the doorbell rings and it is Mr. Hamster, bringing Jeffrey an old felt hat. "Who in the world was that little man?" Dar asks, closing the door. Jeffrey tries the hat on in front of the hall mirror, bending the brim first this way, then that. The hat is perfect. *Showtime!*

On the way into the auditorium, he sees Sean Robertson and Max Gruenwald and tells them a mean joke, meaner than they are. *Why did Helen Keller have a burn on the right side of her face? — She answered the iron. — Why did Helen Keller have a burn on the left side of her face? — They called back.* Sean and Max have white, startled, pimply faces. Jeffrey sweeps past them down the aisle to the front, where he is directed backstage into the greenroom. There are a dozen contestants. He goes on ninth, following Rob Acton's band and Tiffany Bell doing acrobatics and Lydia Wang who is widely considered a child prodigy on the violin. Lydia wins, of course, but Jeffrey will take second place, and he is the one who will get a standing ovation and be hugged by the voluptuous Miss Hanratty to the envy of all as she smashes his face into her huge breasts so hard he sees stars in front of his eyes, a harbinger (word) of things to come.

Big Girl

How did this happen?" the woman asks me so soft I have to lean up in the chair to hear. "When did it start?" A good question. But when does anything start? How far back do you have to go? I was a big girl, now I'm a big woman. My life has been different because of it. Many avenues of opportunity are closed off to a big girl. You can't be a majorette, for instance. You can't be a cheerleader. You dress and undress in the shower stall at gym class. You stand in the back for group pictures. If you ever get elected to anything, it's always treasurer. I never had a date in high school. Boys didn't even notice my big breasts because I was big all over, like the Pillsbury Doughboy, remember him? On the packages of pizza mix and cake mix? I have opened a number of those packages in my time, I might as well admit it. Obviously I'm not a picky eater. Everybody has to be something, I reckon, and I'm a great cook. I tell you that in all honesty. I'm known far and wide for my cakes, my three-cheese lasagna, my chicken and biscuits, and especially my chocolate pecan pie — Billy's favorite.

Used to be his favorite, I should say! During the first six years of our marriage, Billy gained forty pounds, which he complained about, but he didn't really mean it. He needed to beef up some.

He looked better than ever, in my opinion. Maybe I should have paid more attention last spring when he went out and bought that diet stuff at the Whole Earth Store in the mall and said he was going to get back in shape, but I just thought, isn't that nice? A man has got to do *something*, after all, even a man that has got hurt and laid off, and they say walking is good for anybody, though it makes me short of breath, personally. I worked overtime while Billy walked. He walked all summer long.

It never occurred to me to wonder if he had a destination.

"Mrs. Sims, when did you start doing this?" the woman asks again. Her name tag says "Lois Rubin." She's one of those skinny, flat-chested women who wear turtleshell glasses and pull their hair straight back with a barrette and go around writing on clipboards. She's not from around here. I bet she grew up rich. She's rich now, big square-cut diamond ring plus a nice chip-diamond wedding band on her left hand. She's just another do-good rich lady down here at the jailhouse occupying herself while her surgeon husband screws a nurse. Oh Lord! Now where did *that* come from? As a big girl, I'm used to hanging back and not just saying whatever pops into my head, the way I keep doing ever since they brought me in here. I swear, I don't know what has got into me!

Billy always said he was going to get me a diamond but he never did. Though he had the best intentions in the world, poor thing, I still believe this. But life can snatch you up and mess with you in many different ways. Sweet, sweet Billy Sims. None of this is *his* fault, you can count on that.

I take full responsibility for everything.

"Mrs. Sims. Dee Ann." Lois Rubin looks down at her clipboard. "High school graduate, good grades, student government, excellent work record in a number of positions. What happened to you?"

This is the same question asked earlier in the day by my preacher, Rev. Buford Long. Then he laid his hand on my forehead like Jesus and announced he has revved up the prayer chain for me. "Thanks but no thanks," I said. "Get him out of here," I told the deputy, who did it, grinning. This deputy's name is Sam Hicks. Rev. Buford Long was just sputtering and spewing all the way out the door. "Now Dee Ann Sims, I know you are a good girl," he said, working his neck like a chicken. "Why, you are one of my own! I know you don't mean that." He had on this powder blue suit. I knew his wife, Ruth, would be waiting outside in the car, just primed to get the story so she could spread it all over town. All she ever brings to church suppers is three-bean salad.

"Mrs. Sims, let's go back to the beginning," Lois Rubin says so soft her voice is like a voice in my own head. "How did this start?"

THE TRUTH IS THAT most times, you don't even know something has started until you're right in the middle of it, and even then, you don't necessarily recognize what it is. It creeps up on you, like weight.

You wouldn't believe it to look at me now, but I started out as a beanpole. Then they sent Sissy and me to the mission school, where my job was to work in the kitchen. By the time I started working for Mrs. Hawthorne and switched over to regular school, I was about like I am now. I always felt like there was another girl, a little bird girl, trapped inside me. She is quick and fast. She dips and soars. She is everything I'm not. I walked around with her wings beating, beating, beating inside my chest to get out.

I was not a thing like my mama who was movie-star, drop-dead gorgeous, she looked like Elizabeth Taylor. I have a picture of her in my pocketbook right now, which of course they have locked away someplace. I remember being with Mama one time on the street, in Knoxville, downtown, and a man came up and put his hand on her arm. "Who are you?" he said. "Who *are* you?" I don't remember what she said or what happened after that, whether she went off with him or not. I do remember holding Sissy's hand on the street. I always took good care of Sissy when Mama went off "seeking a better association" as she said. And I was glad for Sissy when she got adopted, though she won't hardly give me the time of day now that she has married rich and lives in Boca Raton, Florida. I haven't heard a word from her since last Christmas when we got a basket full of fruit and a card with a picture of their house on it and "Cecelia and Lyman Petersen" in fancy printing. It's a big house too. Pink stucco with palm trees. And I don't care for fruit.

Here's something I've been thinking about ever since they caught me. It does seem like the more you do for somebody, the more they will turn on you in the end. Miss Manners said this once in the newspaper — if you act like a rug, somebody will walk on you. I'm coming to think this is true.

It seems like only yesterday that I used to braid Sissy's hair the same way I braid my own Debbi's hair now. Both of them the kind of little girls that you just naturally love to take care of. I hate to think that Billy's sister Sue is taking care of Debbi right now. Sue will not know to lay down with her on the bed and sing Itsy Bitsy Spider and then say "Now I lay me down to sleep, I pray the Lord my soul to keep" every night, or that Debbi has to have those little ponies lined up in a row on her pillow. Also I can't stand to think about Debbi breathing all of Sue's passive smoke. But Lord knows, Sue owes me — she stayed with us between husbands when she was so nervous. I had to wait on her hand and foot.

I've always been the dependable one, like furniture, like chairs. Like a La-Z-Boy recliner, and I guess you might say Billy was the original La-Z-Boy himself. I don't mean to say that he was lazy, Billy, I mean to say that things have not worked out as he planned. He couldn't help getting his leg hurt, he couldn't help it that Tennessee Power and Light laid him off, or that drinking is genetic in his family, and I know he didn't mean all those ugly things he said to me either. Billy is sweet, sweet. And handsome — Lord! I never could believe he really married me in the first place, with all the girls he had to choose from. He had the whole county to choose from.

Many is the time that I have woke up in the middle of the night with my heart just pounding, to think of it! And then I'd look over at him laying on his back with his hands folded on his belly like a dead man and that little nasal strip over his nose, which he has to use for his sleep apnea, and I'd hear his snuffly breathing, and I'd think, I am the only one who ever sees Billy Sims with his nasal strip on. Then I'd think, Billy Sims is still here in the bed with *me*! After eight years of marriage! It must be a mistake. But it is not.

Was not. It was not. I'd lay there and look at him for hours, listen to him breathing, watch him sleep.

For some reason this reminds me of one time when I was a kid and we were living in that old cabin way out in the woods and I woke up real early for no good reason and walked out on the porch, it was years ago and yet I can remember it like it was yesterday. Mama and Daddy were gone. It was early, early spring and rainy, a little white mist in the trees, sarvis and dogwood in bloom. The cabin was so old that the silvery boards on the porch felt smooth and almost soft to my feet. I walked out real quiet, and there he was. A twelve-point buck standing like a statue just beyond the treeline. He stared straight at me. I stopped dead still and stared back. I felt like he had been watching for me, waiting for me to come out that door. It was like he knew me. And then Sissy called "Dee Ann?" in her little baby voice from inside, and I turned my head for one split second, and when I looked back he was gone. Gone without a trace. Yet I knew he had been there, and for days afterward I felt warm inside, and special, because of it.

I DON'T KNOW WHY I'm telling you all this.

"Just go on," Lois Rubin says.

I WENT OFF TO work every morning after the accident feeling this same way, feeling special, leaving Billy asleep in the bed behind me. He got his nights and days all turned around after he got hurt. First he couldn't get to sleep for the pain, he couldn't get comfortable in spite of the pills. Then he got to where he was sleeping all day and staying up all night long, he'd watch videos, and why not? Poor thing. It killed me to watch him hobbling around the kitchen like a hundred-year old-man with all those pins sticking out of his leg. He was drinking too. It broke my heart.

I could never forget the way he looked running zigzag down the field at the homecoming game senior year, carrying the ball like it was a baby and then throwing it up so high in the end zone, it spun right up out of the light and was lost for good in the sky. That was the winning run.

I saw the whole thing from the student government concession stand where I was making hamburgers and sloppy joes, serving a man who got so excited by Billy's run that he took off toward the field forgetting his change and his fries. Football is real big here. It always has been. And now that they've closed the Piney Creek mine as well as the Resolute No. 4, it's the main thing going on. Everybody in town comes to the games — old people, teenagers, little kids, women holding tiny wrapped-up babies in their arms. We took Debbi to her first game when she was not but four months old, wearing a little purple outfit that Mrs. Francine Butler had knitted for her. People bring whistles and cowbells, streamers to throw, and balloons to let loose at the right moment. Purple and gold. Those are the colors for the Gretna Golden Wave. But it's the men that get into it most, all these men that either used to play football themselves or don't have enough to do since they got laid off. Billy said they even used to come to all the practices, walking up and down the field real serious in their windbreakers, following every play. I guess it made them remember when they were young too, and strong, and ran down the field like the wind. But Billy said they just about drove the coach crazy, giving him so much advice. Then of course they'd go to all the away games too, following the bus.

Anyway, I stood there holding that man's change, looking out at the field where Billy was jumping all around and high-fiving everybody, and he seemed to me like more than a person, like a different kind of thing entirely, like one of those gods and goddesses in Greek mythology. Billy was larger than life. I halfway expected him to leap up off the earth and take his place among the constellations too.

Well, he didn't of course. He graduated and started driving a coal truck for Parker Mining Company right away. He had to. He had to take care of his mother, who had asthma, since his daddy'd got killed in the mine years before, when Billy was a little kid. He can't hardly remember his daddy at all. All he can remember is that his daddy had red hair and whistled. He could whistle any song in the world. Then he'd say, "Why, just a minute there, son! What's that I see?" and pluck a quarter right out of the air behind your ear. Nobody ever figured out how he did it. Billy doesn't really remember him being drunk, though that's *all* his mother remembered. She was sour as a persimmon by the time she died. Warned Billy off of liquor every day.

For a while, that took, and it might of took for good if Anne Patrick Poe hadn't broke his heart. Everybody knew she would. Anne Patrick Poe was the most stuck-up girl in our school, probably the most stuck-up girl in the state. You had to call her by all three names, Anne Patrick Poe. She was Miss Gretna High, Homecoming Queen, and Miss Claytor Lake. She had college written all over her. That is until Billy got her pregnant.

I remember seeing her in the littlest red two-piece bathing suit at the class picnic out at the lake right before graduation. She stood knee deep in the water squealing while Billy splashed her, stomach as flat as a board. I sat up under a canopy with Miss Parsons, the home ec teacher, and Becky Brannon, my best friend, and watched them. Becky sighed. "Aren't they the cutest couple?" she asked, and I said yes. Obviously they were, they'd even been voted Cutest Couple for the yearbook, though secretly I didn't think she was good enough for Billy Sims. I thought she was too self-centered, which was true. I saw how she'd tease him, and toss that ponytail over her shoulder and flirt with other boys such as Coy Eubanks, toying with Billy's affections. I had never spoken to her, not once. I spoke to Billy eight times that year, though he didn't know my name. Why should he? It's a big consolidated high school. Five of those times, he was buying hot dogs from me after games. He always got chili and mustard. The other times were in math, where I got an A and he got a D. Luckily he didn't remember that later, when we got together.

Billy was not a student. But he was a charmer, and the teachers loved him in spite of his grades. Everybody loved him. He has this happy-go-lucky wide-open face with freckles thrown across it like stars, and a way of shuffling just a little when he walks. I saved a paper cup he threw down at the concession stand one time, and a potato chip bag. I flattened them out and put them in my scrapbook, and when Becky Brannon pointed at the page and said, "Now what's *that* all about?" I wouldn't tell her.

But it never crossed my mind that we would ever get together, me and him, not even in my wildest dreams.

Then came Thanksgiving, and Anne Patrick Poe came home from college putting on airs, and then came Christmas vacation and they ran off to South Carolina in her convertible and got married. The Poes almost died. First, Mr. Poe declared he would disown her and shouted out in public that Billy was nothing but trash. Then he calmed down and got Billy a job as a lineman at Tennessee Power and Light. Then he made the down payment for them on a new brick home in Sunnyside subdivision. Then, in April, she lost the baby. What did Mr. Poe think *then*? I reckon he was ready to eat nails, don't you? But they were already married, Billy and Anne Patrick, so there was nothing he could do. She got a job at Susie's Smart Shoppe in the mall, and Billy stayed on at the Power and Light. I'd see them around from time to time, such as at the Kiwanis pancake breakfast. "They look like they ought to be on TV, don't they?" Becky said to me at the time, as we were getting some more pancakes. "Like Luke and Laura on *General Hospital*." I had to agree. Furthermore, Becky was not that far off when she mentioned the soap opera. I'll get to that.

But now, *I* am coming into the picture!

All through high school, as I believe I mentioned, I lived with old Mrs. Hawthorne. I had that little room on the third floor with a slanted ceiling. It was the first room I had ever had all to myself, so I loved it. Not that I didn't appreciate my years at the mission school, but Mrs. Hawthorne's house had pictures on the walls, and flowered rugs, and real silver. She said I could do whatever I wanted to in my room, so I painted it yellow myself, sunshine yellow with white woodwork, and Becky's mother made a yellow flowered spread for my bed. "Oh, Dee Ann," she used to say, brushing my hair, whenever I'd be over there visiting Becky, "whatever will become of you?" She said I had beautiful hair. Becky's mother was real good to me. So was Miss Parsons, who bought me a sewing machine junior year, which sat on its own little table in my room at Mrs. Hawthorne's house. Miss Parsons acted like she won that sewing machine in a contest, so I wouldn't think she had gone out and bought it for me, but of course I knew better all along. She's the one that recommended me to Home Health, which is how I started taking care of Billy's mother. Social services paid for it.

But first, Mrs. Hawthorne died. I will never forget it. I'd been there six years. There is somebody like me in every town, that is good at staying with old people. Just as soon as Mrs. Hawthorne started failing, people started coming up to me in the Food Lion to say that if I ever needed another job, well, *their* mother would be needing some help, too, before long. I could see that the rest of my life was all laid out before me like the flagstone path that went straight from the street to Mrs. Hawthorne's front door. I'd live with first one, then another. I'd take care of everybody.

Mrs. Hawthorne slipped away by degrees until finally there was nothing left in the bed but a little cornhusk doll. She quit talking. She quit eating too. I'd fix boiled custard, tapioca pudding, milk toast, all her favorites. I'd feed her myself with a spoon. Oh, I was desperate! Finally I called her family up long distance, and everybody came. But Mrs. Hawthorne wouldn't talk to them either. She didn't have time to talk. She didn't have time to eat. She didn't have time to sleep, hardly — when I'd go in there at night to check on her, there she'd be with her eyes wide open, clutching her blanket up to her chin, staring fiercely into the dark. Finally she motioned me over with her little clawlike hand. The light from the hall fell across her bed. Her lips were moving. I bent down to hear. "Dee Ann," she said. "Oh, Dee Ann . . ." Her nails bit into my hand. "You must . . ." But I never knew what I must do, for just then a gurgling noise came up in her throat, and when I jerked back to look at her, she was dead. Dead with her eyes and her mouth wide open, teeth in the jar by the bed, cheeks sunk down in her face. I could not quit looking. Her eyes got darker and darker in death, and her mouth got bigger and bigger until I felt that she would swallow the whole world, me included. Yet I couldn't move. I could feel myself going down, down. But just at the last minute I screamed "No," or thought I screamed, and then I was scrambling out, phoning the doctor and the relatives, making coffee for all the folks who'd be coming over. I was just as efficient and dependable as always. Folks marveled at me.

But inside, I was different. For now I realized that I was going to die too, something that had not occurred to me before, in spite of being an orphan and all. Even as I was cutting my pound cake and getting out the folding chairs, I thought about it. I would have given anything to know what she was going to tell me. Anything! And what was I supposed to do? I kept wondering about this, it made me feel wild and crazy. I felt I had a destiny though I didn't know what it was. When I finally got to bed that night, my heart was beating so fast I could hear it in my ears and feel it all through my body.

The very next morning, Home Health called and asked me if I would stay with Mrs. Sims, and I said yes immediately. I knew it was meant to be. But she was a bitter woman, as I said. She'd always had asthma, and now she had congestive heart failure. The house was a wreck. I was cleaning out the kitchen cupboards when Billy showed up the first time. I'd been there three days. It was May, nice and warm. I had opened all the doors and thrown up all the windows. Never mind that Mrs. Sims didn't like this one bit — it was good for her. I was working so hard, banging pots and pans around in the cabinet under the stove, I didn't hear Billy coming — didn't hear his truck, or his step on the squeaky board by the kitchen door, a sound that I grew to love.

"Hey now," he said.

I whirled around.

He stood just outside the screen door. His gold-red hair fell almost down to his shoulders under his TP&L hat. The sun was all in his hair. "I'm Billy, her son," he said.

"I know," I said. I had to sit back on the floor, I thought I was having a heart attack.

He stepped inside the door and squatted down beside me on the floor which I had just washed, thank goodness! "Do I know you?" he asked. Close up, his eyes were greener than ever.

"No," I blurted out, "but I know you." Then I got so embarrassed I liked to have died on the spot, but Billy just grinned, rocking back and forth on his cowboy boots.

"Wait a minute," he said. "High school, am I right?" He snapped his fingers. "Hot dogs," he said. "You used to sell the hot dogs at the games."

I nodded. I couldn't believe he remembered me after all that time.

Then he stood up. "Well, it's a small world, ain't it?" he said, stomping his feet a little bit to get the kinks out of his legs. I couldn't of stood up if I had to. I felt weak all over.

"Now what did you say your name was?" he said, and I told him, and then he said, "Well, me and Anne Patrick, that's my wife, are real glad that you're over here taking care of Mama now. She's been needing somebody full time for a while, and we just can't do it, we both work, and my sisters live away."

Of course I knew that Anne Patrick didn't *have* to work, that it was just a little play job. But I nodded, acting sympathetic.

"How's Mama today?" he called from the hall on his way in there to see her.

"She's doing a lot better now since she's on oxygen all the time," I hollered back. "When she was trying to do for herself, she didn't turn it on enough."

"Well," Billy said from the hall. Men never know what to say in the face of illness. Then I heard him say, "Hey, Mama."

While she was taking her nap that afternoon, I couldn't do a thing but go through every drawer and cubbyhole in that whole house, looking for pictures of Billy. And I found them at every age, school pictures and snapshots, stuck here and there. If it was *my* son, I'd of had them all put together in a nice album. But she wasn't much of a mother, Ruth Sims. I got the idea that she'd spent most of her life laying up in the bed whining and *acting* sick until she really *got* sick, and of course by then she was good at it. Secretly I didn't blame Sue and Darlene for going wild and taking off. Besides, if they'd stuck around and took care of her, I never would have got to step one foot inside the door.

And I was so glad to be in that kitchen with Billy Sims, it seemed like a miracle.

After that, Billy always stopped by about once a week, then twice a week when she started doing poorly, then three times a week when she got real bad. I got used to him coming by any time of the day and on up into the evening, sometimes he'd be as late as 10 p.m. When you work for the power company, you never know when you'll get called out on a job. I kept beer in the refrigerator, coffee on the stove. I made sure I had something good cooked up all the time — chicken and dumplings, beans and ham, vegetable soup. Billy was always hungry, I don't think Anne Patrick ever fixed him a thing. He'd sit right down at the kitchen table and eat, and then he'd lean back and smoke a cigarette and talk to me. Now I was not used to talking to men, so at first this made me nervous. But you can't stay nervous long around Billy. He squints those green eyes and looks right at you as if you've got something to say. And so sure enough I'd find myself just blabbing on and on about everything under the sun, kind of like I'm doing right now. I told Billy Sims things I had never told *anybody* — all about living at the mission school, and with Miss Hawthorne, and the time I went out West on a driving trip with Becky Brannon and her family in a van, and the time I went to Disney World with the church.

"Yeah?" Billy'd say. "Yeah?" He smoked cigarette after cigarette. Then *he'd* start talking, telling me all about growing up here with his whiny mother and those two wild girls. "They used to climb out the bedroom window," he said. "Shimmy down a rope. Then I'd hear them go off in a car. Sometimes I'd know who it was, sometimes not. I hated if it was anybody I knew."

"Was it boys from school?" I asked, thinking of Billy's friends. I knew all their names, of course.

"Naw," he said. "Mostly older guys."

He recounted every game he ever played in high school, every play. "I dropped back to the left," he'd say, "and Clint threw this high pass, I never thought I'd get it — " I remember one night in particular he was going on and on about football and eating a ham biscuit at the same time, and all of a sudden he quit talking and looked at me. "You can't be all that interested in football, Dee Ann," he said.

"Oh, sure I am." I knew I was turning red. I lived for these conversations, though I knew they were nothing to him. He was just being pleasant, shooting the breeze, like he did with everybody. He never mentioned his wife, and I never asked. Though I imagined there was something wrong there, or why would a man like Billy Sims spend so much time talking to a woman like me?

This is how me and Billy got to know each other while his mama died. She was going down a lot faster than Mrs. Hawthorne had, in spite of everything I could do. The county nurse, Mrs. Francine Butler, came around every day to give her a shot, and the doctor came by about every three days. Lots of other people came too, neighbors and cousins and people from her church. But how many times do you think Anne Patrick showed up? I can count them on the fingers of one hand. Lots of makeup, so sweety-sweet it was obviously fake, oh I could see right through her! One afternoon when Billy was there she came by in this little shiny pink outfit, straight from aerobics. I saw how Billy's eyes got all hot and liquid looking at her. He couldn't keep his eyes off that little pink butt.

I felt like such a fool then, for thinking that my destiny was to take care of Mrs. Sims.

"She'll not make it to Christmas," the doctor said in November. By then Mrs. Sims didn't recognize anybody, not even Billy. Then Francine Butler asked me if I'd consider coming to live with *her* mother when Billy's mother died, and I said yes.

Billy came over a lot, sweeping cold air and electricity in the door with him. When he stamped his feet and took off his jacket and his utility belt, the whole house felt suddenly full of life. But Billy *looked* bad, dark circles under those pretty eyes. I knew something was wrong besides his mother dying, though Lord knows that's enough for anybody.

One night in early December, he came in real late. I was still up myself, sitting in the kitchen in my old flannel robe sticking cloves in oranges for a church sale the next day. Billy threw himself down on a kitchen chair and lit a cigarette while I got him some coffee. Then he pulled a little bottle of bourbon out of his jacket pocket and drained it. He rattled the cup in the saucer while he drank the coffee.

"How's Mama?" he asked, and I said she was not doing too good. He knew that. He looked at me through the smoke. His eyes were red. He had just put in a double shift at the power company. "Dee Ann, talk to me," he said. "Tell me something." So I did. For the first time ever, I told what happened when me and Sissy were little girls, that got us put in the home.

It was December then too. We were living out in that cabin

in the woods that I told you about, real far from town. It was a cabin that Daddy had *found,* I think. Maybe the one that owned it was dead, or maybe nobody owned it. Daddy had an old rattle-trap truck then, he'd drive us out to the road so we could catch the bus to school if he was home, and if he was sober, but often we'd stay out there for days by ourselves while him and Mama was off drinking. And then one day he disappeared, just like that. Sissy was too little to understand. "Where's Daddy?" she'd ask. "Where's Daddy?" she kept asking.

"Gone with the wind," said Mama. "Ha ha."

So then I'd have to stay out there with Sissy whenever Mama got a way into town to seek a better association, and sometimes she'd bring a man back with her and sometimes not. Sometimes he'd be nice to us and sometimes not.

But the time I'm talking about was in December, and Sissy was sick. She'd been sick for days, and Mama was gone. I was nine or ten years old. I had to break the ice every morning to get the water from the creek. I could see my breath like a cloud in the air as I went through the snow to get it. We wrapped trash bags around our feet for boots, but Sissy could not get up or go anywhere. And then we ran out of firewood, and I had to gather all the branches I could find fallen down in the woods, and break them up to burn. First we had some potatoes, which I boiled, and some cornmeal, which I mixed up with water and made some little cakes. We had three Coca-Colas which we drank a little bit at a time, to make them last. I had put Sissy right up by the cookstove, by the fire, but she could not quit coughing. And we were hungry, hungry. When you're that hungry, your stomach even stops hurting and you go away in your head someplace, it's hard to describe.

I remember waking up sometime near dawn with Sissy coughing, and going out in the night for water, across the moonlit snow. Oh, it was beautiful! The black trees, the bright snow, the pointed moon sailing like a ship among the clouds. I dipped my pan into the freezing creek and brought it up to drink before I dipped it back down for Sissy. But that cold water sent a jolt straight to my brain. *We're going to die here, Sissy and me,* I thought. *We're dying now.* And then it was like I was flying through the air, up above the cabin, up above the dark trees, into the clear bright beautiful sky and I could look back down and barely see our roof in the little clearing while the woods went on and on forever on every side. A tiny line of smoke came up from the chimney far below. I took another sip of water and then I was running as fast as I could with the trash bags taped over my shoes, back to the cabin where I grabbed Sissy and wrapped her in everything I could find, all the blankets and quilts we had, and pulled her out the door and across the snow to the treeline, and filled up two more garbage bags with all the clothes and things that was ours and Mama's, and pulled *that* out to where Sissy lay in a heap on the snow. I left Mama's hats on the bed. She had two, a blue felt hat with a peacock feather on it, and a big straw hat with a bunch of cherries. Daddy had left a pile of newspapers on the porch. I ripped these up and threw them everywhere. I pulled the furniture kind of together, what there was of it — the table and chairs, an old chester drawers, a rocker, a crib — and then I rolled up a piece of newspaper and lit it at the open door of the stove and went around setting all the other newspapers on fire. When it got to going good, I went out and sat with Sissy.

"Looky," Sissy said. "Looky there."

In no time the cabin was outlined by flames, all four walls and the roofline, like a crayon drawing on fire. After a while the porch fell down, and then the roof caved in, sending a huge column of flames and smoke straight up in the sky like a Roman candle. *Good,* I thought.

The fire had died down some but was still smoking plenty when the people came, I heard their trucks on the road below and their shouts as they came up the holler, though I was too weak by then to answer.

"Good God!" Billy Sims said when I told him this story.

He got up and came over to where I sat in my old bathrobe and hugged me, hard, and then he left.

His mother died the next day. Sue and Darlene came home for the funeral, and then they left, and a week later, Anne Patrick Poe left Billy for Coy Eubanks, from high school. He was a lawyer now, recently divorced. He lived in Memphis. He had come back into her life, she said, when he was in town settling up some family business. Now they were engaged. "Engaged!" Billy said. "But you're already married to me!" "Oh, that was just a boy and girl thing," Anne Patrick said. She said she thought he knew that all along. She said she was moving to Memphis immediately.

Billy woke me up to tell me all this the night it happened, he appeared at my bedside drunk as a lord. "She said she didn't want to leave me until my mama died," Billy said. "Now what kind of shit is that?" Then he staggered and started unbuttoning his shirt, and I realized that his intentions were to get into bed with me. For a moment I was terrified, but then a vision of Mrs. Hawthorne's open mouth came to me out of the blue, and I knew that if I didn't let him, I'd regret it for the rest of my life, no matter how scared I was, and I was plenty scared. But I moved over to make room for him anyway. He climbed into bed with me and cried like a baby for two hours, then shucked off his pants and made my dreams come true.

When I woke up, Billy Sims was gone. Well, I thought as the day passed, that's that. He was drunk, it didn't mean a thing. Probably he won't even remember it. But I couldn't help humming as I walked around packing up and cleaning so the house could be sold. I was moving from there directly out to Mrs. Francine Butler's mother's house in the country, to take care of her. I knew I'd treasure every minute I had spent with Billy Sims and play our conversations over and over in my head, like a tape. But I was kind of looking forward to being out in the country with Mrs. Green. They had a big farm pond out there, and cows, and it was real pretty.

I was all packed up and waiting for Francine Butler to pick me up when Billy's flashy red truck came roaring into the driveway. He opened the door and scoped out the situation. "Where the hell do you think you're going?" he asked, and I told him.

"No, you're not," he said. "Come over here. We're getting married."

For a minute, I didn't go. I had a flash that my memories of Billy might make me happier than Billy himself. But then I saw Mrs. Hawthorne's wide black mouth again, and gave a little scream, and ran straight to him. And we got married as soon as we could, to everyone's total astonishment, I might add, especially those sisters! It was a good marriage too, a happy marriage. I believe that. For Billy and me, we're two of a kind, and he never should have been married to Anne Patrick Poe in the first place. She was not his type. I'm his type! We like the same things — cooking and eating, why Billy even built his own pig cooker, for barbecues — and talking. Lord, that man can talk. And dancing, which he taught me to do. Line dancing, two-step, you name it. I'm a natural, though you might not think it to look at me.

But Billy had developed some mighty expensive tastes living with Anne Patrick, as I soon learned. Nothing they owned was paid for, and Billy had signed for all of it himself. So we were stuck, while Anne Patrick waltzed off to Memphis scot-free. Billy's share of his mama's little house just about got him out of debt, when it finally sold. I didn't have a thing in the world, of course, but I soon got a nice job with some lawyers downtown, a good thing since Billy didn't know beans about money, to my surprise. Why he didn't even write his checks down in the checkbook! He bought such items as a bass boat, a real expensive entertainment center for the family room, some $475 Tony Llama boots, and all this health equipment, weights and such, after he got hurt.

But I'm getting ahead of myself. We loved each other, that was the main thing. And I didn't care about his spending habits. I *wanted* him to have those boots! *Whatever makes Billy happy* was my motto, and I never, ever, said no to anything he wanted, or anything he wanted to do. We went all over the place to Nascar races, for instance. This hobby is not cheap! "Life is short, Dee Ann," Billy used to say. Naturally his attitude alarmed me. But I had never had any fun before in my whole life, and when I got pregnant with Debbi, my happiness was complete.

I will never forget the night I told him, December 8, seven years ago. He was working late, they were wiring the Sugar Fork tipple. I'd already done the test the day before, and it was positive. Then I came home from work and did it again. Positive. So I got in the car and drove out the House Mountain road and on up the mountain, getting there just at dusk. I love a winter sunset, always have. The tipple looked like a giant Tinkertoy outlined against the fiery sky. The clouds were silver. And there was Billy, high up, working. I knew him by the cock of his hip and the way he held his head. He was black against that sky, which faded to orange while I watched. I saw him lean back against the strap and signal to somebody. Then suddenly bright white utility lights went on all over the tipple and everybody cheered. Billy started waving his arms like a kid. I stood on the ground in the dark with his baby in my belly and cried like a baby myself. It was so beautiful.

"Aw, SHOOT," Sam Hicks says.
"Now, now," says Lois Rubin. "Here honey, here's a Kleenex."

BILLY WAS RIGHT beside me in the hospital when Debbi was born, and helped me breathe. But then later he started saying that a baby "cramped his style," for of course we couldn't just pick up and go out like we always had. "You go on," I'd tell him. *"Go."* And so he did, and I was glad he did. You can't expect a man like Billy Sims to stay at home. I was still counting my lucky stars to be with him at all and to be blessed with this perfectly lovely little baby girl too. I loved staying at home with her and would have stayed a lot longer except that the bills were mounting up, and Billy kept pushing me to go back to work. I had to put Debbi into day care at two months, which broke my heart.

She was three when he had the accident.

Billy fell two stories down from that new hospital wing they were wiring. Landed on concrete, broke his jaw, his collarbone, his left arm, his wrist, his leg. If he hadn't of been wearing his hard hat, he'd be dead. I can't stand to think of it, to this day. Pretty Billy Sims laying crumpled up in the parking lot exactly like a bird that's flown into a picture window. Of course the hospital was *right there,* so they rushed him into surgery immediately. I was half out of my mind by the time I made it, I ran all the way across the parking lot dragging Debbi. The doctor met me outside that awful steel door wearing green pajamas, stripping off his gloves.

The good news was that Billy would live. He would have to have pins in his leg, and more surgery followed by physical therapy, but he would be okay.

The bad news was, we didn't have any insurance.

"Tell me that again," I said.

When Debbi was born in that very same hospital, our insurance paid for everything. But Billy had let it go, I learned, so they wouldn't take so much out of his paycheck. Whatever he'd been doing with that extra $280 every month, I didn't know. He probably didn't know either. Money just slipped through his hands like water. Ten here, twenty there. Billy was a high liver, as I said. He cried like a baby when I told him I knew. I couldn't stand this, what with him in pain and all wrapped up in those bandages.

"Just forget it," I told him. "What's done is done, water over the dam."

I put him on the family room couch with everything he needed (TV remote, phone, cooler) close to hand. For once, I was glad he'd bought that fancy entertainment center!

Then I went back to work.

I ran the office for three lawyers: David Martin (tall, thin, sad); Ralph Joiner, a red-headed ball of fire who was in the state house of representatives; and Mr. Longstreet Perkins, old and dignified, a former judge famous for his opinions. I typed all their letters, made up loan packages, deeds, and so on. Typed papers of every sort. I did all the filing, all the accounting. I handled the reconciliation of trust accounts, the payroll, and collected rent for absentee landlords who paid us to perform this service. I made my lawyers' bank deposits, wrote their checks, and paid their taxes. They depended on me totally. "Dee Ann, I don't know how we'd manage without you." David Martin and Ralph Joiner were always telling me that. "Mrs. Sims, you're a wonder," said old Mr. Longstreet Perkins. Meanwhile our own house was a mess with Billy living downstairs in the family room, clothes and plates and magazines and what-have-you strewed all over the place. Men are naturally messy anyway, and Billy was the *worst,* even before the accident. It broke my heart to walk through the family room.

I have to say, it was nice going over to my own little office, which is eggshell blue, where I had put my desk catty-corner so I could see out the window into the street. I kept African violets blooming on my desk, and Tootsie-Roll pops in a jar for anybody that wanted one. You'd be surprised how many takers I had. I kept some M&M's in my top drawer, too, for stress.

Which I had plenty of! Because of course I was the one who paid all the bills at home, and now I just couldn't do it. Even with his disability check, I couldn't make ends meet. I couldn't stand to bother Billy with it either — he was in so much pain, and so blue. I started paying just *some* of the power bill, *some* of the water bill, some of the phone bill, some of the hospital bill, and so on. I'd stay up late figuring all this out while Billy watched TV.

"Aw, don't look so worried, honey," he said to me one night when the cable bill as well as the rent and his truck payment had come due. "It'll work out. Come over here and give your old man some sugar." He was drunk.

But instead of giving him that sugar, I surprised myself by saying, "I fail to see why you have to have such an expensive truck anyway, can you explain this to me?" I heard my voice going up and up like Billy hates. "There wasn't anything wrong with your old truck that I could see." He had bought himself a new one only three months before.

"Goddamnit, Dee Ann." Billy swept everything on the coffee table off onto the floor making the awfullest mess, and then he busted out crying, which was more than I could stand. He looked like the little boy in all his old school pictures. "I'm sorry," he said. "I'm just so goddamn sorry about the whole goddamn thing."

"I'm sorry too," I said.

The next day I went to work, watered my violets, then took two of Martin, Joiner, and Perkins's trust account deposits next door to the bank where I deposited them straight into my own checking account. It was easy. I've known the teller at First Union, Minnie Leola Meadows, for years. She goes to our church. "How's Billy getting along?" she asked as she handed me the deposit slip, and I said, "Better."

That night I finished paying the bills.

As the months passed, I got good at this. Sometimes I'd take the rent checks from the property we managed. Sometimes I'd write a check to "cash" for something I'd make up, such as "supplies" or a phony repairman. I had everybody's air-conditioning worked on, for instance. Sometimes I'd dip it out of the tax money. Most often, though, I simply wrote myself a check off the books, which was easiest of all — and why not? Nobody ever checked the books except me, and I kept them as neat as ever. Plus I never took much, mind you, only what we needed to cover those bills. I was not really stealing either. I fully intended to pay it all back just as soon as Billy started working again.

Finally, they took his leg out of the big cast, pulled out the pins, and put it into a lighter cast which closed with Velcro, so at least he could take a shower. Oh, it just *killed* me to see how little and shriveled up that poor leg had gotten! I massaged it for him every night. But Billy was pepping up some. He started going to physical therapy every day, and then he got on that health kick. He quit drinking so much. He took a long walk every evening, like the doctor said. Sometimes he'd walk for an hour or more.

"I CAN SEE RIGHT where this is going," Sam Hicks speaks up, grinning. Sam Hicks has a big gray mustache that hangs down on both sides of his mouth.

"Hush, Sam," Lois Rubin says, writing on her clipboard.

BUT *I* COULDN'T SEE IT! I still thought Billy Sims hung the moon, and when he finally went back to work, I thought, okay, now we'll be all right. We'll be fine again. I was proud of myself for taking care of our financial problems without having to bother him about it. And the power company turned out to be real nice, giving Billy a sales job at their regional office in Boyd since he can't climb anymore. But it was not the same. Billy was *never* home now, what with commuting to work and the physical therapy and the health club and all. And it seemed like we still kept getting further and further behind financially, no matter how hard I'd scrimp and save or how many times I'd add up the numbers.

"HE WAS HOLDING OUT on you, wasn't he? Holding out! Son of a gun!" says Sam Hicks. "Hee, hee, hee."

"Why you poor thing," says Lois Rubin.

THIS IS HOW I found out.

My friend Becky Brannon, that I have mentioned before, had

just moved into a new town home in the Village Green development, and so one afternoon I decided to ride over there and visit. It was a Sunday afternoon in June. Billy had gone to the lake fishing with Red and Tiny. So here we went, Debbi and me, with a variegated geranium from Food Lion as a house gift. They've tried to make Village Green look like a real village, with flower beds and picket fences and porches on most of the houses. All the streets have flower names — Becky lives on Primrose Circle. I could tell it was just her cup of tea, she's always had ruffled curtains and ducks everyplace. She was already planning to stencil her kitchen.

We found her unpacking boxes. She jumped up to hug me. "Don't you just love it?" she said, and I have to say, I did. Owning a home has always been my own personal dream, but I was real happy for Becky who has always worked so hard and deserves it. All her furniture, which had been too old-timey for her other apartment, fit right in. I was in the process of admiring everything, having fixed Deborah Lynn a Pepsi, when I chanced to look out the kitchen window and received the shock of my life.

For there was Billy Sims, bare chested, wearing cutoff blue jeans, leaning down to turn on a water faucet at the house next door. Then he proceeded to unroll an obviously new, long green hose from one of those spool things, and pull it around the corner of the house out of my view. I walked into the living room where Becky sat on the couch unpacking another box, surrounded by knickknacks and crumpled newspapers.

"Becky," I said, "would you do me the favor of stepping up to your window and looking over there next door and telling me what you see?"

Becky looked at me like I was crazy, and then she got up and did it. She stared back at me speechless.

For there stood Billy Sims, big as life, watering her next-door neighbor's grass, while a red-headed girl in a halter top weeded a flower bed around a birdbath. She had long white legs like pipe cleaners.

I knew who she was.

"That is Miss Lonergan, the physical therapist," I said.

Just at that moment Debbi came into the room and said, "Mama, can we — " and then, "What's the matter?"

"Not a thing, sweetie," Becky said. "Why don't you go in my bedroom and watch TV until your mama gets ready to go?" She took Debbi by the hand. Becky came back with a box of Pepperidge Farm cookies, which she opened without a word. We ate them while waiting for Billy to quit watering Miss Lonergan's yard and go in her house so I could leave, which I finally did. Becky's a big girl too. But the thing about it that just killed me, and kills me to this day, is that Billy never once watered our own yard at home — Billy never showed a *sign* of yard work!

Now, do you remember what I told you Miss Manners said?

I took Debbi by Wendy's on the way home and then watched *The Little Mermaid* tape with her and then put her to bed and went to bed myself. Of course I couldn't sleep! My mind was in a whirl, thinking of what to do. Finally I decided to lay all the cards out on the table, confront him the minute he got home. But then I heard him dragging that leg up the stairs. And then I heard him in the bathroom splashing water on his pretty face. And then here he came, easing himself into the bed (our bedroom suite is not paid for either). He flung one arm across my stomach, the way he always does, and in about one minute flat, he started that little snuffly breathing.

Then I knew I would not say a word. I wanted to keep him

with me as long as I could, you see. I never in the world thought I'd ever have Billy Sims in the first place, and I couldn't stand to lose him. So I wasn't going to speed it up, nor do anything different. I couldn't. I didn't close my eyes that whole night long. Finally I just punched in the alarm thing before it went off, and waited for dawn to come. I made Billy a pan of biscuits to eat when he got up.

"YOU DIDN'T." LOIS RUBIN quits writing at this point. "Weren't you *angry?*"

ANGER HAD NOT YET occurred to me.

That morning I went on to work as usual, and five more weeks passed by. I was holding my breath the entire time. Billy took me and Debbi out to the lake twice, and we also went overnight to a Garth Brooks concert in Lexington. I even got Billy to go to the church homecoming with me. I took two pans of my three-cheese lasagna, by popular request.

Then — now this is *yesterday,* of course, Monday morning — I had no sooner got to work and watered my African violets and sat down at my desk than here came two of my lawyers, Mr. Martin and Mr. Perkins, into my little office. They *knew.* It was written all over their faces. "Dee Ann," Mr. Martin said, "this is terribly hard for us." He looked like his heart would break. "You have been a valued employee, as you know. The best we've ever had. But on last Friday afternoon, after you left, I had occasion to check the George Pendleton trust account, and I was most dismayed to find that no deposit had been recorded this month."

"It hadn't?" I'd kept the check, of course. But I couldn't believe that I had failed to write it in the book. It was my own dumb mistake. If I'd done it right, Mr. Martin never would have known the difference. He's an egghead intellectual, not a practical bone in his body. But this time he fooled me.

"So I decided to check on some of the other trusts," he said. "I took the books home with me this weekend, Dee Ann, and finally ended up calling Longstreet" — he pointed his long bony finger at Mr. Longstreet, who looked like he would rather be anywhere in the world but here — "and as nearly as we can figure, you're into us for about six thousand dollars. Would you say that's fairly accurate?"

"Yes, sir," I said.

Actually it is $13,825.

"We realize you have had some difficult circumstances in your personal life, Dee Ann, so perhaps we can work something out here, among us."

"What do you mean?" I asked.

"Embezzlement is a felony offense," Mr. Martin said kindly. "But perhaps it need not come to that. What would you say if we worked out some sort of a repayment schedule . . ."

"No," I said. "I could never make it. I can't make it now. Go on and do whatever you have to," I said. "I'm through with the whole thing."

Mr. Longstreet Perkins raised one bushy gray eyebrow. "In that case," he said, "I'm afraid we'll need to walk down the street to the police station. I'm so sorry, Dee Ann. Do you want to call Billy first?"

"Hell, no," I said, surprising myself. "He doesn't deserve me."

Lois Rubin flings down her clipboard. "Damn straight!" she says.

"Listen," Sam Hicks says, "there is some men, myself included, that *prefers* a large woman."

"Oh, for Pete's sake," says Lois Rubin.

THE OLD LAWYERS STOOD there looking at each other. "Well, then," Mr. Martin said. I stood up behind my desk and looked them both in the eye, first one, then the other. I'm as tall as they are. I knew they hated this. They hated that I had done it, they hated having to turn me in. And in Mr. Longstreet Perkins's eyes, there was something beyond that even. He understood that anybody could have done what I did in the name of love, anybody at all, that he could even have done it himself. "Ah, Dee Ann," he said.

"Listen," I said. "It's all right."

And it was. It is. As we walked down the street, my heart got lighter and lighter with each step. I was glad to be caught! Mr. Martin and Mr. Perkins spoke to everybody we passed. A summer storm was blowing up by then, as you may recall. Wind whipped down the sidewalk, clouds tore across the sky. Mr. Longstreet Perkins had to hold on to his famous straw hat. It started thundering. Suddenly I felt the way I used to feel when Sissy and me were kids. We'd run up on the top of the mountain to whirl around and around whenever a storm came up. You can smell the lightning in the air, which is real exciting, it doesn't smell like anything else in the world. So that's how I felt, walking down the sidewalk to this jail. Drops of rain as big as silver dollars splattered on the sidewalk. We were getting real wet. My hair lay plastered in strings all down my face. Lightning flashed. It kept on thundering. But my heart rose like a bird with each step we took until I was flying, flying up through the electric air and out among the clouds.

Ultima Thule

"You'll remember to get the Thule put on top of the Volvo, then?" On his way over to the university, Jake turns back to ask her. "And make sure the key works?" He hands her this little bitty key.

"Sure," Nova says, rubbing her eyes, wearing a black number three muscle shirt that used to be her brother's, and nothing else. She knows she can get Theron to do it. "The drug boys are coming today," she says, and Jake nods. He is on the board of Agape, the residential drug treatment program which runs the landscaping and lawn care business that comes to work at their little farm outside Charlottesville, which is not really a farm, any more than they are really farmers, or Jake is an average graduate student, or they are a regular young couple just trying to make ends meet.

No. The big surprise is that Jake has turned out to belong to a very rich family, rich enough to own an entire island in Maine, for instance, which is where they are heading tomorrow morning at the crack of dawn in the Volvo with the Thule on top of it like an enormous coffin filled with their clothes because the dogs will be taking up all the space in the car — Thor, Jake's old black lab, in the backseat, and Odin, the big husky pup, in the back-back. Everybody in Jake's family owns big dogs that wear bandannas and go to Maine. Nova has been there once, last year, when she and Jake had just gotten married.

Everybody in Jake's family called her "The Bride" in a tongue-in-cheek way that made her nervous at first, until she figured out that's just how they all talk, like they are putting quotation marks around everything. Nova recognizes irony, which is what Mrs. Stevenson, her senior English teacher, defined as, "Irony is when the fire chief's house burns down." Part of the irony in calling her "The Bride" came from the fact that Nova was already pregnant, she knew this, too.

"No, this is great, this is awesome, this is seriously great," Jake's brother had assured her in Maine. "We always figured he was gay."

Now Jake blows her a kiss from the yard before he drives off in his old truck. Nova has never known a man before who would blow anybody a kiss, ever, under any circumstances. She rubs her flat stomach, fingering the navel ring. Jake took pictures of her pregnancy, every few days. He used rolls and rolls of film. She lost that baby at five and a half months, and it was a girl, they said. Nova had wanted a girl, she would have taken such good care of it, not like her own mother at all. Nova and Jake had already bought a crib, and gotten Agape to paint the extra bedroom tangerine, her idea. Nova has plenty of ideas, she is not dumb at all. Jake has made her realize this. Now they have closed the door to the little tangerine room, until later.

Good thing they've got these two dogs, which keep her busy, sort of. Nova likes the dogs, but she did not like Maine, an entire state that smells like Pine-Sol, especially Blueberry Island, a very cold and foggy place that is far away from everything, especially the grocery store. Nova does like to cook and it drove her crazy not to be able to go to the grocery store every day, which is what she likes to do at home. Also, the water will freeze your ass off and the grocery store does not even carry grits. Also, there is no TV on Blueberry Island, something Jake forgot to mention in all the times he talked about the island like it was paradise. The only positive thing was that all the Maine women turned out to be big and ugly, almost as if they were doing it on purpose, so this made Nova look like a beauty queen. You should see these women! Nobody wears any makeup or nice clothes. Their hair sticks out on one side and looks awful. This is also true of Jake's mother and sisters, at least in the summertime. Nova does not know if they look any better during the rest of the year or not.

She and Jake did not go up to Connecticut for Christmas, although they were invited, because this is when Nova lost the baby and had to spend several days in the University of Virginia Hospital, very ironic considering that is where she and Jake first met, though Jake was over in Neurosciences and she was working the cash register in the snack bar on the first floor. Jake had been in the hospital for three months when she met him, this is why he had a blue badge and was allowed to come down to the first floor unsupervised. Later he would get a town pass, and still later a day pass that would allow him to take her to the Boars Head Inn and fuck her eyes out. Yes! His brothers would have been so surprised. Nova had never been to the Boars Head Inn before, although she had lived outside Charlottesville all her life. Their room had a sixty-inch TV hidden away inside an antique hutch, she was so surprised. Also a minibar.

Nova had noticed Jake right away because he was so thin. Most of the mental patients are real fat, it is due to their medications. Jake was also sweet, not usually true of doctors or patients either one. The day they met, he was standing patiently in line behind that heavy woman with the big blonde hairdo growing out black at the roots who was so pushy and bought the same thing every day, a cheeseburger and fries and strawberry shortcake, and had a fit whenever they didn't have the strawberry shortcake. That day she forgot her money. When Nova handed her the little piece of paper, she started to cry. The woman had a black mustache, which drove Nova crazy, Nova has got sort of an obsession about facial hair. Maybe she should slip this woman some Nair. "Just go on," Nova told her, looking all around first. "You can pay me tomorrow."

"Oh no . . . I . . ." The woman began to flap her hands.

"Here. Keep the change," Jake said, popping up behind the woman, handing over a ten-dollar bill.

"I'm not allowed to do that," Nova said as the woman started to cry.

"Just add my bill onto hers, then," Jake said.

The woman cried louder, big sobs coming up out of her cleavage.

"Here now, ma'am." He took the woman by the elbow and steered her over to a table, pulling out a chair for her.

Nova rang up the woman's food again, along with three little bowls of macaroni and cheese, and coffee. "That's not a very balanced meal," she said to him when he came back.

"Well." Jake grinned at her. "I'm not a very balanced man. I'm crazy."

"What's your diagnosis?" Nova knew she wasn't supposed to ask.

"Life," he said. "What's your name?"

"Nova," she said. "Named for the car, not the star. My mother got pregnant at a drive-in."

Nova thought he looked like one of those cornhusk dolls her granny used to make, with thin, thin corn silk hair flopping onto his face and a long thin stick nose and big even teeth like a row of corn on the cob and beautiful huge blue eyes like lakes, swimming behind his thick glasses. Or she was swimming in his eyes, that's more like it. Suddenly Nova became very critical of Raymond Crabtree who had given her this job for certain considerations, he had steel blue jaws by five o'clock, and lived for *Monday Night Football*.

"You don't seem very crazy to me," Nova heard herself say, though really he was so thin and pale, he was not her type at all.

"I guess you'll have to get to know me, then," Jake said, and so she did, and still he never did seem very crazy to her, only too sensitive for this world. Jake used to be a rock musician and play in bands, she learned, but now he was a graduate student in American Studies. He used to do a lot of drugs, but now he does oral histories with people such as lobster fishermen in Maine and the drug boys who work for Agape. He has already taped Theron.

The first time Nova went up to visit Jake in the third-floor dayroom in Neurosciences, a skinny blonde woman came over and hugged him and turned to Nova and told her, "You may not know it, but this is Jesus Christ."

"Wow," Nova said.

"All the girls say that," Jake said.

Jake played Pachelbel's Canon in D Major and "Bridge over Troubled Water" for Nova on the piano they had brought into the dayroom for him. Nova started to visit him every afternoon when she got off lunch duty, and one time when she was up there, this little old black man went over and leaned against the piano and started scat-singing along when Jake was playing blues. "I was born down in Savannah," he sang, "under a ugly star." Nurses and aides and other patients gathered around to hear him; this little man had not said a single word since he had been admitted to the hospital months before. Nobody knew who he was or where he had come from or anything of his history. They wrote it down as he sang it, accompanied by Jake.

When Jake got out of the hospital, Nova moved out to his weird house in the country with him. Raymond Crabtree was mad at her now, so she couldn't afford her apartment anymore, but she didn't tell Jake that, and it didn't matter anyway, because by then she was pregnant.

"Honey, if I was you I'd make a good thing of this," Nova's mother said, smoking a cigarette, when Nova went to ask her for money at the dry cleaners where she worked. "You're crazy if you don't." Of course Nova's mother didn't have any money anyway.

And really, Jake was so happy when she told him, and so sweet, he was putty in Nova's hands. She told him she didn't believe in abortion. They got married at the big courthouse downtown. Nova wore a beautiful midcalf flowered dress with a low lacy neckline, while Jake wore some old army pants and a tux jacket. By then she was catching on to how rich people will wear just any old thing. The witnesses at their wedding were a courthouse secretary named Alice Robinson and a black prostitute named Shawndra Day who had been sitting out in the hall waiting to see her court-appointed attorney. Then Jake took Nova down to Richmond for a night in the Jefferson Hotel with its crocodile sculpture and its great dome of stained glass in the lobby like a cathedral, the closest Nova has ever been to one.

When they got back to Charlottesville, there was *his* mother, leaning up against her car parked beside the mailbox. Her car was a navy blue Mercedes with smoked windows, you couldn't tell if she had a driver or anybody else in there with her or not. Jake's mother has dyed red hair and anorexia nervosa even at her age, Nova could tell right off. She recognizes a mental illness when she sees one. Jake's mother's name is Barbara.

Jake got out of the car and Barbara ran over to fling her arms around him dramatically, like a person in a movie. "I can't believe you would do this to me," she sobbed. Jake patted her while extricating himself as best he could, motioning for Nova to get out of the Volvo. "Barbara," he said, "here she is. This is Nova." But Barbara cut loose again and would not even look at her. *Well fuck this,* Nova thought, standing there.

Then the drivers side door of the blue Mercedes opened and Jake's father got out, a horsey-looking man in khaki pants and a pale blue denim shirt. He came over and took both of Nova's hands in his, looking into her eyes in a way that made Nova trust him immediately, as well as feel sort of bad about herself. "Welcome to the family, dear," he said.

"Won't you come in?" Nova said.

"No," said Barbara.

"Sure," said Mr. Valentine.

They had ginger ale and stale cookies and strained conversation, with Barbara sniffling on the old truck seat that served as a sofa, looking all around the crazy living room. "Folk art," Jake explained as his mother took in the old signs and homemade art on the walls, and the chain-saw angel, and the barber's chair that Mr. Valentine was sitting in. Nova went along with Barbara on this. She could not understand why anybody wouldn't have nice comfortable furniture if they could afford it. She hates that chain-saw angel. Nova said she wasn't feeling well and excused herself.

So they didn't know that she was standing right there in the overgrown grape arbor when they left, that she saw Mr. Valentine poke Jake in the side and say, "Way to go!" as Jake turned to leave, or that she heard Barbara say, "I don't like her," when he was out of earshot. "At least he's not gay," Mr. Valentine said as he got in the car.

Now Jake's parents are already in Maine, on the island, with a cook and a housekeeper and a "man" who live in little log cabins out in the piney woods and do everything for them. Nova stands at the screen door and thinks about everything she has got to do to get ready for the trip, besides getting Theron and his boys to put the Thule on top of the Volvo, that's the least of it. Nova does not see why she can't have decent help instead of drug addicts and and crazy people, why they can't have a nice house, why they have to go back to the land. Nova would like to get away from the land! She doesn't understand why they have to go to Maine instead of Hilton Head Island, which is where anybody in their right mind who could afford it would surely go.

But now Nova has got to clean out the refrigerator and wash a load of clothes and go in to town to buy more dog food and sign that little thing in the post office that will cancel their mail delivery while they are gone, though she never gets any mail anyway except stuff from the community college now that Jake has signed her up to take some courses in the fall. She has got to read *The Scarlet Letter* first, which looks awful. Mrs. Stevenson used to want her to go to college too, but then Nova ran off with her mother's boyfriend's brother, a disc jockey from Columbia, South Carolina, ending up in Myrtle Beach doing some things that did not require a degree of any kind. Nova runs her finger along the screen door, she knows she's procrastinating. Actually *procrastinating* was a word on the GED that Nova just did so well on.

Then beyond the mailbox and the meadow she sees a rising plume of dust so she runs back into their bedroom and pulls on some cutoffs and puts on that red halter top and some red lipstick and ties her hair up into a high swingy ponytail on top of her head. She's back at the screen door by the time Theron jumps out of his jeep, looking like an ad for something. Anything! Theron has gray eyes and the most beautiful legs and a café au lait complexion. He says he is Hawaiian but Nova knows he is not. Theron stands for a minute outside the door, peering in.

"Where is everybody?" Nova asks, meaning the rest of the Agape yard crew.

"Taco Bell." Theron unbuttons his shirt.

Nova is naked by the time they hit the bedroom.

Afterward, they share a joint in the unmade bed. Since hiring Agape, Nova has had them clear the meadow and make a stone path out to the old springhouse in the woods that Jake uses for his photography studio. Now she has just decided to make a rock garden out front, on the side of that little hill by the mailbox. It will be a lot of work. Nova smiles, lying flat on her back with her feet up against the wall.

"What you call that thing you want me to put on the car?" Theron is already up, pulling on his pants.

"Thule," she says.

"Funny name." Theron sits back down on the side of the bed to lace up his work boots.

"I thought it was a brand name, but Jake says it means some mythical northern country," Nova says dreamily in that dreamy way she always feels after sex, thinking *Thule, Yule, Thor, Odin,* all of these words that Theron does not and will never know. Thule. It sounds like a kingdom of the olden days. Still, he's gorgeous, those big brown arms.

"Hey babe, you know something?" Now he turns to look at her, he pinches her nipple.

"What." It's hot in the bedroom. A bee buzzes against the screen.

"Well, I been thinking." Now he seems hesitant, for Theron. Usually Theron is right up front. "You know, it wouldn't be too hard for you and me to, you know, do something about Jake. If that's what you wanted me to do, I mean."

Suddenly the whole room goes completely still, like it has turned into a black and white photograph. The air gets thick and hard to breathe.

Nova sits up. "What did you say?" she says.

"You and me, we could, you know." Theron grins at her.

She looks out the window and down the meadow to the road where she sees the dust, which means that Agape is coming up the hill in that old panel truck.

"Hey now, you know, I didn't mean nothing by it." Theron is on his feet, ready to go, smiling at her.

Nova smiles back. "Well, that's good, then."

Maybe that rock garden is not such a good idea, she thinks later, watching Theron lift the Thule like it's nothing. He and his boys attach it securely to the racks on the top of the Volvo. Then they start up their regular mowing and weed eating like crazy. Nova knows they do a lot of unnecessary work out here because they need the money. She doesn't blame them a bit. While they work, she cleans out the refrigerator and finishes the wash and packs her own suitcase, but she knows she can't leave the farm until Agape leaves first, because they will steal something. Of course they will. And why not? They are the underclass, a word she learned last week when she went over to the university with Jake for the opening of that photography exhibit he's in, "The Mind's Eye."

The next morning Nova has to work like an animal because Jake is so disorganized. He forgot to give her the clothes he wanted her to wash, he forgot to pick up his medicine from the pharmacy or the dogs' heartworm pills from the vet, so she has to drive into town to get all this stuff. When she gets back the clothes are dry. They fold them together and then she climbs up on the stepstool and puts them into the Thule as Jake hands them up to her, one item after another in the blazing midday sun, then his tennis racket and his wet suit and all the books and equipment he will need for his various projects — his tripod, his printer, his tape recorder, whatever. Jake makes a huge production about packing everything just so. Nova feels like hitting him, but instead she smiles brightly and says, "Ready?" and Jake reaches up to hug her and says yes, he guesses so. He whistles for the dogs who have been circling the Volvo warily, like fish. He puts Thor into the backseat and opens the back-back door for Odin who will ride behind the pet gate next to Nova's suitcase. Odin jumps in. Jake slams the door.

"Okay, lock it," he calls up to Nova who is getting this god-awful headache now up on this stepstool so close to the sun.

She sticks the little key into the little lock and tries to turn it, but it won't turn. Shit. That's the one thing she forgot to do yesterday, check the goddamn key. But what is she supposed to be anyway, a goddamn hired hand? But she'll have to tell him, won't she? Won't she? Won't they have to go get some bungee cords or something? Nova turns, shielding her eyes from the sun, but now

Jake has disappeared back into the house. He comes out waving *The Scarlet Letter*. "Hey! You almost forgot this!" he yells. He tosses it into the front seat. Right. Like Nova is really going to read *The Scarlet Letter* on this trip. Shit! She's not a hired hand, she's a project.

For the second time that day, Nova has the sense that time has stopped, that she is in one of Jake's photographs. She looks out at the rolling meadow and the little stone farmhouse and the blue line of mountains beyond, where she grew up. She jumps down lightly. When Jake hugs her, she can feel all his ribs.

"Ready?" he says.

She gets in the car.

The next morning, they are on Interstate 81 outside of Chambersburg, Pennsylvania, when the top of the Thule pops up and Jake's clothes start flying out, slowly at first, like something in a dream, scattering all over the interstate behind them. Strangely enough, Nova sees the whole thing, entirely by chance, because she has pulled the passenger-side mirror down to tweeze her face a little bit, those chin hairs. So she just happens to see Jake's red and black checkered L.L. Bean wool shirt out of the corner of her eye as it sails lazily through the air to land on the windshield of a red Chevy Blazer two cars behind them blinding the driver only momentarily but long enough to make her swerve back and forth, back and forth, in larger and larger arcs, the Blazer rocking now until it runs off the road into the median hitting one of those great big rocks like you find in Pennsylvania. Nova puts the tweezers back into her makeup case, which she puts back into her purse. She doesn't say one word to Jake but turns in her seat to watch as his clothes fly through the air faster and faster and all the cars behind them begin to weave and then there's a rattling sound from the top of the Volvo as his printer busts loose to land squarely on the hood of the Subaru wagon just behind them, and his tennis racket bounces off the hood of the little yellow Acura breaking the window and causing the Acura to veer into a silver pickup in the other lane, which hits a Jeep Cherokee, which explodes.

All the cars are running into each other now, out of their nice white lines, crumpling like toy cars. Smoke rises into the sunny air. The dogs start barking. The Cherokee is burning. Now a Mustang convertible, which has slammed into it, is burning too.

Nova knows this is all her fault.

"Oh no! Oh my God! Oh shit!" Now Jake sees it too, he drives right off the road, they are bumping along over big old rocks and then they are in the trees.

Nova never, ever told. She left Jake, who really was too sensitive for this world. She heard he's been dead for a couple of years now. That day on I-81 has come to seem like a film to her, a DVD that she can play at will in her mind's eye, slow or fast, more vivid than anything else in her life before or since. Nova has never made a good thing out of anything, but she's done all right. She gets along okay. They never got to Maine, of course, after the accident, and Nova has never gotten there since. She thinks about it sometimes, though, and it seems so far away to her now, like another country, the country of Thule perhaps with its piney smell and its pointed trees and the freezing water in Blueberry Lake and they are all still there, Jake's whole family and all their dogs and Jake himself, she can still see his swimming blue eyes right now, Lord he was sweet.

Intensive Care

Cherry Oxendine is dying now, and everybody knows it. Everybody in town except maybe her new husband, Harold Stikes, although Lord knows he ought to, it's as plain as the nose on your face. And it's not like he hasn't been *told* either, by both Dr. Thacker and Dr. Pinckney and also that hotshot young Jew doctor from Memphis, Dr. Shapiro, who comes over here once a week. "Harold just can't take it in," is what the head nurse in Intensive Care, Lois Hickey, said in the Beauty Nook last week. Lois ought to know. She's been right there during the past six weeks while Cherry Oxendine has been in Intensive Care, writing down Cherry's blood pressure every hour on the hour, changing bags on the IV, checking the stomach tube, moving the bed up and down to prevent bedsores, monitoring the respirator — and calling Rodney Broadbent, the respiratory therapist, more and more frequently. "Her blood gases is not by twenty-eight," Lois said in the Beauty Nook. "If we was to unhook that respirator, she'd die in a day."

"I would go on and do it then, if I was Harold," said Mrs. Hooker, the Presbyterian minister's wife, who was getting a permanent. "It is the Christian thing."

"You wouldn't either," Lois said, "because she *still knows him.*

That's the awful part. She still knows him. In fact she peps right up ever time he comes in, like they are going on a date or something. It's the saddest thing. And ever time we open the doors, here comes Harold, regular as clockwork. Eight o'clock, one o'clock, six o'clock, eight o'clock, why shoot, he'd stay in there all day and all night if we'd let him. Well, she opens her mouth and says *Hi honey,* you can tell what she's saying even if she can't make a sound. And her eyes get real bright and her face looks pretty good too, that's because of the Lasix, only Harold don't know that. He just can't take it all in," Lois said.

"Oh, I feel so sorry for him," said Mrs. Hooker. Her face is as round and as flat as a dime.

"Well, I don't." Dot Mains, owner of the Beauty Nook, started cutting Lois Hickey's hair. Lois wears it too short, in Dot's opinion. "I certainly don't feel sorry for Harold Stikes, after what he did." Dot snipped decisively at Lois Hickey's frosted hair. Mrs. Hooker made a sad little sound, half sigh, half words, as Janice stuck her under the dryer, while Miss Berry, the old-maid home demonstration agent waiting for her appointment, snapped the pages of *Cosmopolitan* magazine one by one, blindly, filled with somewhat gratuitous rage against the behavior of Harold Stikes. Miss Berry is Harold Stikes's ex-wife's cousin. So she does not pity him, not one bit. He got what's coming to him, that's all, in Miss Berry's opinion. Most people don't. It's a pleasure to see it, but Miss Berry would never say this out loud since Cherry Oxendine is of course dying. Cherry Oxendine! Like it was yesterday, Miss Berry remembers how Cherry Oxendine acted in high school, wearing her skirts too tight, popping her gum.

"The doctors can't do a thing," said Lois Hickey.

Silence settled like fog on the Beauty Nook, on Miss Berry and her magazine, on Dot Mains cutting Lois Hickey's hair, on little Janice thinking about her boyfriend, Bruce, and on Mrs. Hooker crying gently under the dryer. Suddenly, Dot remembered something her old granny used to say about such moments of sudden absolute quiet: "An angel is passing over."

After a while, Mrs. Hooker said, "It's all in the hands of God, then." She spread out her fingers one by one on the tray, for Janice to give her a manicure.

AND AS FOR HAROLD Stikes, he's not even considering God. Oh, he doesn't interfere when Mr. Hooker comes by the hospital once a day to check on him — Harold was a Presbyterian in his former life — or even when the Baptist preacher from Cherry's mama's church shows up and insists that everybody in the whole waiting room join hands and bow heads in prayer while he raises his big red face and curly gray head straight up to Heaven and prays in a loud voice that God will heal these loved ones who walk through the Valley of Death and comfort these others who watch, through their hour of need. This includes Mrs. Eunice Sprayberry, whose mother has had a stroke, John and Paula Ripman, whose infant son is dying of encephalitis, and different others who drift in and out of Intensive Care following surgery or wrecks. Harold is losing track. He closes his eyes and bows his head, figuring it can't hurt, like taking out insurance. But deep down inside, he knows that if God is worth His salt, He is not impressed by the prayer of Harold Stikes, who knowingly gave up all hope of peace on earth and Heaven hereafter for the love of Cherry Oxendine.

Not to mention his family.

He gave them up too.

But this morning when he leaves the hospital after his eight o'clock visit to Cherry, Harold finds himself turning left out of the lot instead of right toward Food Lion, his store. Harold finds himself taking Route 60 just south of town and then driving through those ornate marble gates that mark the entrance to Camelot Hills, his old neighborhood. Some lucky instinct makes him pull into the little park and stop there, beside the pond. Here comes his ex-wife, Joan, driving the Honda Accord he paid for last year. Joan looks straight ahead. She's still wearing her shiny blonde hair in the pageboy she's worn ever since Harold met her at Mercer College so many years ago. Harold is sure she's wearing low heels and a shirtwaist dress. He knows her briefcase is in the backseat, containing lesson plans for today, yogurt, and a banana. Potassium is important. Harold has heard this a million times. Behind her, the beds are all made, the breakfast dishes stacked in the sink. As a home ec teacher, Joan believes that breakfast is the most important meal of the day. The two younger children, Brenda and Harold Jr., are already on the bus to the Academy. James rides to the high school with his mother, hair wet, face blank, staring straight ahead. They don't see Harold. Joan brakes at the stop sign before entering Route 60. She always comes to a complete stop, even if nothing's coming. Always. She looks both ways. Then she's gone.

Harold drives past well-kept lawn after well-kept lawn and lovely house after lovely house, many of them houses where Harold has attended Cub Scout meetings, eaten barbecue, watched bowl games. Now these houses have a blank, closed look to them, like mean faces. Harold turns left on Oxford, then right on Shrewsbury. He comes to a stop beside the curb at 1105 Cambridge and just sits there with the motor running, looking at the house. His house. The Queen Anne house he and Joan planned so carefully, down to the last detail, the fish-scale siding. The house he is still paying for and will be until his dying day, if Joan has her way about it.

Which she will, of course. Everybody is on her side: *desertion*. Harold Stikes deserted his lovely wife and three children for a redheaded waitress. For a fallen woman with a checkered past. Harold can hear her now. "I fail to see why I and the children should lower our standards of living, Harold, and go to the dogs just because you have chosen to become insane in midlife." Joan's voice is slow and amiable. It has a down-to-earth quality which used to appeal to Harold but now drives him wild. Harold sits at the curb with the motor running and looks at his house good. It looks fine. It looks just like it did when they picked it out of the pages of *Southern Living* and wrote off for the plans. The only difference is, that house was in Stone Mountain, Georgia, and this house is in Greenwood, Mississippi. Big deal.

Joan's response to Harold's desertion has been a surprise to him. He expected tears, recriminations, fireworks. He did not expect her calm, reasonable manner, treating Harold the way she treats the Mormon missionaries who come to the door in their black suits, for instance, that very calm, sweet, careful voice. Joan acts like Harold's desertion is nothing much. And nothing much appears to have changed for her except the loss of Harold's actual presence, and this cannot be a very big deal since everything else has remained exactly the same.

What the hell. After a while Harold turns off the motor and walks up the flagstone walk to the front door. His key still fits. All the furniture is arranged exactly the way it was arranged four years ago. The only thing that ever changes here is the display of magazines on the glass coffee table before the fireplace, Joan keeps them up to date. *Newsweek, National Geographic, Good House-keeping, Gourmet.* It's a mostly educational grouping, unlike what Cherry reads — *Parade, Coronet, National Enquirer.* Now these magazines litter the floor at the side of the bed like little souvenirs of Cherry. Harold can't stand to pick them up.

He sits down heavily on the white sofa and stares at the coffee table. He remembers the quiz and the day he found it, four years ago now although it feels like only yesterday, funny thing though he can't remember which magazine it was in. Maybe *Reader's Digest.* The quiz was titled "How Good Is Your Marriage?" and Harold noticed that Joan had filled it in carefully. This did not surprise him. Joan was so law abiding, such a *good girl,* that she always filled in such quizzes when she came across them, as if she *had to,* before she could go ahead and finish the magazine. Usually Harold didn't pay much attention.

This time, he picked the magazine up and started reading. One of the questions said: "What is your idea of the perfect vacation? (a) a romantic getaway for you and your spouse alone; (b) a family trip to the beach; (c) a business convention; (d) an organized tour of a foreign land." Joan had wavered on this one. She had marked and then erased "an organized tour of a foreign land." Finally she had settled on "a family trip to the beach." Harold skimmed along. The final question was: "When you think of the love between yourself and your spouse, do you think of (a) a great passion; (b) a warm, meaningful companionship; (c) an average love; (d) an unsatisfying habit." Joan had marked "(c) an average love." Harold stared at these words, knowing they were true. An average love, nothing great, an average marriage between an average man and woman. Suddenly, strangely, Harold was filled with rage.

"It is not enough!" He thought he actually said these words out loud. Perhaps he *did* say them out loud, into the clean hushed air-conditioned air of his average home. Harold's rage was followed by a brief period, maybe five minutes, of unbearable longing, after which he simply closed the magazine and put it back on the table and got up and poured himself a stiff shot of bourbon. He stood for a while before the picture window in the living room, looking out at his even green grass, his clipped hedge, and the impatiens blooming in its bed, the clematis climbing the mailbox. The colors of the world fairly leaped at him — the sky so blue, the grass so green. A passing jogger's shorts glowed unbearably red. He felt that he had never seen any of these things before. Yet in another way it all seemed so familiar as to be an actual part of his body — his throat, his heart, his breath. Harold took another drink. Then he went out and played nine holes of golf at the country club with Bubba Fields, something he did every Wednesday afternoon. He shot an 82.

By the time he came home for dinner he was okay again. He was very tired and a little lightheaded, all his muscles tingling. His face was hot. Yet Harold felt vaguely pleased with himself, as if he had been through something and come out of the other side of it, as if he had done a creditable job on a difficult assignment. But right then, during dinner, Harold could not have told you exactly what had happened to him that day, or why he felt this way. Because the mind will forget what it can't stand to remember, and anyway, the Stikeses had beef Stroganoff that night, a new recipe that Joan was testing for the Junior League cookbook, and Harold Jr. had written them a funny letter from camp, and for once Brenda did not whine. James, who was twelve that year, actually condescended to talk to his father, with some degree of interest, about baseball, and after supper was over he and Harold went out and pitched to each other until it grew dark and lightning bugs emerged. This is how it's supposed to be, Harold thought, father and son playing catch in the twilight.

Then he went upstairs and joined Joan in bed to watch TV, after which they turned out the light and made love. But Joan had greased herself all over with Oil of Olay, earlier, and right in the middle of doing it, Harold got a crazy terrified feeling that he was losing her, that Joan was slipping, slipping away.

But time passed, as it does, and Harold forgot that whole weird day, forgot it until *right now,* in fact, as he sits on the white sofa in his old house again and stares at the magazines on the coffee table, those magazines so familiar except for the date, which is four years later. Now Harold wonders: If he hadn't picked up that quiz and read it, would he have even *noticed* when Cherry Oxendine spooned out that potato salad for him six months later, in his own Food Lion deli? Would the sight of redheaded Cherry Oxendine, the Food Lion smock mostly obscuring her dynamite figure, have hit him like a bolt out of the blue the way it did?

Cherry herself does not believe there is any such thing as coincidence. Cherry thinks there is a master plan for the universe, and what is *meant* to happen will. She thinks it's all set in the stars. For the first time, Harold thinks maybe she's right. He sees part of a pattern in the works, but dimly, as if he is looking at a constellation hidden by clouds. Mainly, he sees her face.

Harold gets up from the sofa and goes into the kitchen, suddenly aware that he isn't supposed to be here. He could be arrested, probably! He looks back at the living room, but there's not a trace of him left, not even an imprint on the soft white cushions of the sofa. Absentmindedly, Harold opens and shuts the refrigerator door. There's no beer, he notices. He can't have a Coke. On the kitchen calendar, he reads:

Harold Jr. to dentist, 3:30 p.m. Tues.
Change furnace filter 2/18/88 (James)

So James is changing the furnace filters now, James is the man of the house. Why not? It's good for him. He's been given too much, kids these days grow up so fast, no responsibilities, they get on drugs, you read about it all the time. But deep down inside, Harold knows that James is not on drugs and he feels something awful, feels the way he felt growing up, that sick flutter in his stomach that took years to go away.

Harold's dad died of walking pneumonia when he was only three, so his mother raised him alone. She called him her "little man." This made Harold feel proud but also wild, like a boy growing up in a cage. Does James feel this way now? Harold suddenly decides to get James a car for his birthday, and take him hunting.

Hunting is something Harold never did as a boy, but it means a lot to him now. Harold never owned a gun until he was thirty-one, when he bought a shotgun in order to accept the invitation of his regional manager, "Little Jimmy" Fletcher, to go quail hunting in Georgia. He had a great time. Now he's invited back every year, and Little Jimmy is in charge of the company's whole eastern division. Harold has a great future with Food Lion too. He owns three stores, one in downtown Greenwood, one out at the mall, and one over in Indianola. He owned two of them when his mother died, and he's pleased to think that she died proud — proud of the good little boy he'd always been, and the good man he'd become.

Of course she'd wanted him to make a preacher, but Harold

never got the call, and she gave that up finally when he was twenty. Harold was not going to pretend to get the call if he never got it, and he held strong to this principle. He *wanted* to see a burning bush, but if this was not vouchsafed to him, he wasn't going to lie about it. He would just major in math instead, which he was good at anyway. Majoring in math at Mercer College, the small Baptist school his mother had chosen for him, Harold came upon Joan Berry, a home ec major from his own hometown who set out single-mindedly to marry him, which wasn't hard. After graduation, Harold got a job as management trainee in the Food Lion store where he had started as a bag boy at fourteen. Joan produced their three children, spaced three years apart, and got her tubes tied. Harold got one promotion, then another. Joan and Harold prospered. They built this house.

Harold looks around and now this house, his house, strikes him as creepy, a wax museum. He lets himself out the back door and walks quickly, almost runs, to his car. It's real cold out, a gray day in February, but Harold's sweating. He starts his car and roars off toward the hospital, driving — as Cherry would say — like a bat out of hell.

THEY'RE LETTING HAROLD STAY with her longer now. He knows it, they know it, but nobody says a word. Lois Hickey just looks the other way when the announcement "Visiting hours are over" crackles across the PA. Is this a good sign or a bad sign? Harold can't tell. He feels slow and confused, like a man underwater. "I think she looks better, don't you?" he said last night to Cherry's son, Stan, the TV weatherman, who had driven down from Memphis for the day. Eyes slick and bright with tears, Stan went over to Harold and hugged him tight. This scared Harold to death, he has practically never touched his own sons, and he doesn't even *know* Stan, who's been grown and gone for years. Harold is not used to hugging anybody, especially men. Harold breathed in Stan's strong go-get-'em cologne, he buried his face in Stan's long curly hair. He thinks it is possible that Stan has a permanent. They'll do anything in Memphis. Then Stan stepped back and put one hand on each of Harold's shoulders, holding him out at arm's length. Stan has his mother's wide, mobile mouth. The bright white light of Intensive Care glinted off the gold chain and the crystal that he wore around his neck. "I'm afraid we're going to lose her, Pop," he said.

But Harold doesn't think so. Today he thinks Cherry looks the best she's looked in weeks, with a bright spot of color in each cheek to match her flaming hair. She's moving around a lot too. She keeps kicking her sheet off.

"She's getting back some of that old energy now," he tells Cherry's daughter, Tammy Lynn Palladino, when she comes by after school. Tammy Lynn and Harold's son, James, are both members of the senior class, but they aren't friends. Tammy Lynn says James is a "stuck-up jock," a "preppie," and a "country-clubber." Harold can't say a word to defend his own son against these charges, he doesn't even *know* James anymore. It might be true anyway. Tammy Lynn is real smart, a teenage egghead. She's got a full scholarship to Millsaps College for next year. She applied for it all by herself. As Cherry used to say, Tammy Lynn came into this world with a full deck of cards and an ace or two up her sleeve. Also, she looks out for Number One.

In this regard Tammy Lynn is as different from her mama as night from day, because Cherry would give you the shirt off her back and frequently has. That's gotten her into lots of trouble.

With Ed Palladino, for instance, her second husband and Tammy Lynn's dad. Just about everybody in this town got took by Ed Palladino, who came in here wearing a seersucker suit and talking big about putting in an outlet mall across the river. A lot of people got burned on that outlet mall deal. But Ed Palladino had a way about him that made you want to cast your lot with his, it is true. You wanted to give Ed Palladino your savings, your time-sharing condo, your cousin, your ticket to the Super Bowl. Cherry gave it all.

She married him and turned over what little inheritance she had from her daddy's death — and that's the only time in her life she ever had *any* money, mind you — and then she just shrugged and smiled her big crooked smile when he left town under the cover of night. "*C'est la vie,*" Cherry said. She donated the rest of his clothes to the Salvation Army. "*Que será, será,*" Cherry said, quoting a song that was popular when she was in junior high.

Tammy Lynn sits by her mama's bed and holds Cherry's thin dry hand. "I brought you a Chick-fil-A," she says to Harold. "It's over there in that bag." She points to the shelf by the door. Harold nods. Tammy Lynn works at Chick-fil-A. Cherry's eyes are wide and blue and full of meaning as she stares at her daughter. Her mouth moves, both Harold and Tammy Lynn lean forward, but then her mouth falls slack and her eyelids flutter shut. Tammy sits back.

"I think she looks some better today, don't you?" Harold asks.

"No," Tammy Lynn says. She has a flat little redneck voice. She sounds just the way she did last summer when she told Cherry that what she saw in the field was a cotton picker working at night, and not a UFO at all. "I wish I did but I don't, Harold. I'm going to go on home now and heat up some Beanee Weenee for Mamaw. You come on as soon as you can."

"Well," Harold says. He feels like things have gotten all turned around here some way, he feels like he's the kid and Tammy Lynn has turned into a freaky little grown-up. He says, "I'll be along directly."

But they both know he won't leave until Lois Hickey throws him out. And speaking of Lois, as soon as Tammy Lynn takes off, here she comes again, checking something on the respirator, making a little clucking sound with her mouth, then whirling to leave. When Lois walks, her panty girdle goes swish, swish, swish at the top of her legs. She comes right back with the young black man named Rodney Broadbent, Respiratory Therapist. It says so on his name badge. Rodney wheels a complicated-looking cart ahead of himself. He's all built up, like a weightlifter.

"How you doing tonight, Mr. Stipe?" Rodney says.

"I think she's some better," Harold says.

"Well, lessee here," Rodney says. He unhooks the respirator tube at Cherry's throat, sticks the tube from his own machine down the opening, and switches on the machine. It makes a whirring sound. It looks like an electric ice cream mixer. Rodney Broadbent looks at Lois Hickey in a significant way as she turns to leave the room.

They don't have to tell him, Harold knows. Cherry is worse, not better. Harold gets the Chick-fil-A, unwraps it, eats it, and then goes over to the stand by the window. It's already getting dark. The big mercury arc light glows in the hospital parking lot. A little wind blows some trash around on the concrete. He has had Cherry three years, that's all. One trip to Disney World, two vacations at Gulf Shores, Alabama, hundreds of nights in the old metal bed out at the farm with Cherry sleeping naked beside him, her arm thrown over his stomach. They had a million laughs.

"Alrightee," Rodney Broadbent nearly sings, unhooking his machine. Harold turns to look at him. Rodney Broadbent certainly looks more like a middle linebacker than a respiratory therapist. But Harold likes him.

"Well, Rodney?" Harold says.

Rodney starts shadow-boxing in the middle of the room. "Tough times," he says finally. "These is tough times, Mr. Stipe." Harold stares at him. Rodney is light on his feet as can be.

Harold sits down in the chair by the respirator. "What do you mean?" he asks.

"I mean she is drowning, Mr. Stipe," Rodney says. He throws a punch which lands real close to Harold's left ear. "What I'm doing here, see, is suctioning. I'm pulling all the fluid up out of her lungs. But now looka here, Mr. Stipe, they is just too damn much of it. See this little doohickey here I'm measuring it with? This here is the danger zone, man. Now Mrs. Stipe, she has been in the danger zone for some time. They is just too much damn fluid in there. What she got, anyway? Cancer and pneumonia both, am I right? What can I tell you, man? She is *drowning*." Rodney gives Harold a short affectionate punch in the ribs, then wheels his cart away. From the door, apparently struck by some misgivings, he says, "Well, man, if it was me, I'd want to know what the story is, you follow me, man? If it was me, what I'm saying." Harold can't see Rodney anymore, only hear his voice from the open door.

"Thank you, Rodney," Harold says. He sits in the chair. In a way he has known this already, for quite some time. In a way, Rodney's news is no news, to Harold. He just hopes he will be man enough to bear it, to do what will have to be done. Harold has always been scared that he is not man enough for Cherry

Oxendine anyway. This is his worst secret fear. He looks around the little Intensive Care room, searching for a sign, some sign, anything, that he will be man enough. Nothing happens. Cherry lies strapped to the bed, flanked by so many machines that it looks like she's in the cockpit of a jet. Her eyes are closed, eyelids fluttering, red spots on her freckled cheeks. Her chest rises and falls as the respirator pushes air in and out through the tube in her neck. He doesn't see how she can sleep in the bright light of Intensive Care, where it is always noon. And does she dream? Cherry used to tell him her dreams, which were wild, long Technicolor dreams, like movies. Cherry played different parts in them. If you dream in color, it means you're intelligent, Cherry said. She used to tease him all the time. She thought Harold's own dreams were a stitch, dreams more boring than his life, dreams in which he'd drive to Jackson, say, or be washing his car.

"Harold?" It's Ray Muncey, manager of the Food Lion at the mall.

"Why, what are you doing over here, Ray?" Harold asks, and then in a flash he *knows,* Lois Hickey must have called him, to make Harold go on home.

"I was just driving by and I thought, Hey, maybe Harold and me might run by the Holiday Inn, get a bite to eat." Ray shifts from foot to foot in the doorway. He doesn't come inside, he's not supposed to, nobody but immediate family is allowed in Intensive Care, and Harold's glad — Cherry would just die if people she barely knows, like Ray Muncey, got to see her looking so bad.

"No, Ray, you go on and eat," Harold says. "I already ate. I'm leaving right now anyway."

"Well, how's the missus doing?" Ray is a big man, afflicted with big, heavy manners.

"She's drowning," Harold says abruptly. Suddenly he remembers Cherry in a water ballet at the town pool, it must have been the summer of junior year, Fourth of July, Cherry and the other girls floating in a circle on their backs to form a giant flower — legs high, toes pointed. Harold doesn't know it when Ray Muncey leaves. Out the window, the parking lot light glows like a big full moon. Lois Hickey comes in. "You've got to go home now, Harold," she says. "I'll call if there's any change." He remembers Cherry at Glass Lake, on the senior class picnic. Cherry's getting real agitated now, she tosses her head back and forth, moves her arms. She'd pull out the tubes if she could. She kicks off the sheet. Her legs are still good, great legs in fact, the legs of a beautiful young woman.

HAROLD AT SEVENTEEN was tall and skinny, brown hair in a soft flat crew cut, glasses with heavy black frames. His jeans were too short. He carried a pen-and-pencil set in a clear plastic case in his breast pocket. Harold and his best friend, Ben Hill, looked so much alike that people had trouble telling them apart. They did everything together. They built model rockets, they read every science fiction book they could get their hands on, they collected Lionel train parts and Marvel comics. They loved superheroes with special powers, enormous beings who leaped across rivers and oceans. Harold's friendship with Ben Hill kept the awful loneliness of the only child at bay, and it also kept him from having to talk to girls. You couldn't talk to those two, not seriously. They were giggling and bumping into each other all the time. They were immature.

So it was in Ben's company that Harold experienced the most private, the most *personal* memory he has of Cherry Oxendine in high school. Oh, he also has those other memories you'd expect, the big public memories of Cherry being crowned Miss Greenwood High (for her talent; she surprised everybody by reciting "Abou Ben Adhem" in such a stirring way that there wasn't a dry eye in the whole auditorium when she got through), or running out onto the field ahead of the team with the other cheerleaders, red curls flying, green and white skirt whirling out around her hips like a beach umbrella when she turned a cartwheel. Harold noticed her then, of course. He noticed her when she moved through the crowded halls of the high school with her walk that was almost a prance, she put a little something extra into it, all right. Harold noticed Cherry Oxendine then in a way that he noticed Sandra Dee on the cover of a magazine, or Annette Funicello on *American Bandstand*.

But such girls were not for the likes of Harold, and Harold knew it. Girls like Cherry always had boyfriends like Lamar Peebles, who was hers — a doctor's son with a baby blue convertible and plenty of money. They used to drive around town in his car, smoking cigarettes. Harold saw them, as he carried out grocery bags. He did not envy Lamar Peebles, or wish he had a girl like Cherry Oxendine. Only something about them made him stand where he was in the Food Lion lot, watching, until they had passed from sight.

So Harold's close-up encounter with Cherry was unexpected. It took place at the senior class picnic, where Harold and Ben had been drinking beer all afternoon. No alcohol was allowed at the senior class picnic, but some of the more enterprising boys had brought out kegs the night before and hidden them in the woods. Anybody could go back there and pay some money and get some beer. The chaperones didn't know, or appeared not to know. In any case, the chaperones all left at six o'clock, when the picnic was officially over. Some of the class members left then too. Then some of them came back with more beer, more blankets. It was a free lake. Nobody could *make* you go home. Normally, Harold and Ben would have been among the first to leave, but because they had had four beers apiece, and because this was the first time they had ever had *any* beer ever, at all, they were still down by the water, skipping rocks and waiting to sober up so that they would not wreck Harold's mother's green Valiant on the way home. All the cool kids were on the other side of the lake, listening to transistor radios. The sun went down. Bullfrogs started up. A mist came out all around the sides of the lake. It was a cloudy, humid day anyway, not a great day for a picnic.

"If God is really God, how come He let Himself get crucified, is what I want to know," Ben said. Ben's daddy was a Holiness preacher, out in the county.

But Harold heard something. "Hush, Ben," he said.

"If I was God, I would go around and really kick some ass," Ben said.

Harold heard it again. It was almost too dark to see.

"Damn." It was a girl's voice, followed by a splash.

All of a sudden, Harold felt sober. "Who's there?" he asked. He stepped forward, right up to the water's edge. Somebody was in the water. Harold was wearing his swim trunks under his jeans, but he had not gone in the water himself. He couldn't stand to show himself in front of people. He thought he was too skinny.

"Well, *do something.*" It was the voice of Cherry Oxendine, almost wailing. She stumbled up the bank. Harold reached out and grabbed her arm. Close up, she was a mess, wet and muddy, with her hair all over her head. But the thing that got Harold, of course, was that she didn't have any top on. She didn't even try to cover them up either, she stomped her little foot on the bank and said, "I am going to *kill* Lamar Peebles when I get ahold of him." Harold had never even imagined so much skin.

"What's going on?" asked Ben, from up the bank.

Harold took off his own shirt as fast as he could and handed it over to Cherry Oxendine. "Cover yourself," he said.

"Why, thank you." Cherry didn't bat an eye. She took his shirt and put it on, tying it stylishly at the waist. Harold couldn't believe it. Close up, Cherry was a lot smaller than she looked on the stage or the football field. She looked up at Harold through her dripping hair and gave him her crooked grin.

"Thanks, hey?" she said.

And then she was gone, vanished into the mist and trees before Harold could say another word. He opened his mouth and closed it. Mist obscured his view. From the other side of the lake he could hear "Ramblin' Rose" playing on somebody's radio. He heard a girl's high-pitched giggle, a boy's whooping laugh.

"What's going on?" asked Ben.

"Nothing," Harold said. It was the first time he had ever lied to Ben. Harold never told anybody what had happened that night, not ever. He felt that it was up to him to protect Cherry Oxendine's honor. Later, much later, when he and Cherry were lovers, he was astonished to learn that she couldn't remember any of this, not who she was with or what had happened or what she was doing in the lake like that with her top off, or Harold giving her his shirt. "I think that was sweet, though," Cherry told him.

When Harold and Ben finally got home that night at nine or ten o'clock, Harold's mother was frantic. "You've been drinking," she shrilled at him under the hanging porch light. "And where's your shirt?" It was a new madras shirt that Harold had gotten for graduation. Now Harold's mother is out at the Hillandale Rest Home. Ben died in Vietnam, and Cherry is drowning. This time, and Harold knows it now, he can't help her.

OH, CHERRY! WOULD SHE have been so wild if she hadn't been so cute? And what if her parents had been younger when she was born — normal-age parents — couldn't they have controlled her better? As it was, the Oxendines were sober, solid people living in a farmhouse out near the county line, and Cherry lit up their lives like a rocket. Her dad, Martin "Buddy" Oxendine, went to sleep in his chair every night right after supper, woke back up for the eleven o'clock news, and then went to bed for good. Buddy was an elder in the Baptist church. Cherry's mom, Gladys Oxendine, made drapes for people. She assumed she would never have children at all because of her spastic colitis. Gladys and Buddy had started raising cockapoos when they gave up on children. Imagine Gladys's surprise, then, to find herself pregnant at thirty-eight, when she was already old! They say she didn't even know it when she went to the doctor. She thought she had a tumor.

But then she got so excited, that old farm woman, when Dr. Grimwood told her what was what, and she wouldn't even consider an abortion when he mentioned the chances of a mongoloid. People didn't use to have babies so old then as they do now, so Gladys Oxendine's pregnancy was the talk of the county. Neighbors crocheted little jackets and made receiving blankets. Buddy built a baby room onto the house and made a cradle by hand. During the last two months of pregnancy, when Gladys had to stay in bed because of toxemia, people brought over casseroles and boiled custard, everything good. Gladys's pregnancy was the only time in her whole life that she was ever pretty, and she loved it, and she loved the attention, neighbors in and out of the house. When the baby was finally born on November 1, 1944, no parents were ever more ready than Gladys and Buddy Oxendine. And the baby was everything they hoped for too, which is not usually the case — the prettiest baby in the world, a baby like a little flower.

They named her Doris Christine which is who she was until eighth grade, when she made junior varsity cheerleader and announced that she was changing her name to Cherry. Cherry! Even her parents had to admit it suited her better than Doris Christine. As a little girl, Doris Christine was redheaded, bouncy, and busy — she was always into something, usually something you'd never thought to tell her not to do. She started talking early and never shut up. Her old dad, old Buddy Oxendine, was so crazy about Doris Christine that he took her everywhere with him in his old red pickup truck. You got used to seeing the two of them, Buddy and his curly-headed little daughter, riding the country roads together, going to the seed-and-feed together, sharing a shake at the Dairy Queen. Gladys made all of Doris Christine's clothes, the most beautiful little dresses in the world, with hand smocking and French seams. They gave Doris Christine everything they could think of — what she asked for, what she didn't. "That child is going to get spoiled," people started to say. And of course she did get spoiled, she couldn't have helped *that*, but she was never spoiled rotten as so many are. She stayed sweet in spite of it all.

Then along about tenth grade, soon after she changed her name to Cherry and got interested in boys, things changed between

Cherry and the old Oxendines. Stuff happened. Instead of being the light of their lives, Cherry became the bane of their existence, the curse of their old age. She wanted to wear makeup, she wanted to have car dates. You can't blame her — she was old enough, sixteen. Everybody else did it. But you can't blame Gladys and Buddy either — they were old people by then, all worn out. They were not up to such a daughter. Cherry sneaked out. She wrecked a car. She ran away to Pensacola with a soldier. Finally, Gladys and Buddy gave up. When Cherry eloped with the disc jockey, Don Westall, right after graduation, they threw up their hands. They did not do a thing about it. They had done the best they could, and everybody knew it. They went back to raising cockapoos.

Cherry, living up in Nashville, Tennessee, had a baby, Stan, the one who's in his twenties now. Cherry sent baby pictures back to Gladys and Buddy, and wrote that she was going to be a singer. Six years later, she came home. She said nothing against Don Westall, who was still a disc jockey on WKIX, Nashville. You could hear him on the radio every night after 10 p.m. Cherry said the breakup was all her fault. She said she had made some mistakes, but she didn't say what they were. She was thin and noble. Her kid was cute. She did not go back out to the farm then. She rented an apartment over the hardware store, down by the river, and got a job downtown working in Ginger's Boutique. After a year or so, she started acting more like herself again, although not *quite* like herself — she had grown up somehow in Nashville, and quit being spoiled. She put Stan, her kid, first. And if she did run around a little bit, or if she was the life of the party sometimes out at the country club, so what? Stan didn't want for a thing. By then the Oxendines were failing and she had to take care of them too, she had to drive her daddy up to Grenada for dialysis twice a week. It was not an easy life for Cherry, but if it ever got her down, you couldn't tell it. She was still cute. When her daddy finally died and left her a little money, everybody was real glad. Oh *now,* they said, Cherry Oxendine can quit working so hard and put her mama in a home or something and have a decent life. She can go on a cruise. But then along came Ed Palladino, and the rest is history.

Cherry Oxendine was left with no husband, no money, a little girl, and a mean old mama to take care of. At least by this time Stan was in the navy. Cherry never complained, though. She moved back out to the farm. When Ginger retired from business and closed her boutique, Cherry got another job, as a receptionist at Wallace, Wallace and Peebles. This was her undoing. Because Lamar Peebles had just moved back to town with his family, to join his father's firm. Lamar had two little girls. He had been married to a tobacco heiress since college. All this time he had run around on her. He was not on the up-and-up. And when he encountered redheaded Cherry Oxendine again after the passage of so many years, all those old fireworks went off again. They got to be a scandal, then a disgrace. Lamar said he was going to marry her, and Cherry believed him. After six months of it, Mrs. Lamar Peebles checked herself into a mental hospital in Silver Hill, Connecticut. First, she called her laywers.

And then it was all over, not even a year after it began. Mr. and Mrs. Lamar Peebles were reconciled and moved to Winston-Salem, North Carolina, her hometown. Cherry Oxendine lost her job at Wallace, Wallace and Peebles, and was reduced to working at the deli at Food Lion. Why did she do it? Why did she lose all the goodwill she'd built up in this community over so many years? It is because she doesn't know how to look out for Number One. Her own daughter, Tammy Lynn Palladino, is aware of this.

"You have got a fatal flaw, Mama," Tammy said after learning about fatal flaws in English class. "You believe everything everybody tells you."

Still, Tammy loves her mother. Sometimes she writes her mother's whole name, Cherry Oxendine Westall Palladino Stikes, over and over in her Blue Horse notebook. Tammy Lynn will never be half the woman her mother is, and she's so smart she knows it. She gets a kick out of her mother's wild ideas.

"When you get too old to be cute, honey, you get to be eccentric," Cherry told Tammy one time. It's the truest thing she ever said.

It seems to Tammy that the main thing about her mother is, Cherry always has to have *something* going on. If it isn't a man it's something else, such as having her palm read by that woman over in French Camp, or astrology, or the grapefruit diet. Cherry believes in the Bermuda Triangle, Bigfoot, Atlantis, and ghosts. It kills her that she's not psychic. The UFO Club was just the latest in a long string of interests although it has lasted the longest, starting back before Cherry's marriage to Harold Stikes. And then Cherry got cancer, and she kind of forgot about it. But Tammy still remembers the night her mama first got so turned on by UFOs.

RHONDA RAMEY, CHERRY'S BEST friend, joined the UFO Club first. Rhonda and Cherry are a lot alike, although it's hard to see this at first. While Cherry is short and peppy, Rhonda is tall, thin, and listless. She looks like Cher. Rhonda doesn't have any children. She's crazy about her husband, Bill, but he's a workaholic who runs a string of video rental stores all over northern Mississippi, so he's gone a lot, and Rhonda gets bored. She works out at the spa, but it isn't enough. Maybe this is why she got so interested when the UFO landed at a farm outside her mother's hometown of Como. It was first spotted by sixteen-year-old Donnie Johnson just at sunset, as he was finishing his chores on his parents' farm. He heard a loud rumbling sound "in the direction of the hog house," it said in the paper. Looking up, he suddenly saw a "brilliantly lit mushroom-shaped object" hovering about two feet above the ground, with a shaft of white light below and glowing all over with an intensely bright multicolored light, "like the light of a welder's arc."

Donnie said it sounded like a jet. He was temporarily blinded and paralyzed. He fell down on the ground. When he came back to his senses again, it was gone. Donnie staggered into the kitchen where his parents, Durel, fifty-four, and Erma, forty-nine, were eating supper and told them what had happened. They all ran back outside to the field, where they found four large imprints and four small imprints in the muddy ground, and a nearby clump of sage grass on fire. The hogs were acting funny, bunching up, looking dazed. Immediately, Durel jumped in his truck and went to get the sheriff, who came right back with two deputies. All in all, six people viewed the site while the brush continued to burn, and who knows how many people — half of Como — saw the imprints the next day. Rhonda saw them too. She drove out to the Johnson farm with her mother, as soon as she heard about it.

It was a close encounter of the second kind, according to Civil Air Patrol head Glenn Raines, who appeared on TV to discuss it, because the UFO "interacted with its surroundings in a significant way." A close encounter of the first kind is simply a close-range sighting, while a close encounter of the third kind is something like the famous example, of Betty and Barney Hill of Exeter, New Hampshire, who were actually kidnapped by a UFO while they were driving along on a trip. Betty and Barney Hill were taken aboard the alien ship and given physical exams by intelligent humanoid beings. Two hours and thirty-five minutes were missing from their trip, and afterward, Betty had to be treated for acute anxiety. Glenn Raines, wearing his brown Civil Air Patrol uniform, said all this on TV.

His appearance, plus what had happened at the Johnson farm, sparked a rash of sightings all across Mississippi, Louisiana, and Texas for the next two years. Metal disc-like objects were seen, and luminous objects appearing as lights at night. In Levelland, Texas, fifteen people called the police to report an egg-shaped UFO appearing over State Road 1173. Overall, the UFOs seemed to show a preference for soybean fields and teenage girl viewers. But a pretty good photograph of a UFO flying over the Gulf was taken by a retired man from Pascagoula, so you can't generalize. Clubs sprang up all over the place. The one that Rhonda and Cherry went to had seventeen members and met once a month at the junior high school.

Tammy recalls exactly how her mama and Rhonda acted the night they came home from Cherry's first meeting. Cherry's eyes sparkled in her face like Brenda Starr's eyes in the comics. She started right in telling Tammy all about it, beginning with the Johnsons from Como and Betty and Barney Hill.

Tammy was not impressed. "I don't believe it," she said. She was president of the Science Club at the junior high school.

"You are the most irritating child!" Cherry said. "*What* don't you believe?"

"Well, any of it," Tammy said then. "All of it," and this has remained her attitude ever since.

"Listen, honey, *Jimmy Carter* saw one," Cherry said triumphantly. "In nineteen seventy-one, at the Executive Mansion in Georgia. He turned in an official report on it."

"How come nobody knows about it, then?" Tammy asked. She was a tough customer.

"Because the government covered it up!" said Rhonda, just dying to tell this part. "People see UFOs all the time, it's common knowledge, they are trying to make contact with us right now, honey, but the government doesn't want the average citizen to know about it. There's a big cover-up going on."

"It's just like Watergate." Cherry opened a beer and handed it over to Rhonda.

"That's right," Rhonda said, "and every time there's a major incident, you know what happens? These men from the government show up at your front door dressed all in black. After they get through with you, you'll wish you never heard the word *saucer.* You turn pale and get real sick. You can't get anything to stay on your stomach."

Tammy cracked up. But Rhonda and Cherry went on and on. They had official-looking gray notebooks to log their sightings in. At their meetings, they reported these sightings to each other, and studied up on the subject in general. Somebody in the club was responsible for the educational part of each meeting, and somebody else brought the refreshments.

Tammy Lynn learned to keep her mouth shut. It was less embarrassing than belly dancing; she had a friend whose mother took belly dancing at the YMCA. Tammy did not tell her mama about all the rational explanations for UFOs that she found in the school library. They included: (1) hoaxes; (2) natural phenomena, such as fungus causing the so-called fairy rings sometimes

found after a landing; (3) real airplanes flying off course; and
Tammy's favorite, (4) the Fata Morgana, described as a "rare and
beautiful type of mirage, constantly changing, the result of unsta-
ble layers of warm and cold air. The Fata Morgana takes its name
from fairy lore and is said to evoke in the viewer a profound sense
of longing," the book went on to say. Tammy's biology teacher,
Mr. Owens, said he thought that the weather patterns in Mississippi might be especially conducive to this phenomenon. But
Tammy kept her mouth shut. And after a while, when nobody in
the UFO Club saw anything, its membership declined sharply.
Then her mama met Harold Stikes, then Harold Stikes left his
wife and children and moved out to the farm with them, and
sometimes Cherry forgot to attend the meetings, she was so
happy with Harold Stikes.

Tammy couldn't see *why,* initially. In her opinion, Harold
Stikes was about as interesting as a telephone pole. "But he's so
nice!" Cherry tried to explain it to Tammy Lynn. Finally Tammy
decided that there is nothing in the world that makes somebody
as attractive as if they really love you. And Harold Stikes really
did love her mama, there was no question. That old man — what
a crazy old Romeo! Why, he proposed to Cherry when she was
still in the hospital after she had her breast removed (this was back
when they thought that was *it,* that the doctors had gotten it all).

"Listen, Cherry," he said solemnly, gripping a dozen red roses.
"I want you to marry me."

"What?" Cherry said. She was still groggy.

"I want you to marry me," Harold said. He knelt down heavily beside her bed.

"Harold! Get up from there!" Cherry said. "Somebody will
see you."

"Say yes," said Harold.

"I just had my breast removed."

"Say yes," he said again.

"*Yes, yes, yes!*" Cherry said.

And as soon as she got out of the hospital, they were married out in the orchard, on a beautiful April day, by Lew Uggams, a JP from out of town. They couldn't find a local preacher to do it. The sky was bright blue, not a cloud in sight. Nobody was invited except Stan, Tammy, Rhonda and Bill, and Cherry's mother, who wore her dress inside out. Cherry wore a new pink lace dress, the color of cherry blossoms. Tough little Tammy cried and cried. It's the most beautiful wedding she's ever seen, and now she's completely devoted to Harold Stikes.

So Tammy leaves the lights on for Harold when she finally goes to bed that night. She tried to wait up for him, but she has to go to school in the morning, she's got a chemistry test. Her mamaw is sound asleep in the little added-on baby room that Buddy Oxendine built for Cherry. Gladys acts like a baby now, a spoiled baby at that. The only thing she'll drink is Sprite out of a can. She talks mean. She doesn't like anything in the world except George and Tammy, the two remaining cockapoos.

They bark up a storm when Harold finally gets back out to the farm, at one thirty. The cockapoos are barking, Cherry's mom is snoring like a chain saw. Harold doesn't see how Tammy Lynn can sleep through all of this, but she always does. Teenagers can sleep through anything. Harold himself has started waking up several times a night, his heart pounding. He wonders if he's going to have a heart attack. He almost mentioned his symptoms to Lois Hickey last week, in fact, but then thought, What the hell. His heart is broken. Of course it's going to act up some. And everything, not only his heart, is out of whack. Sometimes he'll break into a sweat for no reason. Often he forgets really crucial things, such as filing his quarterly estimated income tax on January 15. Harold is not the kind to forget something that important. He has strange aches that float from joint to joint. He has headaches. He's lost twelve pounds. Sometimes he has no appetite at all. Other times, like right now, he's just starving.

Harold goes in the kitchen and finds a flat rectangular casserole, carefully wrapped in tinfoil, on the counter, along with a Tupperware cake carrier. He lifts off the top of the cake carrier and finds a piña colada cake, his favorite. Then he pulls back the tinfoil on the casserole. Lasagna! Plenty is left over. Harold sticks it in the microwave. He knows that the cake and the lasagna were left here by his ex-wife. Ever since Cherry has been in Intensive Care, Joan has been bringing food out to the farm. She comes when Harold's at work or at the hospital, and leaves it with Gladys or Tammy. She probably figures that Harold would refuse it, if she caught him at home, which he would. She's a great cook, though. Harold takes the lasagna out of the microwave, opens a beer, and sits down at the kitchen table. He loves Joan's lasagna. Cherry's idea of a terrific meal is one she doesn't have to cook. Harold remembers eating in bed with Cherry, tacos from Taco Bell, sour-cream-and-onion chips, beer. He gets more lasagna and a big wedge of piña colada cake.

Now it's two thirty, but for some reason Harold is not a bit sleepy. His mind whirls with thoughts of Cherry. He snaps off all the lights and stands in the darkened house. His heart is racing. Moonlight comes in the windows, it falls on the old patterned rug. Outside, it's as bright as day. He puts his coat on and goes out, with the cockapoos scampering along beside him. They are not even surprised. They think it's a fine time for a walk. Harold goes past the mailbox, down the dirt road between the fields. Out here in the country, the sky is both bigger and closer than it is in town. Harold feels like he's in a huge bowl turned upside down, with tiny little pinpoints of light shining through. And everything is silvered by the moonlight — the old fenceposts, the corn stubble in the flat long fields, a distant barn, the highway at the end of the dirt road, his own strange hand when he holds it out to look at it.

He remembers when she waited on him in the Food Lion deli, three years ago. He had asked for a roast beef sandwich, which come prepackaged. Cherry put it on his plate. Then she paused, and cocked her hip, and looked at him. "Can I give you some potato salad to go with that?" she asked. "Some slaw?"

Harold looked at her. Some red curls had escaped the required net. "Nothing else," he said.

But Cherry spooned a generous helping of potato salad onto his plate. "Thank you so much," he said. They looked at each other.

"I know I know you," Cherry said.

It came to him then. "Cherry Oxendine," said Harold. "I remember you from high school."

"Lord, you've got a great memory, then!" Cherry had an easy laugh. "That was a hundred years ago."

"Doesn't seem like it." Harold knew he was holding up the line.

"Depends on who you're talking to," Cherry said.

Later that day, Harold found an excuse to go back over to the deli for coffee and apple pie, then he found an excuse to look through the personnel files. He started eating lunch at the deli every day, without making any conscious decision to do so. In the afternoons, when he went back for coffee, Cherry would take her break and sit at a table with him.

Harold and Cherry talked and talked. They talked about their families, their kids, high school. Cherry told him everything that had happened to her. She was tough and funny, not bitter or self-pitying. They talked and talked. In his whole life, Harold had never had so much to say. During this period, which lasted for several weeks, his whole life took on a heightened aspect. Everything that happened to him seemed significant, a little incident to tell Cherry about. Every song he liked on the radio he remembered, so he could ask Cherry if she liked it too. Then there came the day when they were having coffee and she mentioned she'd left her car at Al's Garage that morning to get a new clutch.

"I'll give you a ride over there to pick it up," said Harold instantly. In his mind he immediately canceled the sales meeting he had scheduled for four o'clock.

"Oh, that's too much trouble," Cherry said.

"But I insist." In his conversations with Cherry, Harold had developed a brand-new gallant manner he had never had before.

"Well, if you're sure it's not any trouble . . ." Cherry grinned at him like she knew he really wanted to do it, and that afternoon when he grabbed her hand suddenly before letting her out at Al's Garage, she did not pull away.

The next weekend Harold took her up to Memphis and they stayed at the Peabody Hotel, where Cherry got the biggest kick out of the ducks in the lobby and ordering from room service.

"You're a fool," Harold's friends told him later, when the shit hit the fan.

But Harold didn't think so. He doesn't think so now, walking the old dirt road on the Oxendine farm in the moonlight. He loves his wife. He feels that he has been ennobled and enlarged, by knowing Cherry Oxendine. He feels like he has been specially selected among men, to receive a precious gift. He stepped out of his average life for her, he gave up being a good man, but the rewards have been extraordinary. He's glad he did it. He'd do it all over again.

Still walking, Harold suddenly knows that something is going to happen. But he doesn't stop walking. Only, the whole world around him seems to waver a bit, and intensify. The moonlight shines whiter than ever. A little wind whips up out of nowhere. The stars are twinkling so brightly that they seem to dance, actually dance, in the sky. And then, while Harold watches, one of them detaches itself from the rest of the sky and grows larger, moves closer, until it's clear that it is actually moving across the sky, at an angle to the earth. A falling star, perhaps? A comet?

Harold stops walking. The star moves faster and faster, with an erratic pattern. It's getting real close now. It's no star. Harold hears a high whining noise, like a blender. The cockapoos huddle against his ankles. They don't bark. Now he can see the blinking red lights on the top of it, and the beam of white light shooting out the bottom. His coat is blown straight out behind him by the wind. He feels like he's going blind. He shields his eyes. At first it's as big as a barn, then a tobacco warehouse. It covers the field. Although Harold can't say exactly how it communicates to him or even if it does, suddenly his soul is filled to bursting. The ineffable occurs. And then, more quickly than it came, it's gone, off toward Carrollton, rising into the night, leaving the field, the farm, the road. Harold turns back.

It will take Cherry Oxendine two more weeks to die. She's tough. And even when there's nothing left of her but her heart, she will fight all the way. She will go out furious, squeezing Harold's hand at the very moment of death, clinging fast to every minute of this bright, hard life. And although at first he won't want to, Harold will go on living. He will buy another store. Gladys will die. Tammy Lynn will make Phi Beta Kappa. Harold will start attending the Presbyterian church again. Eventually Harold may even go back to his family, but he will love Cherry Oxendine until the day he dies, and he will never, ever, tell anybody what he saw.

Folk Art

Lord have mercy! You liked to scared me to death! Come on out of there this minute. You're tramping on my daylilies. There now. That's better. Let me get a good look at you. You don't say! Why you don't look hardly old enough to be a art professor, I'll tell you that. I would of took you for a boy. Just a little old art boy, how's that? Me, I'm Lily Lockhart. I reckon you know that already. How'd you get in here anyway? Well, it don't matter. Honey, you have come to the right place! Art is my life, if I do say so myself.

Why sure, I'll be glad to show you around my backyard, now that you've got in here. It'd be my pleasure. It's not much to see, though. Not much to show somebody like you. Why thank you. I appreciate that. Mama planted a lot of them herself. She used to say, "Lily, I want our backyard to look just like the Garden of Eden." That's bee balm. Mama planted it years and years ago. Them wild spiky flowers, them's cleomes. And these here is hollyhocks, of course, they're my favorite. Me and Daisy used to take us a blossom and hold it just so, and pretend it was a dolly, going to a dance. See here? This is her party dress. Why no, they're easy, once they get a good start, just like anything else. Once you get something going, it takes on a life of its own, seems like. Looky here how tall they get! Taller than Billy, and Billy's tall. He's in the house, he don't get out much anymore. You're the first visitor I've had in — Lord, I don't know how long! Of course I've got lots of company out here in the yard. You want to meet my people? Come on then. I'll be glad to introduce you.

Now this here is Mama, who loved flowers and songs and every pretty thing. Oh, I wish you could have seen her in life! She was the sweetest thing, she reminded me of a butterfly somehow. Yellow hair hanging down to her waist, and the littlest, whitest feet! She used to paint her toenails fire-engine red, and then she'd paint our little toenails red, too. She'd put cotton between our toes, to let our toenails dry, and then we'd dance and dance in the garden, Daisy and me and Iris Jean, and Mama would sing.

Oh, I don't know. Songs she made up out of her head, I reckon. Daddy didn't like it. He thought all music ought to be church music, but he didn't say a thing. He never spoke a word when it came to Mama, she meant the whole world to him, which was true from the minute he first laid eyes on her at that little church up in the Blackey coal camp where she was born. She was one of nine children, and the oldest, though she was not but fourteen years old when Daddy came riding up the holler to preach that first time. She stood up in front of the altar all by herself and threw back her head and closed her eyes and sang "Beulah Land" in her pure gold voice that never faltered, sang so beautiful Daddy said you could see the notes floating out perfect and visible in the air. Daddy was thirty years old at the time. He had already been out west, gone to jail, married a Mexican, got shot in the leg, you name it! All of these things before he got religion, after which he had took to the road for the Lord. Oh, he'd been places, and seen things. But he had never seen nothing like Mama the day he came to the church at Blackey when she was singing "Beulah Land." Mama noticed him too, of course, the handsome stranger with the snapping black eyes and the big black hat standing thunderstruck in the open door at the back of the church.

And then he *did* preach, though he hardly knew what he said, and after it was all over, Daddy exchanged a few words with Mama and then went right up to her father, old Joe Burns, and said, "Sir, I want to marry your daughter Evalina."

Old Joe Burns looked Daddy in the eye. "I appreciate the offer," he said, "for times is hard, but Evalina is too young, sir. Come back next year and you can have her." And so he did, and brought her over here to Rockhouse Branch, and built this house for her, meantime farming and preaching down at the Mount Gilead church which you must of passed on your way up here.

Why, I don't know as she thought *anything* about it! Girls in those days did as they were told, not like they do now, not like Daisy and Iris Jean have done! Anyway, it was plain to see that Daddy doted on her and got her anything she could think of, though he did not like for her to go off the place except to church. He was always worried that something bad might happen to her. He brought pearl buttons and ribbons and pretty cloth from town, and was real proud of how nice she could sew, and she did make beautiful dresses for us girls and for herself, though there were always those at church that talked about it, and about the sin of vanity.

"My little flowers," Mama called us, and in fact we truly were her garden she said, Iris Jean the oldest, born when Mama was sixteen, and then me and Daisy my sweet twin, and then Billy, three years later. I know it was a lot of children for a slip of a girl to bear, and sometimes I have felt that what happened was *our fault,* somehow, for coming on her so fast.

I remember so clearly one thing I heard her say to Daddy when we were all just little and Billy was newborn. She was lying in the big old bed with Billy nestled up close by her, and Daddy though fully clothed lay by her side and stroked her long bright hair. I stole in the room and stood at the other side of the bed, where they did not see me. "Gabriel Lockhart," Mama said, as if in a dream, "Where did all of them come from? Don't you remember back when it was just me and you? But now there is so many. I keep thinking, oh who are they all? and where have they come from?"

"Now Evalina," Daddy said, "You know they have come from God." And she smiled at him, and then she started humming a little faraway tune while Billy nursed. Everybody was worried about Billy, who came out backward with the cord wrapped around his neck and had terrible seizures as a little child.

I was more worried about Mama, who started talking to Billy in his illness the way you do talk to a baby but then kept on talking to herself, and pacing the house all night. I was not surprised when she left us, as she had been mostly gone in her mind for a while, though Daddy would never admit it. It was true that she might never have left had it not been for John Astor Sneed who came out here from town selling dry goods and notions. He came once, twice, and the third time Mama went with him in that wire-wheeled buggy he had hitched to the cherry tree. John Astor Sneed wore red suspenders, I will never forget it. Had a fat gray horse. Billy stood in the yard and waved good-bye when they left, Billy loves to wave, but I was crying. She said she was coming back, but I knew somehow she never would, not unless I made her, which I have now done. She is the first one I made when I started doing my art.

Shoot, no! Take all the pictures you want. It's real pretty back here, ain't it? Every one of my people has got their own little garden, you might say. Of course it just about kills me, trying to keep it all up. Poor Billy now, he never was a bit of help. Just as soon pull up a rose as a weed. He don't know no better. But he sure has brought me a lot of nice art supplies.

Well, I don't know. I can't exactly tell you. All of a sudden I thought, *Lord, how much I miss Mama!* It had come a real bad thunderstorm that night, and I came out here in the yard to find a big branch snapped right off this little dogwood tree, and something about the way it was standing there, that little jaunty angle of it — see how it looks like it is fixing to dance? — put me in mind of Mama, and how graceful she was, and how light of foot.

The first thing I done was wrap chicken wire all around it, and then I started hauling some clay mud up here from the branch to pack in around it — Daisy and me had always made little people out of that old red clay — but then all of a sudden I thought, *Well, shoot! Why not get some of that instant concrete from the hardware store, might as well be modern.* And so I did, and so I made her. All the quartz? It's down at the branch. That's where the name comes from, Rockhouse Branch. Sure it took a long time. Months. Every day or so I'd put me a little dab of concrete and a little piece of quartz. Gave me something to do. Then Billy got the idea and he started bringing me this mica, see here? Isn't that pretty? Lord knows where he got it, he just walks and walks everplace. That's salvia, blooming at her feet. Fire-engine red! She loves it.

Now what did you say your name was? I was wondering if you

might be kin to any Goodys. You look just like a boy I used to know, name of Ray Goody, a long time back. You kindly favor him.

No? Well, anyway, Daddy was a handsome man as I said, but oh how he declined after Mama left! For he used to call her his little sunshine, and now his sunshine was gone. A blackness fell upon him like a cloak. He turned dark and sad and could not see the good of anything. It seemed like even God had turned His back on Daddy, and on us.

We just did the best we could, naturally. That's all you *can* do! Daddy was so sweet and broken that I had to take care of Billy the best I could, and keep house. Oh, Iris Jean didn't care a fig for all that. It was all school, school, school for Iris Jean, who *was* smart — I'll admit it — but would not stay home from school for one single day, not even when Billy had double pneumonia. Furthermore Iris Jean would not go to church or mention Mama's name, either one. Kept her nose stuck in a book all the time. Poor Daddy! First he lost Mama to John Astor Sneed, then Iris Jean to education. Now I'll tell you frankly, I might of liked some of that education myself — I've always been real smart — but *somebody* had to stay here and cook for Daddy and take care of Billy! Everybody can't just run off and do whatever they please!

Of course Iris Jean came back into the picture from time to time with her fancy degrees and big ideas, such as getting papers on Billy and sending him off to the special school, which liked to kill Daddy and me, though it did not last long, I will tell you. Lord, I won't forget how happy I was the day I was sitting right out here in a lawn chair snapping beans and I heard that little whistle I knew so well, and it was Billy! Grinning like the sun, arms full of old stuff he'd picked up along the way. "Here,

Sissy," he said — that's what he calls me, Sissy. "All for you, Sissy," he said.

I used bottle pieces on Iris Jean — look how they catch the sun! Those blue ones come from Milk of Magnesia bottles, they're my favorite.

And mirror pieces of course for Daisy, who looked like me but did not have any character to speak of, unlike myself. I am afraid Daisy took after our sweet Mama in the worst possible way. It all happened in the blink of an eye. One minute Daisy was playing hollyhock dolls with me, and the next minute she was jumping into pickup trucks with complete strangers. I am not even sure how she met those boys in the first place, as Daddy had started keeping us home from school for our own protection right after we lost Iris Jean. Poor Daddy! He begged and pleaded and cried and prayed over Daisy to no avail. He locked her in her room and switched her with a locust branch until her skinny white legs had long red welts and even I had to feel sorry for her.

I will not forget the time I woke up in the middle of the night to feel a boy's long hard body pressing mine, his warm lips on my face. "Ssshh," he said. In a flash I knew it was Lewjack Jones, sneaking in the wrong window. But I confess I didn't say a word. I lay there and let him kiss me for the longest time before I jumped up and hollered "Daddy!" real loud and scared them all to death. It was funny, really. But then after Daddy ran him and Daisy off, I laid back down on my bed and cried and cried as if my heart would break, as if I even *cared* what that boy and my sister did in the dead of night! So — that's Daisy! Right over there, surrounded by zinnias.

This left Daddy and Billy and me. I got Billy to help me switch the mattresses around until I got the best one, which had been

Iris Jean's, and the prettiest quilt, which used to be on Mama and Daddy's bed. Fan pattern, Mama made it herself. Daddy never missed it. He was not into details by that time, all he did was lie in the bed and cry until finally he lost his church and all of them started coming around here with casseroles, and then they stopped. I love that kind of casserole you make with French-style green beans and mushroom soup and onion rings on top, you know which one I mean? Church women all know how to make that casserole, it must be the law! Well, I miss that. I have never been one to cook, I've got too much to take care of out here in the yard.

Yes, I *did* think about it, just once. It was about then, in fact. Now I was accustomed to walking into town to buy groceries and what all else we needed, such as aspirin from the drug store, or whatever. It *is* a long way. Three miles, I reckon. At least. Well, Daddy used to drive me, but then he got so poorly, and of course I didn't have a driver's license, he never held with us girls driving a car — anyway, I was walking out of the hardware store one day when I heard this high-pitched voice yelling my name. "Lily Lockhart! Lily Lockhart! Wait a minute!" and so I did, and it turned out to be Ray Goody, who worked for Mr. Gray and rented a room right upstairs. Ray Goody was slight-built and sandy-haired, like you are, and had him some of those little gold-frame glasses too. He was real shy. His face turned the brightest red when he talked to you. "Lily Lockhart!" he said again. "I'm going to drive you home." And so he did. And came in the backyard carrying a bag of concrete, and put it down, and admired my people, and said hello to Billy and Daddy who had come out there to gawk at him. Ray Goody acted just like we were anybody. So I did too. "Sit down here and let me get you a cold drink," I said, and he did. He sat on that little stone bench you're sitting on now, and I came back with two glasses of ice water. It was summertime, real hot, and the glasses were all beaded up with sweat by the time I got back with them.

"This is the best water I have ever tasted," Ray Goody said, and proceeded to drink every drop without taking his eyes off me. His eyes looked like china plates behind his glasses. "It's nice here," he said, putting the glass down when he had finally drunk his fill.

"Come back anytime," I said. I don't know what got into me! But the fact is, he did. He came back and sat under the cedar tree and told me how he had been sick in the hospital but was now better and had come to work at Gray's Hardware because Mrs. Gray was his mother's cousin. He was really a writer, he said. "I have been watching you come in the store," he said. "In fact I couldn't take my eyes off of you," he said. This embarrassed us both so much it seemed we might die on the spot, but we did not, and as Ray Goody's visits continued, he started bringing us all manner of gifts from the hardware store, bird feeders and wind chimes and grapefruit spoons with little ridges on them and a new hose and an ashtray shaped like North Carolina. Chewing tobacco for Daddy and butter-rum Life Savers for Billy. Ray Goody spoke of this as his courtship. "How am I doing with my courtship?" he used to ask me, bright red but determined, and soon he took to sneaking up behind me and putting his arms around my waist and rubbing his face in my hair.

As for me, I went around in a dream, and my heart beat too fast all the time. I could see right where we were headed, like leaves floating down Rockhouse Branch to that little waterfall. Then one October day he popped the question. He wanted to marry me, and we would live together in his room in town over the hardware store where I would have a job too, in the arts and crafts. Ray had already asked Mr. Gray about it, and Mr. Gray said it was fine, that he and Mrs. Gray had been thinking about buying an RV vehicle and seeing something of the world themselves.

"What do you say?" Ray Goody asked me, but I was flabbergasted. "Well, think about it," he said, and then he kissed me and drove back into town, saying he'd be back that evening. Well! I had to sit down. I thought about it while scarlet leaves from the maple tree fell on the grass and the wind blew my hair around. My face felt hot, like I had a fever. *Why not?* I thought. *Why not?* I could scarcely breathe. Then I started thinking about making a concrete birdbath shaped like a leaf, and some stepping stones. Those things would be easy to mass produce. My heart on fire, I went in to tell Daddy.

He was standing by the window looking out, and did not turn around when I told him. "Why, that is wonderful," he said. Then he bent over double with the pain that would take several years to kill him. "You go on," he said. "It's not anything. I just want you to be happy," Daddy said. He was so sweet, wanting nothing more than to lie down by himself until it passed. Oh, he was so brave! But of course I did not go with Ray Goody when he came back that evening, I did not go with him then or anytime, and sometime during Daddy's long illness, Ray just slipped away. Left town. I don't know if he told the Grays where he was going or not — he sure didn't tell me! One week he was in there selling nails and saying, "How is your Daddy today, Lil?" and the next week he was gone, that lace curtain fluttering out of his open upstairs window like a sign. Oh, I was a pure-tee fool to think I could have done it anyway! I had to wait on Daddy hand and foot from then on. And he wrestled with the angel of death as hard as he'd wrestled with God, I swear it. You'd think he would have been glad to go, after everything that had happened to him, but he was not. Lord, no! He fought it tooth and nail, I'll tell you. He was all wore out by the end, and light as a feather, and we put him right over there, me and Billy. Sure thing! That's him all right, all them dark rocks in the shape of the cross. Then I built the arbor and planted the grapevine in memory of how hard he hung on, you have to admire that in a man. You have to.

You mean this here pile? Well, I don't know, it gives me something to do while I'm taking care of Billy, he sleeps so much now. Poor thing. He couldn't do without me. And it will not be long, I can tell you. You know how I know? It's when their fingers start curling up like ferns. In fact I may bring me some ferns up here from the creek, now that's a thought. But I'll swear it don't seem like no time at all to me since Billy was just a little boy, making mudpies down there with me and Daisy.

Well, I wish you didn't have to rush off. But you come on back *anytime*! You can sit right there on that bench and write in your notebook, just like you used to. I bet you could get a lot of work done. It's nice, in a garden. Why there's something happening all the time out here, first daffodils and forsythia in the spring, then roses and daylilies and I don't know what all in the summertime, then chrysanthemums and asters and nandina in the fall, everything comes and goes and comes again in its season. You're going to like it out here. It's real peaceful, and there is always a little wind up in them cedar trees, it's like they catch the wind somehow, and trap it up in there, and it sounds so pretty, like wind chimes. Why, you can hear it right now. Just listen.

House Tour

H ave a happy holiday!" The pretty girl in the wine shop is dressed in a red velvet elf suit, with green tights and high black boots. She carries the carton of wine to Lynn's car like it is nothing. When she bends over to put it in the trunk, her tiny skirt hikes up to show her red panties. This is the kind of outfit Lawrence would love, damn his soul. A little kitsch, a little sex, a little irony. Everybody always thought Lawrence was such a genius, but actually he is so predictable as to be boring, really. Lynn recalls that black thong she found in his glove compartment years ago, back when they were first married, she didn't even know what it was.

"I am putty in their hands," he'd said, spreading his. Lawrence has soft, elegant hands with long thin white fingers, he has never done one honest day's work in his life.

"Thanks, Erin, and Merry Christmas to you also," Lynn says, which comes out sounding weird, sort of like English as a second language, but never mind, this Erin girl will get it. She's a smart girl, she has never raised an eyebrow or said one word to Lynn about her solo wine purchases or asked where Lawrence is keeping himself these days. (Guggenheim in Italy? Semester at NYU? Lynn has answers ready.) And when she first broke her ankle, Erin brought a nice bottle of Viognier over to the house herself, a gift. Erin is so nice, really, just like everybody else in town who came by with casseroles or picked up Lynn's mail at the post office for her. This is the benefit of living in a village, though there's a downside too, Lynn thinks darkly. Yes indeed.

For instance, there's no bypass, and right now the traffic is stopped dead, bumper to bumper — where on earth are all these people coming from? Lynn lives right on Main Street, how's she supposed to get home? Finally, she pulls out but is immediately confronted by a young policeman with a whistle which he will *not* stop blowing as he energetically motions her to the left, down Wisteria Way. Lynn is startled to see a giant Cat in the Hat prancing along just beyond him, then a dozen silver-clad majorettes followed by the entire Oakwood High School Marching Band, oh God, it's the Christmas Parade! "Rudolph the Red-Nosed Reindeer" fills the air.

Behind the band, about forty kids from Susie's Dance Studio prance down the hill past the courthouse, turning flips and cartwheels, followed by a giant concrete mixer covered with little children in reindeer hats with antlers, throwing candy to the crowds, which, Lynn notes now, are everywhere, lining Main Street on both sides. A shimmering float sits poised at the top of the hill, covered with beautiful girls undoubtedly freezing to death in their skimpy evening gowns but waving, waving, waving, mouths set in those big sweet smiles. They can do this forever, these girls. Lynn herself was never much good at denial of any sort, not even as a girl, this is why she will never be truly Southern although she has lived down here for twenty-five years now. The band stops still and switches into "Jingle Bells" while the majorettes go into a dance routine. Their batons flash high in the cold bright air.

Lynn drives down Wisteria and heads for home the back way, braking suddenly for a carriage pulled by two big black horses with slavering mouths and real jingle bells and a top-hatted driver like a sudden apparition from the nineteenth century, straight out of Dickens, which Lynn used to teach. Jesus! Where did *he* come from? The fringe on the carriage jiggles. Things have gotten a lot more elaborate since the last Christmas parade Lynn remembers — three years ago, was it? Year before last, they were in Mexico at that conference, and last year they were in San Francisco visiting Anne, who still doesn't know. Nor does Jeffrey, in Rome. Lynn just hasn't told them, that's all. Why should she? Why should *she* have to be the one to do it, when none of it was her fault? And why spoil their Christmases anyway? Why give Lawrence so much power over all their lives?

Evergreen roping is strung from lantern to lantern along the front walkway of the historic Episcopal church. Angels scurry across the lawn, followed by people in choir robes. The minister, Harry Fitzhugh, stands by the open red doors of the church in a long white robe, looking more like Friar Tuck than one of the heavenly host. TOUR SITE #11 reads a placard beside him, printed in somebody's idea of medieval lettering.

Oh shit. It's the Christmas House Tour too, of course it is! There's a TOUR SITE #8 sign in the Woodwards' huge yard; every single window of their antebellum mansion wears a Christmas wreath with a big red bow on it, second floor too. Three costumed ladies stand down by the wrought-iron gate, ready to welcome the onslaught of visitors. Those hoop skirts make them look like bells themselves, belles as bells, Lawrence would have made something clever of it.

Oh, good. Lynn sees that the carriage horses have taken a big shit right in front of Mrs. Gardiner's house, which is on the tour too. Back when Lynn and Lawrence had just moved to town, their first Christmas here, Mrs. Gardiner had stopped Lynn on the street to pluck peevishly at her sleeve and say, "My de-ah, you must know that you should nev-ah, *nev*-ah put colored lights on your home! Only white! *White!*" referring to the Christmas tree Lynn had put out on her front porch, with its old-fashioned round colored bulbs, carefully saved from Lynn's own childhood in Pennsylvania. This was back when Lynn used to decorate her house, back when the children were young.

A shining Moravian star hangs over the Camerons' front door, she sees, while a whole herd of electrical reindeer graze in the McClures' side yard, their bright heads moving up and down. And here comes Lynn's friend Virginia, walking briskly away from her own house while tour guides cluster on the garlanded verandah behind her. Virginia waves cheerily as she turns toward town where she's probably going to watch the parade. Of course Virginia has put her house on the tour; she's unfailingly civic. Virginia has never mentioned Lawrence's absence, either, out of tact or ignorance, Lynn is not sure which. In any case, Virginia *must* leave now, this is the way it works, while volunteers lead the paying public inside to view decorations fashioned by members of the local garden club. Lynn remembers one time when these ladies put a huge wreath made of bagels up over the stove in Marilyn and Don Goodman's gourmet kitchen; the Goodmans invited the entire neighborhood over to eat it the next day for breakfast.

Lynn herself would hate to have the garden club ladies in her own house even more than she would hate to have the public. In this, at least, she and Lawrence were in accord, though they own the kind of house that looks like it *should* be on the house tour, a big old rambling Victorian set way back from Main Street, with gingerbread woodwork all along the deep porches enclosing it on three sides. The previous owners had restored it — Lynn and Lawrence could never have undertaken such a mammoth task, neither one of them being at all handy. They had both been married to other people who were the practical ones. In fact, Lynn has sometimes thought of her sweet, earnest first husband, and his ratchet set, with a certain longing.

But Lawrence made it perfectly plain when he married her: "My dear, I am *not* domestic," he had said straight out, "but whatever it is, I will hire it done."

Not entirely true, but close enough, Lynn supposes, remembering suddenly what he said when that nice tremulous committee lady paid them a surprise call to ask if they would "show their lovely home." Lynn had ushered her straight into Lawrence's office, where he sat in his accustomed gloom, drapes drawn behind him, papers and books strewn across the floor and every available surface. There was nowhere for anyone else to sit.

The lady made her request.

"We shall not be participating in this house tour during my current lifetime," Lawrence had intoned quite formally, giving her the famous stare over his half-glasses.

"Excuse me?" She fluttered her hand to her throat.

"I said, *not bloody likely!*" Then he stood up from his chair, all six and a half skinny, wavering feet of him, towering over this nice lady, who — predictably — fled.

Now Lynn is ashamed to remember how she and Lawrence had high-fived each other, having vanquished, once again, the Philistines. She has come to hate that easy scorn, that superciliousness, that constant depression that was supposed to excuse everything. Of course she knew Lawrence was depressed from the very moment she met him — how could she not know? It was his stock in trade. After all, he was a playwright, the writer in residence. Initially she found it romantic, even somewhat appealing. After all, she was a graduate student. Nobody had told her yet that depression can be catching — or permanent. A worldview. That was a term they used back then, in graduate school. But Lynn always thought she could fix him, anyway, when she wanted to. When she got ready. This turned out to be not true, which came, over time, to enrage her. "I'm *not enough*?" she'd screamed at him more than once.

"Lynn, that's very egotistical," he'd say severely.

She turns into her driveway and pulls up close to the back steps, so she won't have to carry things so far. Her ankle is still bothering her, even though Doug, the physical therapist, has supposedly fixed it.

"You're fine," he said, patting her tibula. "Good to go."

Lynn knows this is not true. She is not good to go. She struggles up the back steps with her groceries, balancing the bag on her hip as she unlocks the door.

They bought this house with the proceeds from *Audubon Park,* Lawrence's big hit, which was just as dark as everything else he'd written, actually, who knows why it was such a success? Six years on Broadway, then the film with Meryl Streep.

Lawrence had disconcerted the perky real estate girl immediately. "Now what are you looking for, in a house?" she had asked, back at the real estate office. "Colonial, modern, near the university, out in the country, what?" She wore a hot pink nubby wool suit, then the height of fashion, her hair caught up in a neat French twist.

Lynn wore jeans.

Lawrence took off his glasses and rubbed his huge watery pale eyes and then put them back on. "What I really want," he said, "is a house I could die in."

Lynn started laughing. The real estate girl rustled her papers and stood up on her tiny heels. "Then let's get going!" she said. She drove them around in her Lincoln Town Car for five hours, until they were punchy and exhausted, finally ending up here just as the sun was setting. It was, Lynn knew immediately, *perfect*. Not quite the House of Usher — new plumbing, thank God, new kitchen, new HVAC — but it was close enough. And a big backyard where their children could play.

"We can make a swing here for our grandchildren," she said dreamily, putting one hand on a huge limb which would be perfect.

"Or I could just use it to hang myself," Lawrence said.

"*Excuse me!*" The real estate girl took off her shoes and ran across the grass in her stocking feet to her car, where she sat chain-smoking Salems until they came over and told her it was a deal.

"You're kidding," she said.

LYNN PUTS THE GROCERIES down on the kitchen counter, then goes back out for the wine. She can hear the parade moving down Main Street in front of her house. The big bass drum sounds like it's beating inside her head. Long shadows slant across the lawn now, it's almost dusk, and suddenly Lynn wonders about that old string of colored lights, someplace down in the basement. She thinks she knows where it is. Maybe she'll just go down there tomorrow and get it and string it around a boxwood. The carton of wine is not as heavy as she'd imagined, but she takes the steps one at a time, carefully. She's still limping, damn it, she is *not* "good to go," no matter what Doug says.

The truth is that Lynn had loved physical therapy, she had loved the sunny, cheerful little gym at Tar Heel Orthopedics with all its primary colors and shiny machines. She loved Doug and Louise and Mike, all of them impossibly young and impossibly fit, she loved the routine of the gym and the easy camaraderie and the way they all encouraged each other, she and the other patients, many of them in far worse shape than she was. They still had pins, stitches, braces, casts. Complications. By contrast, her doctor had said, Lynn's was a clean break. She'd known it the minute she stumbled off the curb and heard the bone pop like a rifle shot.

"The three most important rules of aging," Dr. Lamb had told her as he set it, "are these: *Pay attention, pay attention, pay attention.*"

And now they have released her back into the real and dangerous world, Doug and the doctor. Doug said that she would recover full mobility, and soon she'd be back up to her regular ADL level.

"What does that mean?" she asked. "What is my ADL level?"

"Activities of daily life. Your ADL level ought to be completely normal in no time," Doug told her, not knowing of course that her ADL level has *never* been completely normal.

Lynn manages to open the door and switch on the hall light, but that's depressing because the house is a wreck, it hasn't been cleaned in weeks, nothing is working, nothing seems even capable of getting fixed, of ever working again. Her ADL level is shit, actually. The broken dishwasher sits out in the middle of the broad central hallway where it has been sitting for ten days now, waiting for Mr. Terrell to come and haul it away, while the new one lurks in its huge cardboard box in the kitchen, waiting for a plumber to come and install it. It seems likely that neither one of these people will ever come, that neither one of these things will ever happen.

Lynn sets the carton of wine down on top of the old dishwasher in the hall. Well, okay, she's been drinking too much. Or, possibly, she's not drinking enough. Who can say? Whose goddamn business is it anyway? She takes off her coat and drops it on the bench, then goes into the kitchen with the mail and throws it down on the kitchen table on top of yesterday's mail. Okay, she'll read it all at once. Then she'll pour herself a little glass of wine as a reward. The Pinot, perhaps.

The doorbell rings. Lynn ignores it. She puts the real mail, Christmas cards and letters, into one stack; the bills in another; the year-end pleas for contributions into another. The bell rings again. Lynn starts slitting envelopes open with a paring knife. She reads a Christmas letter which begins, "It's been a big year for the Hobgoods, what with two new grandchildren and an autumn trip to Tuscany for Bill's sixtieth . . ." Sixtieth *what*? Lynn is thinking furiously, she hates it when people leave off the noun.

SUDDENLY LYNN THINKS SHE hears voices in the hall. By the time she has stood up from the kitchen table and walked through the shadowy dining room, she's certain of it. Sure enough, the front door stands wide open, and a whole crowd of women wearing hats (*hats?*) has clustered around in the hallway.

"Hallo? Hallo?" one of them keeps calling.

Another (determined, even bossy) voice says, "Well, let's get some light on *this* subject!" and the hall light is switched on abruptly.

The hats are *red*. The women stand blinking in the light. One, smaller and more frail than the others, leans on her walker. "Robin, I just don't know about this." She sounds fretful.

"Hallo? Hallo?" the tall brunette keeps screaming up the staircase.

Lynn comes to stand in the dining room arch. "Can I help you?" she asks.

"We're here to see the house," announces the very tan blonde standing closest to Lynn.

"This house is not on the tour," Lynn says. "I'm sorry."

"Well, it most certainly *is*! Tour Site number 14!" The brunette abandons the staircase and elbows her way through the group. "Look at this!" Her dark eyes, set too close together, are snapping. She thrusts a brochure at Lynn.

"Let me see that." Luckily Lynn still has her reading glasses on. She examines the map, which has been badly drawn and badly printed. "You're looking for the Barkley School," she explains. "It's on the *next* corner, see? One more block up Main Street. It was a boarding school before the Civil War," she adds, trying to seem friendly.

"But we already walked all the way up this *hill*," moans a pale, plump woman whose red hat is as round as her face.

"Well, I'm sorry, but I can't help that," Lynn says firmly. "As you can see, this house is not on the tour. Just look at it."

"But look at poor little Melissa, why she's just about to die! She pushed her walker all the way up here!" The plump woman points at the older one, who has now turned her walker into a seat and sits upon it, breathing hard. "If we could just stay for a *minute*," Melissa begs softly.

"When was this house built?" the tan one asks. Her cap of

blonde hair sits on her head like a mushroom. "You ought to be on the tour anyway. This a lot better than the last house we went in."

"We're not, though," Lynn says hopelessly. "We're not on the tour."

But now they are all milling about, widening their area, peeping into other doors that open off the central hall. "That's a beautiful sideboard." Several peer past Lynn into the dining room.

"Rita, come look at this, you won't believe such a mess!" The mushroom blonde peers into Lawrence's study, where no one is allowed. "Why, it's just a pigpen in there."

Suddenly Lynn can't help it, she starts laughing uncontrollably.

"Now come on." The tall brunette nudges Lynn. "Can't you just let us look around for a minute? After all," she adds reasonably, "we're already *here*."

"Well, you certainly are," Lynn hears herself say, then, "Okay. What the hell? Why the hell not?" Some of the ladies glance at each other, suddenly wary, when she says "hell." But Lynn continues, "Come on. Sure. I'll give you your own personal house tour. Why not? I haven't got one other single goddamn thing to do."

"I think we'd better go." A thin redhead wearing a lot of gold jewelry speaks up for the first time.

"Georgia, are you *crazy*?" somebody else says. "Think about that hill. We'd have to walk all the way down it, then go a whole block up again, to that school, then climb up *that* hill . . ."

"Who cares about a school anyway?" the pale fat one says. "I vote we stay here."

"Then we'd better introduce ourselves." The brunette with the too-close-together eyes is obviously the leader, she reminds Lynn of a high school principal. No! Of an *assistant* high school principal. "I am Robin Atwater," she says, "and this is Mary Lane Faucette" — gesturing toward the pale plump woman who looks like a snow lady, Lynn realizes now, exactly like the snow lady and snowman her kids used to build out there on the front lawn every winter. "Angela Flack" — Robin indicates the blonde. "Melissa Cheatham," who nods from her walker, hand to chest. What if she *dies* in my front hall? Lynn is thinking. What then? Georgia Mayo is the thin redhead with the gold jewelry. Rita Goins is the big-haired one wearing the mink coat and all the makeup; she used to be very pretty, Lynn can tell. You can always tell. But that Angela Flack looks like she has spent half her life in a tanning booth. What is it with all this tanning anyway? Lynn has always wondered. Doesn't Angela know how bad this is for her? Doesn't she even read *Parade* magazine?

Robin introduces them all, then pauses expectantly.

But instead of introducing herself in return, Lynn asks, "So what's with the red hats?"

"Oh, don't you *know*?" several of them cry out, obviously surprised. "Don't you know who we are?"

Lynn shakes her head. "Sorry," she says.

"It's all based on a poem," the snow lady offers.

"What poem?" Lynn is really surprised.

"It's this poem that goes, 'When I am an old woman, I shall wear purple / with a red hat . . .' and I forget the rest . . ."

"Who's it by?"

"Oh, who cares?" Robin snaps. "The point is how we interpret it, what we *do*."

"But what *do* you do?" Lynn asks. *Besides breaking into innocent people's houses,* she does not say.

The women look at each other. Then Georgia stands to attention. She looks like a soldier in her bright red blazer and all that gold jewelry. "Nothing!" she cries.

"What?" Lynn must have misunderstood.

"Nothing! I said, *nothing*!" Georgia shrieks, giggling.

The others chime in like a high Greek chorus: "We've been doing things for other people our whole lives, and now it's time for *us* to enjoy ourselves . . . so we take trips, we go out to lunch . . . Our entire purpose is having fun! We are releasing our inner child!"

"Well, I suppose the least I can do is show you around the house, then," Lynn says. "Let's start with the pigpen. But just stick your heads in the door, please, there's really no place to stand, as you will see."

Obediently, they bunch up at the study door.

"My goodness, I have never seen that many books in one place in my life except in a library," Angela remarks. "Who reads?"

It's like an accusation. They all turn to stare at Lynn.

"Well, we both do," she says finally.

"You do? All these books?"

"Yes, we both read quite a lot. In fact, we've both been teachers all our lives, and actually, my husband is a writer, as well. Quite a famous writer. And I used to be a writer too." Lynn can't imagine why she's adding this part. But now they are all staring at her.

"Oh, that must be so *boring*," Georgia — the redhead — finally says.

"Why, what do you mean?"

"I mean, well . . . you have to write all those 'he saids' and 'she saids' all the time, don't you get really tired of it? I *would*," Georgia announces decisively.

"I guess I've never thought of it quite that way," Lynn says politely, thinking *damn good point* as she ushers them into the living room.

"Well, you certainly haven't decorated for Christmas, have you?" Robin asks pointedly.

"I'm not on the tour," Lynn reminds them, overwhelmed suddenly by the clutter of their lives, which now strikes her as appalling rather than eclectic — hodgepodge furniture bought here and there; her grandmother's antique crewel-work armchair; that huge, square glass coffee table they got in New York, covered with art books, most of them Lawrence's beloved German expressionism; the Chinese porcelain vases they brought back from China when Lawrence was invited to participate in that PEN tour (and they went down the Yangtze in that yellow boat just at dawn, oh God); and that half-woman, half-horse sculpture from New Mexico bolted to the chimney (Lynn has never been sure whether Lawrence was fucking the sculptor or not). The rugs from Turkey, the brass elephant from Morocco, the Tibetan temple door on the landing, the tapestry they bought from the old man in Turkey. Lynn loved Africa best of all, the Serengeti, looking out across those endless plains.

The women stop before one of Lawrence's treasured Max Beckmann prints hanging in the hallway, a formally dressed man holding a cigarette in one hand, staring insolently out of the frame. Rita says, "I think that's what you call undressing somebody with your eyes," while the rest of them giggle. "I wouldn't have that man in my house!" somebody else declares.

Lynn points to a sketch of San Galgano, in Tuscany. "I did that," she says, and they turn to stare at her.

"You *did*?" says Georgia, as if she doesn't quite believe it.

"And this watercolor too." Lynn indicates a placid canal in

Belgium, a trip they took with their best friends from Berkeley, the Hoffbergers, long since divorced.

"Now that's a nice one." Robin pauses at an old photograph of Lynn's family out on the rocky shore of their house at Cape Breton, Lawrence in his most disreputable fishing hat, the children in shorts, herself in rolled-up jeans throwing a stick for their beloved dogs Plato and Emily Dickinson, long since dead. Maybe Lynn should get herself a dog, now there's a thought.

"Those must be your children?" Robin prompts, and Lynn says yes, that Anne lives in California with her husband and two daughters, both adopted — little Chinese girls — and Jeffrey is in Rome for the year on a fellowship.

"*Really?*" This idea seems to strike Robin as radical. "They're not coming home for Christmas? Your son will be over there all by himself?"

"Well." Lynn tries to hide a smile. "He's thirty-five, and he has a partner." An Italian hairdresser, she does not say, whom they have never met.

"I see." Robin squinches her eyes even closer together.

Lynn is beginning to hate her.

But the women will not move on. "And when was this picture taken?" Angela asks.

"Oh, years ago," Lynn says, "but we still have this house in Nova Scotia, we go up there every summer. We've been going for thirty years. The children love it, they always come for a while, no matter where they're living, especially for the Fourth of July. That's sort of what we do instead of Christmas. We boil lobsters out on the beach, and corn and clams in this big iron pot . . ." Lynn goes on and on describing their Fourth of July ritual, unable to stop, furious at herself for telling these women these details. Because this will be the sore point, the sticking point, won't it? Who will get this house? This house that you can't quite see in this photograph, hidden back there behind the birches. This house where the children spent every summer of their childhoods, which the children love. Which Lawrence loves, and she loves too, thinking of those long red sunsets and the spray in her face as they head out into the bay in the ancient Boston Whaler which used to belong to Lawrence's first wife's first husband. Could these women even follow that? Could they ever understand anything at all about our lives?

"Dave and I went to Canada once," Mary Lane says, "but the water was too cold to swim."

Lynn hears Georgia say to Robin in an undertone, "You know, you could really do something with this house if you got all the junk out of it. Look at all this crown molding," as the group goes through the dining room.

"Wait, oh wait!" Melissa cries piteously, falling behind on her walker.

The kitchen is such a disaster (dishes in the sink, groceries still in their paper bags on the counter) that Lynn tries to rush the red hat ladies on through, but by now they're totally into the tour, pausing to exclaim over the ferns that Lynn has brought inside for the winter — "Why, it's practically a greenhouse in here!" — and the hand-painted tiles all around the sink and stove, tiles which Lynn carried back so carefully from Italy where they had had that lovely high pink house in Lucca with a view of the sea from the bedroom window and those long lace curtains sweeping the floor, that passionate year of fights (that cleaning girl) and then making up, why once she'd let the baby — this was Anne — cry for half the morning while she made love to Lawrence, swept up in overwhelming guilt and desire. She and Lawrence used to dance out on the balcony too, as she recalls, to the music of the village band coming up from the piazza, and once they had danced in the kitchen, to no music at all. What would the red hat ladies think of that? But surely they had had *some* fun with their own husbands? Surely it hadn't been all duty, all carpools and PTA?

But she too has spent a large part of her life taking care of others, Lynn realizes. She is as old as these red hat ladies, even older than Georgia and Robin. So why isn't she out there fulfilling herself too, having fun? Releasing her own inner child? Or does she still have one? Maybe that child has been killed off now by too much drinking and too many very long dinner parties with other overeducated supercilious people such as herself and Lawrence. Maybe she ought to join the red hat ladies. Or maybe she ought to become a Republican. She'd been amazed when Gore lost. She'd been amazed every time Jesse Helms won, all these years of living in North Carolina and they'd never known one single person, not one, who ever admitted to voting for Jesse Helms. But somebody did, because then the vote rolled in. Lynn bets that most of the people in that Christmas parade voted for him, possibly some of these ladies in the red hats as well. Some of them must be Republicans. Robin is one for sure. Momentarily Lynn envies them, at least if she were a Republican, she could be so goddamn *positive* about things, about *something* at least, about anything. Anything at all. She'd like to become a truly positive person like Doug and Mike and Louise at physical therapy, and improve her ADL. Improvement is possible, Doug has said so. Doug has promised. A great deal of improvement is still possible! Things can be fixed! Maybe Lynn should just break her other ankle, so she can go back to the cheerful little gym — no, that's ridiculous!

She leads the women into the back hallway.

"Well!" Robin stops dead in her tracks, eyeing the broken dishwasher with the box of wine on top of it.

"Oh. Who drinks?" Angela asks, and Lynn says, "I do."

This cracks them up, these red hat ladies, but Lynn has had about enough of them by now. She shows them the music room. "Is that really a Steinway?" Georgia wants to know, and Lynn says yes, it is, adding that Jeffrey is really a concert pianist. She leads them down the hall toward the front door, but clearly they don't want to leave yet, they dawdle, they don't want to set off down that long hill.

"So!" Robin stops by the newel post. "Aren't there any ghost stories associated with this old house?"

SOMETHING SNAPS INSIDE LYNN's head. "Why, yes," she says. "As a matter of fact, we *do* have a ghost, because actually there was a terrible death right here."

"Right *where*?" The ladies peer nervously about themselves. It's getting dark outside, and it's a little spooky in this hallway, even with the chandelier on. It's always been dark in here. Lynn decides she's going to paint the entire downstairs a sort of creamy eggshell color, brighten it up some.

"Right *there*!" She points to the dark at the top of the stairs. "Now here's the story."

They draw in closer.

"It was back in the nineteen twenties," Lynn says, "when this house was owned by a very attractive couple awaiting the birth of their first child. The husband had been sent here to open a new bank, the Carolina Southern, right down the street there in that old stone building next to the pharmacy." Everybody nods. Lynn continues, amazed at herself, "Nobody knew much about this young husband — he seemed to have risen up out of nowhere, though he was perfectly charming and clearly very smart — but *she* came from one of the oldest and wealthiest families in Wilmington. He was a gambler and a spendthrift, though nobody knew it yet, and the new bank was in serious trouble when her mother — now, this is the wife's mother, Mrs. Mildred Osgood, a widow, one of the Cape Fear Osgoods — came up from Wilmington to spend the Easter holiday and stay on for the birth of her first grandchild, as this daughter was her only child. So it was Easter Sunday, nineteen twenty-three, when the tragedy occurred."

"What tragedy?" Mary Lane breathes.

"Well, the daughter was downstairs all ready for church — they belonged to the Episcopal church — but her husband and her mother were still upstairs dressing, and she was afraid they were going to be late, so she called up the staircase and begged them to hurry. Later, she could have bit off her tongue, because her mother appeared briefly at the top of these stairs and then tripped somehow, breaking her ankle, and fell all the way down this entire staircase, head over heels, landing in a crumpled heap right there." Lynn points dramatically to the hooked rug at the bottom of the stairs. "She died instantly. And of course the young couple was just distraught, overcome with sorrow, and in fact they never got over it."

"Never?" It's Mary Lane again.

"No. Never. Because after the mother's death, there was a presence in the house, a certain presence, you would feel someone beside you when no one was there, you would sense a presence in the room, and when she got old enough, the baby would smile at it, at the person who wasn't there. So the young couple left, after a few years, but things did not go well for them. He died in an automobile accident, drove his car off the bridge into the Neuse River, and she became an alcoholic back in Wilmington. She drank white wine all day long."

"What happened to the child, then, their baby?"

"I don't know," Lynn says.

"Do *you* think he did it? The husband, I mean? Do you think he pushed her down the stairs, for the money?" Robin Atwater's mind is just clicking away.

"It's possible. I just don't know. There are some things we can never know," Lynn says.

A silence falls around them then, like snow. Down at the end of the front yard, the streetlights come on along Main Street.

"Have *you* ever felt that . . . that presence?" Angela asks softly.

"Oh yes," Lynn says. "Many times."

There's an audible intake of breath, an involuntary drawing together.

"And I'll tell you something else." Now Lynn is getting reckless, she knows she's going to blow it, but she can't resist, she just *can't*.

"*What?*"

"When Mrs. Osgood fell down the staircase, she was wearing a *red hat*!"

Nobody says a word.

"Oh, you're kidding, right? You just made that up," Georgia Mayo says finally.

"Did you make it *all* up?" Mary Lane sounds very disappointed.

"I think that's just *mean*!" Melissa Cheatham, in her walker, sounds like she's going to cry.

"Well, girls, it's getting late, I think we'd better be going on now." Robin takes control again. "Thanks so much," she says briskly, extending her hand but pulling it back when Lynn has barely touched her long, sharp, manicured nails. "Quite entertaining, I must say! And now, good-bye, and Merry Christmas." Robin shepherds them out the door. It's drizzling now, getting dark. Lynn turns on the porch light and stands to watch as they straggle over to the side street, helping Melissa along, then moving in their group down the long hill, farther and farther away. Carolers are singing someplace nearby, their voices float out on the chilly air.

"Merry Christmas!" Lynn calls after the ladies. "Merry Christmas!" She watches them until they turn the corner and disappear, heading back down Main Street. Obviously they have decided to skip the Barkley School after all.

Now, finally, she'll get that drink. Lynn laughs as she closes the door behind her and walks back down the long haunted hallway to grab the Pinot. She's still smiling when she goes into the kitchen to open it and finds Lawrence sitting at the kitchen table, wearing his overcoat, going through the mail.

HE LOOKS UP AT her over the half-glasses, white hair floating out all around his head like a dandelion gone to seed. God, he's aged, he looks really old now, like some character out of *Alice in Wonderland*. "Bravo, bravo!" He starts that slow deliberate sort of clapping he does which always drove Lynn mad. "Well done, well done, my dear! Very creative! I commend you."

"You were here? You heard all that?"

"Ah yes, my dear, I had just come slinking home through the back door, appropriately enough, dragging my tail behind me."

Lynn glances out into the back hall. She didn't notice any luggage when she passed the broken dishwasher. No, his bag is not there, it's definitely not there. So what does this mean? Does he imagine that he has come home for good? Or is he just visiting? Lawrence stands up to take off the huge overcoat, which strikes Lynn now as an affectation, especially that capey thing, and the belt — why, it's downright theatrical, really. Lawrence seems theatrical too, an old ham, a joke.

He says, "I especially liked the mother-in-law's name, Mrs. Mildred Osgood, and that line, 'one of the Cape Fear Osgoods.' That was quite good, you know."

Lynn had somehow forgotten about his deep, stupid voice-of-God voice, which they all love so much on NPR. And that accent — almost English, isn't it? Lawrence claims he got it at Harvard, but plenty of people who went to Harvard don't sound like that, do they? She opens the bottle.

"And that detail about the baby smiling at the presence in the room, very nice. You should go back to writing fiction, you know. You really should. You've a gift for it."

"I won't, though. I have other plans," Lynn hears herself saying.

"Well, what are they?" he asks. "Good works? Ha ha." He does his harumphing laugh, he's being ironic, of course.

"Perhaps." Lynn gets herself a jelly jar from the sink and pours some wine into it. "If I ever do go back to writing, the first thing I'm going to write is a long epic poem titled 'Irony Sucks.'"

He raises those scraggly white eyebrows. "Aha! A manifesto? You *are* interesting, you know. You are still interesting."

"Thank you." Her ankle hurts. She walks over to sit down at the littered table.

Lawrence gets up, opens the china cabinet. "Bravo!" he says again. "In any case, bravo! You have vanquished the opposition." He takes down one of those little green glasses they got in Venice, actually at Murano, out in the lagoon, where there'd been some sort of a workingman's organization holding a celebration, singing and dancing, arms linked, all of them singing and dancing as one. Lawrence and Lynn had stood up and joined them. Come to think of it, that might be as close as they ever got to feeling like part of something else, like part of a group. Usually, it had been the two of them against the world.

He fills the delicate green glass and lifts it. "To you, my dear."

"To Deborah Woodley," Lynn says instead, raising hers. "So, where is she?"

"Gone." He lowers his glass. "Gone with the wind. Or so it would seem."

Lynn lifts an eyebrow, sipping her wine.

"Yes," he says. "I 'brought her down,' apparently. 'You bring me down,' is what she told me, to be precise. She is considerably younger than I, as you know. We had gone to a holiday party where she had a wonderful time, as usual, and I did *not,* again as usual. And on the way home in the car, she said she was tired of me bringing her down."

"Just like that? What else did you say?"

"What do you mean?"

"I mean, what else had you said — before that, I mean — to bring her down?"

"Oh, well, I suppose I had said something to the effect . . . oh yes, I remember now. I had remarked that I hate it whenever she has a good time."

"And then *she* said . . ."

"And then she said she was tired of me bringing her down."

"So here you are."

"So here I am."

Lynn starts laughing and can't stop.

"What? What is it?" He leans forward frowning.

"Do you remember when we first moved to North Carolina?" she asked. "And I was working for the newspaper? And I had to write all those headlines and cutlines?"

"Yes . . ." He's nodding his wispy white head.

"Well, I can just see the headline now," she says. "Debbie Dumps Depressive"

Lawrence starts laughing too. "Oh, that's good," he says. "That's rich, that's really good. 'Debbie Dumps Depressive,' very nice."

They are still laughing when Mary Lane Faucette, the snow lady, pokes her red hat around the back door. "Hello — oh!" she carols. And here comes Georgia Mayo smiling her bright red smile, advancing into the kitchen, with Rita Goins tap-tapping along right behind her on those ridiculous spike heels.

Oh God. Will Lynn *never* be rid of these women?

"You must be the husband," Georgia says to Lawrence.

"In a manner of speaking." Lawrence drains his glass and pours another.

"Well, pardon me," Georgia says. Actually she looks like the Little Drummer Boy in that red blazer with all the gold jewelry. "Pardon me, but we just had to come back and make sure . . . That wasn't really true, was it? That part about the mother-in-law falling down the staircase?"

"No," Lynn says.

"I *told* you," Rita says.

"Well, why did you say it, then?" Mary Lane's feelings have obviously been hurt.

"I don't know," Lynn says.

"Ladies . . ." Lawrence begins, then pauses. "Ladies, pardon me.

But could you explain your attire to me, please? Are you members of a club? An organization?"

"Not really," Rita says.

"We're a *dis*organization," Georgia explains. "The only rule is that you have to be over fifty. And basically we're all tired of doing things for other people. We just want to have some fun. We're releasing our inner child," she adds.

Lawrence laughs, a short, abrupt bark.

Oh no, Lynn is thinking. Now he will destroy them.

But instead, Lawrence says, "There are those who feel that my inner child has been released entirely too much already. In fact, it seems entirely possible that I am nothing but an old fool, an idiot."

Lynn can feel him looking at her.

"Who are you, again?" Georgia asks him point-blank.

"I am no one. *No one,*" Lawrence intones in the voice-of-God voice.

"Are you really the husband?" she persists.

"In a manner of speaking." Lawrence drains his glass, then pours another. He stands up.

Now, Lynn is thinking. Now he will destroy them.

But instead, he makes a stagy little bow. "Ladies, please," he says. "Please. Sit down. Have a drink."

They look at each other.

"I don't mind if we do," Mary Lane says. "It was *hard,* getting back up that hill." She sinks gratefully into the chair which Lawrence pulls out for her. Rita takes off her mink coat and does the same, while Georgia sits gingerly on the very edge of her chair, looking all around the messy kitchen.

Lawrence refills Lynn's jelly jar, then pours each of them a little green glass of wine. "*Salut!*" he says. "To you!"

"Thank you." Mary Lane Faucette seems shy, suddenly. She drains her glass. Then she clears her throat and says, "My son is gay too. He lives in Atlanta, and he's just wonderful. He's the sweetest thing. In fact, he has always been the light of my life . . . of all our lives, really. He was the only truly lighthearted one in our family. But my husband won't accept it, he just can't. At first I thought, Oh, he'll come around, it'll just take time, but he can't. He just can't. In fact, he won't even talk about it. He won't mention his name."

"That's rough," Lawrence says. "Hard on you."

Lynn stares at him. Who's this? Sigmund Freud?

"It's been hard for all of us," Mary Lane says, "especially at Christmas. It's especially sad for Libbie, that's his twin sister, they used to be so close."

"I would imagine that it's harder on your husband than anybody else," Lawrence says. "That's how men are, we'll hold on to an idea we can't live with until it kills us."

"Well, that's just crazy!" Georgia Mayo says decisively, tipping her glass up to get the last bit.

"But people *are* crazy. Not just men." Rita leans forward on the kitchen table, propping her pretty face up in her hands. "I mean, you never know what is going to happen in this world, do you? For instance, I used to be Miss South Carolina?" Her voice goes up at the end. "And now I have a double mastectomy? And my husband left right in the middle of all the chemo and radiation and everything, he just couldn't take it? But guess what?"

"What?" Lynn can't imagine.

"The radiologist and I fell in love? And my children just had a fit because of course he's eleven years younger than I am, but that's not much, is it? And we didn't care, we went right ahead and got married anyway? Before my hair even came back? Because you just never know how much time you've got, do you? And now we are so happy, I mean, so happy, I just had no idea! And then we bought this house down at Hilton Head? And I have actually become a *bird-watcher*? And the children all got over it eventually, why between us we've got five grandchildren, I've got my 'brag book' right here." She produces a small pink photo album from her voluminous purse and puts it on the table, flipping the pages one by one.

"Oh, look at that darling little towhead boy," Mary Lane says. "I could just eat him up with a spoon."

Lawrence opens another bottle of Pinot Noir, and the Viognier, for her.

Lynn rummages in a kitchen drawer and pulls out a picture of her granddaughters, taken this past summer at Cape Breton. She puts it on the table.

"Why, aren't they cute?" Georgia exclaims. "And their eyes look just like anybody's! Why, I'll say!"

You'll say what? Lynn is thinking furiously. *What?* But she holds her tongue, and they all have another drink, and then another, and some of that poundcake Virginia brought over yesterday, and it's nearly seven o'clock when the three women struggle back into their coats and leave. Lynn and Lawrence stand together in the wide open front door, hands not touching, to watch them walk down the hill.

Lawrence makes his harumphing sound. "Well?" he asks.

"Well, *what*?" Lynn says. In her mind, her doctor is saying, *Pay attention, pay attention, pay attention.* She has had a clean break, though there are often complications. And her ADL level is still shit, though Doug has said she is "good to go." But improvement is possible, Doug has also said this. A great deal of improvement is still possible. For instance, she is going to put colored lights on that boxwood. And she is going to buy some sexy high heels like Rita's. She is going to buy a dog. She is going to paint the entire downstairs: eggshell. A cold breeze lifts her hair. The parade is long since over, the carolers and tourists have all gone home. The rain is past too, though dark clouds race across the dark sky, chasing a sickle moon. Lynn and Lawrence stand together in the doorway, not quite touching. In the darkened room behind them, Lynn senses their inner children sitting on the edge of their chairs, just waiting to see what will happen.

The Southern Cross

Mama always said, "Talk real sweet and you can have whatever you want." This is true, though it does not hurt to have a nice bust either. Since I was blessed early on in both the voice and bosom departments, I got the hell out of eastern Kentucky at the first opportunity and never looked back. That's how Mama raised us, not to get stuck like she did. Mama grew up hard and married young and worked her fingers to the bone and wanted us to have a better life. "Be nice," she always said. "Please people. Marry rich."

After several tries, I am finally on the verge of this. But it has been a lot of work, believe me. I'm a very high-maintenance woman. It is *not easy* to look the way I do. Some surgery has been involved. But I'll tell you, what with the miracles of modern medicine available to our fingertips, I do not know why more women don't go for it. *Just go for it!* This is my motto.

Out of Mama's three daughters, I am the only one that has gotten ahead in the world. The only one who really listened to her, the only one who has gone places and done things. And everywhere I go, I always remember to send Mama a postcard. She saves them in a big old green pocketbook that she keeps right by her bed for this very purpose. She's got postcards from Las Vegas and Disney World and Los Angeles and the Indianapolis 500 in there. From the Super Bowl and New York City and Puerto Vallarta. Just this morning, I mailed her one from Miami. I've been everywhere.

As opposed to Mama herself, who still cooks in the elementary school cafeteria in Paradise, Kentucky, where she has cooked for thirty years, mostly soup beans. Soup beans! I wouldn't eat another soup bean if my life depended on it, if it was the last thing to eat on the earth. Give me caviar. Which I admit I did not take to at first as it is so salty, but now have acquired a taste for, like scotch. There are some things you just have to like if you want to rise up in the world.

I myself am upwardly mobile and proud of it, and Mama is proud of me too. No matter what kind of lies Darnell tries to tell her about me. Darnell is my oldest sister, who goes to church in a mall where she plays tambourines and dances all around. This is just as bad as being one of those old Holiness people up in the hollers handling snakes, in my opinion. Darnell tells everybody I am going to Hell. One time she chased me down in a car to lay hands on me and pray out loud. I happened to have a new boyfriend with me at the time and I got so embarrassed I almost died.

My other sister, Luanne, is just as bad as Darnell but in a different way. Luanne runs a ceramics business at home, which has allowed her to let herself go to a truly awful degree, despite the fact that she used to be the prettiest one of us all, with smooth creamy skin, a natural widow's peak, and Elizabeth Taylor eyes. Now she weighs over two hundred pounds and those eyes are just slits in her face. Furthermore, she is living with a younger man who does not appear to work and does not look American at all. Luanne claims he has Cherokee blood. His name is Roscoe Ridley and he seems nice enough, otherwise I never would let my little Leon stay with them, of course it is just temporary until I can get Larry nailed down. I feel that Larry is finally making a real commitment by bringing me along this weekend, and I have cleared the decks for action. Larry has already left his marriage psychologically, so the rest is just a matter of time.

But speaking of decks, this yacht is not exactly like the *Love Boat* or the one on *Fantasy Island,* which is more what I had in mind. Of course, I am not old enough to remember those shows, but I have seen the reruns. I never liked that weird little dwarf guy, I believe he has died now of some unusual disease. I hope so. Anyway, thank goodness there is nobody like that on *this* boat. We have three Negroes who are nice as you please. They smile and say yes ma'am and will sing calypso songs upon request, although they have not done this yet. I am looking forward to it, having been an entertainer myself.

"Well, baby, whaddaya think? Paradise, huh?" This is my fiancé and employer Larry Marcum who certainly deserves a little trip to paradise if anybody does. I have never known anybody to work so hard. Larry started off as a paving contractor and still thinks you can never have too much concrete.

This is also true of gold, in my opinion, as well as shoes.

Now Larry is doing real well in commercial real estate and property management. In fact we are here on this yacht for the weekend thanks to his business associate, Bruce Ware, one of the biggest developers in Atlanta, though you'd never know it by looking at him. When he met us at the dock in Barbados wearing those hundred-year-old blue jeans, I was so surprised. I believe that in general, people should look as good as they *can*. Larry and I had an interesting discussion about this in which he said that from his own observation, *really* rich people like Bruce Ware will often dress down, and even drive junk cars. Bruce Ware drives an old jeep, Larry says! I cannot imagine.

And I can't wait to see what Bruce Ware's wife will have on, though I *can* imagine this, as I know plenty of women just like her — "bowheads" is what I call them, all those Susans and Ashleys and Elizabeths, though I would never say this aloud, not even to Larry. I have made a study of these women's lives, which I aspire to, not that I will ever be able to wear all those dumb little bows without embarrassment.

"Honey, this is fabulous!" I tell Larry, and it is. Turquoise blue water so clear you can see right down to the bottom where weird fish are swimming around, big old birds, strange jagged picturesque mountains popping up behind the beaches on several of the islands we're passing.

"What's the name of these islands again?" I ask, and Larry tells me, "The Grenadines." "There is a drink called that," I say, and Larry says, "Is there?" and kisses me. He is such a hard worker that he has missed out on everything cultural.

Kissing Larry is not really great but okay.

"Honey, you need some sunscreen," I tell him when he's through. He has got that kind of redheaded complexion that will burn like mad in spite of his stupid hat. "You need to put it everywhere, all over you, on your feet and all. Here, put your foot up on the chair," I tell him, and he does, and I rub sunscreen all over his fat white feet one after the other and his ankles and his calves right up to those baggy plaid shorts. This is something I will not do after we are married.

"Hey, Larry, how'd you rate that kind of service?" It's Bruce Ware, now in cutoffs, and followed not by his wife but by some young heavy country-club guy. I can feel their eyes on my cleavage.

"I'm Chanel Keen, Larry's fiancée." I straighten up and shake their hands. One of the things Larry does not know about me is that my name used to be Mayruth, back in the Dark Ages. Mayruth! Can you imagine?

Bruce introduces the guy, who turns out to be his associate, Mack Durant, and then they both stand there grinning at me. I can tell they are surprised that Larry would have such a classy fiancée as myself.

"I thought your wife was coming," I say to Bruce Ware, looking at Larry.

"She certainly intended to, Chanel," Bruce says, "but something came up at the very last minute. I know she would have enjoyed being here with you and Larry." One thing I have noticed about very successful people is that they say your name all the time and look right at you. Bruce Ware does this.

He and Mack sit down in the deck chairs. I imagine their little bowhead wives back in Atlanta shopping or getting their legs waxed or fucking the kids' soccer coach.

Actually I am relieved that the wives stayed home. It is less competition for me, and I have never liked women much anyway. I never know what to say to them, though I am very good at drawing a man out conversationally, any man. And actually a fiancée such as myself can be a big asset to Larry on a business trip, which is what this is anyway, face it, involving a huge mall and a sports complex. It's a big deal. So I make myself useful, and by the time I get Bruce and Mack all settled down with rum and tonic and sunscreen, they're showing Larry more respect already.

Bruce Ware points out interesting sights to us, such as a real volcano, as we cruise toward Saint-Philippe, the little island where we'll be anchoring. It takes three rum and tonics to get there. We go into a half-moon bay that looks exactly like a postcard, with palm trees like Gilligan's Island. The Negroes anchor the yacht and then take off for the island in the dinghy, singing a calypso song. It is *really foreign* here! Birds of the sort you find in pet stores, yachts and sailboats of every kind flying flags of every nationality, many I have never seen before. "This is just *not American* at all, is it?" I remark, and Bruce Ware says, "No, Chanel, that's the point." Then he identifies all the flags for Larry and me. Larry acts real interested in everything, but I can tell he's out of his league. I bet he wishes he'd stayed in Atlanta to make this deal. Not me! I have always envisioned myself on a yacht, and am capable of learning from every experience.

For example, I am interested to hear Bruce Ware use a term I have not heard before, *Eurotrash,* to describe some of the girls on the other yachts. Nobody mentions that about half the women on the beach are topless, though the men keep looking that way with binoculars. I myself can see enough from here — and most of those women would do a lot better to keep their tops on, in my opinion. I could show them a thing or two. But going topless is not something which any self-respective fiancée such as myself would ever do.

The Negroes come back with shrimp and limes and crackers, and so on. I'm so relieved to learn that there's a store someplace on this island, as I foresee running out of sunscreen before this is all over. While the Negroes are serving hors d'oeuvres, I go down to put on my suit, which is a little white bikini with gold trim that shows off my tan to advantage. I can't even remember what we did before tanning salons! (But then I *do* remember, all of a sudden, laying out in the sun on a towel with Darnell and Luanne, we had painted our boyfriends' initials in fingernail polish on our stomachs so we could get a tan around them. C. B., I had painted on my stomach for Clive Baldwin who was the cutest thing, the quarterback at the high school our senior year, he gave me a pearl ring that Christmas, but then after the wreck I ran off to Nashville with Mike Jenkins. I didn't care what I did. I didn't care about anything for a long, long time.)

"You feel okay, honey?" Larry says when I get to the top of the stairs, where at first I can't see a thing, the sun is so bright, it's like coming out of a movie.

"Sure I do." I give Larry a wifely peck on the cheek.

"*Damn,*" Mack Durant says. "You sure *look* okay." Mack himself looks like Burt Reynolds but fatter. I choose to ignore that remark.

"Can I get somebody to run me in to the beach?" I ask. "I need to make a few purchases."

"Why not swim in?" Bruce suggests. "That's what everybody else is doing." He motions to the other boats, and this is true. "Or you can paddle in on the kickboard."

"I can't swim," I say, which is not technically true, but I have no intention of messing up my makeup or getting my hair wet, plus also I have a basic theory that you should never do anything in front of people unless you are really good at it, this goes not just for swimming but for *everything*.

Bruce claps his hands and a Negro gets the dinghy and I ride to the beach in style, then tell him to wait for me. I could get used to this! Also I figure that my departure will give the men a chance to talk business.

There's not actually much on the island that I can see, just a bunch of pathetic-looking Negroes begging, which I ignore, and selling their tacky native crafts along the beach. These natives look very unhealthy to me, with their nappy hair all matted up and their dark skin kind of dusty looking, like they've got powder on. The ones back in Atlanta are much healthier, in my opinion, though they all carry guns.

I buy some sunscreen in the little shack of a store that features very inferior products, paying with some big green bills that I don't have a clue as to their value, I'm sure these natives are cheating me blind. Several Italian guys try to pick me up on the beach, wearing those nasty little stretch briefs. I don't even bother to speak to them. I just wade out into the warm clear water to the dinghy and ride back and then Larry helps me up the ladder to the yacht, where I land flat on my butt on the deck, to my total dismay. "It certainly is hard to keep up your image in the tropics!" I make a little joke as Larry picks me up.

"Easier to let it go," Bruce Ware says. "Go native. Let it all hang out."

In my absence, the men have been swimming. Bruce Ware's gray chest hair looks like a wet bath mat. He stands with his feet wide apart as our boat rocks in the wake of a monster sailboat. Bruce Ware looks perfectly comfortable, as if he grew up on a yacht. Maybe he did. Larry and I didn't, that's for sure! We are basically two of a kind, I just wish I'd run into him earlier in life, though better late than never as they say. This constant rocking is making me nauseous, something I didn't notice before when we were moving. I am not about to mention it, but Bruce Ware must have noticed because he gives me some Dramamine.

Larry and I go down below to dress up a little bit for dinner, but I won't let Larry fool around at all as I am sure they could *hear* us. Larry puts on khaki pants and a nice shirt and I put on my new white linen slacks and a blue silk blouse with a scoop neck. The Negroes row us over to the island. I am disappointed to see that Bruce and Mack have not even bothered to change for dinner, simply throwing shirts on over their bathing suits, and I am further disappointed by the restaurant, which we have to walk up a long steep path through the actual real jungle to get to. It's at least a half a mile. I'm so glad I wore flats.

"This better be worth it!" I joked, but then I am embarrassed when it's not. The restaurant is nothing but a big old house with Christmas lights strung all around the porch and three mangy yellow dogs in the yard. Why, I might just as well have stayed in eastern Kentucky! We climb up these steep steps onto the porch and sit at a table covered with oilcloth and it *is* a pretty view, I must admit, overlooking the harbor. There's a nice breeze too. So I am just relaxing a little bit when a chicken runs over my foot, which causes me to jump a mile. "Good Lord!" I say to Larry, who says, "Shhh." He won't look at me.

Bruce Ware slaps his hand on the table. "This is the real thing!" He goes on to say that there are two other places to eat, on the other side of the island, but this is the most authentic. He says it is run by two native women, sisters, who are famous island cooks, and most of the waitresses are their daughters. "So what do you think, Chanel?"

"Oh, I like it just fine," I say. "It's very interesting," and Larry looks relieved, but frankly I am amazed that Bruce Ware would want to come to a place like this, much less bring a lady such as myself along.

"Put it right here, honey," Bruce says to a native girl who brings a whole bottle of Mount Gay rum to our table and sets it down in front of him, along with several bottles of bitter lemon and ice and drinking glasses, which I inspect carefully to choose the cleanest one. None of them look very clean, of course they can't possibly have a dishwasher back in that kitchen, which we can see into, actually, every time the girls walk back and forth through the bead curtain. Two big fat women are back there cooking and laughing and talking a mile a minute in that language which Bruce Ware swears is English though you can't believe it.

"It's the rhythm and the accent that make it sound so different," Bruce claims. "Listen for a minute." Two native men are having a loud back-slapping kind of conversation at the bar right behind us. I can't understand a word of it. As soon as they walk away, laughing, Bruce says, "Well? Did you get any of that?"

Larry and I shake our heads no, but Mack is not even paying attention to this, he's drinking rum at a terrifying rate and staring at one of the waitresses.

Bruce smiles at us like he's some guy on the Discovery Channel. "For example," he lectures, "one of those men just said, 'Me go she by,' which is really a much more efficient way of saying, 'I'm going by to see her.' This is how they talk among themselves. But they are perfectly capable of using the King's English when they talk to us."

I make a note of this phrase, *the King's English*. I am always trying to improve my vocabulary. "Then that gives them some privacy from the tourists, doesn't it?" I remark. "From people like us."

"Exactly, Chanel." Bruce looks very pleased and I realize how much I could learn from a man like him.

"Well, this is all just so interesting, and thanks for pointing it out to us," I say, meaning every word and kicking Larry under the table. He mumbles something. Larry seems determined to match Mack drink for drink, which is not a good idea. Larry is not a good drunk.

But unfortunately I have to go to the bathroom (I can't imagine what *this* experience will be like!), so I excuse myself and make my way through the other tables, which are filling up fast. I can feel all those dark native eyes burning into my skin. When I ask for the ladies' room, the bartender simply points out into the jungle. I ask again and he points again. I am too desperate to argue. I stumble out there and am actually thankful to find a portable toilet such as you would see at a construction site. Luckily I have some Kleenex in my purse.

It is all a fairly horrifying experience made even worse by a man who's squatting on his haunches right outside the door when I exit. "Oh!" I scream, and leap back, and he says something. Naturally I can't understand a word of it. But for some reason I am rooted to the spot. He stands up slow and limber as a leopard and then we are face to face and he's looking at me like he knows me. He is much lighter skinned and more refined looking than the rest of them. "Pretty missy," he says. He touches my hair.

I'm proud to say I do not make an international incident out of this, I maintain my dignity while getting out of there as fast as possible, and don't even mention it to the men when I get back, as they are finally talking business, but of course I will tell Larry later.

So I just pour myself a big drink to calm down, and Larry reaches over to squeeze my hand, and there we all sit while the sun sets in the most spectacular fiery sunset I have ever seen in real life and the breeze comes up and the chickens run all over the place, which I have ceased to mind, oddly enough, maybe the rum is getting to me, it must be some really high proof. So I switch to beer, though the only kind they've got is something called Hairoun which does not even taste like beer in my opinion. The men are deep in conversation, though Mack gets up occasionally and tries to sweet-talk the pretty waitress, who laughs and brushes him off like he is a big fat fly. I admire her technique as well as her skin, which is beautiful, rich milk chocolate. I laugh to think what Mack's little bowhead wife back in Atlanta would think if she could see him now! The strings of Christmas lights swing in the breeze and lights glow on all the boats in the harbor. Larry scoots closer and nuzzles my ear and puts his arm around me and squeezes me right under the bust which is something I wish he would not do in public. "Having fun?" he whispers in my ear, and I say, "Yes," which is true.

I am expanding my horizons as they say.

This restaurant does not even have a menu. The women just serve us whatever they choose, rice and beans and seafood mostly, it's hard to say. I actually prefer to eat my food separately rather than all mixed up on a plate which I'm sure is not clean anyway. The men discuss getting an 85 percent loan at 9 percent and padding the specs, while I drink another Hairoun.

The man who touched my hair starts playing guitar, some kind of island stuff, he's really good. Also he keeps looking at me and I find myself glancing over at him from time to time to see if he is still looking, this is just like seventh grade. Still it gives me something to do since the men are basically ignoring me, which begins to piss me off after a while since Mack is *not* ignoring the pretty waitress. The Negro with the guitar catches me looking at him and grins. I am completely horrified to see that his two front teeth are gold. People start dancing. "I don't know," Larry keeps saying to Bruce Ware. "I just don't know."

I have to go to the bathroom again and when I come back

there's a big argument going on involving Mack, who has apparently been slapped by the pretty waitress. Now she's crying and her mother is yelling at Mack who is pretty damn mad, and who can blame him? Of course he didn't mean anything by whatever he did, he certainly wasn't going to sleep with that girl and get some disease. "Goddamn bitch," he says, and Bruce tells Larry and me to get him out of there, which we do, while Bruce gets into some kind of fight himself over the bill. These Negroes have overcharged us. Bruce's behavior at this point is interesting to me. He has gone from his nice Marlin Perkins voice to a real J. R. Ewing obey-me voice. *Thank God there is somebody here to take charge,* I'm thinking as I stand at the edge of the jungle with a drunk on each arm and watch the whole thing happening inside the house like it's on television. The ocean breeze lifts my hair off my shoulders and blows it around and I don't even care that it's getting messed up. I am so mad at Larry for getting drunk.

"You okay, honey?" Bruce Ware says to me when he gets everything taken care of to his satisfaction, and I say, "Yes." Then Bruce takes Mack by the arm and I take Larry and we walk back down to the beach two by two, which seems to take forever in the loud rustling dark. I wouldn't be a bit surprised if a gorilla jumped out and grabbed me, after everything that's happened so far! Bruce goes first, with the flashlight.

I love a capable man.

When we finally make it down to the beach, I am so glad to see our Negroes waiting, but even with their help it's kind of a problem getting Mack into the dinghy, in fact it's like a slapstick comedy, and I finally start laughing. At this point Mack turns on me. "What are you laughing at, bitch?" he says, and I say, "Larry?" but all Larry says is, "Sshhh."

"Never mind, Chanel," Bruce tells me. "Mack's just drunk, he won't even remember this tomorrow. Look at the stars."

By now the Negroes are rowing us out across the water.

"What?" I ask him.

"Look at the stars," Bruce says. "You see a lot of constellations here that you never get to see at home, for instance that's the Southern Cross over there to your left."

"Oh yes," I say, though actually I have never seen any constellations in my life, or if I did I didn't know it, and certainly did not know the names of them.

"There's Orion right overhead," Bruce says. "See those three bright stars in a row? That's his belt."

Of course I am acting as interested as possible, but by then we've reached the yacht and a Negro is helping us all up (he has quite a job with Mack and Larry), and then two of them put Mack to bed. "Scuse me," Larry mutters, and goes to the back of the boat to hang his head over and vomit. Some fiancé! I stand in the bow with Bruce Ware, observing the southern sky, while the Negroes say good night and go off with a guy who has come by for them in an outboard. Its motor gets louder and louder the farther they get from us, and I am privately sure that they are going around to the other side of the island to raise hell until dawn.

Bruce steps up close behind me. "Listen here, whatever your real name is," he says, "Larry's not going to marry you, you know that, don't you?"

Of course this is none of Bruce Ware's business, so it makes me furious. "He most certainly *is*!" I say. "Just as soon as — "

"He'll never leave Jean," Bruce says into my ear. *"Never."*

Then he sticks his tongue in my ear, which sends world-class shivers down my whole body.

"Baby — " It's Larry, stumbling up beside us.

"Larry, I'm just, we're just . . ." Now I'm trying to get away from Bruce Ware but he doesn't give an inch, pinning me against the rail. He's breathing all over my neck. "Larry," I start again.

"Hey, baby, it's okay. Go for it. I know you like to have a good time." Larry is actually saying this, and there was a time when I would have actually had that good time, but all of a sudden I just can't do it.

Before either my ex-fiancé or his associate can stop me, I make a break for it and jump right down into the dinghy and pull the rope up over the thing and push off and grab the oars and row like mad toward the shore. I use the rowing machine all the time at the health club, but this is the first time I have had a chance at the real thing. It's easy.

"Come back here," yells Bruce Ware. "Where the hell do you think you're going?"

"Native," I call back to them across the widening water. "I'm going native!"

"Shit," one of them says, but by now I can barely hear them. What I hear is the slapping sound of my oars and the occasional bit of music or conversation from the other boats, and once somebody says, "Hey, honey," but I keep going straight for the beach, which lies like a silver ribbon around the bay. I look back long enough to make sure that nobody's coming after me. At least those natives can speak the King's English when they want to, and I can certainly help out in the kitchen if need be. I grew up cooking beans and rice. Anyway, I'm sure I can pay one of them to take me back to Barbados in the morning. Won't that surprise my companions? Since I am never without some "mad money" and Larry's gold card, this is possible, although I did leave some brand-new perfectly gorgeous shoes and several of my favorite outfits on the yacht.

A part of me can't believe I'm acting this crazy, while another part of me is saying, "Go, girl." A little breeze comes up and ruffles my hair. I practice deep breathing from aerobics and look all around. The water is smooth as glass. The whole damn sky is full of stars. It is just beautiful. All the stars are reflected in the water. Right overhead I see Orion and then I see his belt, as clear as can be. I'm headed for the island, sliding through the stars.

Between the Lines

"Peace be with you from Mrs. Joline B. Newhouse" is how I sign my columns. Now I gave some thought to that. In the first place, I like a line that has a ring to it. In the second place, what I have always tried to do with my column is to uplift my readers if at all possible, which sometimes it is not. After careful thought, I threw out "Yours in Christ." I am a religious person and all my readers know it. If I put "Yours in Christ," it seems to me that they will think I am theirs because I am in Christ, or even that they and I are in Christ *together,* which is not always the case. I am in Christ, but I know for a fact that a lot of them are not. There's no use acting like they are, but there's no use rubbing their faces in it either. "Peace be with you," as I see it, is sufficiently religious without laying all the cards right out on the table in plain view. I like to keep an ace or two up my sleeve. I like to write between the lines.

This is what I call my column, in fact: Between the Lines, by Mrs. Joline B. Newhouse. Nobody knows why. Many people have come right out and asked me, including my best friend, Sally Peck, and my husband, Glenn. "Come on, now, Joline," they say. "What's this Between the Lines all about? What's this Between the Lines supposed to mean?" But I just smile a sweet mysterious smile and change the subject. I know what I know.

And my column means everything to folks around here. Salt Lick community is where we live, unincorporated. I guess there is not much that you would notice, passing through — the post office (real little), the American oil station, my husband Glenn's Cash 'N' Carry Beverage Store. He sells more than beverages in there, though, believe me. He sells everything you can think of, from thermometers and rubbing alcohol to nails to frozen pizza. Anything else you want, you have to go out of the holler and get on the interstate and go to Greenville to get it. That's where my column appears, in the *Greenville Herald,* fortnightly. Now there's a word with a ring to it: *fortnightly.*

There are seventeen families here in Salt Lick — twenty, if you count those three down by the Five Mile Bridge. I put what they do in the paper. Anybody gets married, I write it. That goes for born, divorced, dies, celebrates a golden wedding anniversary, has a baby shower, visits relatives in Ohio, you name it. But these mere facts are not what's most important, to my mind.

I write, for instance: "Mrs. Alma Goodnight is enjoying a pleasant recuperation period in the lovely, modern Walker Mountain Community Hospital while she is sorely missed by her loved ones at home. Get well soon, Alma!" I do not write that Alma Goodnight is in the hospital because her husband hit her up the side with a rake and left a straight line of bloody little holes going from her waist to her armpit after she yelled at him, which Lord knows she did all the time, once too often. I don't write how Eben Goodnight is all torn up now about what he did, missing work and worrying, or how Alma likes it so much in the hospital that nobody knows if they'll ever get her to go home or not. Because that is a *mystery,* and I am no detective by a long shot. I am what I am, I know what I know, and I know you've got to give folks something to hang on to, something to keep them going. That is what I have in mind when I say *uplift,* and that is what God had in mind when He gave us Jesus Christ.

My column would not be but a paragraph if the news was all I told. But it isn't. What I tell is what's important, like the bulbs coming up, the way the redbud comes out first on the hills in the spring and how pretty it looks, the way the cattails shoot up by the creek, how the mist winds down low on the ridge in the mornings, how my wash all hung out on the line of a Tuesday looks like a regular square dance with those pants legs just flapping and flapping in the wind! I tell how all the things you ever dreamed of, all changed and ghostly, will come crowding into your head on a winter night when you sit up late in front of your fire. I even made up these little characters to talk for me, Mr. and Mrs. Cardinal and Princess Pussycat, and often I have them voice my thoughts. Each week I give a little chapter in their lives. Or I might tell what was the message brought in church, or relate an inspirational word from a magazine, book, or TV. I look on the bright side of life.

I've had God's gift of writing from the time I was a child. That's what the B. stands for in Mrs. Joline B. Newhouse — Barker, my maiden name. My father was a patient strong God-fearing man despite his problems and it is in his honor that I maintain the B. There was a lot of us children around all the time — it was right up the road here where I grew up — and it would take me a day to tell you what all we got into! But after I learned how to write, that was that. My fingers just naturally curved to a pencil and I sat down to writing like a ball of fire. They skipped me up one, two grades in school. When I was not but eight, I wrote a poem named "God's Garden," which was published in the church bulletin of the little Methodist church we went to then on Hunter's Ridge. Oh, Daddy was so proud! He gave me a quarter that Sunday, and then I turned around and gave it straight to God. Put it in the collection plate. Daddy almost cried he was so proud. I wrote another poem in school the next year, telling how life is like a maple tree, and it won a statewide prize.

That's me — I grew up smart as a whip, lively, and naturally good. Jesus came as easy as breathing did to me. Don't think I'm putting on airs, through: I'm not. I know what I know. I've done my share of sinning too, of which more later.

Anyway, I was smart. It's no telling but what I might have gone on to school like my own children have and who knows what all else if Mama hadn't run off with a man. I don't remember Mama very well, to tell the truth. She was a weak woman, always lying in the bed having a headache. One day we all came home from school and she was gone, didn't even bother to make up the bed. Well, that was the end of Mama! None of us ever saw her again, but Daddy told us right before he died that one time he had gotten a postcard from her from Tampa, Florida, years and years after that. He showed it to us, all wrinkled and soft from him holding it.

Being the oldest, I took over and raised those little ones, three of them, and then I taught school and then I married Glenn and we had our own children, four of them, and I have raised them too and still have Marshall, of course, poor thing. He is the cross I have to bear and he'll be just like he is now for the rest of his natural life.

I was writing my column for the week of March 17, 1976,

when the following events occurred. It was a real coincidence because I had just finished doing the cutest little story named "A Red-Letter Day for Mr. and Mrs. Cardinal" when the phone rang. It rings all the time, of course. Everybody around here knows my number by heart. It was Mrs. Irene Chalmers. She was all torn up. She said that Mr. Biggers was over at Greenville at the hospital, very bad off this time, and that he was asking for me and would I please try to get over there today as the doctors were not giving him but a 20 percent chance to make it through the night. Mr. Biggers has always been a fan of mine, and he especially liked Mr. and Mrs. Cardinal. "Well!" I said. "Of course I will! I'll get Glenn on the phone right this minute. And you calm down, Mrs. Chalmers. You go fix yourself a Coke." Mrs. Chalmers said she would and hung up. I knew what was bothering her, of course. It was that given the natural run of things, she would be the next to go. The next one to be over there dying. Without even putting down the receiver, I dialed the beverage store. Bert answered.

"Good morning," I said. I like to maintain a certain distance with the hired help although Glenn does not. He will talk to anybody, and anytime you go in there, you can find half the old men in the county just sitting around that stove in the winter or outside on those wooden drink boxes in the summer, smoking and drinking drinks which I am sure they are getting for free out of the cooler although Glenn swears it on the Bible they are not. Anyway, I said good morning.

"Can I speak to Glenn?" I said.

"Well now, Mrs. Newhouse," Bert said in his naturally insolent voice — he is just out of high school and too big for his britches — "he's not here right now. He had to go out for a while."

"Where did he go?" I asked.

"Well, I don't rightly know," Bert said. "He said he'd be back after lunch."

"Thank you very much, there will not be a message," I said sweetly, and hung up. I *knew* where Glenn was. Glenn was over on Caney Creek where his adopted half sister Margie Kettles lived, having carnal knowledge of her in the trailer. They had been at it for thirty years and anybody would have thought they'd have worn it out by that time. Oh, I knew all about it.

The way it happened in the beginning was that Glenn's father had died of his lungs when Glenn was not but about ten years old, and his mother grieved so hard that she went off her head and began taking up with anybody who would go with her. One of the fellows she took up with was a foreign man out of a carnival, the James H. Drew Exposition, a man named Emilio something. He had this curly-headed dark-skinned little daughter. So Emilio stayed around longer than anybody would have expected, but finally it was clear to all that he never would find any work around here to suit him. The work around here is hard work, all of it, and they said he played a musical instrument. Anyway, in due course this Emilio just up and vanished, leaving that foreign child. Now that was Margie, of course, but her name wasn't Margie then. It was a long foreign name, which ended up as Margie, and that's how Margie ended up here, in these mountains, where she has been up to no good ever since. Glenn's mother did not last too long after Emilio left, and those children grew up wild. Most of them went to foster homes, and to this day Glenn does not know where two of his brothers are! The military was what finally saved Glenn. He stayed with the military for nine years, and when he came back to this area he found me over here teaching school and with something of a nest egg in hand, enabling him to start the beverage store. Glenn says he owes everything to me.

This is true. But I can tell you something else: Glenn is a good man, and he has been a good provider all these years. He has not ever spoken to me above a regular tone of voice nor raised his hand in anger. He has not been tight with the money. He used to hold the girls in his lap of an evening. Since I got him started, he has been a regular member of the church, and he has not fallen down on it yet. Glenn furthermore has that kind of disposition where he never knows a stranger. So I can count my blessings too.

Of course I knew about Margie! Glenn's sister Lou-Ann told me about it before she died, that is how I found out about it originally. She thought I *should* know, she said. She said it went on for years and she just wanted me to know before she died. Well! I had had the first two girls by then, and I thought I was so happy. I took to my bed and just cried and cried. I cried for four days and then by gum I got up and started my column, and I have been writing on it ever since. So I was not unprepared when Margie showed up again some years after that, all gap toothed and wild looking, but then before you knew it she was gone, off again to Knoxville, then back working as a waitress at that truck stop at the county line, then off again, like that. She led an irregular life. And as for Glenn, I will have to hand it to him, he never darkened her door again until after the birth of Marshall.

Now let me add that I would not have gone on and had Marshall if it were left up to me. I would have practiced more birth control. Because I was old by that time, thirty-seven, and that was too old for more children I felt, even though I had started late of course. I had told Glenn many times, I said three normal girls is enough for anybody. But no, Glenn was like a lot of men, and I don't blame him for it — he just had to try one more time for a boy. So we went on with it, and I must say I had a feeling all along.

I was not a bit surprised at what we got, although after wrestling with it all for many hours in the dark night of the soul, as they say, I do not believe that. Marshall is a judgment on me for my sin. He is one of God's special children, is how I look at it. Of course he looks funny, but he has already lived ten years longer than they said he would. And has a job! He goes to Greenville every day on the Trailways bus, rain or shine, and cleans up the Plaza Mall. He gets to ride on the bus, and he gets to see people. Along about six o'clock he'll come back, walking up the holler and not looking to one side or the other, and then I give him his supper and then he'll watch something on TV like *The Brady Bunch* or *Family Affair,* and then he'll go to bed. He would not hurt a flea. But oh, Glenn took it hard when Marshall came! I remember that night so well and the way he just turned his back on the doctor. This is what sent him back to Margie, I am convinced of it, what made him take up right where he had left off all those years before.

So since Glenn was up to his old tricks I called up Lavonne, my daughter, to see if she could take me to the hospital to see Mr. Biggers. Why yes she could, it turned out. As a matter of fact she was going to Greenville herself. As a matter of fact she had something she wanted to talk to me about anyway. Now Lavonne is our youngest girl and the only one that stayed around here. Lavonne is somewhat pop eyed, and has a weak constitution. She is one of those people that never can make up their minds. That day on the phone, I heard a whine in her voice I didn't like the sound of. Something is up, I thought.

First I powdered my face, so I would be ready to go when Lavonne got there. Then I sat back down to write some more of my column, this paragraph I had been framing in my mind for weeks about how sweet potatoes are not what they used to be. They taste gritty and dry now, compared to how they were. I don't know the cause of it, whether it is man on the moon or pollution in the ecology or what, but it is true. They taste awful.

Then my door came bursting open in a way that Lavonne would never do it and I knew it was Sally Peck from next door. Sally is loud and excitable but she has a good heart. She would do anything for you. "Hold on to your hat, Joline!" she hollered. Sally is so loud because she's deaf. Sally was just huffing and puffing — she is a heavy woman — and she had rollers still up in her hair and her old housecoat on with the buttons off.

"Why, Sally!" I exclaimed. "You are all wrought up!"

Sally sat down in my rocker and spread out her legs and started fanning herself with my *Family Circle* magazine. "If you think I'm wrought up," she said finally, "it is nothing compared to what you are going to be. We have had us a suicide, right here in Salt Lick. Margie Kettles put her head inside her gas oven in the night."

"Margie?" I said. My heart was just pumping.

"Yes, and a little neighbor girl was the one who found her, they say. She went over to borrow some baking soda for her mama's biscuits at seven o'clock a.m." Sally looked real hard at me. "Now wasn't she related to you all?"

"Why," I said just as easily, "why, yes, she was Glenn's adopted half sister, of course, when they were nothing but a child. But we haven't had anything to do with her for years as you can well imagine."

"Well, they say Glenn is making the burial arrangements," Sally spoke up. She was getting her own back that day, I'll have to admit it. Usually I'm the one with all the news.

"I have to finish my column now and then Lavonne is taking me in to Greenville to see old Mr. Biggers who is breathing his last," I said.

"Well," Sally said, hauling herself up out of my chair, "I'll be going along then. I just didn't know if you knew it or not." Now Sally Peck is not a spiteful woman in all truth. I have known her since we were little girls sitting out in the yard looking at a magazine together. It is hard to imagine being as old as I am now, or knowing Sally Peck — who was Sally Bland then — so long.

Of course I couldn't get my mind back on sweet potatoes after she left. I just sat still and fiddled with the pigeonholes in my desk and the whole kitchen seemed like it was moving and rocking back and forth around me. Margie dead! Sooner or later I would have to write it up tastefully in my column. Well, I must say I had never thought of Margie dying. Before God, I never hoped for that in all my life. I didn't know what it would do to *me,* in fact, to me and Glenn and Marshall and the way we live because you know how the habits and the ways of people can build up over the years. It was too much for me to take in at one time. I couldn't see how anybody committing suicide could choose to stick their head in the oven anyway — you can imagine the position you would be found in.

Well, in came Lavonne at that point, sort of hanging back and stuttering like she always does, and that child of hers, Sherry Lynn, hanging on to her skirt for dear life. I saw no reason at that time to tell Lavonne about the death of Margie Kettles. She would hear it sooner or later anyway. Instead, I gave her some plant food that I had ordered two for the price of one from Montgomery Ward some days before.

"Are you all ready, Mama?" Lavonne asked in that quavery way she has, and I said indeed I was, as soon as I got my hat, which I did, and we went out and got in Lavonne's Buick Electra and set off on our trip. Sherry Lynn sat in the back, coloring in her coloring book. She is a real good child. "How's Ron?" I said. Ron is Lavonne's husband, an electrician, as up and coming a boy as you would want to see. Glenn and I are as proud as punch of Ron, and actually I never have gotten over the shock of Lavonne marrying him in the first place. All through high school she never showed any signs of marrying anybody, and you could have knocked me over with a feather the day she told us she was secretly engaged. I'll tell you, our Lavonne was not the marrying sort! Or so I thought.

But that day in the car she told me, "Mama, I wanted to talk to you and tell you I am thinking of getting a d-i-v-o-r-c-e."

I shot a quick look into the backseat, but Sherry Lynn wasn't hearing a thing. She was coloring Wonder Woman in her book.

"Now, Lavonne," I said. "What in the world is it? Why, I'll bet you can work it out." Part of me was listening to Lavonne, as you can imagine, but part of me was still stuck in that oven with crazy Margie. I was not myself.

I told her that. "Lavonne," I said, "I am not myself today. But I'll tell you one thing. You give this some careful thought. You don't want to go off half cocked. What is the problem, anyway?"

"It's a man where I work," Lavonne said. She works in the Welfare Department, part time, typing. "He is just giving me a fit. I guess you can pray for me, Mama, because I don't know what I'll decide to do."

"Can we get an Icee?" asked Sherry Lynn.

"Has anything happened between you?" I asked. You have to get all the facts.

"Why, *no*!" Lavonne was shocked. "Why, I wouldn't do anything like that! Mama, for goodness' sakes! We just have coffee together so far."

That's Lavonne all over. She never has been very bright. "Honey," I said, "I would think twice before I threw up a perfectly good marriage and a new brick home for the sake of a cup of coffee. If you don't have enough to keep you busy, go take a course at the community college. Make yourself a new pantsuit. This is just a mood, believe me."

"Well," Lavonne said. Her voice was shaking and her eyes were swimming in tears that just stayed there and never rolled down her cheeks. "Well," she said again.

As for me, I was lost in thought. It was when I was a young married woman like Lavonne that I committed my own great sin. I had the girls, and things were fine with Glenn and all, and there was simply not any reason to ascribe to it. It was just something I did out of loving pure and simple, did because I wanted to do it. I knew and have always known the consequences, yet God is full of grace, I pray and believe, and His mercy is everlasting.

To make a long story short, we had a visiting evangelist from Louisville, Kentucky, for a two-week revival that year. John Marcel Wilkes. If I say it myself, John Marcel Wilkes was a real humdinger! He had the yellowest hair you ever saw, curly, and the finest singing voice available. Oh, he was something, and that very first night he brought two souls into Christ. The next day I went over to the church with a pan of brownies just to tell him how much I personally had received from his message. I thought, of course, that there would be other people around — the Reverend Mr. Clark, or the youth director, or somebody cleaning. But to my surprise that church was totally empty except for John Marcel Wilkes himself reading the Bible in the fellowship hall and making notes on a pad of paper. The sun came in a window on his head. It was early June, I remember, and I had on a blue dress with little white cap sleeves and open-toed sandals. John Marcel Wilkes looked up at me and his face gave off light like the sun.

"Why, Mrs. Newhouse," he said. "What an unexpected pleasure!" His voice echoed out in the empty fellowship hall. He had the most beautiful voice too — strong and deep, like it had bells in it. Everything he said had a ring to it.

He stood up and came around the table to where I was. I put the brownies down on the table and stood there. We both just stood there, real close without touching each other, for the longest time, looking into each other's eyes. The he took my hands and brought them up to his mouth and kissed them, which nobody ever did to me before or since, and then he kissed me on the mouth. I thought I would die. After some time of that, we went together out into the hot June day where the bees were all buzzing around the flowers there by the back gate and I couldn't think straight. "Come," said John Marcel Wilkes. We went out in the woods behind the church to the prettiest place, and when it was all over I could look up across his curly yellow head and over the trees and see the white church steeple stuck up against that blue, blue sky like it was pasted there. This was not all. Two more times we went out there during that revival. John Marcel Wilkes left after that and I have never heard a word of him since. I do not know where he is, or what has become of him in all these years. I do know that I never bake a pan of brownies, or hear the church bells ring, but what I think of him. So I have to pity Lavonne and her cup of coffee if you see what I mean, just like I have to spend the rest of my life to live my sinning down. But I'll tell you this: if I had it all to do over, I would do it all over again, and I would not trade it in for anything.

Lavonne drove off to look at fabric and get Sherry Lynn an Icee, and I went to the hospital. I hate the way they smell. As soon as I entered Mr. Biggers's room, I could see he was breathing his last. He was so tiny in the bed you almost missed him, a poor little shriveled-up thing. His family sat all around.

"Aren't you sweet to come?" they said. "Looky here, honey, it's Mrs. Newhouse."

He didn't move a muscle, all hooked up to tubes. You could hear him breathing all over that room.

"It's Mrs. Newhouse," they said, louder. "Mrs. Newhouse is here. Last night he was asking for everybody," they said to me. "Now he won't open his eyes. You are real sweet to come," they said. "You certainly did brighten his days." Now I knew this was true because the family had remarked on it before.

"I'm so glad," I said. Then some more people came in the door and everybody was talking at once, and while they were doing that, I went over to the bed and got right up by his ear.

"Mr. Biggers!" I said. "Mr. Biggers, it's Joline Newhouse here."

He opened one little old bleary eye.

"Mr. Biggers!" I said right into his ear. "Mr. Biggers, you know those cardinals in my column? Mr. and Mrs. Cardinal? Well, I made them up, Mr. Biggers. They never were real at all." Mr. Biggers closed his eye and a nurse came in and I stood up.

"Thank you so much for coming, Mrs. Newhouse," his daughter said.

"He is one fine old gentleman," I told them all, and then I left.

Outside the hall, I had to lean against the tile wall for support while I waited for the elevator to come. Imagine, me saying such a thing to a dying man! I was not myself that day.

Lavonne took me to the big Kroger's in north Greenville and we did our shopping, and on the way back in the car she told me she had been giving everything a lot of thought and she guessed I was right after all.

"You're not going to tell anybody, are you?" she asked me anxiously, popping her eyes. "You're not going to tell Daddy, are you?" she said.

"Why, Lord no, honey!" I told her. "It is the farthest thing from my mind."

Sitting in the backseat among all the grocery bags, Sherry Lynn sang a little song she had learned at school. "Make new friends but keep the old, some are silver but the other gold," she sang.

"I don't know what I was thinking of," Lavonne said.

Glenn was not home yet when I got there — making his arrangements, I suppose. I took off my hat, made myself a cup of Sanka, and sat down and finished off my column on a high inspirational note, saving Margie and Mr. Biggers for the next week. I cooked up some ham and red-eye gravy, which Glenn just loves, and then I made some biscuits. The time seemed to pass so slow. The phone rang two times while I was fixing supper, but I just let it go. I thought I had received enough news for *that* day. I still couldn't get over Margie putting her head in the oven, or what I had said to poor Mr. Biggers, which was not at all like me you can be sure. I buzzed around that kitchen doing first one thing, then another. I couldn't keep my mind on anything I did.

After a while Marshall came home, and ate, and went in the front room to watch TV. He cannot keep it in his head that watching TV in the dark will ruin your eyes, so I always have to go in there and turn on a light for him. This night, though, I didn't. I just let him sit there in the recliner in the dark, watching his show, and in the pale blue light from that TV set he just looked like anybody else.

I put on a sweater and went out on the front porch and sat in the swing to watch for Glenn. It was nice weather for that time of year, still a little cold but you could smell spring in the air already and I knew it wouldn't be long before the redbud would come out again on the hills. Out in the dark where I couldn't see them, around the front steps, my crocuses were already up. After a while of sitting out there I began to take on a chill, due more to my age no doubt than the weather, but just then some lights came around the bend, two headlights, and I knew it was Glenn coming home.

Glenn parked the truck and came up the steps. He was dog tired, I could see that. He came over to the swing and put his hand on my shoulder. A little wind came up, and by then it was so dark you could see lights on all the ridges where the people live. "Well, Joline," he said.

"Dinner is waiting on you," I said. "You go on in and wash up and I'll be there directly. I was getting worried about you," I said.

Glenn went on and I sat there swaying on the breeze for a

minute before I went after him. Now where will it all end? I ask you. All this pain and loving, mystery and loss. And it just goes on and on, from Glenn's mother taking up with dark-skinned gypsies to my own daddy and his postcard to that silly Lavonne and her cup of coffee to Margie with her head in the oven, to John Marcel Wilkes and myself, God help me, and all of it so long ago out in those holy woods.

Tongues of Fire

The year I was thirteen — 1957 — my father had a nervous breakdown, my brother had a wreck, and I started speaking in tongues. The nervous breakdown had been going on for a long time before I knew anything about it. Then one day that fall, Mama took me downtown in the car to get some Baskin-Robbins ice cream, something she never did, and while we were sitting on the curly chairs facing each other across the little white table, Mama took a deep breath, licked her red lipstick, leaned forward in a very significant way, and said, "Karen, you may have noticed that your father is *not himself* lately."

Not himself! Who was he, then? What did she mean? But I had that feeling you get in your stomach when something really important happens. I knew this was a big deal.

Mama looked all around, as if for spies. She waited until the ice cream man went through the swinging pink doors, into the back of his shop.

"Karen," she said, so low I could hardly hear her, "your father is having a nervous breakdown."

"He is?" I said stupidly.

The ice cream man came back.

"Sshhh," Mama said. She caught my eye and nodded gravely, once. "Don't eat that ice cream so fast, honey," she said a minute later. "It'll give you a headache."

And this was the only time she ever mentioned my father's nervous breakdown out loud, in her whole life. The older kids already knew, it turned out. Everybody had wanted to keep it from me, the baby. But then the family doctor said Mama *ought* to tell me, so she did. But she did not elaborate, then or ever, and in retrospect I am really surprised that she ever told me at all. Mama grew up in Birmingham, so she talked in a very southern voice and wore spectator heels and linen dresses that buttoned up the front and required a great deal of ironing by Missie, the maid. Mama's name was Dee Rose. She said that when she married Daddy and came up here to the wilds of north Alabama to live, it was like moving to Siberia. It was like moving to Outer Mongolia, she said. Mama's two specialties were Rising to the Occasion and Rising Above It All, whatever "it" happened to be. Mama believed that if you can't say something nice, say nothing at all. If you don't discuss something, it doesn't exist. This is the way our family handled all of its problems, such as my father's quarrel with my uncle Dick or my sister's promiscuity or my brother's drinking.

Mama had long red fingernails and shiny yellow hair that she wore in a bubble cut. She looked like a movie star. Mama drank a lot of gin and tonics and sometimes she would start on them early, before five o'clock. She'd wink at Daddy and say, "Pour me one, honey, it's already dark underneath the house." Still, Mama had very rigid ideas, as I was to learn, about many things. Her ideas about nervous breakdowns were:

1. The husband *should not* have a nervous breakdown.
2. Nobody can mention the nervous breakdown. It is shameful.
3. The children must *behave* at all times during the nervous breakdown.
4. The family must keep up appearances at all costs. *Nobody should know.*

Mama and I finished our ice cream and she drove us home in the white Cadillac, and as soon we got there I went up in my treehouse to think about Daddy's breakdown. I knew it was true. *So this is it,* I thought. This had been it all along. This explained the way my father's eye twitched and watered now, behind his gold-rimmed glasses. My father's eyes were deep set and sort of mournful at best, even before the twitch. They were an odd, arresting shade of very pale blue which I have never seen since, except in my sister, Ashley. Ashley was beautiful, and my father was considered to be very good looking, I knew that, yet he had always been too slow moving and thoughtful for me. I would have preferred a more military model, a snappy go-getter of a dad. My dad looked like a professor at the college, which he was not. Instead he ran a printing company with my uncle Dick, until their quarrel. Now he ran it by himself — or rather his secretary, Mrs. Eunice Merriman, ran it mostly by herself during the time he had his nervous breakdown. Mrs. Eunice Merriman was a large, imposing woman with her pale blonde hair swept up in a beehive hairdo as smooth and hard as a helmet. She wore glasses with harlequin frames. Mrs. Merriman reminded me of some warlike figure from Norse mythology. She was not truly fierce, however, except in her devotion to my father, who spent more and more time lying on the daybed upstairs in his study, holding books or magazines in his hands but not reading them, looking out the bay window, at the mountains across the river. What was he thinking about?

"Oh *honestly,* Karen!" my mother exploded when I asked her this question. My mother was much more interested, on the day I asked her, in the more immediate question of whether or not I had been invited to join the Sub-Deb Club. The answer was yes.

But there was no answer to the question of what my father might be thinking about. I knew that he had wanted to be a writer in his youth. I knew that he had been the protégé of some old poet or other down at the university in Tuscaloosa, that he had written a novel, which was never published, that he had gone to the Pacific Theater in the War. I had always imagined the Pacific Theater as a literal theater, somewhat like the ornate Rialto in Birmingham with its organ that rose up and down mechanically from the orchestra pit, its gold-leaf balconies, its chandelier as big as a Chevrolet. In this theater, my father might have watched movies such as *Sands of Iwo Jima* or *To Hell and Back.* Now it occurred to me, for the first time, that he might have witnessed horrors. Horrors! Sara Nell Buie, at school, swore that *her* father had five Japanese ears in a cigar box from the Philippines. Perhaps my father had seen horrors too great to be borne. Perhaps he too had ears.

But this did not seem likely, to look at him. It seemed more like mononucleosis to me. He was just *lying on the daybed.* Now he'd gotten his days and nights turned around so that he had to take sleeping tablets; he went to the printing company for only an hour or two each day. He rallied briefly at gin-and-tonic time, but his conversation tended to lapse in the middle of itself during dinner, and frequently he left the table early. My mother rose above these occasions in the way she had been trained to do as a girl in Birmingham, in the way she was training Ashley and me to do; she talked incessantly, about anything that entered her head, to fill the void. This was another of Mama's rules:

A lady never lets a silence fall.

Perhaps the most exact analysis of my father's nervous breakdown was provided by Missie one day when I was up in the treehouse and she was hanging out laundry on the line almost directly below me, talking to the Gardeners' maid from next door. "You mean Missa Graffenreid?" Missie said. "He have *lost his starch,* is all. He be getting it back directly."

In the meantime, Mama seemed to grow in her vivacity, in her busyness, taking up the slack. Luckily my sister, Ashley, was a senior at Lorton Hall that year, so this necessitated a lot of conferences and visits to colleges. The guidance counselor at Lorton Hall wanted Ashley to go to Bryn Mawr, up north, but after the visit to Bryn Mawr my mother returned with her lips pressed tight together in a little red bow. "Those girls were *not ladies,*" she reported to us all, and Bryn Mawr was never mentioned again except by Ashley, later, in fits of anger at the way her life turned out. The choices narrowed to Converse College in Spartanburg, South Carolina; Meredith College in Raleigh, North Carolina; Sophie Newcomb in New Orleans; and Sweet Briar in Virginia. My mama was dead set on Sweet Briar.

So Mama and Ashley were very busy with college visits and with all the other activities of Ashley's senior year at Lorton Hall. There were countless dresses to buy, parties to give and go to. I remember one Saturday that fall when Ashley had a Coke party in the back garden, for the senior girls and their mothers. Cokes and finger sandwiches were served. Missie had made the sandwiches the day before and put them on big silver trays, covered by damp tea towels. I watched the party from the window of my room upstairs, which gave me a terrific view of the back garden and the red and yellow fall leaves and flowers, and the girls and their mothers like chrysanthemums themselves. I watched them from my window — just as my father watched them, I suppose, from his.

My mother loved to shop, serve on committees, go to club meetings, and entertain. (Probably she should have been running Graffenreid Printing Co. all along — I see this now — but of course such an idea would not have entered anyone's head at the time.) Mama ran the Flower Guild of the Methodist church, which we attended every Sunday morning, minus my father. She was the recording secretary of the Ladies' Auxiliary, which literally *ran the town* as far as I could see; she was a staunch member of the Garden Club and the Bluebird Book Club.

Her bridge club met every Thursday at noon for lunch and bridge, rotating houses. This bridge club went on for years and years beyond my childhood, until its members began to die or move to Florida. It fascinated me. I loved those summer Thursdays when I was out of school and the bridge club came to our house — the fresh flowers, the silver, the pink cloths on the bridge tables that were set up for the occasion in the Florida room, the way Mama's dressing room smelled as she dressed, that wonderful mixture of loose powder (she used a big lavender puff) and cigarette smoke (Salems) and Chanel No. 5. The whole bridge club dressed to the hilt. They wore hats, patent-leather shoes, and dresses of silk shantung. The food my mama and Missie gave them was wonderful — is still, to this day, my very idea of elegance, even though it is not a menu I'd ever duplicate; and it was clear to me, even then, that the way these ladies were was a way I'd never be.

But on those Thursdays, I'd sit at the top of the stairs, peering through the banisters into the Florida room, where they lunched in impossible elegance, and I got to eat everything they did, from my own plate which Missie had fixed specially for me: a pink molded salad that melted on the tongue, asparagus-cheese souf-flé, and something called Chicken Crunch that involved mush-room soup, chicken, Chinese noodles, pecans, and Lord knows what else. All of Mama's bridge-lunch recipes required gelatin or mushroom soup or pecans. This was Lady Food.

So — it was the year that Mama was lunching, Daddy was lying on the daybed, and Ashley was Being a Senior. My brother, Paul, had already gone away to college, to Washington and Lee up in Virginia. At that time in my life, I knew Paul only by sight. He was incredibly old. Nice, but very old and very busy, riding around in cars full of other boys, dashing off here and there when he was home, which was seldom. He used to tell me knock-knock jokes and come up behind me and buckle my knees. I thought Paul's degree of bustle and zip was *promising,* though. I certainly hoped he would be more active than Daddy. But who could tell? I rarely saw him.

I rarely saw *anybody* in my family, or so I felt. I floated through it all like a dandelion puff on the air, like a wisp of smoke, a ghost. During the year of my father's nervous breakdown, I became invisible in my family. But I should admit that even before my invisibility I was scarcely noticeable, a thin girl, slight, brown haired and brown eyed, *undeveloped* (as Mrs. Black put it deli-cately in health class). There was no sign of a breast anyplace on my chest even though some other girls my age wore B and even

C cups, I saw them in gym. I had gone down to Sears on the bus by myself the previous summer and bought myself two training bras, just so I'd have them, but my mother had never mentioned this subject at all, of course. And even after I got the training bras, I remained — I felt — still ugly, and still invisible in the midst of my gorgeous family.

Perhaps it is not surprising that I turned to God.

I had always been *interested* in religion anyway. When I was a little girl, my favorite part of the summer was Vacation Bible School, with the red Kool-Aid in the little Dixie cups and the Lorna Doone cookies at break. I loved to color in the twelve disciples. I loved to make lanyards. I loved to sing "You Are My Sunshine" and "Red and Yellow, Black and White, They Are Precious in His Sight." I loved to hold hands with Alice Field, who was my best friend for years and years until her family moved to Little Rock, Arkansas. I loved Mrs. Treble Roach, the teacher of Vacation Bible School, a plump soft woman like a beanbag chair, who hugged us all the time. Mrs. Treble Roach gave us gold stars when we were good, and I was *very* good. I got hundreds of gold stars over the years and I believe I still have them upstairs someplace in a jewelry box, like ears.

I had always liked church too, although it was less fun. I associated church with my grandparents, since we sat with them every Sunday, third pew from the back on the left-hand side of the little stone Methodist church that my grandfather had attended all his life, that my grandmother had attended since their marriage fifty years before. Usually my mother went to church too; sometimes Ashley went to church, under duress ever since she became an atheist in tenth grade, influenced by an English teacher who was clearly *not a lady;* my father attended only on Easter. Frankly, I liked those Sundays when none of them made it, when Mama just dropped me off in front of the church and I went in all alone, clutching my quarter for the collection plate, to sit with my grandparents. Even though I was invisible in my own family, my grandparents noticed me plenty. I was their good, good little girl . . . certainly, I felt, their favorite. I did everything I could to ensure that this was true.

My grandmother had wispy blue hair and a whole lot of earrings and brooches that matched. She was the author of four books of poems which Daddy had printed up for her at the printing company. She suffered from colitis, and was ill a lot. One thing you never wanted to do with Grandmother was ask her how she felt — she'd *tell* you, gross details you didn't want to know. My mama, of course, was entirely above this kind of thing, never referring to her own or anybody else's body in any way. My grandfather wore navy blue suits to church with red suspenders underneath. He was a boxy little man who ran the bus station and had a watch that could tell you the time in Paris, London, and Tokyo. I coveted this watch and had already asked Grandaddy to leave it to me when he died, a request that seemed to startle him.

After church, I'd walk up the street with my grandparents to their house on the corner across from the Baptist church and eat lunch, which frequently ended with lemon meringue pie, my favorite. I kept a close eye out the window for Baptists, whose service was dismissed half an hour later than ours. There were so many Baptists that it took them longer to do everything. In pretty weather, I sat out on the front porch so that I could see the Baptists more clearly. They wore loud suits and made more noise in general than the quiet Methodists.

Our church had only forty-two members and about twenty

of them, like my grandparents, were so old as to be almost dead already. I was not even looking forward to joining the MYF, which I'd be eligible for next year, because it had only eight members, two of them definite nerds. All they did was collect food for the poor at Thanksgiving, and stuff like that. The BTU, on the other hand, did great stuff such as have progressive dinners and sweetheart banquets and go on trips to Gulf Shores. The BTU was a much snappier outfit than the MYF, but I knew better than to ask to join it. My mother had already explained to me the social ranking of the churches: Methodist at the top, attended by doctors and lawyers and other "nice" families; Presbyterian slightly down the scale, attended by store owners; then the vigorous Baptists; then the Church of Christ, who thought they were the only real church in town and said so. They said everybody else in town was going to hell except for them. They had hundreds of members. And then, of course, at the *very bottom* of the church scale were those little churches out in the surrounding county, some of them recognizable denominations (Primitive Baptist) and some of them not (Church of the Nazarene, Tar River Holiness) where people were reputed to yell out, fall down in fits, and throw their babies. I didn't know what this *meant,* exactly, but I knew I'd love to see it, for it promised drama far beyond the dull responsive readings of the Methodists and their rote mumbling of the Nicene Creed.

Anyway, I had been sitting on my grandparents' front porch for years eating pie and envying the Baptists, waiting without much hope to be seized by God for His heavenly purpose, bent to His will, as in *God's Girl,* my favorite book — a biography of Joan of Arc.

So far, nothing doing.

But then, that fall of Daddy's nervous breakdown, the Methodist church was visited by an unusually charismatic young preacher named Bobby Rock Malone while Mr. Treble Roach, our own preacher, was down at Duke having a hernia operation. I was late to church that day and arrived all by myself, after the service had already started. The congregation was on its feet singing "I Come to the Garden Alone," one of my favorite hymns. One unfamiliar voice led all the rest. I slipped in next to Grandaddy, found the right page in the hymnal, and craned my neck around Miss Eulalie Butter's big black hat to see who was up there singing so nice. It looked like one of the disciples to me — his long brown hair hung down past the open collar of his white shirt. And he was so *young* — just out of seminary, somebody said after the service. It was a warm fall Sunday, and rays of colored light shot through the stained-glass windows at the side of the church to glance off Bobby Rock Malone's pale face. "He *walks* with me, and He *talks* with me," we sang. My heart started beating double time. Bobby Rock Malone stretched out his long thin arms and spread his long white fingers. "Beloved," he said, curling his fingers, "let us pray." But I never closed my eyes that day, staring instead at the play of light on Bobby Rock Malone's fair face. It was almost like a kaleidoscope. Then the round rosy window behind him, behind the altar, began to *pulse* with light, to glow with light, now brighter now not, like a neon sign. I got the message. I was no dummy. In a way, I had been waiting all my life for this to happen.

The most notable thing about me as a child — before I got religious, I mean — was my obsessive reading. I had always been an inveterate reader of the sort who hides underneath the covers with a flashlight and reads *all night long*. But I did not read casually, or for mere entertainment, or for information. What I wanted was to feel all wild and trembly inside, an effect first produced by *The Secret Garden,* which I'd read maybe twenty times. And the Reverend Bobby Rock Malone looked exactly the way I had always pictured Colin! In fact, listening to him preach, I felt exactly the way I felt when I read *The Secret Garden,* just exactly.

Other books that had affected me strongly were *Little Women,* especially the part where Beth dies, and *Gone with the Wind,* especially the part where Melanie dies. I had long hoped for a wasting disease, such as leukemia, to test my mettle. I also loved *Marjorie Morningstar, A Tree Grows in Brooklyn, Heidi,* and books like *Dear and Glorious Physician, The Shoes of the Fisherman, Christy,* and anything at all about horses and saints. I had read all the Black Stallion books, of course, as well as all the Marguerite Henry books. But my all-time favorite was *God's Girl,* especially the frontispiece illustration picturing Joan as she knelt and "prayed without ceasing for guidance from God," whose face was depicted overhead, in a thunderstorm. Not only did I love Joan of Arc, I wanted to *be* her.

The only man I had ever loved more than Colin of *The Secret Garden,* to date, was Johnny Tremain, from Esther Forbes's book of that title. I used to wish that it was *me* — not Johnny Tremain — who'd had the hot silver spilled on my hand. I would have suffered anything (everything) for Johnny Tremain.

But on that fateful Sunday morning, Bobby Rock Malone eclipsed both Colin and Johnny Tremain in my affections. It was a wipeout. I felt as fluttery and wild as could be. In fact I felt too crazy to pay attention to the sermon which Bobby Rock Malone was, by then, almost finished with. I tried to concentrate, but my mind was whirling. The colors from the windows seemed to deepen and swirl. And then, suddenly, I heard him loud and clear, reading from Revelation: "And I saw a great white throne, and Him that sat on it, from whose face the earth and heaven fled away; and there was found no place for them. And I saw the dead, small and great, stand before God, and the books were opened . . . and whosoever was not found written in the book of life was cast into the lake of fire."

I can't remember much about what happened after that. I got to shake hands with him as we left the church, and I was surprised to find that his hand was cool, not burning hot — and, though bony, somehow as soft as a girl's. I looked hard at Bobby Rock Malone as he stood in front of our pretty little church, shaking hands. He was on his way to someplace else, over in Mississippi. We would never see him again. *I* would never see him again. And yet somehow I felt exhilarated and *satisfied,* in a way. I can't explain it. Back at my grandparents' house, I couldn't even eat any lemon meringue pie. I felt shaky and hot, like I might be getting a virus. I went home early.

My father was upstairs in his study, door closed. Nobody else was home. I wandered the house. Then I sat in the Florida room for a while, staring out at the day. After a while, I picked up my mother's sewing basket from the coffee table, got a needle and threaded it with blue thread, and sewed all the fingers of my left hand together, through the cuticle. Then I held my hand out and admired it, wishing desperately for my best friend Alice Field, of Little Rock. I had no best friend now, nobody to show my amazing hand to. Weird little Edwin Lee lived right across the street, but it was inconceivable that I would show *him,* the nerd, such a hand as this. So I showed it to nobody. I left it sewed up until Mama's white Cadillac pulled in the driveway, and then I cut the thread between my fingers and pulled it all out.

It was about this time too that I began to pray a lot (*without ceasing* was my intention) and set little fires all around the neighborhood. These fires were nothing much. I'd usually take some shredded newspapers or some Kleenex, find a few sticks, and they'd burn themselves out in a matter of minutes. I made a fire in my treehouse, in our garage, in the sink, in the basement, on Miss Butter's back patio, on Mr. and Mrs. Percy Castle's front porch, and in little Charlotte Lee's playhouse. Here I went too far, singeing off the hair of her Barbie doll. She never could figure out how it happened.

I entertained visions of being a girl evangelist, of appearing with Billy Graham on television, of traveling throughout Mississippi with Bobby Rock Malone. I'd be followed everywhere I went by a little band of my faithful. I made a small fire in the bed of Ashley's new boyfriend's pickup truck while he and my sister were in the den petting and watching *Your Hit Parade*. They didn't have any idea that I was outside in the night, watching them through the window, making a fire in the truck. They all thought I was in bed!

Although I was praying a lot, my prayers were usually specific, as opposed to *without ceasing*. For instance I'd tell one friend I'd go shopping with her, and then something I really wanted to do would come up, and I'd call back and say I couldn't come after all, that my grandmother had died, and then I would go to my room and fling myself to the floor and pray without ceasing that my lie would not be found out, and that my grandmother would not really die. I made big deals with God — if He would make sure I got away with it this time, I would talk to Edwin Lee for five minutes on the bus, three days in a row, or I would clean out my closet. He did His part; I did mine. I grew in power every day.

I remember so well that important Friday when I was supposed to spend the night with Margaret Applewhite. Now Margaret Applewhite was totally boring, in my opinion — my only rival in the annual spelling bee (she won in third, I won in fourth and fifth, she beat me out in sixth with *catarrh,* which still rankled). Margaret Applewhite wore a training bra too. Our mothers, who played bridge together, encouraged our friendship. I'd rather do just about *anything,* even watch Kate Smith on TV, than spend time with boring Margaret Applewhite. Still, earlier that week when she'd called and invited me, I couldn't for the life of me think of any good reason to say no, so I'd said yes. Then that Friday right before sixth period, Tammy Lester came up to my locker popping her gum (against the rules: we were not allowed to chew gum in school) and — wonder of wonders — asked me to come home with her after school that very day and spend the night.

Tammy Lester! Shunned by Sub-Debs, sent to Detention, noticed by older boys. I couldn't believe it. I admired Tammy Lester more than any other girl in my entire class, I'd watched her from afar the way I had watched the Baptists. Tammy Lester lived out in the country someplace (in a trailer, it was rumored), she was driven to school each morning by one or the other of her wild older brothers in a red pickup truck (these brothers slicked back their hair with grease, they wore their cigarette packs rolled up the sleeves of their T-shirts), and best of all, she was missing a tooth right in front, and nobody had taken her to the dentist yet to get it fixed. The missing tooth gave Tammy a devilish, jaunty look. Also, as I would learn later, she could whistle through this hole, and spit twenty feet.

Her invitation was offhand. "You wanna come home with me today?" she asked, in a manner that implied she didn't give a hoot whether I did or not. "Buddy's got to come into town tomorrow morning anyway, so he could bring you back."

"All right," I said, trying to sound casual.

"I'll meet you out in front when the bell rings." Tammy flashed me her quick dark grin. She popped her gum, and was gone.

I didn't hesitate for a minute. I stopped Margaret Applewhite on her way to health class. "Listen," I said in a rush, "I'm so sorry I can't come spend the night with you, but my mother is having an emergency hysterectomy today, so I have to go straight home and help out." I had just learned about hysterectomies from a medical book in the library.

Margaret's boring brown eyes widened. "Is she going to be all right?"

I sucked in my breath dramatically and looked brave. "We hope so," I said. "They think they can get it all."

Margaret walked into health. I sank back against the mustard yellow tile walls as, suddenly, it hit me: Margaret's mother knew my mother! What if Margaret's mother called my mother, and Mama found out? She'd be furious, not only because of the lie but because of the nature of the lie — Mama would *die* before she'd ever mention something like a hysterectomy. Mama referred to everything below the belt as "down there," an area she dealt with darkly, indirectly, and only when necessary. "Trixie Vopel is in the hospital for tests," she might say. "She's been having trouble *down there*." *Down there* was a foreign country, like Africa or Nicaragua.

What to do? I wrote myself an excuse from gym, signed my mother's name, turned it in, and then went to the infirmary, where I lay down on a hard white cot and prayed without ceasing for upward of an hour. I promised a lot: If Mama did not find out, I would sit with Lurice May at lunch on Monday (a dirty fat girl who kept her head wrapped up in a scarf and was rumored to have lice), I would be nice to Edwin Lee three times for fifteen minutes each, I would clean out under my bed, I would give back the perfume and the ankle bracelet I had stolen from Ashley, and I would put two dollars of my saved-up babysitting money in the collection plate at church on Sunday. It was the best I could do. Then I called my mother from the infirmary phone, and to my surprise, she said, "Oh, of course," in a distracted way when I asked if I could spend the night with Tammy Lester. She did not even ask what Tammy's father did.

Then "*Karen,*" she said in a pointed way that meant this was what she was *really* interested in, "do you have any idea where your sister is right now?"

"What?" I couldn't even remember *who* my sister was, right now.

"*Ashley,*" Mama said. "The school called and asked if she was sick. Apparently she just never showed up at school today."

"I'll bet they had some secret senior thing," I said.

"Oh." Mama sounded relieved. "Well, maybe so. Now who is it you're spending the night with?" she asked again, and I told her. "And what did you say her father does?"

"Lawyer," I said.

SPENDING THE NIGHT WITH Tammy Lester was the high point of my whole life up to that time. She did *not* live in a trailer, as rumored, but in an old unpainted farmhouse with two boarded-up windows, settled unevenly onto cinder-block footings. A mangy dog lay up under the house. Chickens roamed the property. The porch sagged. Wispy ancient curtains blew out eerily at the upstairs windows. The whole yard was strewn with parts of things — cars, stoves, bedsprings, unimaginable machine parts rusting among the weeds. I loved it. Tammy led me everywhere and showed me everything: her secret place, a tent of willows, down by the creek; the grave of her favorite dog, Buster, and the collar he had worn; an old chicken house that her brothers had helped her make into a playhouse; a haunted shack down the road; the old Packard out back that you could get in and pretend you were taking a trip. "Now we're in Nevada," Tammy said, shifting gears. "Now we're in the Grand Canyon. Now we're in the middle of the desert. It's hot as hell out here, ain't it?"

I agreed.

At suppertime, Tammy and I sat on folding chairs pulled up to the slick oilcloth-covered table beneath a bare hanging light-bulb. Her brothers had disappeared. Tammy seemed to be cooking our supper; she was heating up Dinty Moore stew straight out of the can.

"Where's your daddy?" I asked.

"Oh, he's out west on a pipeline," she said, vastly unconcerned.

"Where's your mama?" I said. I had seen her come in from work earlier that afternoon, a pudgy, pale redheaded woman who drove a light blue car that looked like it would soon join the others in the backyard.

"I reckon she's reading her Bible," Tammy said, as if this were a perfectly ordinary thing to be doing on a Friday night at gin-and-tonic time. "She'll eat after while."

Tammy put half of the Dinty Moore stew into a chipped red bowl and gave it to me. It was delicious, lots better than Lady Food. She ate hers right out of the saucepan. "Want to split a beer?" she said, and I said sure, and she got us one — a Pabst Blue

Ribbon — out of the icebox. Of course I had never tasted beer before. But I thought it was great.

That night, I told Tammy about my father's nervous breakdown, and she told me that her oldest brother had gone to jail for stealing an outboard motor. She also told me about the lady down the road who had chopped off her husband's hands with an ax while he was "laying up drunk." I told her that I was pretty sure God had singled me out for a purpose He had not yet revealed, and Tammy nodded and said her mother had been singled out too. I sat right up in bed. "What do you mean?" I asked.

"Well, she's real religious," Tammy said, "which is why she don't get along with Daddy too good." I nodded. I had already figured out that Daddy must be the dark handsome one that all the children took after. "And she was a preacher's daughter too, see, so she's been doing it all her life."

"Doing what?" I asked into the dark.

"Oh, talking in tongues of fire," Tammy said matter-of-factly, and a total thrill crept over me, the way I had always wanted to feel. I had hit pay dirt at last.

"I used to get embarrassed, but now I don't pay her much mind," Tammy said.

"Listen," I said sincerely. "I would give *anything* to have a mother like that."

Tammy whistled derisively through the hole in her teeth.

But eventually, because I was already so good at collective bargaining, we struck a deal: I would get to go to church with Tammy and her mother, the very next Sunday if possible, and in return, I would take Tammy to the country club. (I could take her when Mama wasn't there; I was allowed to sign for things.) Tammy and I stayed up talking nearly all night long. She was even more fascinating than I'd thought. She had breasts, she knew how to drive a car, and she was part Cherokee. Toward morning, we cut our fingers with a kitchen knife and swore to be best friends forever.

The next day, her brother Buddy drove me into town at about one o'clock. He had to see a man about a car. He smoked cigarettes all the way, and scowled at everything. He didn't say a word to me. I thought he was wonderful.

I arrived home just in time to intercept the delivery boy from the florist's. "I'll take those in," I said, and pinched the card which said, "For Dee Rose. Get well soon. Best wishes from Lydia and Lou Applewhite." I left the flowers on the doorstep, where they would create a little mystery later on, when Mama found them, and went upstairs to my room and prayed without ceasing, a prayer of thanksgiving for the special favors I felt He had granted me lately. Then before long I fell asleep, even as a huge argument raged all over the house, upstairs and down, between Mama and my sister Ashley who had *just come in,* having stayed out all day and all night long.

"If a girl loses her reputation, she has lost *everything,*" Mama said. "She has lost her Most Precious Possession."

"So what? So what?" Ashley screamed. "All you care about is appearances. Who cares what I do, in this screwed-up family? Who really cares?"

It went on and on, while I melted down and down into my pink piqué comforter, hearing them but not really hearing them, dreaming instead of the lumpy sour bed out at Tammy's farm, of the moonlight on the wispy graying curtains at her window, of a life so hard and flinty that it might erupt at any moment into tongues of fire.

NOT ONLY WAS THE fight over with by Sunday morning, but it was so far over with as not to have happened at all. I came in the kitchen late, to find Mama and Ashley still in their bathrobes, eating sticky buns and reading the funnies. It looked like nobody would be available to drive me to church. Clearly, both Ashley and Mama had Risen Above It All — Mama, to the extent that she was virtually levitating as the day wore on, hovering a few feet off the floor in her Sunday seersucker suit as she exhorted us all to hurry, hurry, hurry. Our reservations were for one o'clock. The whole family was going out for brunch at the country club.

Daddy was going too.

I still wonder what she said to him to get him up and dressed and out of there. I know it was the kind of thing that meant a lot to her — a public act, an event that meant *See, here is our whole happy family out together at the country club; see, we are a perfectly normal family; see, there is nothing wrong with us at all.* And I know that Daddy loved her.

Our table overlooked the first tee of the golf course. Our waiter, Louis, had known Daddy ever since he was a child. Daddy ordered a martini. Mama ordered a gin and tonic. Ashley ordered a lemon Coke. I ordered a lemonade. Mama was so vivacious that she almost gave off light. Her eyes sparkled, her hair shone, her red lipstick glistened. She and Ashley were discussing which schools her fellow seniors hoped to attend, and why. Ashley was very animated too. Watching them, I suddenly realized how much Ashley was like Mama. Ashley laughed and gestured with her pretty hands. I watched her carefully. I knew Mama thought Ashley had lost her Most Precious Possession (things were different *down there*), yet she didn't look any different to me. She wore a hot pink sheath dress and pearls. She looked terrific.

I turned my attention to Daddy, curiously, because I felt all of a sudden that I had not really seen him for years and years. He might as well have been off on a pipeline, as far as I was concerned. Our drinks arrived, and Daddy sipped at his martini. He perked up. He looked weird, though. His eyes were sunken in his head, like the limestone caves above the Tombigbee River. His skin was as white and dry as a piece of Mama's stationery. My father bought all his clothes in New York so they were always quite elegant, but now they hung on him like a coat rack. How much weight had he lost? Twenty pounds? Thirty? We ordered lunch. Daddy ordered another martini.

Now he was getting entirely too perky, he moved his hands too much as he explained to Ashley the theory behind some battle in some war. He stopped talking only long enough to stand up and shake hands with the friends who came by our table to speak to him, friends who had not seen him for months and months. He didn't touch his food. Underneath my navy blue dress with the sailor collar, I was sweating, in spite of my mother's pronouncement: *Horses sweat, men perspire, and women glow.*

I could feel it trickling down my sides. I wondered if, as I grew up, this would become an uncontrollable problem, whether I would have to wear dress shields. We all ordered Baked Alaska, the chef's specialty, for dessert. My mother smiled and smiled. I was invisible. When the Baked Alaska arrived, borne proudly to our table by Louis, nobody could put out the flames. Louis blew and blew. Other waiters ran over, beating at it with linen napkins. My mother laughed merrily. "For goodness' sakes!" she said. My daddy looked stricken. Finally they got it out and we all ate some, except for Daddy.

Gazing past my family to the golfers out on the grass beyond us, I had a sudden inspiration. I knew what to do. I emerged from invisibility long enough to say, "Hey, Daddy, let's go out and putt," and he put his napkin promptly on the table and stood right up. "Sure thing, honey," he said, sounding for all the world like my own daddy. He smiled at me. I took his hand, remembering then who I had been before the nervous breakdown: Daddy's little girl. We went down the stairs, past the snack bar, and out to the putting green at the side of the building.

My dad was a good golfer. I was not bad myself. We shared a putter from the Pro Shop. We started off and soon it was clear that we were having a great time, that this was a good idea. The country club loomed massively behind us. The emerald grass, clipped and even, stretched out on three sides in front of us, as far as we could see, ending finally in a stand of trees here, a rolling hill there. This expanse of grass, dotted with pastel golfers, was both comforting and exhilarating. It was a nine-hole putting green. On the seventh hole, we were tied, if you figured in the handicap that my father had given himself. I went first, overshooting on my second stroke, sinking it with a really long shot on my third. I looked back at Daddy to make sure he had seen my putt, but clearly he had not. He was staring out over the grass toward the horizon, beyond the hill.

"Your turn!" I called out briskly, tossing him the putter. What happened next was awful.

In one terrible second, my father turned to me, face slack, mouth agape, then fell to his knees on the putting green, cowering, hands over his face. The putter landed on the grass beside him. He was crying. I didn't know what to do. I just stood there, and then suddenly the putting green was full of people — the pro, Bob White, in his jacket with his name on it, helping Daddy to his feet; our dentist, Dr. Reap, holding him by the other elbow as they walked him to our white Cadillac, which Mama had driven around to pick us up in. Ashley cried all the way home. So did Daddy.

It was not until that day that I realized that the nervous breakdown was real, that Daddy was really sick.

I ran upstairs and prayed without ceasing for a solid hour, by the clock, that Daddy would get well and that we would all be *all right,* for I had come to realize somehow, during the course of that afternoon, that we might *not* be. We might never be all right again.

AT LEAST I HAD a New Best Friend. I banished all memory of Alice Field, without remorse. Tammy Lester and I became, for the rest of that spring, inseparable. The first time I brought her to my house, I did it without asking. I didn't want to give Mama a chance to say no. And although we had not discussed it, Tammy showed up dressed more like a town girl than I had ever seen her — a plaid skirt, a white blouse, loafers, her dark hair pulled back and up into a cheerful ponytail. She could have been a cheerleader. She could have been a member of the Sub-Deb Club. No one could have ever guessed what she had in her pocket — a pack of Kents and a stolen kidney stone once removed from her neighbor, Mrs. Gillespie, who had kept it in a jar on her mantel. But even though Tammy looked so nice, Mama was giving her the third degree. "How many brothers and sisters did you say you had?" and "Where was your Mama *from?*"

This interrogation took place upstairs in Mama's dressing room. Suddenly, to everyone's surprise, Daddy lurched in to fill the doorway and say, "Leave those little girls alone, Dee Rose, you've got your hands full already," and oddly enough, Mama *did* leave us alone then. She didn't say another word about it at the time, turning back to her nails, or even later, as spring progressed and Ashley's increasing absences and moodiness became more of a problem. Before long, Daddy refused to join us even for dinner. Mama did have her hands full. If I could occupy myself, so much the better.

I will never forget the first time I was allowed to go to church with Tammy and her mother. I spent the night out at the farm, and in the morning I was awake long before it was time to leave. I dressed carefully, in the yellow dress and jacket Mama had ordered for me only a couple of months before from Rich's in Atlanta. It was already getting too small. Tammy and her mother both looked at my outfit with some astonishment. They didn't have any particular church clothes, it turned out. At least, they didn't have any church clothes as fancy as these. Tammy wore a black dress that was much too old for her, clearly a hand-me-down from someplace, and her mother wore the same formless slacks and untucked shirt she always wore. I could never tell any of her clothes apart. For breakfast that morning we had Hi-Ho cakes, which we ate directly from their cellophane wrappers, and Dr Pepper. Then we went out and got into their old blue car, which threatened not to start. *Oh no!* I found myself suddenly, terribly upset. I realized then how very much I was dying to hear Tammy's mother speak in tongues of fire, a notion that intrigued me more and more the better I got to know her, because usually she *didn't speak at all.* Never! Her pale gray eyes were fixed on distance, the way my daddy's had been that day on the golf course. The engine coughed and spluttered, died. Then finally Tammy's mother suggested that Tammy and I should push her down the muddy rutted driveway and she'd pop the clutch. I had never heard of such a thing. In my family, a man in a uniform, from a garage, came to start cars that wouldn't start. Still, we pushed. It started. I got mud all over the bottom of my yellow dress.

Which didn't matter at all, I saw as soon as we got to the church. There were old men in overalls, younger men in coveralls with their names stitched on their pockets, girls in jeans, boys in jeans. The men stood around by their trucks in the parking lot, smoking cigarettes. The women went on in, carrying food. Tammy's mother had a big bag of Fritos. The church itself was a square cinder-block building painted white. It looked like a convenience store. Its windows were made of the kind of frosted glass you would find in restrooms. The only way you could tell it was a church was from the hand-lettered sign on the door, MARANATHA APOS-TOLIC CHURCH, ALL COME IN. I asked Tammy what "Maranatha" meant and she said she didn't know. Tammy would rather be at my house on Sundays, so she could look through Mama's jewelry, eat lemon meringue pie at my grandmother's, and stare at Baptists. She had made this plain. I'd rather be at her house, in general; she'd rather be at mine. We walked into her church.

"*This way.*" Tammy was pulling my arm. Men sat on the right-hand side of the church. Women sat on the left. There was no music, no Miss Eugenia Little at the organ. Men and women sat still, staring straight ahead, the children sprinkled among them like tiny grave adults. The pews were handmade, hard, like benches, with high, straight backs. There was no altar, only the huge wooden cross at the front of the church, dwarfing everything, and a curtain, like a shower curtain, pulled closed behind it. A huge Bible stood open on a lectern with a big jug (of what? water?) beside it. More people came in. My heart was beating a mile a minute. The light that came in through the frosted-glass windows produced a soft, diffuse glow throughout the church. Tammy popped her gum. Tammy's mother's eyes were already closed. Her pale eyelashes fluttered. Her mouth was moving and she swayed slightly, back and forth from the waist up. Nothing else was happening.

Then four women, all of them big and tough looking, went forward and simply started singing "Rock of Ages," without any warning or any introduction at all. I almost jumped right out of my seat. Some of the congregation joined in, some did not. It seemed to be optional. Tammy's mother did not sing. She did not open her eyes either. The women's voices were high and mournful, seeming to linger in the air long after they were done. "Praise God!" "Yes, Jesus!" At the conclusion of the song, people throughout the church started shouting. I craned my neck around to see who was doing this, but the back of the pew was too high, blocking a lot of my view. They sang again. I had never heard any music like this music, music without any words at all, or maybe it was music without any music. It seemed to pierce my brain. I was sweating under my arms again.

The preacher, Mr. Looney, entered unobtrusively from the side during the singing. Initially, Mr. Looney was a disappointment. He was small and nondescript. He looked like George Gobel. Tammy had told me he was s security guard at the paper mill during the week. He spoke in a monotone with a hick accent. As he led us all in prayer — a prayer that seemed to go on forever, including everybody in the church by name — my mind wandered back to a time when I was little and our whole family had gone to the Gulf Shores for a vacation, and Ashley and Paul were there too, and all of us worked and worked, covering Daddy up with sand,

and Mama wore a sailor hat. By the end of the prayer, I was crying, and Mr. Looney had changed his delivery, his voice getting stronger and more rhythmical as he went into his message for the day. This message was pretty simple, one I had heard before. God's wrath is awful. Hell is real and lasts forever. It is not enough to have good intentions. The road to Hell is paved with those. It is not enough to do good works, such as taking care of the sick and giving to the poor. God will see right through you. The only way you can get to Heaven is by turning over your whole will and your whole mind to Jesus Christ, being baptized in the name of the Father, Son, and Holy Ghost, and born again in Glory.

"Does sprinkling count?" I whispered to Tammy. I had been sprinkled in the Methodist church.

"No," she whispered back.

Mr. Looney went on and on, falling into chant now, catching up his sentences with an "Ah!" at the end of each line. People were yelling out. And then came, finally, the invitational, "Just as I am, without one plea, but that Thy blood was shed for me, O Lamb of God, I come, I come!"

The stolid-looking young woman sitting two seats over from us surprised me by starting to mumble suddenly, then she screamed out, then she rushed forward, right into Mr. Looney's arms.

I twisted my head around to see what would happen next. Mr. Looney blessed her and said that she would "pass through to Jesus" by and by.

"What does he mean, 'pass through to Jesus'?" I was still whispering, but I might as well have been speaking aloud; there was so much commotion now that nobody else could have heard me.

Tammy jerked her head toward the front of the church. "Through them curtains, I reckon," she said.

"What's back there?" I asked, and Tammy said it was a swimming pool that people got baptized in.

And sure enough, it was not long before Mr. Looney pulled back the curtains to reveal a kind of big sliding glass door cut in the wall, with a large wading pool right beyond it, the kind I had seen in the Sears catalog. Mr. Looney pulled the heavy young woman through the curtains and hauled her over the edge of the pool. The water reached up to about midthigh on both of them. I couldn't believe they would just walk into the water like that, wearing all their clothes, wearing their *shoes*! Mr. Looney pulled back the woman's long hair and grasped it firmly. Her face was as blank and solid as a potato. "In the name of the Father and the Son and the Holy Ghost!" Mr. Looney yelled, and dunked her all the way under, backward. Although she held her nose, she came up sputtering.

Now people were jumping up all over the church, singing out and yelling, including Tammy's mother, who opened her mouth and screamed out in a language like none I had ever heard, yet a language which I felt I knew immediately, somehow, better than I knew English. It was *my language,* I was sure of it, and I think I might have passed out right then from the shock of sheer recognition except that Tammy grabbed my arm and yanked like crazy.

"Get ready!" she said.

"What?"

"She's fixing to fall," Tammy said just as her mother pitched backward in a dead faint. We caught her and laid her out on a pew. She came to later, when church was over, and then we all had dinner on the ground out back of the church. Later I sneaked back into the fellowship hall on the pretext of going to the bathroom, so I could examine the pool in greater detail. It was in a little anteroom off the fellowship hall, right up against the double doors that led from the sanctuary, now closed. It was a plain old wading pool, just as I'd thought, covered now by a blue tarpaulin. I pulled back the tarp. The water was pretty cold. A red plastic barrette floated jauntily in the middle of the pool. I looked at it for a long time. I knew I would have to get in that water sooner or later. I would have to get saved.

I was so moved by the whole experience that I might have actually broken through my invisible shield to tell Daddy about it, or even Ashley, but Mama met me at the door that afternoon with an ashen face and, for once, no makeup.

"Where in the world have you all *been*?" she shrilled. "I've been trying to call you all afternoon."

"We ate lunch out at the church," I said. "They do that." Out of the corner of my eye, I watched Tammy and her mother pull away in the battered blue car and wished I were with them, anywhere but here. I didn't want to know whatever Mama had to say next. In that split second, several possibilities raced through my mind:

1. Grandmother really *has* died.
2. Ashley is pregnant.
3. Ashley has eloped.
4. Daddy has killed himself.

But I was completely surprised by what came next.

"Your brother has been in the most terrible wreck," Mama said, "up in Virginia. He's in a coma, and they don't know if he'll make it or not."

PAUL HAD BEEN DRUNK, of course. Drunk, or he might not have lived at all, somebody said later, but I don't know whether that was true or not. I think it is something people say after wrecks, whenever there's been drinking. He had been driving back to W&L from Randolph-Macon, where he was dating a girl. This girl wrote Mama a long, emotional letter on pink stationery with a burgundy monogram. Paul was taken by ambulance from the small hospital in Lexington, Virginia, to the University of Virginia hospital in Charlottesville, one of the best hospitals in the world. This is what everybody told me. Mama went up there immediately. Her younger sister, my aunt Liddie, came to stay with us while she was gone.

Aunt Liddie had always been referred to in our family as "flighty." Aunt Liddie "went off on tangents," it was said. I wasn't sure what this meant. Still, I was glad to see her when she arrived, with five matching suitcases full of beautiful clothes and her Pekingese named Chow Mein. Back in Birmingham she was a Kelly girl, so it was easy for her to leave her job and come to us. The very first night she arrived, Liddie got me to come out on the back steps with her. She sat very close to me in the warm spring night and squeezed both my hands. "I look on this as a wonderful opportunity for you and me to get to know each other better," Aunt Liddie said. "I want you to tell me *everything.*"

But I would tell her nothing, as things turned out. This was to be our closest moment. The very next week, Liddie started dating Mr. Hudson Bell, a young lawyer she met by chance in the bank. Immediately, Liddie and Hudson Bell were *in love,* and Ashley and I were free — within the bounds of reason — to come and go as we pleased. Aunt Liddie asked no questions. Missie cooked the meals.

This was just as well with me, for I had serious business to tend to.

I knew it was up to me to bring Paul out of that coma. I would pray without ceasing, and Tammy would help me. The first week, we prayed without ceasing only after school and on the weekend. Paul was no better, Mama reported from Charlottesville. The second week, I gave up sitting on soft chairs and eating chocolate. I paid so much attention to the unfortunate Lurice May that she began avoiding me. Paul had moved his foot, Mama said. I doubled my efforts, giving up also Cokes and sleeping in bed. (I had to sleep flat on the floor.) Also, I prayed without ceasing all during math class. I wouldn't even answer the teacher, Mrs. Lemon, when she called on me. She sent me to Guidance because of it. During this week, I began to suspect that perhaps Tammy was not praying as much as she was supposed to, not keeping up her end of the deal. Still, I was too busy to care. I gave up hot water; I had to take cold showers now.

The third weekend of Mama's absence and Paul's coma, I spent Saturday night with Tammy, and that Sunday morning, at Tammy's church, I got saved.

When Mr. Looney issued his plea, I felt that he was talking right to me. "With every head bowed and every eye closed," he said, "I want you to look into your hearts and minds this morning. Have you got problems, brother? Have you got problems, sister? Well, give them up! Give them over to the Lord Jesus Christ. If His shoulders are big enough to *bear the cross,* they are big enough to take on your little problems, beloved. Turn them over to Him. He will help you now in this life, here in this vale of tears. And He will give you Heaven Everlasting as a door prize. Think about it, beloved. Do you want to burn in Hell forever, at the Devil's barbecue? Or do you want to lie in banks of flowers, listening to that heavenly choir?"

I felt a burning, stabbing sensation in my chest and stomach — something like heartburn, something like the hand of God. The idea of turning it all over to Him was certainly appealing at this point. Another week of prayer, and I'd flunk math for sure. The choir sang, "Softly and tenderly, Jesus is calling, calling for you and for me." Beside me, Tammy's mama was starting to mumble and moan.

Mr. Looney said, "Perhaps there is one among you who feels that his sin is too great to bear, but no sin is too black for the heavenly laundry of Jesus Christ, He will turn you as white as snow, as white as the driven snow, hallelujah!" Mr. Looney reached back and pulled the curtains open, so we could all see the pool. Tammy's mama leaped up and called out in her strangely familiar language. Mr. Looney went on, "Perhaps there is a child among you who hears our message this morning, who is ready now for Salvation. Why, a little child can go to Hell, the same as you and me! A little child can burn to a crisp. But it is also true that a little child can come to God — right now, right this minute, this very morning. God don't check your ID, children. God will check your souls."

"Come home, come home," they sang.

Before I even knew it, I was up there, and we had passed through those curtains, and I was standing in the water with my full blue skirt floating out around me like a lily pad. Then he was saying the words, shouting them out, and whispering to me, "Hold your nose," which I did, and he pushed me under backward, holding me tightly with his other hand so that I felt supported, secure, even at the very moment of immersion. It was like being dipped by the big boys at ballroom dancing, only not as scary. I came up wet and saved, and stood at the side of the pool while Mr. Looney baptized Eric Blankenship, a big gawky nineteen-year-old who came running and sobbing up the aisle just as Mr. Looney got finished with me. Eric Blankenship was confessing all his sins, nonstop, throughout his baptism. His sins were a whole lot more interesting than mine, involving things he'd done with his girl-friend, and I strained to hear them as I stood there, but I could not, because of all the noise in the church.

And then it was over and everyone crowded forward to hug us, including Tammy. But even in that moment of hugging Tammy, who of course had been baptized for years and years, I saw something new in her eyes. Somehow, now, there was a difference between us, where before there had been none. But I was wet and freezing, busy accepting the congratulations of the faithful, so I didn't have time to think any more about it then. Tammy gave me her sweater and they drove me home, where Aunt Liddie looked at me in a very fishy way when I walked in the door.

"I just got baptized," I said, and she said, "Oh," and then she went out to lunch with Hudson Bell, who came up the front walk not a minute behind me, sparing me further explanations.

Aunt Liddie came back from that lunch engaged, with a huge square-cut diamond. Nobody mentioned my baptism.

But the very next night, right after supper, Mama called to say that Paul was fine. All of a sudden, he had turned to the night nurse and asked for a cheeseburger. There seemed to be no brain damage at all except that he had some trouble remembering things, which was to be expected. He would have to stay in the hospital for several more weeks, but he would recover completely. He would be just fine.

I burst into tears of joy. I knew I had done it all. And for the first time, I realized what an effort it had been. The first thing

I did was go into the kitchen and fix myself a milk shake, with Hershey's syrup. And my bed felt so good that night, after the weeks on the floor. I intended to pray without ceasing that very night, a prayer of thanksgiving for Paul's delivery, but I fell asleep instantly.

When Mama came back, I hoped she would be so busy that my baptism would be overlooked completely, but this was not the case. Aunt Liddie told her, after all.

"Karen," was Mama's reaction, "I am *shocked*! We are not the kind of family that goes out into the county and immerses ourselves in water. I can't imagine what you were thinking of," Mama said.

I looked out the window at Mama's blooming roses. It was two weeks before the end of school, before Ashley's graduation.

"Well, *what*?" Mama asked. She was peering at me closely, more closely than she had looked at me in years.

"Why did you do it?" Mama asked. She lit a cigarette.

I didn't say a thing.

"Karen," Mama said. "I asked you a question." She blew a smoke ring.

I looked at the roses. "I wanted to be saved," I said.

Mama's lips went into that little red bow. "I see," she said.

So later, that next weekend when she refused to let me spend the night out at Tammy's, I did the only thing I could: I lied and said I was going to spend the night with Sara Ruth Johnson, and then prayed without ceasing that I would not be found out. Since it was senior prom weekend and Mama was to be in charge of the decorations and also a chaperone, I felt fairly certain I'd get away with it. But when the time came for the invitational that Sunday morning in the Maranatha church, I simply could not resist.

I pushed back Tammy's restraining hand, rushed forward, and rededicated my life.

"I don't think you're supposed to rededicate your life right after you just dedicated it," Tammy whispered to me later, but I didn't care. I was wet and holy. If I had committed some breach of heavenly etiquette, surely Mr. Looney would tell me. But he did not. We didn't stay for dinner on the ground that day either. As soon as Tammy's mother came to, they drove me straight home, and neither of them said much.

Mama's Cadillac was parked in the drive.

So I went around to the back of the house and tiptoed in through the laundry room door, carrying my shoes. But Mama was waiting for me. She stood by the ironing board, smoking a cigarette. She looked at me, narrowing her eyes.

"Don't drip on the kitchen floor, Missie just mopped it yesterday," she said.

I climbed up the back stairs to my room.

The next weekend, I had to go to Ashley's graduation and to the baccalaureate sermon on Sunday morning in the Confederate Chapel at Lorton Hall. I sat between my grandparents. My aunt Liddie was there too, with her fiancé. My daddy did not come. I wore a dressy white dress with a little bolero jacket and patent-leather shoes with Cuban heels — my first high heels. I felt precarious and old, grown up, and somehow sinful, and I longed for the high hard pews of the Maranatha church and the piercing, keening voices of the women singers.

But I never attended the Maranatha church again. As soon as my school was over, I was sent away to Camp Alleghany in West Virginia for two months — the maximum stay. I didn't want to go, even though this meant that I would finally have a chance to learn horseback riding, but I had no choice in the matter. Mama made this clear. It was to separate me from Tammy, whom Mama had labeled a Terrible Influence.

"And by the way," Mama said brightly, "Margaret Applewhite will be going to Camp Alleghany too!" Oh, I could see right through Mama. But I couldn't do anything about it. Camp started June 6, so I didn't have time to pray for a change in my fate. She sprang it on me. Instead, I cried without ceasing all that long day before they put me and my trunk, along with Margaret Applewhite and her trunk, on the train. I tried and tried to call Tammy and tell her good-bye, but a recorded message said that her line had been disconnected. (This had happened several times before, whenever her mama couldn't pay the bill.) My father would be going away too, to Shepherd Pratt Hospital in Baltimore, Maryland, and Ashley was going to Europe.

Sitting glumly by Mama at the train station, I tried to pray but could not. Instead, I remembered a game we used to play when I was real little, Statues. In Statues, one person grabs you by the hand and swings you around and around and then lets you go, and whatever position you land in, you have to freeze like that until everybody else is thrown. The person who lands in the best position wins. But what I remembered was that scary moment of being flung wildly out into the world screaming, to land however I hit, and I felt like this was happening to us all.

To MY SURPRISE, I loved camp. Camp Alleghany was an old camp, with rough-hewn wooden buildings that seemed to grow right out of the deep woods surrounding them. Girls had been carving their initials in the railings outside the dining hall for years and years. It was a tradition. I loved to run my fingers over these initials, imagining these girls — M. H., 1948; J. B., 1953; M. N., 1935. Some of the initials were very old. These girls were grown up by now. Some of them were probably dead. This gave me an enormous thrill, as did all the other traditions at Camp Alleghany. I loved the weekend campfire, as big as a tepee, ceremoniously lit by the Camp Spirit, whoever she happened to be that week. The Camp Spirit got to light the campfire with an enormous match, invoking the spirits with an ancient verse that only she was permitted to repeat. At the end of each weekly campfire, a new Camp Spirit was named, with lots of screaming, crying, and hugging. I was dying to be Camp Spirit. In fact, after the very first campfire, I set this as my goal, cooperating like crazy with all the counselors so I would be picked. But it wasn't hard for me to cooperate.

I loved wearing a uniform, being a part of the group — I still have the photograph from that first session of camp, all of us wearing our navy shorts, white socks, and white camp shirts, our hair squeaky clean, grinning into the sun. I loved all my activities — arts and crafts, where we made huge ashtrays for our parents out of little colored tiles; swimming, where I already excelled and soon became the acknowledged champion of the breaststroke in all competitions; and drama, where we were readying a presentation of *Spoon River*. My canoeing group took a long sunrise trip upstream to an island where we cooked our breakfast out over a fire: grits, sausage, eggs. Everything had a smoky, exotic taste, and the smoke from our breakfast campfire rose to mingle with the patchy mist still clinging to the trees, still rising from the river. I remember lying on my back and gazing up at how the sunshine looked, like light through a stained-glass window, emerald green and iridescent in the leafy tops of the tallest trees. The river was as smooth and shiny as a mirror. In fact it reminded me of a mirror, of Ashley's mirror-topped dressing table back at home.

And the long trail rides — when we finally got to take them — were even better than the canoe trips. But first we had to go around and around the riding ring, learning to post, learning to canter. The truth was, I didn't like the horses nearly as much as I'd expected to. For one thing, they were a lot *bigger* than I had been led to believe by the illustrations in my horse books. They were as big as cars. For another thing they were not lovable either. They were smelly, and some of them were downright mean. One big old black horse named Martini was pointed out to us early on as a biter. Others kicked. On a trail ride, you didn't want to get behind one of these. Still the trail rides were great. We lurched along through the forest, following the leader. I felt like I was in a Western movie, striking out into the territory. On the longest trail ride, we took an overnight trip up to Pancake Mountain, where we ate s'mores (Hershey bars and melted marshmallows smashed into a sandwich between two graham crackers), told ghost stories, and went to sleep finally with the wheezing and stamping of the horses in our ears.

Actually, I liked the riding counselors better than I liked the horses. The regular counselors were sweet, pretty girls who went to school at places like Hollins and Sweet Briar, or else maternal, jolly older women who taught junior high school during the regular year; but the riding counselors were tough, tan, muscular young women who squinted into the sun and could post all day long if they had to. The riding counselors said "shit" a lot, and smoked cigarettes in the barn. They did not speak of college.

My only male counselor was a frail, nervous young man named Jeffrey Long, reputed to be the nephew of the owner. He taught nature study, which I loved. I loved identifying the various trees (hickory, five leaves; ironwood, the satiny metallic trunk; maple, the little wings; blue-berried juniper; droopy willow). We made sassafras toothbrushes, and brushed our teeth in the river.

On Sundays, we had church in the big rustic assembly hall. It was an Episcopal service, which seemed pretty boring to me in comparison with the Maranatha church. Yet I liked the prayer book, and I particularly liked one of the Episcopal hymns, which I had never heard before, "I Sing a Song of the Saints of God," with its martial, military tune. I imagined Joan of Arc striding briskly along in a satin uniform, to just that tune. I also liked the hymn "Jerusalem," especially the weird lines that went, "Bring me my staff of burnished gold, bring me my arrows of desire." I loved the "arrows of desire" part.

We all wore white shirts and white shorts to church. After church we had a special Sunday lunch, with fried chicken and ice cream. "I scream, you scream, we all scream for ice cream!" we'd shout, banging on the tables before they brought it out. (In order to have any, you had to turn in an Ice Cream Letter — to your parents — as you came in the door.)

On Sunday nights, we all climbed the hill behind the dining hall for vespers. We sat on our ponchos looking down on the camp as the sun set, and sang, "Day Is Done." We bowed our heads in silent prayer. Then, after about ten minutes of this, one of the junior counselors played "Taps" on the bugle. She played it every night at lights out too. I much admired the bugler's jaunty, boyish stance. I had already resolved to take up the bugle, first thing, when I got back home.

And speaking of home, I'd barely thought of it since arriving at Camp Alleghany. I was entirely too busy. I guess that was the idea. Still, every now and then in a quiet moment — during silent prayer at vespers, for instance; or rest hour after lunch, when we usually played Go Fish or some other card game, but sometimes, *sometimes* I just lay on my cot and thought about things; or at night, after "Taps," when I'd lie looking up at the rafters before I fell asleep — in those quiet moments, I did think of home, and of my salvation. I didn't have as much time as I needed, there at camp, to pray without ceasing. Besides, I was often too tired to do it. Sometimes I just forgot. To pray without ceasing requires either a solitary life or a life of invisibility such as I had led within my family for the past year.

What about my family, anyway? Did I miss them? Not a bit. I could scarcely recall what they looked like. Mama wrote that Paul was back home already and had a job at the snack bar at the country club. Ashley was in France. Daddy was still in Baltimore, where he would probably stay for six more months. Mama was very busy helping Aunt Liddie plan her wedding, which I would be in. I would wear an aqua dress and dyed-to-match heels. I read Mama's letter curiously, several times. I felt like I had to translate it, like it was written in a foreign language. I folded this letter up and placed it in the top tray of my trunk, where I would find it years later. Right then, I didn't have time to think about my family. I was too busy doing everything I was supposed to, so that I might be picked as Camp Spirit. (Everybody agreed that the current Camp Spirit, Jeannie Darling from Florida, was a stuck-up bitch who didn't deserve it at all.) At the last campfire of First Session, I had high hopes that I might replace her. We started out by singing all the camp songs, first the funny ones such as "I came on the train and arrived in the rain, my trunk came a week later on." Each "old" counselor had a song composed in her honor, and we sang them all. It took forever. As we finally sang the Camp Spirit song, my heart started beating like crazy.

But it was not to be. No, it was Jeanette Peterson, a skinny boring redhead from Margaret Applewhite's cabin. I started crying but nobody knew why, because by then everybody else was crying too, and we all continued to cry as we sang all the sad camp songs about loyalty and friendships and candle flames. This last campfire was also Friendship Night. We had made little birchbark boats that afternoon, and traded them with our best friends. At the end of the campfire, the counselors passed out short white candles, which we lit and carried down to the river in solemn procession. Then we placed the candles in our little boats and set them in the water, singing our hearts out as the flotilla of candles entered the current and moved slowly down the dark river and out of sight around the bend. I clung to my New Best Friend and cried. This was Shelley Williams from Leesburg, Virginia, with a freckled, heart-shaped face and a pixie haircut, who talked a mile a minute all the time. It was even possible that Shelley Williams had read more books than I had, unlike my Old Best Friend Tammy back at home in Alabama, who had not read any books at all, and did not intend to. Plus, Shelley Williams owned a pony and a pony cart. She had shown me a picture of herself at home in Leesburg, driving her pony cart. Her house, in the background, looked like Mount Vernon. I was heartbroken when she left, the morning after Friendship Night.

It rained that morning, a cold drizzle that continued without letup for the next two days. About three-quarters of the campers left after First Session, including everybody I liked. Margaret Applewhite stayed. My last vision of the departing campers was a rainy blur of waving hands as the big yellow buses pulled out, headed for the train station and the airport. All the girls were singing at the top of their lungs, and their voices seemed to linger in the air long after they were gone. Then came a day and a half of waiting around for the Second Session campers to arrive, a day and a half in which nobody talked to me much, and the counselors were busy doing things like counting the rifle shells. So I became invisible again, free to wander about in the rain, free to pray without ceasing.

Finally the new campers arrived, and I brightened somewhat at the chance to be an Old Girl, to show the others the ropes and teach them the words to the songs. My New Best Friend was Anne Roper, from Lexington, Kentucky. She wasn't as good as Shelley, but she was the best I could do, I felt, considering what I had to pick from. Anne Roper was okay.

But my new counselor was very weird. She read aloud to us each day at rest hour from a big book called *The Fountainhead,* by Ayn Rand. Without asking our parents, she pierced all our ears. Even this ear piercing did not bring my spirits up to the level of First Session, however. For one thing, it never stopped raining. It rained and rained and rained. First we couldn't go swimming — the river was too high, too cold, too fast. We couldn't go canoeing either. The tennis courts looked like lakes. The horses, along with the riding counselors, stayed in their barn. About all we could do was arts and crafts and Skits, which got old fast. Lots of girls got homesick. They cried during "Taps."

I cried then and at other odd times too, such as when I walked up to breakfast through the constant mist that came up now from the river, or at church. I was widely thought to be homesick. To cheer me up, my weird counselor gave me a special pair of her own earrings, little silver hoops with turquoise chips in them, made by Navahos.

Then I got bronchitis. I developed a deep, thousand-year-old Little Match Girl cough that started way down in my knees. Because of this cough, I was allowed to call my mother, and to my surprise, I found myself asking to come home. But Mama said no. She said, "We always finish what we start, Karen."

So that was that. I was taken into town for a penicillin shot, and started getting better. The sun came out too.

But because I still had a bad cough, I did not have to participate in the all-camp Game Day held during the third week of Second Session. I was free to lounge in my upper bunk and read the rest of *The Fountainhead,* which I did. By then I had read way ahead of my counselor. I could hear the screams and yells of the girls out on the playing fields, but vaguely, far away. Then I heard them all singing, from farther up the hill, and I knew they had gone into Assembly to give out the awards. I knew I was probably expected to show up at Assembly, too, but somehow I just couldn't summon up the energy. I didn't care who got the awards. I didn't care which team won — the Green or the Gold, it was all the same to me — or which cabin won the ongoing competition among cabins. I didn't even care who was Camp Spirit. Instead I lolled on my upper bunk and looked at the turning dust in a ray of light that came in through a chink in the cabin. I coughed. I felt that I would die soon.

This is when it happened.

This is when it always happens, I imagine — when you least expect it, when you are least prepared.

Suddenly, as I stared at the ray of sunshine, it intensified, growing brighter and brighter until the whole cabin was a blaze of light.

I sat right up, as straight as I could. I crossed my legs. I knew I was waiting for something. I knew something was going to happen. I could barely breathe. My heart pounded so hard I feared it might jump right out of my chest and land on the cabin floor. I don't know how long I sat there like that, waiting.

"Karen," He said.

His voice filled the cabin.

I knew immediately who it was. No question. For one thing, there were no men at Camp Alleghany except for Mr. Grizzard, who cleaned out the barn, and Jeffrey Long, who had a high, reedy voice.

This voice was deep, resonant, full of power.

"Yes, Lord?" I said.

He did not speak again. But as I sat there on my upper bunk I was filled with His presence, and I knew what I must do.

I jumped down from my bunk, washed my face and brushed my teeth at the sink in the corner, tucked in my shirt, and ran up the hill to the assembly hall. I did not cough. I burst right in through the big double doors at the front and elbowed old Mrs. Beemer aside as she read out the results of the archery meet to the rows of girls in their folding chairs.

Mrs. Beemer took one look at me and shut her mouth.

I opened my mouth, closed my eyes, and started speaking in Tongues of Fire.

I came to in the infirmary, surrounded by the camp nurse, the doctor from town, the old lady who owned the camp, the Episcopal chaplain, my own counselor, and several other people I didn't even know. I smiled at them all. I felt great, but they made me stay in the infirmary for two more days to make sure I had gotten over it. During this time I was given red Jell-O and Cokes, and the nurse took my temperature every four hours. The chaplain talked to me for a long time. He was a tall, quiet man with wispy white hair that stood out around his head. I got to talk to my mother on the telephone again, and this time she promised me a kitten if I would stay until the end of camp. I had always, always wanted a kitten, but I had never been allowed to have one because it would get hair on the upholstery and also because Ashley was allergic to cats.

"What about Ashley?" I asked.

"Never you mind," Mama said.

So it was decided. I would stay until the end of camp, and Mama would buy me a kitten.

I got out of the infirmary the next day and went back to my cabin, where everybody treated me with a lot of deference and respect for the rest of Second Session, choosing me first for softball, letting me star in Skits. And at the next-to-last campfire, I was named Camp Spirit. I got to run forward, scream and cry, but it was not as good as it would have been if it had happened First Session. It was an anticlimax. Still, I did get to light the very last campfire, the Friendship Night campfire, with my special giant match and say ceremoniously:

> *Kneel always when you light a fire,*
> *Kneel reverently,*
> *And thankful be*
> *For God's unfailing majesty.*

Then everybody sang the Camp Spirit song. By now, I was getting *really tired of singing.* Then Anne Roper and I sailed each other's little birchbark boats off into the night, our candles guttering wildly as they rounded the bend.

All the way home on the train the next day, I pretended to be asleep while I prayed without ceasing that nobody back home would find out I had spoken in tongues of fire. For now it seemed to me an exalted and private and scary thing, and somehow I knew it was not over yet. I felt quite sure that I had been singled out for some terrible, holy mission. Perhaps I would even have to *die,* like Joan of Arc. As the train rolled south through Virginia on that beautiful August day, I felt myself moving inexorably toward my Destiny, toward some last act of my own Skit, which was yet to be played out.

THE MINUTE I WALKED onto the concrete at the country club pool, I knew that Margaret Applewhite (who had flown home) had told everybody. Dennis Jones took one look at me, threw back his head, and began to gurgle wildly, clutching at his stomach. Tommy Martin ran out on the low board, screamed in gibberish, and then flung himself into the water. Even I had to laugh at him. But Paul and his friends teased me in a more sophisticated manner. "Hey, Karen," one of them might say, clutching his arm, "I've got a real bad tennis elbow here, do you think you can heal it for me?"

I was famous all over town, I sort of enjoyed it. I began to feel popular and cute, like the girls on *American Bandstand.*

But the kitten was a disaster. Mama drove me out in the county one afternoon in her white Cadillac to pick it out of a litter that the laundry lady's cat had had. The kittens were all so tiny that it was hard to pick — little mewling, squirming things, still blind. Drying sheets billowed all about them, on rows of clotheslines. "I want *that* one," I said, picking the smallest, a teeny little orange ball. I named him Sandy. I got to keep Sandy in a shoe box in my room, then in a basket in my room. But as time passed (Ashley came home from Europe, Paul went back to W&L), it became clear to me that there was something terribly wrong with Sandy. Sandy *mewed too much,* not a sweet mewing, but a little howl like a lost soul. He never purred. He wouldn't grow right either, even though I fed him half-and-half. He stayed little and jerky. He didn't act like a cat. One time I asked my mother, "Are you *sure* Sandy is a regular cat?" and she frowned at me and said, "Well, of *course* he is, what's the matter with you, Karen?" but I was not so sure. Sandy startled too easily. Sometimes he would leap straight up in the air, land on all four feet, and just stand there quivering, for no good reason at all. While I was watching him do this one day, it came to me.

Sandy was a Holy Cat. He was possessed by the spirit, as I had been. I put his basket in the laundry room. I was fitted for my aqua semiformal dress, and wore it in Aunt Liddie's wedding. Everybody said I looked grown up and beautiful. I got to wear a corsage. I got to drink champagne. We had a preschool meeting of the Sub-Deb Club, and I was elected secretary. I kept trying to call Tammy, from pay phones downtown and the phone out at the country club, so Mama wouldn't know, but her number was still out of order. Tammy never called me.

Then Ashley invited me to go to the drive-in movie with her and her friends, just before she left for Sweet Briar. The movie was *All That Heaven Allows,* which I found incredibly moving, but Ashley and her friends smoked cigarettes and giggled through the whole thing. They couldn't be serious for five minutes. But they were being real nice to me, so I volunteered to go to the snack bar for them the second or third time they wanted more popcorn. On the way back from the snack bar, in the window of a red Thunderbird with yellow flames painted on its hood, I saw Tammy's face.

I didn't hesitate for a minute. I was so glad to see her! "Tammy!" I screamed. The position of My Best Friend was, of course, vacant. I ran right over to the Thunderbird, shifted all the popcorn boxes over to my left hand, and flung open the door. And sure enough, there was Tammy, *with the whole top of her sundress down*. It all happened in an instant. I saw a boy's dark hair, but not his face — his head was in her lap.

Tammy's breasts loomed up out of the darkness at me. They were perfectly round and white, like tennis balls. But it seemed to me that they were too high up to look good. They were too close to her chin.

Clearly, Tammy was Petting. And in a flash I remember what Mama had told me about Petting, that

> a nice girl does not Pet. It is cruel to the boy to allow him to Pet, because he has no control over himself. He is just a boy. It is all up to the girl. If she allows the boy to Pet her, then he will become excited, and if he cannot find relief, then the poison will all back up into his organs, causing pain and sometimes death.

I slammed the car door. I fled back to Ashley and her friends, spilling popcorn everyplace as I went.

On the screen, Rock Hudson had been Petting too. Now we got a close-up of his rugged cleft chin. "Give me one of those cigarettes," I said to Ashley, and without batting an eye, she did. After three tries, I got it lit. It tasted great.

The next day, Ashley left for Sweet Briar, and soon after that, my school started too. Whenever I passed Tammy in the hall, we said hello, but did not linger in conversation. I was put in the Gifted and Talented group for English and French. I decided to go out for JV cheerleader. I practiced and practiced and practiced. Then, one day in early September, my cat Sandy — after screaming out and leaping straight up in the air — ran out into the street in front of our house and was immediately hit by a Merita bread truck.

I knew it was suicide.

I buried him in the backyard, in a box from Rich's department store, along with Ashley's scarab bracelet, which I had stolen sometime earlier. She wondered for years whatever happened to that bracelet. It was her favorite.

I remember how relieved I felt when I had smoothed the final shovelful of dirt over Sandy's grave. Somehow, I knew, the last of my holiness, of my chosenness, went with him. Now I wouldn't have to die. Now my daddy would get well, I would make cheerleader, and go to college. Now I could grow up, get breasts, and have babies. Since then, all these things have happened. But there are moments yet, moments when in the midst of life a silence falls, and in these moments I catch myself still listening for that voice. "*Karen,*" He will say, and I'll say, "Yes, Lord. Yes."

Fried Chicken

Here comes the murderer's mother, Mrs. Polly Pegram. She walks to Jitney Jungle every other day, then carries her paper bag of groceries home. When the boy at Jitney Jungle says "Paper or plastic, ma'am?" as if he doesn't already know the answer, as if he doesn't know who she is, she always says "Paper, please," and she always walks the same way home, past the tanning salon, past Lil's Beauty, past the Baptist church with its rosebushes blooming out front and its green Astroturf entrance and hymns floating out its open windows. She used to be a Baptist, years back. She used to bring Leonard here for Sunday school. He could sing like an angel, as a boy. Now he is forty-one years old.

Leonard used to drive Mrs. Pegram everywhere, so she never bothered to get her driver's license, she never needed it. She doesn't need it now, though Miss Bright — this is the social worker who won't leave her alone — keeps suggesting it. It's true that Leonard's red car is just sitting out there in the driveway. Sometimes when she's working in her garden, she'll rinse it off with the hose. But if she did learn to drive it, where in the world would she go? Miss Bright swears that the driving instructor from the high school will drive right up to Mrs. Pegram's door to pick her up for her lessons. He will ring her doorbell, she'll come out, and off they'll go in the special car together.

The thought of this sets Mrs. Pegram's heart aquiver. For nobody comes to this little house, nobody ever came. Her husband, Royal Pegram, did not like visitors, and Leonard did not like visitors either. Oh, she knows what they said about Leonard! *Loner. Lives with his mother.* As if it were a crime. Anyway, Leonard had plenty of friends. This is one thing that never came out in court, how popular he was, though he would never invite them over to the house, preferring to go out, as young people will. Sometimes Mrs. Pegram pages through the magazines as she stands in the checkout line at Jitney Jungle, lingering over the cookouts. She used to wish Leonard would have a cookout, but he never did.

Mrs. Pegram unlocks her door and walks through the front room where the TV is, past the closed door of Leonard's room, into the spotless little yellow kitchen where she puts the milk in the refrigerator and the two packages of cellophane-wrapped chicken out on the countertop. She buys Pick O' the Chick, all breasts and legs and thighs, it's more expensive, but it's worth it if you want to fix really good fried chicken. Mrs. Pegram knows that the girls behind the meat counter whispered to each other after she was gone, saying, "What do you reckon she's going to do with all that chicken, now that he's in the pen?" Well, they would be real surprised to find out, that's for sure!

Leonard just loved her fried chicken, she used to fix it for him on Sundays and he would eat it every bit up, except for one piece, which is all she ever ate. Mrs. Pegram just pecks at her food like a bird. She's a tiny little thing anyway, hardly five foot tall and shrinking.

Mrs. Pegram takes the cellophane off the packages and rinses the chicken under running water. But before she gets started cooking, she'd better take off these nice shoes and put on her house shoes, fuzzy old things, and put on her apron too. Chicken spatters. She's got to save her good clothes. Now that she's not working for Mrs. Calhoun any more, she won't be getting any of Mrs. Calhoun's old clothes, which were actually not old at all, just things that Mrs. Calhoun had grown tired of. Well, most of them were too big anyway.

The awful fact is that soon after the verdict, in spite of all their years together, Mrs. Calhoun let Mrs. Pegram go. Oh, Mrs. Pegram saw it coming. She saw Mrs. Calhoun grow more and more nervous as the trial went on, acting exactly like she had when she was going through the change of life, or when her daughter, Alicia, was getting her divorces, or when Mr. Calhoun had cancer of the prostate. Mrs. Calhoun got to where she wouldn't look Mrs. Pegram in the eye anymore, and she never, ever mentioned the trial.

Finally there came the morning when Mrs. Calhoun did not come downstairs at all. Instead, Mr. Johnny Calhoun sat waiting at the breakfast table, wearing his three-piece suit. "Natalie wants you to know how much she has valued her association with you over the years," he said in his courtroom voice, "but she feels that with the children grown, we need to economize, and she wants to do some of the housework herself, for the exercise, and have a cleaning service come in once a month, which is all we really need. Natalie knew you would understand." Then Johnny Calhoun handed Mrs. Pegram a check for a thousand dollars. During the years she'd been working for the Calhouns, his hair had turned from black to silver. Now he was a very distinguished man.

Mrs. Pegram looked at him until he looked away. "I under-stand," she said. Of course he was lying through his teeth, Natalie Calhoun would kill herself before she'd touch a can of Comet. She didn't even know where the dust rags were kept. But who could blame Mrs. Calhoun, after all? Who could blame her for firing the murderer's mother, for not wanting the murderer's mother to be the one who knew where she hid her Xanax in the false bottom of her jewelry box, who knew that Johnny Pegram required clean sheets every single day and wanted his underwear ironed, who knew that their daughter was an alcoholic? Who would want a murderer's mother to know these things? Mrs. Pegram can't blame her.

Of course she was disappointed, because she had thought Natalie Calhoun was her *friend* too, though Leonard had snorted at this idea. "Mrs. Calhoun is a bitch, Ma," he'd said. "Don't kid yourself."

For years Leonard had been after her to get a better job, but this was what she knew how to do, wait on people, take good care of their things. At least she still has Mr. and Mrs. Joyner two days a week, they're so out of it, poor souls, it is possible they don't even know about Leonard's case.

Mrs. Pegram puts flour, salt, pepper, and paprika in a plastic bag and shakes it. She puts Wesson oil in the skillet. She used to try to get Leonard to eat baked chicken the way she fixed it for the Calhouns, but he wouldn't have it. He liked it fried. Mrs. Pegram knew this was bad for him because he was such a big boy, she was sure his cholesterol was real high, but he wouldn't even get it checked for free in the booth at the mall.

You couldn't do a thing with Leonard when it came to his habits. For instance he wore the same outfit to his job at Lowes warehouse winter and summer, a flannel shirt and army work pants, and he had to have the same thing in his lunch box every day too — three bologna sandwiches with Miracle Whip on the bread, two packages of Little Debbie oatmeal cakes with cream filling. Then he'd buy himself some chocolate milk at the 7-Eleven to go with it. Mrs. Pegram had wished that Leonard would reduce and dress better so he'd have more of a chance with the girls, but actually he never showed any interest in nice girls or in marriage, either one. She always acted like she didn't know about the pile of nasty magazines in his closet, but so what? Plenty of people buy those magazines, there's a stack of them under Mr. Johnny Calhoun's side of the bed right now. Plus, Leonard was interested in plenty of other magazines too, such as those military magazines. Mrs. Pegram has always felt it was a shame that the army wouldn't take Leonard, it might have been the making of him.

Mrs. Pegram shakes each piece of chicken up in the plastic bag, coating it with the flour mixture, then slips it into the sizzling pan. This is the part where you have to pay attention, you want to get a nice crispy coating on all sides, but you can't let it burn. Mrs. Pegram stands close to the stove, turning the chicken frequently in the big old iron skillet. Royal Pegram hit her once with this skillet, years ago, she can't even remember the circumstances.

Mrs. Pegram is still not sure how it happened that Royal turned so mean. She'd met him in the little store up on Piney Ridge when she was not but sixteen, and him the same. He'd come into the county with a logging operation run by his older brother. Maybe it was because he was a stranger that she took to him so, since she didn't know anybody in the world that she hadn't been knowing her whole life long. They fell upon each other like they were meant to. Looking back, Mrs. Pegram thinks of the young Royal Pegram as a different person from the one she was married to for so long. That boy had black hair and black eyes and a sweet, dreamy way about him. He was from West Virginia and proposed to go back over there to work in the mines, and proposed to take her with him. *Go,* her mama said. *Go on while you've got the chance,* for there were seven more at home and this would be one less mouth to feed.

It was the first time she'd been out of the county, not to mention the state of Virginia, and at first it was fine, he mined for the company and she got a job keeping house for the company doctor's wife, a tall sad woman from Alabama who taught her how to set the table and polish silver with a toothbrush and slice ham real thin.

During those days Royal used to sit on the front porch and pick his guitar while she was stringing beans of a Sunday. He used to wear a straw hat with a feather stuck in the brim. Sometimes they went fishing in the river, and once he took her to the West Virginia State Fair. Then she had the baby, Martha Sue, who was sickly, and Royal didn't like her whining and crying so much because he was working the night shift, and needed to get his sleep. But Martha Sue cried and cried and did not grow. She had something wrong with her blood, and there was nothing they could do about it, and she died right before her third birthday. She was buried in a little pine box on a mountainside that was later strip mined.

After Martha Sue's death, Royal would not allow her name to be mentioned in his presence, and he burned her clothes and the two pictures they had of her, so that now Mrs. Pegram has none, and sometimes she wonders if she ever had that little baby girl at all, just as she wonders if those slow sweet days over in West

Virginia right after they got married were some kind of a dream. Because it all becomes a blur after that, her life a kind of a whirlwind. The mine fell in, and Royal got trapped for a day and a half next to a dead man, and so they left there and went to another mining town, and she had the twin boys, Roger and Royal Junior, and Royal got laid off and started drinking pretty bad, and then they moved again. And again. Finally she got to where she never unpacked the boxes, and she learned to stay away from him when he was drinking, and never to answer him back. Leonard was born at a free clinic over in Kentucky.

Everywhere they ever lived, Mrs. Pegram had a job keeping house for somebody, because she had a nice genteel way about her and she was quiet, and she knew how to do things right. The homes where she worked were a comfort to her, the shining windows, the orderly flower beds, the pale expanses of wall-to-wall carpet. At her own place it was nothing but yelling and broken things, except for Leonard.

Leonard was the joy of his mother's life. And he was certainly *not* retarded, no matter what anybody says now. When he was not but five, he'd play Chinese checkers with his mother by the hour. He loved Chinese checkers. He always picked the blue marbles to be his, and to this day Mrs. Pegram cannot see the color blue without thinking of her little boy, fat and serious, with eyes as round and as blue as those marbles. Leonard knew the words to all the popular songs too, he'd sing right along with the radio. He especially liked "Kaw-liga" about the wooden Indian, which they played on the radio a lot then. There was nothing retarded about him!

Now Mrs. Pegram puts a tablespoon of water right into the hot grease and turns the heat down and covers the pan quickly, to trap the steam inside. This is the real secret of good fried chicken, this is what most people don't know how to do. This is what makes the meat tender, so it just melts in your mouth like it ought to. After ten minutes of steaming, Mrs. Pegram takes the lid off the chicken and turns the heat back up and fries it some more, turning it constantly, so the nice brown coating gets crispy again.

People who are so quick to judge ought to know that Leonard was the one who ran his daddy off finally, as soon as he got bigger than Royal Pegram. The other boys were long gone by then, and who could blame them? It was the day after Christmas and Royal had been on the wagon — he'd bought her a new car coat for Christmas, and a Schwinn bike for Leonard, sometimes he could still be real sweet — but then he'd started up again, and by the time Leonard came in the house from riding his bike, she was on the couch crying, too dizzy to get up. Leonard was thirteen years old then and they wanted her to sign the papers to send him off, but she wouldn't, she needed him at home too bad, though of course she couldn't explain this to his teacher.

"Ma?" Leonard called, coming in. Then he came over and looked at her and then he went in the kitchen and then he came back and sat down in the ladder-back chair by the door. She kept falling in and out of sleep. When Royal came in, Leonard hit him in the face with a ball-peen hammer and then kicked him in the side when he fell. He kept kicking him. Leonard would have broken every bone in Royal's body if she had not gotten up and gotten in between them finally. By then the neighbors were there, and the police came.

The upshot of it was that a judge sent Leonard off to the special school after all, and when Royal got out of the hospital, he moved back over to West Virginia and died there several years later of cirrhosis of the liver. His sister wrote to Mrs. Pegram that Royal turned yellow at the end, and spoke her name before he died.

After that, Mrs. Pegram kept to herself. She worked steadily and lived frugally and paid off her little house. When Leonard came back from the special school, she was glad for his company, though he didn't talk much. But it was a steady life, a good life, hers and Leonard's. Leonard was nothing if not dependable, regular as a clock. He kept things fixed around the house and took the trash out. You could set your watch by Leonard. This was such a comfort to Mrs. Pegram after all those years of uncertainty and constant moving. And though she was never one to put herself forward, Mrs. Pegram made quiet little friendships all over town. Besides the people she worked for, such as the Calhouns of course and the Joyners and the Streets who moved away, she came to know Mr. Harris the pharmacist, Betty at the bank, Lil who did her hair, and the Banner sisters who ran the fabric shop and took her out to eat at the Western Sizzlin on the bypass, though Leonard didn't really like for her to go.

Now, since the trial, Mrs. Pegram has been wishing she lived in a big city, so she could be anonymous. Here, everybody knows her. Everywhere she goes, they're whispering behind their hands, "Look! Here she comes! It's the murderer's mother!" They all think it is somehow her fault. Even when they pretend to be nice, such as when the Banner sisters asked her to go to the outlets with them or when Preacher Rose came by to invite her to prayer meeting or when Margie Niles from next door brought her a piece of red velvet cake, Mrs. Pegram did not respond. She heard what Hubert Liles, the manager at Lowes, said about him at the trial. She knows they are only acting out of pity, all of them. Or perhaps they are acting out of curiosity, perhaps they are all just dying to know what it's like to be the murderer's mother! Well, she will not give them the satisfaction, she will give them the cold shoulder instead. Completely alone now, the murderer's mother feels somehow exhilarated, exalted, singled out.

This chicken is perfect. Mrs. Pegram lifts it out of the frying pan and puts it on paper towels so it won't be greasy. Suddenly she recalls Royal Pegram telling somebody, years ago, that he married her for her fried chicken. She blushes hot all over for a minute, remembering this. Then Mrs. Pegram takes off her apron and her house shoes and puts her good shoes back on. She goes in the bedroom to comb her hair, powder her face, and put on her little black hat. She looks nice. Anybody would know, just from looking at her, that she is a nice woman. That girl was *not nice,* this certainly came out in the trial, ditto those other girls who came up to testify against him, just look at the way they were dressed. Look at the way *she* was dressed, of course he didn't have to do what he did to her. Mrs. Pegram pushes these awful thoughts out of her mind. She never, *ever,* thinks about it. And today, she's got places to go! People to see!

She goes back in the kitchen and lines a basket with more paper towels, then carefully transfers the chicken to it, piece by piece. The phone rings, startling her, just as she finishes putting tinfoil over the top.

"It's Heidi Bright," the cheerful voice says on the other end of the phone. This is that pesky social worker. "It's such a beautiful Sunday afternoon, I thought you might like to go for a drive with me. Maybe we could drive out to the lake."

"Thank you so much," Mrs. Pegram says, adopting the tone Mrs. Calhoun always used when she wanted to get rid of visiting Mormons, "but I've already made plans."

"Oh, you *have*!" Miss Bright sounds encouraging. She'd really like to know, wouldn't she, just what kind of plans a murderer's mother makes!

"Yes," Mrs. Pegram says, "I've got an appointment. Thanks so much for asking, though." Then she hangs up, before Miss Bright can say another word. An appointment! She likes the sound of it.

Mrs. Pegram takes her basket and her purse and steps outside, turning to lock the door behind her. It *is* a beautiful day, Indian summer they call it, lovely warm sun and the leaves just beginning to turn. Leonard never appreciated nature at all. Still, he was the cutest little boy, hair so blond it was white. Mrs. Pegram walks past the Baptist church, Lil's Beauty, and the tanning salon, past Jitney Jungle, which is real busy now, on downtown past the bank and all the closed shops, past the Presbyterian church, which the Calhouns attend, past Hardee's.

She goes into the big new Trailways bus station and sits on a bench to wait for the new bus from Charlotte, due in at three thirty. It's three twenty-five. Mrs. Pegram peers around. She has never seen the man behind the desk, a good-looking young man with a mustache, she's sure he's not from around here. She doesn't know him, he doesn't know her, and he would never suspect of course that such a nice-looking little woman could possibly be a murderer's mother. Not in a million years! Then the bus from Charlotte comes in, a flood of strangers. The young man calls out connections for Roanoke, for Atlanta. People go this way, that way. It's exciting. Mrs. Pegram watches the crowd.

Finally she moves over to take a seat beside a tired-looking young blond mother and a squirmy little boy. Sometimes it's a mother with several children, sometimes it's a child traveling alone, sometimes it's a whole family.

"Where are you going?" she'll ask pleasantly after a while, and the young mother will say Atlanta or Norfolk or Richmond or Washington, even L.A., it could be anyplace, and then Mrs. Pegram will ask where they're from, and the young mother will tell her, and then Mrs. Pegram will say, "My goodness, that's quite a trip," and the young mother, warming to her, will tell all about it, why they're going and how long they'll be there, and sometimes it will be a long story and sometimes not. The little boy will be climbing all over his mother, eyeing Mrs. Pegram's basket. Finally she will say, "I'm just taking my son some fried chicken, it's real good and I've got plenty, would you like a piece?" and when she takes off the tinfoil, the heavenly smell of fried chicken will be everywhere as she offers it to them. The mother will eat a breast, then a thigh. "It's so good!" she'll cry. The little boy will eat all the drumsticks. His eyes are as round as a plate, he's so cute, he is the most important thing in the world to his mother, he is her whole life. The good-looking young man will call their bus. Mrs. Pegram will wrap up two more pieces in tinfoil and insist upon giving them to the mother as they hurry to get in line. It's okay — she's got plenty of chicken left. Plenty! Mrs. Pegram clutches the basket to her beating heart and waits for the next bus to come.

The Happy Memories Club

I may be old, but I'm not dead.

Perhaps you are surprised to hear this. You may be surprised to learn that people such as myself are still capable of original ideas, intelligent insights, and intense feelings. Passionate love affairs, for example, are not uncommon here. Pacemakers cannot regulate the strange unbridled yearnings of the heart. You do not wish to know this, I imagine. This knowledge is probably upsetting to you, as it is upsetting to my sons, who do not want to hear, for instance, about my relationship with Dr. Solomon Marx, the historian. "Please, Mom," my son Alex said, rolling his eyes. "Come on, Mama," my son Robert said. "Can't you maintain a little dignity here?" *Dignity,* said Robert, who runs a chain of miniature golf courses! "I have had enough dignity to last me for the rest of my life, thank you," I told Robert.

I've always done exactly what I was supposed to do — now I intend to do what I want.

"Besides, Dr. Solomon Marx is the joy of my life," I told them all. This remained true even when my second surgery was less than successful, obliging me to take to this chair. It remained true until Solomon's most recent stroke five weeks ago, which has paralyzed him below the waist and caused his thoughts to become disordered, so that he cannot always remember things, and he cannot always remember the words for things. A survivor himself, Solomon is an expert on the Holocaust. He has numbers tattooed on his arm. He used to travel the world, speaking about the Holocaust. Now he can't remember the name of it.

"Well, I think it's a blessing," said one of the nurses — that young Miss Rogers. "The Holocaust was just awful."

"It is not a blessing, you ignorant bitch," I told her. "It is the end. Our memories are all we've got." I put myself in reverse and sped off before she could reply. I could feel her staring at me as I motored down the hall. I am sure she wrote something in her ever-present notebook. *Inappropriate* and *unmanageable* are some of the words they use, unpleasant and inaccurate adjectives all.

The words that Solomon can't recall are always nouns.

"My dear," he said to me one day recently, when they had wheeled him out into the Residence Center lobby, "what did you say your name was?" He knew it, of course, in his heart's deep core, as well as he knew his own.

"Alice Scully," I said.

"Ah. Alice Scully," he said. "And what is it that we used to do together, Alice Scully, that brought me such intense . . . oh, so big . . ." His eyes were like bright little beads in his pinched face. "It was of the greatest, ah . . ."

"Sex," I told him. "You loved it."

He grinned at me. "Oh, yes," he said. "Sex. It was sex, indeed."

"Mrs. Scully!" his nurse snapped.

Now I have devised a game to help Solomon remember nouns. It works like this. Whenever they bring him out, I go over to him and clasp my hands together, as if I were hiding something in them. "If you can guess what I've got here," I say, "I'll give you a kiss."

He squints in concentration, fishing for nouns. If he gets one, I give him a kiss.

Some days are better than others.

This is true for us all, of course. We can't be expected to remember everything we know.

IN MY LIFE I was a teacher, and a good one. I taught English in the days when it was English, not "language arts." I taught for thirty years at the Sandy Point School in Sandy Point, Virginia, where I lived with my husband, Norman Scully, and brought up four sons, three of them Norman's. Norman owned and ran the Trent Riverside Pharmacy until one day he dropped dead in his drugstore counting out antibiotic capsules for a high school girl. His mouth and eyes were wide open, as if whatever he found on the other side surprised him mightily. I was sorry to see this, as Norman was not a man who liked surprises.

I must say I gave him none. I was a good wife to Norman, although I was initially dismayed to learn that this role entailed taking care of his parents from the day of our marriage until their deaths. They both lived long lives, and his mother went blind at the end. But we lived in their house, the largest house in Sandy Point, right on the old tidal river, and their wealth enabled us to send our own sons off to the finest schools, and even, in Steven's case, to medical school.

Norman's parents never got over his failure to get into medical school himself. In fact, he barely made it through pharmacy school. As far as I know, however, he was a good pharmacist, never poisoning anybody or mixing up prescriptions. He loved to look at the orderly rows of bottles on his shelves. He loved labeling. Often he dispensed medical advice to his customers: which cough medicine worked best, what to put on a boil. People trusted him. Norman got a great deal of pleasure from his job and from his standing in the community.

I taught school at first, because I was trained to do it and because I wanted to. It was the only way in those days that a woman could get out of the house without being considered odd. I was never one to plan a menu or clip a recipe out of a magazine. I left all that to Norman's mother and to the family housekeeper, Lucille.

I loved teaching. I loved to diagram sentences on the blackboard, precisely separating the subject from the predicate with a vertical line, the linking verb from the predicate adjective with a slanted line, and so forth. The children used to try to stump me by making up long sentences they thought I couldn't diagram, sentences so complex that my final diagram on the board looked like a blueprint for a cathedral, with flying buttresses everywhere, all the lines connecting.

I loved geography as well — tracing roads, tracing rivers. I loved to trace the route of the Pony Express, of the Underground Railroad, of De Soto's search for gold. I told them the story of that bumbling fool Zebulon Pike who set out in 1805 to find the source of the Mississippi River and ended up instead at the glorious peak they named for him, Pikes Peak, which my sister, Rose, and I visited in 1926 on our cross-country odyssey with our brother, Clyde, and his wife. In the photograph taken at Pikes Peak, I am seated astride a donkey, wearing a polka-dot dress and a floppy hat, while the western sky goes on and on endlessly behind me.

I taught my students these things: the first sustained flight in a power-driven airplane was made by Wilbur and Orville Wright at Kitty Hawk, North Carolina, on December 17, 1903; Wisconsin is the "Badger State"; the Dutch bought Manhattan Island from the Indians for twenty-four dollars in 1626; you can't sink in the Great Salt Lake. Now these facts ricochet in my head like pinballs, and I do not intend, thank you very much, to enter the Health Center for "better care."

I never tired of telling my students the story of the Mississippi River — how a scarlet oak leaf falling into Lake Itasca, in Minnesota, travels first north and then east through a wild, lonely landscape of lakes and rapids as if it were heading for Lake Superior, then over the Falls of St. Anthony, then down through Minneapolis and St. Paul, past bluffs and prairies and islands, to be joined by the Missouri River just above St. Louis, and then by the Ohio, where the water grows very wide — you can scarcely see across it. My scarlet leaf meanders with eccentric loops and horseshoe curves down, down, down the great continent through the world's biggest delta, to New Orleans and beyond, past the huge fertile mud plain shaped like a giant goose's foot, and into the Gulf of Mexico.

"And what happens to the leaf *then,* Mrs. Scully?" some student would never fail to ask.

"Ah," I would say, "then our little leaf becomes a part of the universe" — leaving them to ponder *that*!

I was known as a hard teacher but a fair one, and many of my students came back in later years to tell me how much they had learned.

HERE AT MARSHWOOD, A "total" retirement community, they want us to become children again, forgoing intelligence.

This is why I was so pleased when the announcement went up on the bulletin board about a month ago.

Writing Group to Meet Wednesday, 3 P.M.

Ah, I thought, that promising infinitive "to meet." For, like many former English teachers, I had thought that someday I might like "to write."

At the appointed day and hour, I motored over to the library (a euphemism, since the room contains mostly well-worn paperbacks by Jacqueline Susann and Louis l'Amour). I was dismayed to find Martha Louise Clapton already in charge. The idea had been hers, I learned; I should have known. She's the type who tries to run everything. Martha Louise Clapton has never liked me, having had her eye on Solomon, to no avail, for years before my arrival. She inclined her frizzy blue head ever so slightly to acknowledge my entrance.

"As I was just saying, Alice, several of us have discovered in mealtime conversation that in fact we've been writing for years, in our journals and letters and whatnot, and so I said to myself, 'Martha Louise, why not form a writing group?' and *voilà*!"

"*Voilà*," I said, edging into the circle.

So it began.

BESIDES MARTHA LOUISE AND myself, the writing group included Joy Richter, a minister's widow with a preference for poetry; Miss Elena Grier, who taught Shakespeare for years and years at a girls' preparatory school in Nashville, Tennessee; Frances Weinberg, whose husband lay in a coma over at the Health Center (a euphemism — you never leave the Health Center); Shirley Lassiter, who had buried three husbands and still thought of herself as a belle; and Vern Hofstetter, retired lawyer, deaf as a post. We agreed to meet again in the library one week later. Each of us should bring some writing to share with the others.

"What's that?" Vern Hofstetter said. We wrote the time and place down on a piece of paper and gave it to him. He folded the paper carefully and put it in his pocket. "Could you make copies of the writing, please?" he asked. He inclined his silver head and tapped his ear significantly. We all agreed. Of course we agreed, we outnumber the men four to one, poor old things. In a place like this, they get more attention than you would believe.

Then Joy Richter said that she probably couldn't afford to make copies. She said she was on a limited budget.

I pointed out that there was a free Xerox machine in the manager's office and I felt sure that we could use it, especially since we needed it for the writing group.

"Oh, I don't know." Frances Weinberg started wringing her hands. "They might not let us."

"I'll take care of it," Martha Louise said majestically. "Thank you, everyone, for joining the group."

I HAD WONDERED if I might suffer initially from "writer's block," but nothing of that sort occurred. In fact, I was flooded by memories — overwhelmed, engulfed, as I sat in my chair by the picture window, writing on my lap board. I was not even aware of the world outside, my head was so full of people and places of the past, rising up in my mind as they were then, in all the fullness of life, and myself as I was then, that headstrong girl longing to leave her home in eastern Virginia and walk in the world at large.

I wrote and wrote. I wrote for three days. I wrote until I felt satisfied, and then I stopped. I felt better than I had in years, filled with new life and freedom (a paradox, since I am more and more confined to this chair).

During that week Solomon guessed "candy," "ring," and "Anacin." He was getting better. I was not. I ignored certain symptoms in order to attend the Wednesday meeting of the writing group.

Martha Louise led off. "They just don't make families like they used to," she began, and continued with an account of growing up on a farm in Ohio, how her parents struggled to make ends meet, how the children strung popcorn and cut out paper ornaments to trim the tree when there was no money for Christmas, how they pulled taffy and laid it out on a marble slab, and how each older child had a little one to take care of. "We were poor but we were happy," Martha Louise concluded. "It was an ideal childhood."

"Oh, Martha Louise," Frances Weinberg said tremulously, "that was just beautiful."

Everyone agreed.

Too many adjectives, I thought, but I held my tongue.

Next, Joy Richter read a poem about seeing God in everything: "the stuff of day" was a phrase I rather liked. Joy Richter apparently saw God in a shiny red apple, in a dewy rose, in her husband's kind blue eyes, in the photographs of her grandchildren. It was a pretty good poem, but it would have been better if she hadn't tried so hard to rhyme it. Miss Elena then presented a sonnet comparing life to a merry-go-round. The final couplet went:

> *Lost children, though you're old, remember well*
> *the joy and music of life's carousel.*

This was not bad, and I said so. Frances Weinberg read a reminiscence about her husband's return from the Second World War, which featured the young Frances "hovering upon the future" in a porch swing as she "listened for the tread of his beloved boot." The military theme was continued by Vern Hofstetter, who read (loudly) an account of army life titled "Somewhere in France." Shirley Lassiter was the only one whose story was not about herself. Instead it was fiction evidently modeled upon a romance novel, for it involved a voluptuous debutante who had to choose between two men. Both of them were rich, and both of them loved her, but one had a fatal disease, and for some reason this young woman didn't know which one.

"Why not?" boomed the literal Vern.

"It's a mystery, silly," Shirley Lassiter said. "That's the plot." Shirley Lassiter had a way of resting her jeweled hands upon her enormous bosom as if it were a shelf. "I don't want to give the plot away," she said. Clearly, she did not have a brain in her head.

Then it was my turn.

I began to read the story of my childhood. I had grown up in the tiny coastal town of Waterville, Maryland. I was the fourth in a family of five children, with three older brothers and a baby sister. My father, who was in the oyster business, killed himself when I was six and Rose was only three. He went out into the Chesapeake Bay in an old rowboat, chopped a hole in the bottom of it with an ax, and then shot himself in the head with a revolver. He meant to finish the job. He did not sink as planned, however, for a fisherman witnessed the act and hauled his body to shore.

This left Mama with five children to bring up and no means of support. She was forced to turn our home into a boardinghouse, keeping mostly teachers from Goucher College and salesmen passing through, although two old widows, Mrs. Flora Lewis and Mrs.

Virginia Prince, stayed with us for years. Miss Flora, as we called her, had to have a cup of warm milk every night at bedtime; I will never forget it. It could be neither too hot nor too cold. I was the one who took it up to her, stepping so carefully up the dark back stair.

Nor will I forget young Miss Day from Richmond, a teacher, who played the piano beautifully. She used to play "Clair de Lune" and "Für Elise" on the old upright in the parlor. I would already have been sent to bed, and so I'd lie trembling in the dark, seized by feelings I couldn't name, as the notes floated up to me and Rose in our attic room, in our white iron bed wrought with roses and figures of nymphs. Miss Day was jilted some years later, we heard, her virtue lost and her reputation ruined.

Every Sunday, Mama presided over the big tureen at breakfast, when we would have boiled fish and crisp little johnnycakes. Mama's face was flushed, and her hair escaped its bun to curl in damp tendrils as she dished up the breakfast plates. I thought she was beautiful. I'm sure she could have married again had she chosen to do so, but her heart was full of bitterness at the way her life had turned out, and she never forgave our father or looked at another man.

Daddy had been a charmer, by all accounts. He carried a silver-handled cane and allowed me to play with his gold pocket-watch when I was especially good. He took me to the harness races with him, where we cheered for the horse he owned, a big roan named Joe Cord. On these excursions I wore a white dress and stockings and patent-leather shoes. And how Daddy could sing! He had a lovely baritone voice. I remember him on bended knee singing, "Daisy, Daisy, give me your answer, do," to Mama, who pretended to be embarrassed but was not. I remember his bouncing Rose up and down on his lap and singing, "This is the way the lady rides."

After his death the boys went off to sea as soon as they could, and I was obliged to work in the kitchen and take care of Rose. Kitchen work is never finished in a boardinghouse. This is why I have never liked to cook since, though I know how to do it, I can assure you.

We had a summer kitchen outside, so it wouldn't heat up the whole house when we were cooking or canning. It had a kerosene stove. I remember one time when we were putting up blackberry jam, and one of those jars simply exploded. We had blackberry jam and broken glass all over the place. It cut the Negro girl, Ocie, who was helping out, and I was surprised to see that her blood was as red as mine.

As time went on, Mama grew sadder and withdrew from us, sometimes barely speaking for days on end. My great joy was Rose, a lively child with golden curls and skin so fair you could see the blue veins beneath it. We slept in the same bed every night and played every day. Since Mama was indisposed, we could do whatever we wanted, and we had the run of the town, just like boys. We'd go clamming in the bay with an inner tube floating out behind us, tied to my waist by a rope. We'd feel the clams with our feet and rake them up, then flip them into a net in the middle of the inner tube. Once we went on a sailing trip with a cousin of ours, Bud Ned Black, up the Chickahominy River for a load of brick. But the wind failed and we got stuck there. We just *sat* on that river, for what seemed like days and days. Rose fussed and fumed while Cap'n Bud Ned drank whiskey and chewed tobacco and did not appear to mind the situation so long as his supplies held out. But Rose was impatient — always, always so impatient.

"Alice," she said dramatically as we sat staring out at the shining water, the green trees at its edge, the wheeling gulls, "I will *die* if we don't move, I will die here," Rose said, though Bud Ned and I laughed at her.

But Rose meant it. As she grew older, she had to go here, go there, do this, do that — have this, have that — she hated being poor and living in the boardinghouse and could not wait to grow up and go away.

We both developed a serious taste for distance when our older brother, Clyde, and his wife took us motoring across the country. I was sixteen. I loved that trip, from the first stage of planning our route on the map to finally viewing the great mountains, which sprang straight up from the desert like apparitions. Of course we had never seen such mountains; they took my breath away. I remember how Rose flung her arms out wide to the world as we stood in the cold wind on Pikes Peak. I believe we would have gone on driving and driving forever. But of course we had to return, and I had to resume my duties, letting go the girl Clyde had hired so Mama would permit my absence. Clyde was our sweetest brother, but they are all dead now, all my brothers, and Rose too.

I have outlived everyone.

Yet it seems like only yesterday that Rose and I were little girls playing that game we loved so well, a game that strikes me now as terribly dangerous. This memory is more vivid than any other in my life.

It is late night, summertime. Rose and I have sneaked out of the boardinghouse, down the tiny dark back stair, past the gently sighing widows' rooms; past Mama's room, door open, moonlight ghostly on the mosquito netting draped from the canopy over her bed; past the snoring salesmen's rooms, stepping tiptoe across the wide-plank kitchen floor, wincing at each squeak. Then out the door into moonlight so bright that it leaves shadows. Darting from tree to tree, we cross the yard and attain the sidewalk, moving rapidly past the big sleeping houses with their shutters yawning open to the cool night air, down the sidewalk to the edge of town where the sidewalk ends and the road goes on forever through miles and miles of peanut fields and other towns and other fields, toward Baltimore.

Rose and I lie down flat in the middle of the road, which still retains the heat of the day, and let it warm us head to toe as we dream aloud of what the future holds. At different times Rose planned to be an aviator, a doctor, and a film actress living in California, with an orange tree in her yard. Even her domestic dreams were grand. "I'll have a big house and lots of servants and a husband who loves me *so much,*" Rose would say, "and a yellow convertible touring car and six children, and we will be rich and they will never have to work, and I will put a silk scarf on my head and we will all go out riding on Sunday."

Even then I said I would be a teacher, for I was always good in school, but I would be a missionary teacher, enlightening natives in some far-off corner of the world. Even as I said it, though, I believe I knew it would not come to pass, for I was bound to stay at home, as Rose was bound to go.

But we'd lie there looking up at the sky, and dream our dreams, and wait for the thrill of an oncoming vehicle, which we could hear coming a long time away and could feel throughout the length of our bodies as it neared us. We would roll off the pavement and into the peanut field just as the car approached, our hearts pounding. Sometimes we nearly dozed on that warm road — and once we were almost killed by a potato truck.

Gradually, as Mama retreated to her room, I took over the running of the boardinghouse, and Mama's care as well. At eighteen, Rose ran away with a fast-talking furniture salesman who had been boarding with us. They settled finally in Ohio and had three children, and her life was not glamorous in the least, though better than some, and we wrote to each other every week until her death of lung cancer at thirty-nine.

This was as far as I'd gotten.

I quit reading aloud and looked around the room. Joy Richter was ashen, Miss Elena Grier was mumbling to herself, Shirley Lassiter was breathing heavily and fluttering her fingers at her throat. Vern Hofstetter stared fixedly at me with the oddest expression on his face, and Frances Weinberg wept openly, shaking with sobs.

"Alice! Now just look what you've done!" Martha Louise said to me severely. "Meeting adjourned!"

I HAD TO MISS the third meeting of the writing group because Dr. Culbertson stuck me into the Health Center for treatment and further tests (euphemisms both). In fact, Dr. Culbertson then went so far as to consult with my son, Steven, a doctor as well, about what to do with me next. Dr. Culbertson was of the opinion that I ought to move to the Health Center for "better care." Of course I called Steven immediately and gave him a piece of my mind.

That was yesterday.

I know they are discussing me by telephone — Robert, Alex, Steven, and Carl. Lines are buzzing up and down the East Coast.

I came here when I had to, because I did not want any of their wives to get stuck with me, as I had gotten stuck with Norman's mother and father. Now I expect some common decency and respect. It is a time when I wish for daughters, who often, I feel, have more compassion and understanding than sons.

Even Carl, the child of my heart, says I had "better listen to the doctor."

Instead, I have been listening to this voice too long silent inside me, the voice of myself, as I write page after page propped up in bed at the Health Center.

It is Wednesday. I have skipped certain of my afternoon medications. At two fifteen I buzz for Sheila, my favorite, a tall young nurses' aide with the grace of a gazelle. "Sheila," I say, "I need for you to help me dress, dear, and then roll my chair over here, if you will. My own chair, I mean. I have to go to a meeting."

Sheila looks at my chart and then back at me, her eyes wide. "It doesn't say," she begins.

"Dr. Culbertson said it would be perfectly all right," I assure her. I pull a twenty-dollar bill from my purse, which I keep right beside me in bed, and hand it to her. "I know it's a lot of trouble, but it's very important," I say. "I think I'll just slip on the red sweater and the black wraparound skirt — that's so easy to get on. They're both in the drawer, dear."

"Okay, honey," Sheila says, and she gets me dressed and sets me in my chair. I put on lipstick and have Sheila fluff up my hair in the back, where it's gotten so flat from lying in bed. Sheila hands me my purse and my notebook and then I'm off, waving at the girls at the nurses' station as I purr past them. They wave back. I feel fine now. I take the elevator down to the first floor and then motor through the lobby, speaking to acquaintances. I pass the gift shop, the newspaper stand, and all the waiting rooms.

It's chilly outside. I head up the walkway past the par 3 golf course, where I spy Parker Howard, ludicrous in those bright green pants they sell to old men, putting on the third hole. "Hi, Parker!" I cry.

"Hello, Alice," he calls. "Nice to see you out!" He sinks the putt.

I enter the multipurpose building and head for the library, where the writers' group is already in progress. It has taken me longer to drive over from the Health Center than I'd supposed.

Miss Elena is reading, but she stops and looks up when I come in, her mouth a perfect *O*. Everybody looks at Martha Louise.

"Why, Alice," Martha Louise says. She raises her eyebrows. "We didn't expect that you would be joining us today. We heard that you were in the Health Center."

"I was," I say. "But I'm out now."

"Evidently," Martha Louise says.

I ride up to the circular table, set my brake, get out my notebook, and ask Miss Elena for a copy of whatever she's reading. Wordlessly, she slides one over. But still she does not resume. They're all looking at me.

"What is it?" I ask.

"Well, Alice, last week when you were absent, we laid out some ground rules for this writing group." Martha Louise gains composure as she goes along. "We are all in agreement here, Alice, that if this is to be a pleasant and meaningful club for all of us, we need to restrict our subject matter to what everyone enjoys."

"So?" I don't get it.

"We've also adopted an official name for the group." Now Martha Louise is cheerful as a robin.

"What is it?"

"It's the Happy Memories Club," she announces, and they all nod.

I am beginning to get it.

"You mean to tell me — " I start.

"I mean to tell you that if you wish to be a part of this group, Alice Scully, you will have to calm yourself down and keep your subject matter in check. We don't come here to be upset," Martha Louise says serenely.

They are all watching me closely now, Vern Hofstetter in particular. I think they expect an outburst.

But I won't give them the satisfaction.

"Fine," I say. This is a lie. "That sounds just fine to me. Good idea!" I smile at everybody.

There is a perceptible relaxation then, an audible settling back into chairs, as Miss Elena resumes her reading. It's a travelogue piece entitled, "Shakespeare and His Haunts," about a tour she made in England several years ago. But I find myself unable to listen. I simply can't hear Elena, or Joy, who reads next, or even Vern.

"Well, is that it for today? Anybody else?" Martha Louise raps her knuckles against the table.

"I brought something," I say, "but I don't have copies."

I look at Vern, who shrugs and smiles and says I should go ahead anyway. Everybody else looks at Martha Louise.

"Well, go on then," she directs tartly, and I begin.

After Rose's disappearance, my mother took to her bed and turned her face to the wall, leaving me in charge of everything. Oh, how I worked! I worked like a dog, long hours, a cruelly unnatural life for a spirited young woman. Yet I persevered. People in the town, including our minister, complimented me; I was discussed and admired. Our boardinghouse stayed full, and somehow I managed, with Ocie's help, to get the meals on the table. I smiled and chattered at mealtime. Yet inside I was starving, starving for love and life.

Thus it is not surprising, I suppose, that I should fall for the first man who showed any interest in me. He was a schoolteacher who had been educated at the University in Charlottesville, a thin, dreamy young man from one of the finest families in Virginia. His grandfather had been the governor. He used to sit out by the sound every day after supper, reading, and one day I joined him there. It was a lovely June evening; the sound was full of sailboats, and the sky above us was as round and blue as a bowl.

"I was reading a poem about a girl with beautiful yellow hair," he said, "and then I look up and what do I see? A real girl with beautiful yellow hair."

For some reason I started to cry, not even caring what my other boarders thought as they sat up on the porch looking out over this landscape in which we figured.

"Come here," he said, and he took my hand and led me behind the old rose-covered boathouse, where he pulled me to him and kissed me curiously, as if it were an experiment.

His name was Carl Redding Armistead. He had the reedy look of the poet, but all the assurance of the privileged class. I was older than he, but he was more experienced. He was well educated and had been to Europe several times.

"You pretty thing," he said, and kissed me again. The scent of the roses was everywhere.

I went that night to his room, and before the summer was out, we had lain together in nearly every room at the boardinghouse. We were crazy for each other by then, and I didn't care what might happen, or who knew. On Saturday evenings I'd leave a cold supper for the rest, and Carl and I would take the skiff and row out to Sand Island, where the wild ponies were, and take off all our clothes and make love. Sometimes my back would be red and bleeding from the rough black sand and the broken shells on the beach.

"Just a minute! Just a minute here!" Martha Louise is pounding on the table, and Frances Weinberg is crying as usual. Vern Hofstetter is staring at me in a manner that indicates he has heard every word I've said.

"Well, I think that's terrific!" Shirley Lassiter giggles and bats her painted blue eyelids at us all.

Of course our romance did not last. Nothing that intense can be sustained, although the loss of such intensity can scarcely be borne. Quite simply, Carl and I foundered upon the prospect of the future. He had to go on to that world that awaited him; I could not leave Mama. Our final parting was bitter — we were spent, exhausted by the force of what had passed between us. He did not even look back as he sped away in his red sports car, nor did I cry.

Nor did I ever tell him about the existence of Carl, my son, whom I bore defiantly out of wedlock eight months later, telling no one who the father was. Oh, those were hard, black days! I was ostracized by the very people who had formerly praised me, and ogled by the men in the boardinghouse, who now considered me a fallen woman. I wore myself down to a frazzle taking care of Mama and the baby at the same time.

One night, I was so tired I felt that I would actually die, yet little Carl would not stop crying. Nothing would quiet him — not rocking, not the breast, not walking the room. He had an unpleasant cry, like a cat mewing. I remember looking out my window at the quiet town, where everyone slept — everyone on this earth, I felt, except for me. I held Carl out at arm's length and looked at him good in the streetlight, at his red, twisted little face. I had an awful urge to throw him out the window —

"That's enough!" several of them say at once. Martha Louise was standing.

But it is Miss Elena who speaks, "I cannot believe," she says severely, "that out of your entire life, Alice Scully, this is all you can find to write about. What of your long marriage to Mr. Scully? Your seven grandchildren? Those of us who have not been blessed with grandchildren would give — "

Of course I loved Norman Scully. Of course I love my grandchildren. I love Solomon too. I love them all. Miss Elena is like my sons, too terrified to admit to herself how many people we can love, how various we are. She does not want to hear it, any more than they do, any more than you do. You all want us to *never change, never change.*

I did not throw my baby out the window, after all, and my mother finally died, and I sold the boardinghouse then and was able, at last, to go to school.

Out of the corner of my eye I see Dr. Culbertson appear at the library door, accompanied by a man I do not know. Martha Louise says, "I simply cannot believe that a former *English teacher* — "

This strikes me as very funny. My mind is filled with enormous sentences as I back up my chair and then start forward, out the other door and down the hall and outside into the sweet spring day, where the sunshine falls on my face as it did in those days on the beach, my whole body hot and aching and sticky with sweat and salt and blood, the wild ponies paying us no mind as they ate the tall grass that grew at the edge of the dunes. Sometimes the ponies came so close that we could reach out and touch them. Their coats were shaggy and rough and full of burrs, I remember.

Oh I remember everything as I cruise forward on the sidewalk that neatly separates the rock garden from the golf course. I turn right at the corner, instead of left toward the Health Center. "Fore!" shouts Parker Howard, waving at me. *A former English teacher,* Martha Louise said. These sidewalks are like diagrams, parallel lines and dividers: oh, I could diagram anything. The semicolon, I used to say, is like a scale; it must separate items of equal rank, I'd warn them. Do not use a semicolon between a clause and a phrase or between a main clause and a subordinate clause. Do not write, *I loved Carl Redding Armistead; a rich man's son.* Do not write, *If I had really loved Carl Armistead; I would have left with him despite all obstacles.* Do not write, *I still feel his touch; which has thrilled me throughout my life.*

I turn at the top of the hill and motor along the sidewalk toward the Residence Center, hoping to see Solomon. The sun is in my eyes. Do not carelessly link two sentences with only a comma. Do not write, *I want to see Solomon again, he has meant so much to me.* To correct this problem, subordinate one of the parts. *I want to see Solomon, because he has meant so much to me.* Because he has meant. So much. To me. Fragments. Fragments all. I push the button to open the door into the Residence Center, and sure enough, they've brought him out. They've dressed him in his madras plaid shirt and wheeled him in front of the television, which he hates. I cruise right over.

"Solomon," I say, but at first he doesn't respond when he looks at me. I come even closer. "Solomon!" I say sharply, bumping his wheelchair. He notices me then, and a little light comes into his eyes.

I cup my hands. "Solomon," I say. "I'll give you a kiss if you can guess what I've got in my hands."

He looks at me for a while longer.

"Now Mrs. Scully," his nurse starts.

"Come on," I say. "What have I got in here?"

"An elephant," Solomon finally says.

"Close enough!" I cry, and lean right over to kiss his sweet old cheek, being unable to reach his mouth.

"Mrs. Scully," his nurse starts again, but I'm gone, I'm history, I'm out the front door and around the parking circle and up the long entrance drive to the highway. It all connects. Everything connects. The sun is bright, the dogwoods are blooming, the state flower of Virginia is the dogwood, I can still see the sun on the Chickahominy River and my own little sons as they sail their own little boats in a tidal pool by the Chesapeake Bay, they were all blond boys once, though their hair would darken later, Annapolis is the capital of Maryland, the first historic words ever transmitted by telegraph came to Maryland: "What hath God wrought?" The sun is still shining. It glares off the snow on Pikes Peak, it gleams through the milky blue glass of the old apothecary jar in the window of Norman Scully's shop, it warms the asphalt on that road where Rose and I lie waiting, waiting, waiting.

Stevie and Mama

Roxy pushes the buttons that roll all the windows down as she drives across the long bridge to Amelia Island. It's dead low tide. On either side of the bridge, mud flats stretch out for miles, broken up by glistening streams of water winding through patches of tall green grass. Roxy pulls the rubber band off her ponytail and lets her hair blow back in the rush of funky, fishy air. She puts her cigarette out and breathes in deeply. No other air, anyplace else in the world, smells anything like this. March — it's already the first of March. It's been way, way too long. Roxy follows A1A through Yulee past the tourist places selling pecans and gator heads and Indian River oranges, noticing the fancy new sign at the right turn down to the southern point where the Ritz-Carlton is. That is not their end of the island, hers and Willie's.

Roxy turns left toward Fernandina Beach, which still looks mostly like it did back when they bought the beach house years ago with that little windfall they got when his mother died. Miss Rowena! *Lord.* First Roxy thought Miss Rowena would never die. Then she thought she would never get over it. They bought the house for thirty thousand dollars cash, can you believe that? Now the land alone is probably worth five times this much. Roxy drives past the old amusement park, now closed. Not only closed but condemned, she hates this. She and Willie used to neck on the Ferris wheel, way up high. From the top, you could see all the way across the island. But now teardowns are starting, even on their own sandy street. That little yellow house on the corner where the Cardinales used to live is totally gone, as if it had never existed. A brand-new house is already framed up, under construction in its place. Roxy remembers back when Lou Cardinale built that tiki bar out back, he used to be so proud of his mai tais, but they were way too sweet. Soon, Fernandina Beach won't even exist anymore, not *this* Fernandina Beach, not theirs. The kids have been calling it a time warp for years.

Roxy pulls into their driveway which is almost covered by the winter's blowing sand, as usual. She'll have to get out here and sweep like hell. Somehow she is always surprised to find the cottage still here. When she doesn't see it for a while, she starts thinking maybe she just dreamed it up. She feels like that about Willie too. She forgets what he looks like whenever he's away — she still can't believe she ever met him, she still can't believe he's hers, even after all these years. *Lord!* Where did the years go, anyway? The little ramshackle frame house has been added on to haphazardly from time to time, a room here, a room there, like a house built by children. The deck sags. It's still painted white, but peeling, with green woodwork and a Pepto-Bismol pink front door, the same colors it had when they bought it. Willie likes for everything to stay the same.

Roxy takes the door key out from under the rubber mat that says GO AWAY!

Their sentiments exactly.

She lets herself in, then goes around raising all the shades. She slides the glass doors open onto the deck and the beach. They're hard to push on their gritty tracks. A red paper Japanese lantern hangs down low over the big battered oak table, always littered with whatever Willie has found on the beach. Every morning he walks for miles, then makes a different arrangement to amuse her. Often, *I love you* in shells — oyster shells, mussel shells, shiny coquina shells. Today there's a funny cat face left over from last fall, with round startled shell eyes, a giant curved rusty nail for a mouth, and seaweed whiskers. The iron smile looks wry and seductive. Roxy remembers sitting at this table herself with Lilah and her little friends, making ballerinas out of pipe cleaners, using those delicate white hinged shells as the skirts. Sometimes they even glued on yarn for hair. Sometimes Willie still quotes that poem he used to say to her, the one about loving all the little things, and that's still true. He still does. Roxy loves it when Willie says poetry out loud to her, she never heard anybody do this before she met him.

Roxy runs her hand over the pile of starfish and horseshoe crabs on the end of the table. Used to be, she didn't give a damn about stuff like this. She would have thrown this whole mess in the trash. In a certain way, Willie has given her the natural world, as he has given her a stepdaughter, Lilah, the joy of their hearts. Pictures of Lilah are everywhere. Roxy believes in lots of pictures, though she has taken down almost all the photographs of little Alice now. Todd and Seth, her sons by her first marriage, are everywhere too: nice-looking boys, nice-looking men. She got their names from TV, to give them a good start in life, a plan that has clearly worked.

Willie likes to say that Roxy saved him, which is not true. It's more true that *he* saved *her,* from a regular comfortable life of schedules and dinner parties and country clubs. Not that there is anything wrong with such a life. But if she had met Willie first, it would have been another story. She didn't, though.

Willie is the love of her life. And actually, she met him *twice*.

THE FIRST TIME, Roxy was married to the father of her sons, a law student named Livingston Lovett Carter the Fourth, like a king of England. "But what do people *call* him?" Roxy's sister, Frances, had asked, wrinkling her nose, when Roxy took him up home. Roxy just looked at her. "They call him Livingston," she said. This should have been a warning, but it wasn't.

Roxy was crazy about Livingston from the first time she saw him at a wedding reception at the country club in Athens, Georgia, where she worked sometimes catering parties, one of three part-time jobs she took on during her sophomore year to supplement her scholarship. Frances kept telling her that she ought to just bag it and come back home and take classes at the community college like everybody else, and Roxy knew that made good sense, but she just loved Athens. She felt like *herself* in Athens, some way, which she never had back home in Rose Hill where she'd felt like an impostor in her own family all along. She knew this was crazy, but it was true. She could be Roxy in Athens but she was still Shelby Roxanne back in Rose Hill where she had been everything: a cheerleader, the vice president of the Beta Club, a star in all the plays.

She had even been crowned Miss Rose Hill in a pageant, reciting a poem she had written herself as her talent. That poem has been lost for years now. As Miss Rose Hill, Shelby Roxanne won a set of white Samsonite luggage and a steam iron, gifts which seemed to carry opposing messages: stay home and get married and iron your brains out, versus *travel*. She had picked travel, over everyone's objections, accepting the scholarship in Athens. Her family was a close family, nobody had ever left the county. Roxy's mother was one of the very few outsiders; she had come there to teach home economics in the high school, and fallen in love with Roxy's dad, and then she never left either.

Roxy's mother had made her and her sisters join the 4-H Club against their wishes, but then Roxy loved it, she loved to go off to 4-H conventions and contests in other towns, and to 4-H camp in Homosassee, Florida, where she got a new and better boyfriend every year. She loved the home demonstration part of 4-H, where you got to stand up in front of the judge and make a speech about whatever you were demonstrating, it was just exactly like being in a play. When she was a junior, Shelby Roxanne developed her own recipe for potato salad (her secret: the dressing was half French, half mayonnaise, so the potato salad was sort of pink). She learned all about the nutrient values of the potato and the history of the potato, including the Irish potato famine. She delivered her potato salad speech wearing a red and white checked blouse and a blue denim skirt, made by her mother and designed to look both patriotic *and* country at the same time (this was Shelby Roxanne's own idea). She was the cutest girl in the contest. Her potato salad, prepared ahead of time and tasted by the judges, was good too. In fact, it was delicious. She won at the local level, then went on to the state contest in Atlanta where she lost in the finals because she didn't wear a hairnet.

But she got her picture in the *Rose Hill Record* wearing her potato outfit anyway, along with a "little write-up" as her aunt Suetta always called it. Her aunt Suetta was making a scrapbook about her. Everything she did went into this scrapbook — every program from the times she sang in church, every play she ever starred in, the invitation to her high school graduation, the announcement of her scholarship to the university. The summer before she left, Shelby Roxanne and Frances and their first cousin, Darlene, got up a little trio named the Gospel Girls and sang at revivals and church homecomings all over their area, chauffeured by Aunt Suetta.

Later, in Athens, Roxy sang with a rock group named Steel Wool and slept with the bass player, named Skye Westbrooke. Skye thought the potato salad story was a riot, he was always getting her to tell it to his friends. At first Roxy enjoyed doing this, she enjoyed the big laugh she got every time, but after a while, she began to feel disloyal to *somebody* . . . her family? Or maybe her old self, that good, sweet Shelby Roxanne? She wasn't exactly sure. So she quit, she refused to tell the potato story anymore, and she and the bass player had a fight, and that's when she met Livingston at that wedding reception at the Athens country club in 1965, wearing the little black skirt and white blouse of caterers everywhere, serving tiny crab cakes on a silver tray.

Or to be exact, when Livingston met her.

Because whatever happened, Livingston took it over. This was his nature. He would make it *his* thing, and then he would make everything happen *his* way, whatever he wanted. It never occurred to him not to do this. And it never occurred to Roxy not to go along with it, either, because whatever Livingston wanted, he wanted in the most intense and focused way imaginable. So of course she was flattered — who wouldn't be? There is nothing as persuasive as somebody who wants you very, very much.

Livingston was cute, too, in a preppy way, before Roxy had ever heard that word. He had perfect blond hair that fell forward into his eyes just a little bit, and loafers with no socks ("Where are his socks?" Frances asked). He wore knit shirts with the collars turned up, which looked stupid in Roxy's opinion, though she held her tongue. She would hold her tongue for years and years, about everything.

Now she is ashamed of this. But she felt guilty because she got pregnant. The modest wedding reception was held at that same Athens country club, paid for by Livingston's mother and father who actually turned out to have a lot less money than a person might have supposed. Mostly what they had was a sense of style, like Livingston. They had expected him to marry money, and were disappointed when he didn't. They were disappointed by the circumstances, as well. So it was Roxy's own idea to invite only her own immediate family to the wedding, not all those tacky cousins from up in the hollers.

"Listen," Frances whispered fiercely in the moment just before Roxy and their dad started down the aisle, "*Don't do it*. Just don't do it. This is not the love of your life." Frances herself was holding out for Mr. Right. But Roxy did it anyway. It was also her own idea to drop out of college and start working a series of jobs to put Livingston through law school, where he was fast becoming a star: editor of the *Law Review*, Order of the Coif. He studied all the time. He was there, but not there. Of course she was very proud of him.

Roxy put the baby, Todd, in day care and worked as the receptionist at an insurance office, then as the manager at a swim club, and then she sold ads for the newspaper. Meanwhile her own degree hung out there in the future like a sign on an inn, lit up in the foggy night someplace on the other side of town. She always thought she'd finish it, but she never did. She was so good at jobs, so good with people. Everybody liked her. After Seth was born, Roxy stayed home and started selling Mary Kay cosmetics at night, at Mary Kay parties in people's homes. Soon she was a Ruby, then a Double Ruby, then a Diamond, then a Double Diamond, moving right up the Mary Kay pyramid. She was about to earn a pink Cadillac. Roxy was making a small fortune selling Mary Kay when she found out that both her mother-in-law and the dean's wife were scandalized by this career, that Mary Kay was considered somehow low class. It "would not do" for a lawyer's wife to drive a pink Cadillac. So Roxy switched to real estate when Livingston finally graduated and got a job clerking for the federal judge in Macon. Real estate gave her more flexible hours for the little boys, anyway, and this is how she met Willie the first time, at an open house.

THIS HOUSE HAD BEEN on the market for almost two years because the owners were asking too much for it. It was an ultramodern split-level overlooking Lake Heron, north of town. Everything in it was chrome, beige, or black. Cold. Roxy could see why the people who lived here had split up, she couldn't have lived in a house like this for five minutes herself. But you couldn't have guessed this if you had come to the open house that Sunday afternoon, and Roxy had showed you around. The *real* problem, she soon figured out, was that people old enough to afford this house were put off by the style, and people young enough to appreciate the style didn't have the money.

The open house had already been going on for two hours when Willie showed up with his wife, Lucinda, who was very tall, very pregnant, and incredibly beautiful. Roxy noticed her right off. You couldn't help it. Lucinda had enormous blue eyes, like Lake

Heron, and waist-length naturally blonde hair, as opposed to Roxy's own not naturally blonde hair. Lucinda had a Kim Novak nose and a small pretty mouth with perfect white teeth. She wore a glittering lavender top over a flowing patchwork skirt. She was the most beautiful person that Roxy had ever seen in real life, like a movie star, or somebody on television. Maybe this was actually true, because she looked down all the time, like she was afraid of being recognized. Willie was sort of scruffy and nondescript beside his huge beautiful wife, a normal-size red-bearded man who wore a weird medallion on a chain. Willie had long scraggly red hair and an open shirt that showed even more red hair on his chest. Both of them were barefooted. Of course it *was* the early seventies, but *still* — this was *Georgia,* for Pete's sake!

WILLIE INTRODUCED HIMSELF, then Lucinda, first names only, then went straight over to the refreshment table where he poured himself a plastic cupful of wine right up to the top and drank it all down in one gulp, then another. There was nothing to eat, all the peanuts and Roxy's homemade cheese straws were long gone. She had already decided that these people couldn't possibly afford this house when Lucinda went over to Willie and took his hand tentatively and whispered something in his ear. Lucinda moved slowly, like a woman walking through water.

Willie cleared his throat. "I guess we'd like to look at it," he told Roxy.

"Okay." She went into her spiel. "There's a whole master suite upstairs with its own balcony overlooking the lake, and a choice of other rooms for the baby." Though she couldn't imagine anybody having a baby in this house — would it have a chrome crib? "And this is a great area for children," she added. "There's a Montessori school about a mile up the road." These people looked like Montessori types to Roxy.

Lucinda gave her a shy half smile, then looked back down. Willie poured himself another cup of wine ("A traveler?" Roxy almost asked him) for the house tour. Upstairs and down they all went, then into the enormous gleaming kitchen where Lucinda barely glanced at the state-of-the-art appliances, clinging to her husband's hand. Something was wrong with her, Roxy decided. Maybe she was terminally ill like Ali McGraw in *Love Story,* which had just come out. Or maybe she was on drugs. Actually they *both* looked like they might be on drugs.

Other visitors stared at them curiously as they came back down the winding staircase, holding hands. Roxy thought Willie and Lucinda would leave then, but they didn't. Instead, they suddenly turned around at the bottom and went back up the stairs and stood in front of the long window on the landing for half an hour, whispering. Willie kept his arm around his wife and massaged her shoulder the whole time. At one point Roxy started up the stairs to speak to them, then just stopped on a step below, looking up at them from behind. The sun fell through the long window, spinning their hair into gold, as in a fairy tale. *He really loves her,* she thought. *Really really really.* Suddenly Roxy felt empty and foolish standing there in her little red suit and patent-leather pumps watching them. She felt hollow and fragile, like a wind chime, a thought so crazy that she went back downstairs and got a cup full of wine herself despite a frown from Irene Kramer, her more experienced co-worker.

Finally Willie and Lucinda headed back down the stairway like a bridal couple making an entrance. Lucinda was blushing, though she still looked down.

"We'll take it," Willie told Roxy when they reached the bottom.

"Don't you want to look at the lower floor?" she asked. "The basement? There's a whole guest suite down there, and an office — "

Willie looked at his wife, who shook her head slightly: no.

"That's okay," he said.

"Really?" Roxy knew she was being unprofessional, but she couldn't believe it. And they still hadn't asked the price.

"We're sure." For the first time, Willie smiled directly at *her,* and then she could see the appeal, all right.

Irene Kramer moved forward like a bitch on wheels. "I'll be glad to discuss terms with you," she said. "We can step back here into the study."

"Oh, we'll just pay cash," Willie's wife spoke for the first time, in a surprising little-girl voice. Then she wrote out a check for ten thousand dollars and handed it to Roxy. "Is that enough for now?" she asked, and Roxy said it was plenty.

They left in an old red convertible with the top down, her yellow hair flying out behind them like a banner in the breeze as Willie gunned it down the long driveway. Willie always drove convertibles, and he always drove too fast. He always cooked on high, too. But Roxy would learn all this much later.

"Well, I swan!" she said, reverting to an old mountain expression of her mother's, which covered just about everything.

But Irene smiled a practiced, calculating smile that crinkled her makeup. "Music people," she said. "Wait and see. You run into every damn thing in this business."

THE SECOND TIME ROXY met Willie was twelve years after that, when she took a poetry class by mistake over at the college. It all started the day after Livingston told her that he was contemplating a run for the state legislature. "Why not?" he'd said, striding back and forth across the new Oriental rug. He'd made partner at Massengale, Frankstone, and Hogue, he'd made over ten million dollars winning personal injury suits, his specialty. Both boys had just left for Virginia Episcopal School, the same prep school Livingston himself had gone to. They were doing great. Roxy's decorator, David, had just put the finishing touches on this house they'd built at the Ambassador's Club — right on the seventh hole, for luck. Now, Livingston said, he *felt* lucky. For years, people had been after him to run for office. He had headed up a list of volunteer organizations and fund drives as long as your arm, he had served on many boards. It was time.

Roxy cleared her throat. "Actually," she'd said, "I was just thinking it's also about time for me to go back to school and get that degree. I'd like to teach, like Mama. Maybe home ec, don't laugh. Or maybe special ed. I'd like to be useful in the world." She didn't know she was going to say this before she said it, it popped right into her head. *Well, I swan!* she thought. *I sound just like Mama,* who had recently died. Roxy had been feeling sort of shaky and weird ever since. Sometimes she felt like she was floating above herself, watching herself walk and talk and smile like an idiot. Or like she was in a play, or a pageant.

"Honey," Livingston said, "you *are* useful in the world. You're useful right here." Livingston had been walking all around the new living room. Now he stopped and poured her a glass of wine. "I need you — the boys need you — just think how much I'll need you when we run."

"*We,*" he said, not "I." And "*when,*" not "if."

Immediately Roxy saw herself in a series of photographs taken on a series of platforms, herself and Livingston, smiling, smiling, smiling ever more broadly until her whole face was stretched tight. He would need her on those platforms, and he would need her as a hostess too, for Roxy was already a famous hostess in Macon, where her Christmas Eve parties had become a tradition, with homemade gumbo and jambalaya and a Christmas tree in every room, each tree with a different theme. She'd always loved people, and she loved to cook. But suddenly Roxy had a vision of herself cleaning up from those parties, putting the Christmas ornaments into those special boxes with the little dividers, each box clearly marked with its own theme label, for all the Christmases of all the years of her life to come.

She raised her glass to Livingston. "To you," she said. "Go for it, honey!"

But she called Continuing Education over at the college that very day and signed up for a class named Kid Stuff: Special Topics in Special Education.

FIRST SHE COULDN'T FIND a parking space on campus, and then she couldn't find Lenore Hall, and then the doorknob wouldn't turn, or at least she couldn't turn it, maybe because her hands were sort of sweaty because she couldn't find the elevator either and she'd had to walk up three flights of stairs, so that she burst, literally *burst,* into the classroom, immediately dropping her purse, which fell wide open spilling change and makeup and her driver's license and about a million credit cards all over the floor.

"Is this it?" she asked wildly.

Fifteen blank young faces turned around to look back at her.

"Well, is this it or not?" she said into the silence.

Willie stood up at his desk. "Maybe, maybe not," he said. "But why don't you just take a seat and we'll find out?"

IRENE KRAMER HAD BEEN right, of course. Willie turned out to be Willie Cocker who used to play with Lynard Skynard and then started the legendary group Desperado. They had had that huge hit back in the late sixties with "Heat Lightning," which he wrote. In fact the whole album went platinum. Lucinda had left him three years after they bought the house, taking their only child, a girl, with her. A year after that, Lucinda killed herself. Willie got the child, Lilah, at that point, but since he was in no condition to take care of her, Lilah had lived with his mother, Miss Rowena, in the big house over on Virginia Place until he got out of rehab.

So Lilah, not Roxy, was the one who had actually saved Willie, in Roxy's opinion. From then on, he raised Lilah by himself, if anybody could have been said to have raised Lilah at all. Mostly she raised herself, or maybe she raised *him*. Willie quit the band so he wouldn't have to travel and started teaching music lessons at home, plus the occasional English course over at the college, his original occupation. He was keeping it, he told everybody, *very simple.* They lived in an old bungalow near the campus. Lilah was the envy of all her friends, with a bead-curtain door and a television and refrigerator in her own room, plus her own dog, Possum, who slept on her waterbed with her. Possum was mostly Lab. They had found him lost in the mountains while on a camping trip. Willie had a dog too — Gator, found injured in a ditch beside the road when they were driving through the Okeefenokee Swamp. "Shot and left for dead!" Lilah liked to announce dramatically, pointing at Gator, a big friendly yellow mutt with floppy ears.

Roxy thought it was so weird for them both to have dogs named for other animals.

And there were other weird things about them too, but what could you expect? After all, Willie was a genius, with a lot of fancy degrees from fancy schools up north, and geniuses are even weirder than rock stars, everybody knows that. Roxy was a practical person. Later, she would clean out their cabinets, get rid of the mold everyplace, buy new sheets that matched, and plant an herb garden. Willie was a gourmet cook but a terrible housekeeper, though a series of girlfriends (there was always a girlfriend, and she was always nice) had tried their best to organize him. "I have my own system," he would explain, referring to the piles of papers and records and sheet music on the floor as his "files," and in time these nice women would give up on organizing him, if their pet allergies or his unwillingness to commit hadn't already driven them away.

The bungalow's living room was filled with pianos, keyboards, and recording equipment, while the dining room table was piled high with papers and books. Willie slept downstairs back then, in the little room off the dining room, which used to be a sun porch. He liked it out there. He liked the weather, hot or cold. He liked to see the japonica bloom in the spring and watch the dogwood leaves turn red in the fall, up close. He wanted the moonlight to fall across his bed.

Lilah had the big sunny corner bedroom upstairs. She was never exactly sure who might turn up in the other two bedrooms when she woke up in the morning. Students, fans, relatives, friends — Lilah and Willie had a lot of friends. Sometimes the friends stayed for weeks. Sometimes Miss Rowena sent her hired man, Horace, over there to clean. Horace moved through the house mournfully and purposefully, mopping and vacuuming, clicking his tongue; after he'd left, they couldn't find *anything* for the longest time, until they had messed it all up again.

Yet Lilah emerged from this crazy house on time for school every morning, neat as a pin, and marched off to the Harper Hill Academy in her uniform, the blue blazer and plaid skirt and knee-socks in winter, the white blouse and khaki Bermuda shorts and sneakers in spring and fall. She always had perfect attendance and perfect grades. It was a miracle; *she* was a miracle. Lilah grew into a tall, blonde, beautiful girl like her mother but so thin that her knees knocked together when she walked. Roxy had an immediate impulse to feed her. Lilah had the same huge blue eyes that Roxy remembered so well, the same Kim Novak nose, but a big, generous mouth like Julia Roberts so that when she smiled, which she did often, she gave off light like the sun.

Or like a lighthouse, Roxy thinks now, walking out on the sagging deck to look across the marsh at her favorite view, the black and white striped Cape Plenty lighthouse built in 1910 and still in use. Roxy identifies with this lighthouse — she and Willie are getting pretty old themselves now, but by God they are still in use, both of them. Everything still works — *everything.* Suddenly she can't wait for him to get here, she hasn't seen him for three days because he's been in Atlanta scoring a documentary film. Roxy smiles, putting cushions out on the heavy old cedar deck chairs, gray with age. She looks out at the horizon and remembers the night they pulled the mattress out here and drank champagne and watched the Perseid shower, those shooting stars all night long. She has just gone back into the house and gotten another armful of cushions when the phone rings. She puts the cushions down and picks the receiver up; somehow, she knows it's going to be important.

"ROXY?" LILAH'S VOICE IS about an octave higher than usual.

"Hi honey, what's going on? I thought you were going to some golf tournament or conference or something with Kyle this weekend."

Kyle is the current boyfriend.

"We are — I mean, we *were,* but then Kyle changed his mind and now he wants to drive down to the beach all of a sudden, so is that okay with you guys?"

"Well, sure, but you know it's still kind of cold out on the island, and it's a pretty long drive, and it's not great weather or anything yet. In fact, I just got here myself, I'm just starting to clean up the house."

"What about Daddy? Isn't Daddy there? Kyle says he especially wants to see Daddy."

"Lilah, tell me what's going on. Are you okay?" Roxy sits down on Miss Rowena's old sofa, she called it her davenport.

"I'm fine," Lilah says in a cheery voice, though it's clear that she's not. "Where's Daddy?"

"He's coming, sweetheart. He's driving down from Atlanta, I'm not quite sure what time he'll get here. In a little while."

"Well, we ought to get there about.... What time did you say? Just a minute." Though Lilah has put her hand over the receiver, Roxy hears a man's voice in the background — clearly she's talking to Kyle.

"*Today?* You mean you're coming today?" Roxy wedges the receiver under her chin as she lights a cigarette.

"Actually we're already on the road," Lilah says. "Kyle says we'll be there by six."

"Oh great! Can't wait to see you!" Roxy lies, hanging up the phone. Well shit. She sits on the davenport looking out at the line of waves on the empty beach. What if Lilah's pregnant? But that's impossible. Lilah has always been the sanest, smartest, most capable child in the world; now she's got an MBA degree and carries a briefcase. MBAs don't get pregnant, do they? But what else could it be? Now Roxy's just *dying* to talk to Willie, but of course he doesn't have a cell phone. He refuses to get one. He's such a throwback, he won't do e-mail either. He's on the road by now too, loud music playing on his old tape deck, driving like a bat out of hell.

ROXY REMEMBERS HOW MISS Rowena used to push that imaginary brake pedal on the floor whenever she rode with her son. "Slow down, honey, for pity's sake!" she'd beg, stomping on the floorboard.

"Brake-dancing," Willie called this.

Roxy herself wasn't much better, also terrified by his driving, always telling him to slow down, or pointing out whatever was happening on the road ahead, just in case he didn't see it, *backseat driving* even when she was riding shotgun in the front seat — but Willie was such a scary driver that she just couldn't help it. It was mostly a matter of his driving *style,* she had to admit, since he'd never had a real accident although he'd had plenty of fender-benders and gotten a lot of speeding tickets and even lost his license once for a year. But Roxy, like Miss Rowena, just couldn't control herself whenever she rode with him. She couldn't shut up. She couldn't stop shouting out; she couldn't stop giving pointers and issuing warnings. It got to be a real problem. Finally Willie had rescued them both by making a game out of it.

The game had started about ten years ago when they were

driving up to the North Carolina mountains for MerleFest, Doc Watson's bluegrass festival held in memory of his son, Merle. Roxy and Willie had never missed it.

They were barreling up I-77 north of Charlotte in his old white Dodge Dart convertible, taking the curves like a piece of cake, when all of a sudden the giant red tractor-trailer ahead of them slowed down to a virtual stop in its lane, without putting its turn signal on. "Willie," she yelled, "Watch out! This truck is going to turn, or get off, or something. Look out, honey! Slow down! Or maybe you should try to switch lanes — " which Willie obviously couldn't do because the other lane was clogged bumper-to-bumper with traffic.

"You're going to hit it! We're going to hit it, honey — " Roxy's whole life began to flash before her, as it often did on a car trip with Willie. The last actual thing she saw before she ducked was the Ohio license tag of the truck, close up.

"Is that a fact, Mama? Is that right? You got to hep me, Mama, I can't see a thing. I'm blind, Mama. Don't you forget I'm blind. Now where is that truck? I swear I jus can't see a thing out here on this highway, where is we, Mama? Where we going?" Willie went into his best Stevie Wonder imitation. Roxy sat back up to see that the truck had turned off and Willie was rocking back and forth, head cocked and bobbing, grinning from ear to ear. "Did you say they is a truck out here, Mama?" he hollered. "Where that truck at? You got to tell me, Mama, I can't see nothing, I blind, Mama. I be just blind as a bat out here."

She started laughing and fell right into it. "Stevie, you crazy thing! You slow down now, you just slow down and listen to yo Mama." Even in Roxy's own opinion, she sounded great. Willie wasn't the only one who could do Stevie Wonder.

"Yas, Mama. Anything you says, Mama. Little Stevie gone get you there, you don't got to worry about a thing. Little Stevie sure gone get you there bye and bye." Willie threw back his head and started singing "I Was Made to Love Her." Roxy joined him on "Work out, Stevie, work out," singing at the top of her lungs.

Willie had explained that if she was going to treat him like a blind man, he might as well *be* one. After this, they played Mama and Stevie every time Roxy started backseat driving. It always slowed him down, and it took the pressure off too.

THE STEVIE AND MAMA routine still cracks Willie and Roxy up, though it scandalizes their three politically correct, super-high-achieving children, whose major rebellion lies in their straightness. *Oh well, at least they aren't Republicans.* Roxy sighs, starting to clean. Or at least not *yet,* though nobody is really sure about this Kyle fellow. He's brand new . . . Jesus, this living room looks like *archaeology* with its layers and layers of clutter: papers, clothes, books, shoes. Oh well. Roxy will just have to do the best she can, and the hell with it. She moves into higher gear. She puts the rest of the cushions out on the deck furniture, then sweeps the winter's sand off the deck, then goes back inside and puts sheets on their bed and on the double beds in two of the other little rooms, who knows? Maybe Lilah and Kyle will make a pretense of sleeping in separate rooms. They are *so straight.*

Roxy shakes her head, remembering herself and Willie at the same point in their relationship, about two months after she started taking that poetry class. Because Willie *was* the love of her life — she knew it immediately too. She had never met anybody like him — anybody so brilliant and wild and funny, yet so educated — why, she was just *crazy* about him! She couldn't believe that he actually seemed to like her back; she knew she didn't deserve him. She is still convinced that she doesn't deserve him, especially after losing Alice. If Roxy actually had to say what her best trait is, she would say, reliable. *Hardworking.* That's pathetic, isn't it? Even *mules* are hardworking. Horses! Even dogs. But she has a good bustline too and a good heart which is capable of intense love, so much love that it has surprised her and even scared her to death upon occasion when it has caused her to do the wildest things, things she would have thought nobody her age would ever do, especially a realtor. She has never been his equal. She is just a normal person who got hooked up to a genius, sort of like a car that gets its battery charged by a Rolls Royce. This is a metaphor, which means saying one thing in terms of another, such as, "My love is like a red, red rose." This is one thing she learned in Willie's class.

They met for a cup of coffee to discuss the poem she had written for her first assignment, and after that, she couldn't help it. Any of it. They were immediate soul mates, *old souls,* Willie called it. Roxy had never had a soul mate before. In fact, she hadn't had any fun for years either, and Willie was so much fun. They snuck around. They had picnics out in the silent, secret black-water swamp. They spent afternoons at the Bambi Lynn Motel in Montezuma, where all the pictures on all the walls showed the same thing, the same locomotive coming around a bend. The Bambi Lynn Motel must have bought a truckload of those pictures. They made love on the new Oriental rug in Roxy's living room while the boys were off at school and Livingston was at the legislature; they got rug burns, at their age. *Rug burns!* Roxy looked at them in the mirror and giggled. "Oh, that's eczema," she told Livingston when he asked. Sometimes they made love in Roxy's own king-size bed with its dual controls of mattress firmness;

she is not proud of this. Sometimes Roxy wore her old majorette uniform, which still fit, and one time when Livingston was at a meeting in Washington, she met Willie at the door wearing nothing but white high heels and her Miss Rose Hill banner and her rhinestone tiara.

They were crazy, and of course they got caught. But the big surprise was that Livingston did not appear to care too much one way or the other, certainly not as much as Roxy would have thought. In fact, this almost hurt her feelings, at least until his bland little administrative assistant, Miss Porterfield, came forward and stepped right into Roxy's shoes without missing a beat. Claudia Porterfield had graduated from Sweetbriar College and gotten a master's degree in public policy from Georgetown. She was much more suitable for Livingston in every way. They had actually *done him a favor,* Willie said, which must have been true, since Livingston was reelected easily the next two terms, and then ran for attorney general.

Now Livingston remains just as stuffy as he ever was, but whoever thought their own Lilah would turn out to be more like him than her own real biological father? Lilah works incredibly long hours and has her calendar and address book and 401(K) plan and long-range plans and God knows what all on her blackberry or raspberry or whatever that little thing is that she carries around with her all the time. *Lord!* Roxy's got so much to do before they get here: Lilah has such high standards, who would have thought it, this child of their hearts?

Roxy glances up at the Elvis clock on the kitchen wall, which says 4 p.m. already. Elvis's pelvis swivels, his black and white checkered legs swing back and forth, back and forth, beneath his cool blue sports jacket. Lilah has called this clock retro and

offered to sell it on e-Bay for them. Roxy and Willie have said no
thanks. But now Roxy will have to get something ready for dinner, won't she? She'll have to go to the store. At least she brought
that big tin of chocolate chip cookies along. *Thank God.* Roxy
decides to take all these old magazines and newspapers to the
dump on her way to the grocery store — and she'll leave Willie a
note too, so he'll know what's going on. He might get here sooner
than she thinks. But first she'd better put clean towels out in the
bathrooms, she might forget later. Roxy is very dismayed to find
that there's no overhead light in the tiny guest bath; this is a fixture she hates, you have to take the whole damn thing down to
put in a new bulb. She gets a bulb and stool to stand on. Well,
shit! Now she remembers. You have to have a Phillips head screwdriver too. Damn. She knows they've got one someplace. Roxy
looks in the bottom drawer in the kitchen, then in the tool chest
on the shelf above the washer and dryer where she finds every
kind and size of screwdriver in the world except for a Phillips
head. Wouldn't you just know it? Meanwhile Elvis swivels on,
tick tock tick tock tick tock. If you wind him up, he sings, Down
at the end of Lonely Street, it's Heartbreak Hotel.

Finally she looks in Willie's rusted old tackle box, jammed into
the back of their bedroom closet. It's not in the top layer, filled
with hooks and lures and pliers and knives and loose change and
God knows what all. She starts to close the top, then — she will
never know why she does this — she lifts that tray out and finds
the stack of letters in the bottom of the box, bound with a rubber band.

THERE ARE MANY LETTERS, written in a large, loopy
though somehow feminine hand, all addressed to Willie at a

post office box — since when does he have a PO box? Roxy goes
hot, then cold. She picks up the entire tackle box and goes over
to sit down on the blue rocking chair in the corner beneath the
cross-stitched sampler on the wall, made by her grandmother up
home. It says, "Peace be with you while you stay, God be with
you on your way." Roxy can hardly breathe. She takes an envelope at random — not the top envelope — and smooths the letter
out on her knees. It's dated September 18, 1990, five months after
Alice died.

Honey
    You have just left and I am laying here on the bed still
thinking about you and everything we do together and I
can tell you, it means the world. I don't know what I would
of done if it was not for you, me or Ricky, ether one. I am so
glad he is out of here now he is doing so good isnt he. I do not
know what would have happened to him if he would not have
met you. If I would not have met you ether. I just hope he can
stay off the drugs, what do you think about that. Oh honey I
hate to get up from here I can still smell you in this bed and
feel your arms around me. You are so good to find some time
for me I know it is hard for you to get away. You know I want
you when ever I can get you honey but don't worry I do not
expect a thing, I am just so happy to see you whenever you
come in this door with your big smile. I am just going to lay
here for a wile and think about you honey then I am going to
get up and take a bath and go over to the rest home and see
Bill as it is Sunday thogh he don't know it of course. But then
sometimes I think, well he might, so I will go over there and
take him some potato chips, he loves potato chips, and feed

them to him one by one and tell him things just like he can hear me such as how the Atlanta Braves are doing, because who knows? Who knows a damn thing in this world? not me that is for sure ha ha except I am just happy that you are in it with me ever minute that I can get with you it makes all the difference. I will see you when I see you

I love you love you.

Love you
Mary Etta

Roxy's hands are shaking so much that it's hard for her to fold this letter back up and put it back in its envelope, one of those cheap oblong envelopes from the dime store. The return address reads

1104 Peach Road
Holly Springs
GA 30456

Which Roxy knows to be a country town someplace south of Macon, an old mill town she thinks, but definitely below the gnat line. A sleepy dead little redneck racist mill town, lots worse than Rose Hill. She grabs up another letter and reads

Bo,

Sometimes I think, well, what if I had never met you? What if Ricky had not gone up before that nice lady judge who sent him to the special school where you taught him music and saved his life? what if he had just went straight to prison instead, which he probably should of. Then he never would of met you, I never would of met you. What would of happened to us then, I wonder? and now Ricky is doing great at Ga. Southern, he has got a 3.5 average, did I tell you that, and a nice regular girlfriend and the band has got as many gigs as they can take while still in school, it sounds like too many to me tho. Sometimes I worry that there is something real bad out there waiting on Ricky around the bend but lord I hope not. I know I have got to quit thinking like that. I worry that he will go crazy because Bill was pretty crazy you know, even before the accident. I have not told you the half of it, the accident was just the last straw. Though I can not say that I did not love him, I did with all my heart, tho we was just kids of course at the time. And at least he got me out of that house. And Bill done the best he could, I will have to hand it to him. He did not deserve what has happened to him but then nobody does.

Bo? Where did that Bo come from? Roxy feels like she doesn't know Willie at all, like she never knew him. Furiously she tears through the pile of letters, lines jumping out at her.

> I wish you could come over here more but I know you can not Believe me I apreciate every minute of your time I can get I know it is hard

and

> Bill apreciates that new TV so much I know even if he can not talk, it is company for him. Thank you so much you are so good to do it. You are so good to all of us.

Jesus! What does Willie think he is, the fucking United Way?

Bo,

    If there is one thing I can not stand, it is for you to feel sorry for me. I am glad to do an honest days work too. Cleaning is honest work. I have done worse, believe me. Plus I make more money than Rita, you remember Rita that lives in number 14? And she is a substute teacher at the high school. I know this is a shame but it is true. They is something wrong with this country. Also I can quit a person anytime if I want to, and not lose my job. I do not have to pay SS ether, ha! I have done a lot worse as you know, right after the accident when Bill was in the hospital and I had those little children at home, I am ashamed of what I done sometimes to put bread on the table. Well I was drinking then too. That was in Florida, down at Tampa, all them tourists in the plaid shorts. Well you never know what you will do until you have to. It is just a good thing Bill had been in the army or we would of all been up shit creek without a paddle, but at least he got the medical and now he is in the VA. I truly do not know what we would of done without the VA. Lord I was not but 22 when it happened, I am not even old now, you know it? I forget. I have felt old as the hills for years now but I am not relly. You make me feel young again, you have gave me back some of my life honey.

    And to tell the truth, I like to clean, I am good at it too. I have got an eye for it according to all. It makes a body feel good to straighten up peoples shelves and fold their laundry and put the magazines in stacks on their coffee tables and line up all the chairs and leave everything so clean and neat and straight as it is not in life, ha! Where everything is a goddamn mess. I will even iron their pillowcases if I have got time. Mister Souci says I am the best he ever saw, he swears by me. He is the one that owns Pinetops. So do not pity me, I do not want your pity honey, just save some of the other stuff for me, ha!

Your Mary Etta

and

Well of course your wife is sad what in the world can you expect. It is harder for the mother, it just takes a long long time honey. There is a lot of us that lives in sad houses believe you me. But you go on, you have to. You will too. After Bills accident somebody told me it is like walking cross a big field in the dark all you can do is put one foot in front of the other and keep on walking and some day you will get there. You will too.

Roxy remembers something her own mother used to say when times got tough, that you just have to "keep on keeping on." In spite of herself, Roxy sort of likes this Mary Etta, Mary Etta is her kind of girl. Plus Mary Etta can't help any of this, she is just a poor dumb woman, a *maid* for Gods sake! with about a sixth grade education. A poor disadvantaged person that Willie has clearly taken advantage of, damn his sorry hide.

This reminds Roxy of that poem from Willie's class, the one about the girl that got raped by the swan. What was that girl's name? Leda! Roxy still remembers the ending. "Did she put on his knowledge with his power, before the indifferent beak could let her drop?" and clearly the answer is No, she did not. She did not put on one damn bit of knowledge or power either one, clearly

---

she was an ignorant slut to begin with and she is still an ignorant slut today. She did not take in a damn thing, Roxy thinks furiously, but she is not really furious, not entirely, because there is something so sad and so sweet about this woman, oh Roxy *gets it*. She gets it all too well. Willie is a sucker for a sad story. But he is not a psychiatrist, damn him.

It is not really Mary Etta's fault at all. This makes Roxy madder than ever, she's going to wring Willie's neck when he gets here. And then she is going to divorce him. Willie can keep his bass boat and his damn convertibles. She is going to keep the 4Runner and the house in town and the rental properties which they never would have owned if wasn't for her anyway. But oh God, who will get *this* little house? She reads on.

Honey,

You have just left but I cant do a thing, I can not come back down to earth. I can not ever thank you enogh for taking me to Daytona, it is the nicest thing that anybody has ever done for me, ever. I loved that hotel and even roses in the room. It is a birthday I will always remember. I loved the white cloths and the candles on the tables and the moon on the water when we walked out onto the beach and you said that beautiful poem to me the one about that other beach, I will never forget it. Also what we did on the balcony, it is probably against the law ha ha! I will never forget that ether. Honey I could just eat you up with a spoon. I have got to calm down I have got to get some sleep you know tomorrow is my longest day first the Armstrongs then Mrs. Johnson then the Pinetops Motel. I think I will just stand dreaming at every bed thinking of you. Well thanks. Thanks thanks thanks baby, I am yours for ever no matter what.

Mary Etta

Dover Beach! Roxy can't believe he said "Dover Beach" to her. This is unforgivable, the worst thing of all. This is *their* poem, hers and Willie's. *Was.* This was their poem which has always reminded her of this very place, Fernandina Beach, where they have spent so many days and nights and hours of their lives, where Roxy thought they were so happy. *Ah love, let us be true / To one another!*

Right. Roxy puts this letter back into the stack and sticks them all in the bottom of the tackle box and puts it back in the closet and closes the closet door. She is never going to look at them again. They are too upsetting. She does not *need* this! She is either going to kill him or leave him, one, she just can't decide which.

Roxy drives down the beach to Food City and buys red potatoes and celery and eggs and mayonnaise and French dressing and everything else she needs to make her famous potato salad because she can't think of anything else to make right now. She buys a Hormel Cure 81 ham and cloves to stick into it, and bananas and Cool Whip and vanilla wafers and pudding mix for banana pudding, which used to be Lilah's favorite when she was a little girl. After all, Lilah is bringing this brand-new boyfriend to their home for the first time, they'll have to eat *something,* it is certainly not Lilah's fault that her daddy is an adulterer.

Roxy buys two bottles of white wine and two bottles of red and a six-pack of imported beer because who knows what this boy will want to drink? They've already got plenty of liquor back at the house. Roxy drives home and makes herself a gin and tonic and unloads her groceries and boils the potatoes and the eggs and sticks little cloves into the ham like it is Willy's head, and puts it in the oven. She probably *is* going to kill him, but not in front of Lilah. She is not going to embarrass Lilah no matter what. She chops up the celery and the onion and the pickle and adds it to the potato salad, which turns out to be delicious. Good. The smell of the ham cooking fills the house. Maybe she'll make some corn bread too. Roxy makes great corn bread.

She takes a nice long shower and washes her hair and puts on some sexy new underwear from Victoria's Secret and even perfume, so Willie will see what he's missing. She puts on her aqua V-neck top and some white pedal pushers and gold high-heel sandals and sits at the old oak table waiting and watching Elvis's legs swing back and forth, back and forth, back and forth. *Down at the end of Lonely Street at Heartbreak Hotel. You make me so lonely, baby, I get so lonely, I get so lonely I could die.* The sun puts on a big Technicolor show going down, but nobody cares. Nobody comes. Roxy smokes a cigarette and taps her foot. She pours herself some more gin. She takes the ham out of the oven and makes the banana pudding.

She has never been so mad in her life.

She can't decide whether she's going to confront Willie immediately, before Lilah and Kyle arrive, or wait until after they've left. Obviously it would be better to wait until they've left, but the question is, *can* she wait? Can she even keep herself from dumping this banana pudding all over Willie's head the very minute she sees him? But then nobody would get to eat any of it after she has gone to all the trouble of making it, and anyway, it's Lilah's favorite. Lilah sounded so weird on the phone. Roxy feels weird too, right now, but not like she is floating above herself, the way she has often felt before. She feels like she is somehow *concentrated,* more herself than she has ever been. She feels strong. And she can do it, she can wait. She's got to, for Lilah's sake, because they could never fake it for the rest of the weekend, her and Willie. They have never faked anything.

Oh, but that's a lie, isn't it? Willie's been faking it for years, the son of a bitch, while she thought he loved her so much. She tries to remember back to that time which is all a blur anyway. But wasn't it the summer of 1990 that Willie took her on that Blues Cruise out of Miami, with Taj Mahal and Sleepy LaBeef? And Roxy thought they had so much fun? Now she feels like a fool, an idiot. And wasn't that the same year they went up to Gatlinburg for Valentine's Day and rented that chalet with the hot tub? Was Willie thinking about this woman, this maid, the whole time he was fucking *her*? And Roxy is pretty sure that 1991 was when Willie Nelson played MerleFest, the first year they got the back-stage passes. *Oh God, who will get the backstage passes to Merle-Fest?* These letters have taken it all away somehow — all the good times, her whole marriage, her whole life with Willie is suddenly gone like a shooting star.

If Willie had pulled into the driveway right then, Roxy definitely would have let him have it, first thing. But this doesn't happen. She smokes another cigarette and drinks another gin which she can't even feel, she's so mad. She's in a zone right now where she could drink a whole bottle and it wouldn't even touch her. She makes the corn bread to calm herself down, Paula Deen's recipe with the canned corn and the cheese in it, now Paula Deen is a woman who knows how to cook for men. But who gives a damn. Roxy pours the batter into her hot iron skillet and then puts the skillet back in the oven at 450 degrees just like her mama taught them, her and Frances, so long ago. Every girl has to have an iron skillet to be a wife, Mama said. But Frances never married, bless her heart, and she was still waiting for Mr. Right when she was killed in an automobile accident on the Atlanta belt line in 1994. Frances held out for love, but Roxy was the one who got it. The one who *thought* she got it, Roxy corrects herself. Well, shit. What a crock of shit. It all seems so sad and so stupid and so long ago, oh those sweet sweet hopeful girls they used to be.

Roxy is taking the corn bread out of the oven when Willie and the kids all arrive at the same time, first the Mustang convertible, then the navy blue Saab, with lots of spewing sand, slamming doors, and crying out hello, hello. *Shit.* Roxy puts on her biggest smile and runs out to hug everybody. "Finally!" she says. "At last! I was starting to get real worried about you all."

"Mmmmm." Willie breathes into her hair, tickling her ear with his bristly beard and mustache, squeezing her hard against him before turning to Lilah. "Baby! What a surprise. I didn't know you were going to be down here." He gives her a big hug. "*Man.* This is fantastic."

"You would have known if you had a cell phone," Lilah teases him.

"And this is . . ." Willie turns to the boyfriend, holding out a hand.

"Kyle. Pleased to meet you, sir." Kyle steps forward. Willie registers the "sir." Roxy hides a smile, watching Kyle crunch his hand, that's the way they do it, these manly types. Then she remembers that she's furious.

"We're so glad to have you. Come on in the house," she says sweetly to everybody. "Here, let me take that." She grabs for Lilah's bag, but Kyle has already got it. He's a dark-haired substantial fellow with nice brown eyes and regular, pleasant features, wearing khaki pants and a white shirt, tucked in. Most of them wear their shirttails out these days, Roxy has noticed. Kyle manages to carry everything *and* hold the door open for everybody else. They all stand blinking in the sudden overhead light.

"Well! Babe, you look great," Willie says, squeezing Lilah's shoulder a bit tentatively, as if he's testing to make sure she's real. They haven't seen her for, how long now? Four months, maybe? And there's something different about her tonight, for sure. Lilah is, well, *beautiful.* She wears a long-sleeved T and black pants, a pink sweater tied around her waist, her long blonde hair springing out all around her shoulders. She's curled it, or something. She looks animated, like she's giving off sparks. "See?" she says, grabbing Kyle's arm. "Isn't this place just like I told you, just exactly?"

"You nailed it, hon," he says, looking around. "I'm so happy to be here."

Roxy is glad she had time to clean up. Still, she can't imagine exactly what Lilah has told him. And she's not sure she likes that "hon." "I've got dinner all ready," she says brightly. "But why don't you take your stuff on back, settle in, and we'll all have a drink first?"

"Mmmm. Ham, right?" Lilah says. "I can smell it. And some banana pudding for me, I hope?"

Kyle clears his throat. "Actually," he says in the deep noncommittal voice of, say, a news broadcaster, "I've got a little surprise for Lilah. I've already made reservations for the two of us down at the Ritz-Carlton for dinner. It's going to be a special night. She didn't know anything about it," he adds, seeing Roxy's surprised face. "And I know we'll want some of that ham for sandwiches tomorrow."

"Oh, Kyle!" Lilah claps her hands, a favorite gesture from childhood. "You are too sweet! He's just crazy," she tells Roxy and Willie. "He's always springing these surprises on me, I just never know what he's going to do next." Her hand flies up to her mouth. "Oh no," she says. "I think that's a really fancy place, honey. I don't have a thing with me that I could possibly wear."

But Kyle, it seems, cannot stop grinning. "Look in your bag."

"What do you mean?"

"Just look in your bag," he says. "And why don't you go ahead and take a shower, too? While I run a quick errand. Our reservation is at eight thirty, we don't want to be late. This is going to be a very special occasion."

Lilah grabs up her bags and runs down the tiny hallway, giggling.

Kyle turns to Willie. "How about taking a little ride with me, sir?" he asks. "I want to buy her some flowers."

"You can get some over at Food City," Roxy suggests. "They've got plenty. I just saw them, I was just there. In the display case right next to the produce. Or you could just pick some of that forsythia blooming right next door, by the Connors' garage. They're not even here, they'd never know. They're real nice anyway."

Over Kyle's head, Roxy sees Willie grinning at her, then making a kissy face with his mouth.

"No," Kyle says. "I mean real flowers. Roses. And actually there's a florist at 311 Hatch Street. Do you know where Hatch Street is, sir?"

"*Willie*," Willie says.

"Sir?" Kyle blinks. "Do you know where that is?"

"Call me Willie, I mean," Willie says, "and hell yes, of course I know where that is. Come on, Romeo, we'd better get a move on." He grabs two beers from the refrigerator and throws one to Kyle, rolling his eyes at Roxy as they leave. Roxy sinks down on the davenport, feeling like a hurricane has just hit this little house. Down the hall she can hear water running and Lilah singing at the top of her lungs, belting out "Angel from Montgomery" in the shower. She's got a great voice, just like her dad.

Roxy tries to relax and act normal but then suddenly she just can't stand it, she jumps up and rushes back to their bedroom locking the door behind her and takes the tackle box back out and shuffles through the letters like a deck of cards, looking at the dates. Actually they're *all* a long time back, aren't they? The most recent ones she can find are dated 1991. Roxy takes a deep breath and smooths them out on her lap.

Bo,

I saw you there in the back at Bills funeral honey, you were so sweet to come. I wish I could of spoken to you. Did you see Rita? And little Billy and Vicki and the kids came in from Panama City, did you see them? She is getting sort of fat. My daughter Lisa is the one that is beautiful and cried real loud. And of course Ricky, I bet you would not of reconized Ricky if you had seen him in the street, now would you? Doesn't he look good thogh? And that sweet girl, could you tell she is pregnant? Ricky jumped all over my brother Wayne for saying Bill's death is a blessing, but I told him, this is just what people say at a funeral. And of course it IS a blessing after all these long years but it is so sad too, Lord I don't know what I will do with myself, without Bill laying over there in the VA to tell you the truth. He never showed a sign that he could tell I was there, but I belive he did know it somehow, it was just something I felt way deep down always.

> Well goodbye for now,
> Mary Etta

Bo,

   I appreciate yr letters and yr concern. I am sorry I did not write or call you back, I could not. I just went all to pieces when Bill died if you want to know the truth, I did not expect that to happen but there it is. Seems like I could not see you any more, nor write, I can not explain this ether, thogh you have been so good to me. But do not worry, things have turned out for the best after all. I have a suprise for you! I have married Mr. Souci, that I used to tell you about, that owns the motel where I used to clean, his wife had died some time previous. He will not let me clean any more, and treats me great! We are running this motel together now. And I am wishing you the very best Bo now and always. You know you saved my life.

> Yr. grateful friend for ever and ever,
> Mrs. Mary Etta Souci

Way to go, Mary Etta! A part of Roxy is cheered up by this news. She *admires* Mary Etta, she can't help it. She ruffles through the stack again to make sure there are no more recent letters. But that's it. Shit! Twenty years ago. This whole thing was over twenty years ago. Over and done with. Ships that passed in the night, water under the bridge. The only problem is Roxy's problem now, the only problem is that she knows. That her heart is broken, that she is devastated, that's all.

She knows.

THE DOORBELL RINGS, a sound Roxy hasn't heard in years. Usually everybody just bursts in here. It rings again, a tinny blast from the past. Shit! Why are they ringing the bell, why don't they just come on in the house? Hastily she stuffs the letters back in the tackle box and shoves it back in the closet. She runs a brush through her hair and slashes on some lipstick (*Red,* God damn him!), then hurries out into the tiny hall where she almost collides with Lilah, enveloped in a cloud of perfume and wearing a low-cut black dress, where did she get *that*? Lilah has never owned such a dress in her life. And where did that cleavage come from?

The doorbell rings again.

"You answer it." Lilah pushes Roxy down the hall. "You get it . . . please?"

Roxy gives her a quick fierce hug and strides to the door. "Hel-*lo* there!" She sings out flinging it open and there stands Kyle holding the biggest bouquet of red roses in the world and smiling a goofy smile. His hair looks wet, slicked back. Somehow he has acquired a jacket and a tie. "Good evening, ma'am," he says like a boy in a play.

"Good evening, Kyle." Roxy feels like she's in the play too. She peers over his shoulder to see Willie out there in the shrubbery drawing an imaginary knife across his throat and rolling his eyes back in his head like he's dying, this would be funny if Roxy didn't hate him so much and wish he were dead.

"Come on in." She steps back.

Kyle comes in then stands there like a deer in the headlights holding his ridiculous roses as Lilah walks forward to greet him. "Oh wow, you look beautiful, hon," he says. One thing about Kyle is, he's sincere. Or he certainly seems to be. Actually he looks like he's going to pass out. He thrusts the bouquet at Lilah.

"Oh Kyle, how gorgeous," she says. Her blonde hair bounces all around her shoulders, her lips are glistening with some of that wet-look lipstick. Everybody looks wet these days.

Suddenly Kyle sticks his hand in his pocket and comes up with a shiny little camera. "Can you take our picture, ma'am?" he asks Roxy. "See, just hold it out and look in here. You can see us. That's it. Okay." He shows Roxy how to do it then springs back over to Lilah's side, pulling her close. She smiles brilliantly — they both smile brilliantly — into the tiny camera, into the future stretched out before them.

"Oh, it worked!" Roxy cries. "Look at this, it's perfect!"

"Thanks," Kyle says. "Now I guess we'd better get going."

"Okay, but I . . ." Clearly Lilah doesn't know what to do with the enormous roses until her daddy takes them from her, kissing her lightly on the forehead.

"Have fun, bunny," he says, his old name for her.

"Don't wait up for us," Lilah calls back, laughing. Her perfume still hangs in the air.

"Bye," Roxy yells out the door.

"Whew." Willie slams it. "Oh honey — " He goes straight to Roxy and hugs her tight, a big long bear hug. "He's going to marry my baby," Willie says into her hair. "He's going to fucking marry her."

"What? Are you sure?" Roxy pulls back to get a good look at him.

"Yeah, fuck yeah, he is. He really is." Willie is sort of grinning and sort of crying at the same time. "He's going to ask her tonight."

"You're kidding. How do you know?"

"Because he asked me first, damn it. He asked me for her hand in marriage. That was the whole point of making me go on that little ride with him. He told me he would always love her and protect her and cherish her. He did everything except get down on one knee."

"*Cherish?* He said cherish?"

"Yeah. Cherish." Willie puts the roses down on the old oak table.

"So then what did *you* say?"

"Well, what could I say? I said yes, damn it, sure, if that's what she wants to do. I said it's all up to Lilah."

"Then what?"

"Then he started grinning, then he hit me on the back so hard I almost fell down, then he hugged me."

Roxy can't even picture this. Willie is not a hugger of men.

"Then he shook my hand for about a half an hour, liked to kill me." Willie goes into the kitchen and makes himself a gin and tonic. "I see you've been hitting the bottle here." He grins at Roxy.

"Well, just a little. I guess I was nervous, I could tell something was up the minute she called." Roxy follows him.

"Wait, I didn't even tell you the punch line." Willie takes a long swallow. "*Then* he gets out this little box and opens it up and shows me the ring."

"He did?" Suddenly Roxy's getting light-headed, she's got to sit down. "So what does it look like?"

"Hell, I don't know. It's just a regular engagement ring, all right?" Willie pulls a chair over next to hers and sits down too. He puts his hand on her thigh.

"I mean, does it have a round diamond? Or an emerald cut, or is it square, or what? Is it gold or white gold?" Roxy hears herself rattling on and on.

Willie starts laughing. "Damned if I know. It's pretty, though. It's real big, real sparkly and everything. The works. The real thing."

"Oh my." Roxy can hardly breathe now.

Willie's massaging her knee, almost reflexively. "Seems like he's a real old-fashioned, stand-up kind of guy. He even offered to help pay for the wedding, what do you think of that?"

"Really? What did you say?"

"I said hell no, of course. I've only got one baby, damned if I won't pay for her whole wedding. Then he said, 'Well sir, I appreciate that, and of course I haven't discussed this with Lilah yet, but we may want a pretty big wedding,' and I said, 'Well then, we'll have the biggest goddamn wedding you've ever seen.'"

"They *are* grown-ups," Roxy reminds him. "I'm sure they have a lot of friends and business associates, and just think of all the people we might want to ask, too. Not to mention Kyle's family and their friends." Roxy has always, always wanted to run a big wedding, maybe because she didn't really get to have one herself. The first time, she was pregnant, and the second time, she and Willie got married by a justice of the peace wearing a Gamecocks cap under a hanging lightbulb in Darlington, South Carolina. Seth and Todd both had nice weddings, but she did not get to run them because she was only the mother of the groom, not the bride, everything would have been very different if she'd been in charge. For instance she would never have a sit-down meal because that is the kiss of death, it just stops the flow of a party dead. Roxy would have a lot of little feeding stations instead, each one with a different kind of food so everybody can move around and mingle and visit with each other. And fireworks! She's always thought a wedding should end with fireworks, though of course that would mean an evening wedding instead of afternoon.

"Be right back, honey." Willie squeezes her thigh and disappears down the hall.

Actually Roxy won't mind if Lilah and Kyle choose autumn instead of summer, autumn weddings can be so much more colorful, not to mention comfortable. The weekend after Thanksgiving would be perfect for a wedding. Or even Christmas. What about the weekend just before Christmas? The decorations could be so cute, so original. Red and green. Glitter — Roxy loves glitter. But what is she thinking? She and Willie will be split up by Christmas, God damn him, she'll be long gone. She might have another life in another town. Lilah will have to hire a wedding planner. Maybe Roxy won't even be invited.

But she can still plan Alice's wedding, can't she? as she has planned all of Alice's birthday parties and Halloween costumes and trips and school clothes and Christmas presents over the years. Alice was born on Christmas Eve 1987, they put a Christmas angel and a gold star on her crib at the hospital. She died April 20, 1990. She was almost two and a half. It was a picnic at Highland Park for all the families of the girls on Lilah's soccer team. Willie, in an apron, was grilling burgers while Roxy kept an eye on Alice and chatted with the other mothers as they set out all the food on the long table. Roxy was opening a box of paper napkins when all of a sudden she couldn't see Alice anywhere among the other kids, and then the screams went up. Alice had run out into the parking lot after a ball just as Dave Bridges backed up his SUV, going after more ice. Somehow, Willie was there already, covering the small body with his own, while Alice's blood pooled out all around him. "She's dead," he said to everybody. "Go on home, please, take the girls. Just remember Alice, just remember how she was." Roxy has relived this moment over and over and over, thousands of times. She was watching Alice and then Alice wasn't there. Everybody said it was not Roxy's fault, again and again. It was not Dave Bridges's fault either, he couldn't see her at all. It was just one of those things. But Roxy can't let it go. She has kept this terrible doubt in her mind, just as she has kept the Christmas angel and the gold star all these years, wrapped in tissue paper in the secret pigeonhole of Mama's old desk from up home. She has kept all of Alice's baby clothes too.

And over the years, she has kept on imagining Alice — little Alice here at the beach, walking hand in hand with her dad, making sandcastles, flying her kite, feeding the seagulls; sturdy Alice at eight, strong square knees and flyaway red curls; Alice a tomboy in ragged jeans at ten, surveying the world from her clubhouse up in the apple tree behind the house in Macon; Alice at thirteen, pigtailed, crazy about horses, leaning forward in her stirrups to ride through a golden field; Alice a high school cheerleader, turning cartwheels across a floodlit football field; or Alice right now, at twenty, a very good student at a very good school somewhere in New England, she's still wearing jeans and those kind of combat boots like they all wear now, all the smart girls, she's got little old-fashioned granny glasses and dreamy blue eyes and a sweet look about her, like an old-fashioned girl, like an angel. She's biting her lip as she writes in the notebook on her lap, she's sitting on the grass under one of those huge old trees that they have up there on campuses in New England. Alice hasn't even *thought* about getting married yet! And she's got plenty of time — all the time in the world.

"Honey? Honey? What's the matter?" Willie's behind her now, he's nuzzling her neck with his prickly beard, bringing her back, as he has done time and time again. Oh how she will miss him.

When Alice died, Roxy's grief was like a big dark, windy place that she was lost in, like the old abandoned Preston mine shaft that they used to sneak up the mountain to visit when she was a girl — its long twisting corridors opening into a cavern so vast that the beam of your flashlight finally disappeared into darkness, illuminating nothing, while your voice bounced back and forth, back and forth, fainter and fainter. She had stayed in this cavern for months, refusing therapy and drugs and all Willie's attempts to divert her, even for a little bit, until finally he let her be, and just tended her, waiting. For a long time Roxy was dedicated to that darkness, that intensity, sensing that to lose it would be to lose little Alice forever. This has proved partly true. But finally she went out and got a pedicure, she got her hair streaked again, she and Willie went to MerleFest, then he took her on that blues cruise. Lilah graduated from high school. Seth was accepted into law school at UVA, Todd got married. Livingston ran for governor, Roxy saw his big face every day on the billboard at the turn off the interstate to the Reliable Real Estate office where she worked.

"Honey? What's the matter?"

"Nothing," she says, setting the table. "I guess we'd better go on and eat."

Willie slices the ham while she puts a piece of corn bread and a helping of potato salad on each of their plates. She grabs the honey mustard from the refrigerator. "Okay, then," she says. He puts on a CD and they sit down where they always sit, facing each other. The seashell cat smiles its iron smile at the end of the table. Elvis's legs swing back and forth. "Time's the revelator," sings Gillian Welch. Roxy pushes potato salad around on her plate. Actually *she's* the revelator, she is, Roxy.

She can tell, or not tell. She can tell it now, or later. Or not at all. Never. But actually she doesn't know if she's capable of not telling it, of keeping such a big secret. She's still so mad. She can't eat a bite. She looks over at Willie, who's almost finished already.

Suddenly he stands up. "This is big, isn't it, baby? This is as big as it gets. Come on." He pulls out her chair.

"What? Where do you think we're going? I haven't even done the dishes, you know. They'll be back before long."

"No they won't," he says. "And even if they are, so what? Come on. It's a full moon out there. Let's take a drive down the beach like we used to."

"Right *now*?"

"Right now." He's got her by the shoulders, he's hustling her along.

"I . . . I can't," she says, meaning, *I can't do this, any of it, any longer. The truth is what you get with Roxy, she's so reliable, you can count on her.*

But he's breathing into her hair.

"Why not?" he asks.

"I . . . I . . ."

Willie draws back. He stops pushing her. He's waiting. Elvis's legs swing back and forth, back and forth. *Down at the end of Lonely Street, it's Heartbreak Hotel and I'm so lonely baby, I'm just so lonely I could die.* The hands of the clock move to nine.

"I've got to get a sweater." Roxy darts into the bedroom and opens the closet door and pushes the tackle box back where it belongs, back into the back of the closet, and piles an old quilt and some outgrown jackets and coats on top for good measure. There now! *Archaeology.* Nobody will ever know the tackle box is back there, and Roxy will never read those letters again. She feels her secret blooming like a great red rose inside her — a metaphor! Or, her secret is blooming like a great red rose *inside the garden of her body,* an extended metaphor, a beautiful image seen by no one. Known by no one except herself. Suddenly Roxy is damn proud of keeping this secret, of not hurting Willie, her soul mate, her old true love.

"Roxy, get a move on! What are you doing in there?" he's yelling out in the hall.

"Just hold your horses!" she yells back, because she's his equal now, isn't she? Finally, after all these years. She thinks of herself and Frances on that seesaw Daddy made when lightning split the old poplar — two little sisters always teetering, but perfectly balanced. Another metaphor. She remembers Frances's red wool coat and her flyaway dark curls in the April wind.

"Roxy, goddamnit! Come on!"

"Coming!" Roxy throws on her aqua scarf and grabs up the faux fur jacket she bought in Nashville. Outside it's a big full moon but a windy night. Cold. Thank God he's got the top up for once. She jumps in the convertible and Willie guns it down the driveway throwing sand everywhere. The seashell road stretches out white in the moonlight past all the dark houses ahead. *The road is a ribbon of moonlight over the purple moor.* This is a poem from high school, when Roxy was Miss Rose Hill and potato salad queen. *May the road rise to meet you.* This is an old Irish toast that Willie taught her. Willie is Irish. But Roxy is nothing but Roxy, squealing as he accelerates, just like she used to do on the Ferris wheel, way up high. Then the houses are gone and they're flying out toward the point past scrub pines and beach grass and sandy hills briefly illumined then lost in darkness as the land falls away behind them on either side. When they get to the little park at the end, Willie slows down enough to drive across the parking lot, right past all the POSTED AND STOP signs then out between the dunes and onto the beach itself.

Surely they'll be arrested.

Luckily it's low tide.

The moon is as bright as a headlight making a path across the water straight to them, it reminds Roxy of that locomotive at the Bambi Lynn Motel, its headlight bearing down upon such scenes, good Lord, some of them against the law. Suddenly Willie switches off the lights and now there's nothing but moonlight everywhere, *the moon lies fair upon the straits,* the wide beach rising to meet them like a ribbon of moonlight itself until suddenly it's all obscured by a bank of clouds. Now Roxy can't see a thing. It's black as pitch, dark as a dungeon, dark as a mine. Roxy can't see the water, she can't see the sand or the dunes beyond. If they die out here, that'll ruin Lilah's big wedding for sure. Plus it would be so stupid. She grabs his jacket, then his arm.

"Now Stevie," she says sternly. "You watch where you're going, honey. It's a mighty big ocean over there."

"Shut up, Mama," Stevie hollers. "You just stick with me," as they keep on driving down the beach into the windy dark.

Mrs. Darcy and the Blue-Eyed Stranger

It was cocktail time. The sun, which had been in and out all day, now found a crack in the piles of gray cloud and shone brilliantly, falsely, down the length of the beach, even though thunder rolled on in the distance. The ocean was full of whitecaps. Its color went from a mean gray, far out near the horizon under those clouds, to steely blue patches closer in where the sun hit it. The tide was coming in, running about a foot higher than usual, eating up the beach, bunching the people on the beach closer and closer together. It was unreliable, irritating weather, unusual for August. A strong wind had come up after the most recent shower, blowing straight in from the ocean over the waves. This wind was perfect for kites and kites had sprung up everywhere, flown mostly by grandchildren who tangled their strings or let them get caught on TV antennas and then had to have another one, immediately, from El's Hardware Store on the mainland. It was this day, August 25, nearing sunset, cocktail time in kite weather, when Mrs. Darcy received her first vision.

Below the house, Mrs. Darcy's daughters had arranged themselves together on the beach. Tall, graceful women like flowers, they leaned delicately toward one another and sipped their gin and tonics and shouted into the wind. Their family resemblance was noticeable, if not particularly striking: the narrow forehead, the high cheekbones, the dark eyes set a fraction of an inch too close together: the long straight nose, rather imperious, aristo-cratic, and prone to sinus. They were good-looking women.

Yet try as she might — and she *had* tried, all their years of growing up — Mrs. Darcy was unable to find anything of her-self in them. Mrs. Darcy was short, blonde, and overweight, with folds of flesh that dangled like dewlaps from her upper arms. She had been a pretty girl once, but she had never been a thin girl, or a fashionable girl, or a fashionable young woman. These girls took after their father; they had his long, thin hands. Inside the house, Mrs. Darcy leafed through the pile of craft books that Trixie had brought her, and looked down at her daughters on the beach. Craft books! Mrs. Darcy thought. Craft books. What does she know? Wrapping her robe about her, Mrs. Darcy moved to stand at the door.

"WHAT WAS SHE DOING when you came out?" Trixie asked. Trixie was the oldest, with three teenagers of her own. Her close-cut hair was streaked with gray, and her horn-rimmed glasses sat squarely on her nose. "What was she *doing*?" Trixie asked again, over the wind.

Maria, the middle sister, shifted her position on the quilt. "Not much, I think. Puttering around the kitchen."

"Well, there's nothing to do for supper," Trixie pointed out. "It's already done."

"I don't know," said Maria, who always deliberated, or gave the impression of deliberating, before she spoke. "I think some of the children had come in and gotten a drink or something."

"I tried to get her to help cook," Trixie said. "Remember how she used to cook?"

"You know what really drove me mad?" Ginny said suddenly. "I was telling my shrink this the other day. I mean, whenever I think of Mama, you know what I think of her doing? I think of her putting leftovers in a smaller container. Like, say, we've had a roast, right? And if it were *me,* I'd leave the roast in the pan it was in. But oh no. After dinner, she had to find a smaller pan, right? For the refrigerator. Tupperware or something. The Tupperware post-roast container. Then somebody makes a sandwich maybe, and one inch of the roast is gone, so she had to find another container. Then another, then another, then another. She must have gone through about fifteen containers for every major thing she fixed. That's all I can remember of childhood." Ginny had been leaning forward intensely, sucking on a Winston in the wind. Now she stabbed the cigarette out in the sand and flung herself back flat and her long black hair fanned out on the quilt.

"You're feeling very angry about this," Maria said in her precise, well-modulated voice. Maria was a psychologist, married to another psychologist, Mark, who sat some thirty yards behind the sisters on the deck at the back of the house, observing things through his binoculars. "Your anger seems oddly out of proportion to the event," Maria remarked.

"No kidding," Ginny said.

One of Maria's children, Andrew, came up to get his shoe tied. "*Why* can't we buy any firecrackers?" he wailed, and then ran off, a blur of blue jean legs, without waiting for the answer.

"Now, then," Trixie said. The wind had died down, it was possible to talk, and Trixie liked to get right to the heart of the matter. "It does seem to me, as I wrote to both of you, that a certain amount of, er, *aimlessness* is understandable under the circumstances. But as I said before, when I went to Raleigh last month, I just couldn't believe it. I couldn't believe the way she was living. Dust on everything, and you know how she always was about dust. She was drinking Coca-Colas. Hawaiian Punch. Frozen pizza in the refrigerator — *pizza,* can you imagine?"

Maria smiled at the idea of pizza, the mere mention of it so incongruous with their childhood dinners in Raleigh. She remembered the long shining expanse of mahogany, the silver, the peacocks on the wallpaper, the crimson-flowered Oriental rug. "Pizza!" Maria said softly. "Pop would have died."

"He did," Ginny pointed out.

"Really!" Trixie said.

"I think there has to be a natural period of mourning," Maria said, not meaning to lecture. "It's absolutely essential in the cycle of regeneration."

"But it's not mourning, exactly," Trixie said. "It's just being not interested. Not interested in anything, that's the only way I can describe it. Lack of interest in life."

"I can understand that," Ginny said.

"That could be a form of mourning," Maria said. "No two people mourn alike, of course."

"Different strokes for different folks," Ginny said. They ignored her.

"But you know how she used to keep herself so busy all the time," Trixie said. "She always had some craft project going, always. She was always doing volunteer work, playing bridge, you know how she was."

"She wore spectator heels and stockings every day," Ginny said in a passing-judgment tone.

"Yes, well, that's what I mean," Trixie went on. "And now what is she wearing? Rubber flip-flops from Kmart. She's let Lorene go, too. Lorene only comes in once a week now and does the bathrooms and the floors."

"I can't imagine that house without Lorene," Maria said. Lorene had been a central figure in their girlhood, skinny as Olive Oyl in her starched white uniform.

"Well, Lorene is just as worried about Mama as she can be," Trixie said. "As you might well imagine. I went over to see her in the projects and gave her some money and I wrote down my number for her, at home, and told her to call me up any time. Any time she goes over there to clean and anything worries her."

"That's a good idea, Trixie," Maria said.

"Well," Trixie said. Trixie saw her two daughters, tan, leggy Richmond girls, far down the beach, walking toward them in the foaming line of surf. "I'll tell you what I told Mother," Trixie continued. "I said, 'Why don't you start going to church again? Why don't you join one of these retirement clubs in town? They have all sorts of them now, you wouldn't believe it. They go to the mountains and they go to New York to see plays and everything is all arranged for them ahead of time. Why, we saw a group of them at Disney World in Florida, having a perfectly wonderful time!'"

"I can't see that," Ginny said.

"Of course you can't, you're twenty-seven years old," Trixie snapped. Sometimes she felt as though Ginny were her daughter instead of her sister.

"Still, she did show some interest in coming down here," Maria pointed out. "Surely that's something."

"Interest but no initiative," Trixie said. "I suggested it, I picked her up."

"Aren't you something?" Ginny said.

"Ginny, I realize that you're going through a difficult period of adjustment yourself, but that is no excuse, no excuse at all for childish behavior. I think we have to start thinking in terms of a nursing home, is what I think. Caswell agrees, incidentally. Of course that would involve selling the Raleigh house: it would all be quite complicated. But I do see that as a distinct possibility."

"There's Margaret, why don't you ask her what she thinks?" Maria said. "She came over to see Mama this morning."

"When?" Trixie asked sharply.

"Oh, about ten o'clock. You were at the Hammock Shop, I think."

"Gotcha!" Ginny said.

MARGARET DALE WHITTED, who had divorced one husband and buried two, made her slow majestic way across the sand. A white caftan billowed about her and she carried a martini balanced carefully in one hand. "Cheers!" Margaret said when she reached them, steadying herself with a hand on Trixie's shoulder. "My God, dears, it's not worth it, is it? Nature, I mean." Margaret's voice was raspy and decisive, the voice of someone who has always had money. She had known their mother for forty summers more or less, since the time when Lolly and Pop had built their house, the Lollipop, next to Margaret's Sand Castle. There had been nothing, almost nothing, on the south end of the island then. They had been pioneers.

"Margaret, how are you?" Ginny asked. Ginny had always liked Margaret.

"Oh, there's some life in the old girl yet." Margaret gave her famous wink. "I'm having some trouble, though, just between us girls, with this shoulder. I fell, you know, in March."

They didn't know.

Margaret sipped her martini and stared out to sea, breathing heavily. Ginny stood up and dusted the sand off her jeans. Margaret's gold medallion winked in the fitful sun.

"We wanted to ask you about Mama. What you think, I mean," Trixie said. Trixie noticed how her own daughters had seated themselves just far enough away so that no one could connect them with her at all.

"Mama, Mama, it's all tangled up," wailed Christy, Maria's six-year-old daughter.

"Take it to Daddy," Maria said. "He'll have to cut some string."

Trixie and Maria stood up.

"Well," Margaret rasped. "I'll tell you what, girls. It's hell to get old." Margaret laughed and steadied herself on Trixie's elbow. The wind blew Margaret's huge white skirt about their legs, entwining them. Suddenly Ginny dashed off after a Frisbee, got it, and threw it back to Bill, Trixie's son. Maria picked up the quilt, shook it, and walked back up toward the Lollipop, the deck, her husband. Through the binoculars, he stared toward the ocean, his red beard curled around his pipe. The screen door of the Lollipop opened and Mrs. Darcy came slowly out, blinking in the sun.

Down on the beach, Margaret raised her silver cup aloft, "Cheers, honey," she said to Trixie.

"Look, Mama, look!" Christy and Andrew started up a howl. "Look, Mama, a rainbow, a rainbow!"

Maria nodded to them, with exaggerated gestures, from the deck.

"How's it going, honey?" Mark asked without lowering the binoculars. "Getting everything worked out?"

"Oh, it's just so difficult." Maria put the quilt over the rail and sat down in a chair. "Ginny is so difficult, for one thing. I hate these whole-family things, I always have. There are so many things to work through. So many layers of meaning to sort out."

"Actually, there's a great deal to be said for the nuclear family structure," said Mark, focusing his binoculars on the sight he had been viewing for some time now, Ginny's breasts moving beneath her pink T-shirt as she played Frisbee with his nephew.

But Ginny stopped playing Frisbee then and turned to stare out at the ocean and Bill did too, as all movement stopped along the beach.

"Mama, Mama, Mama!" Christy screamed.

"I'll be damned," Mark said, putting the binoculars down. "A double rainbow." Mark put an arm around his wife and they stood together on the deck, nuclear and whole, like a piece of architecture against the wind.

"All the summers we've been here, I've never seen one of those," Trixie remarked to Margaret.

A giant rainbow shimmered above the horizon, pink and blue and yellow and blue again, above the mass of clouds, and as they all watched, the clouds parted and a second rainbow — almost iridescent at first, the merest hint of color — arced across the sky beneath the first, spreading color until the rainbows seemed to fill the sky. The children on the beach, caught in motion as definitely as if they had been playing Statues, broke up with a whoop and began to cavort madly, whirling around and around in all directions. Sand and Frisbees flew. Up on the porch, behind Maria and her son-in-law, Mrs. Darcy moved hesitantly at first, in an oddly sidewise, crablike fashion, farther out into the afternoon. Mrs. Darcy wore her flip-flops and a flowered housecoat. She raised her arms suddenly, stretching them up and out toward the rainbows. "Ai-yi-yi!" she wailed loudly. "Yi-yi-yi!" Mrs. Darcy stood transfixed then fell forward into the sandy deck in a dead faint.

THE NEXT MORNING DAWNED clear and beautiful. The joggers were at it early, pounding the road from one end of the island to the other. Fishermen lined the bridge over the sound to the mainland, dropping their lines straight down into the outgoing tide. Marsh grass waved in the wind and strange South Carolina birds flew overhead. Somebody caught a blowfish. Along the road beside the biggest houses, white-uniformed maids came out to dump the bottles and trash from the night before, getting their houses ready for the next day, lingering to gossip in the sun. Children ran out onto the piers that protruded far into the marsh, checking crab traps, squealing at the catch.

At the far south end of the island, Ginny prowled the beach for sand dollars, watching the shifting tide pools as the tide rushed out to sea. She remembered getting on her raft in the sound at about the middle of the island, drifting lazily through the marsh grass past all the piers, gaining speed as the tide picked up, rocketing around the south end of the island finally, right here, jetting out to sea to be knocked back at last by the waves. Ginny remembered the final, absolute panic each time in the rush to the sea, how strong the current was. In this memory she seemed to be always alone. Maria never wanted to do it, Trixie had been too old, off at school or something. But there had been friends every summer. Ginny remembered the Mitchells from Columbia, whose house had been sold five years ago. Johnny Bridgely, her first beau. The Padgetts who always had birthday parties with piñatas. Ginny sat in a tide pool and played with the hermit crabs. The water was so clear you couldn't tell it was there sometimes. She could feel the sun, already hot on her shoulders, and nothing seemed worth the effort it took.

At the Lollipop, Mrs. Darcy lay back on a daybed in the big rustic living room, surrounded by children and friends who urged her back each time she attempted to rise.

"I still think, Mama, that it would be very silly — I repeat, very silly — for you not to let us take you right up to the doctor in Myrtle Beach. Or down to Georgetown if you prefer. But you cannot just ignore an attack like this," Trixie said.

"I wonder if this might not be some sort of ploy," Maria whispered to Mark in the kitchen. "An attention-getting thing. Unconscious, of course."

"It's possible," Mark said. "Or she might have had a slight stroke."

"A stroke!" Maria said. "Do you think so?"

"No, but it's possible," Mark said. Mark got a cup of coffee and went out onto the beach. His nieces, already oiled, lay on their stomachs reading books from their summer book list. His own children were making a castle in the wet sand, farther out.

"I think I'll scramble some eggs," Mrs. Darcy said, but the lady from across the street, Susie Reynolds, jumped up and began doing it for her.

There was something new about Mrs. Darcy, something ethereal, this morning. Had she had a brush with death? A simple fall? Or what? Why did she refuse to see the doctor? Mrs. Darcy looked absurdly small lying there on the rather large daybed, surrounded by pillows. She still wore the flowered housecoat. Her small fat ankles stuck out at the bottom, the bare feet plump and blue veined, with a splotch or two of old red nail polish on the yellowed toenails. Her arms were folded over her stomach, the hands clasped. Her hair curled white and blonde in all directions, but beneath the wild hair, her wrinkled face had taken on a new, luminous quality, so that it appeared to shine.

Trixie, looking at her mother, grew more and more annoyed. Trixie remembered her mother's careful makeup, her conservative dress. Why couldn't she be reasonable, dress up a little, like the other old ladies out on the beach? Even Margaret, with her martinis and her bossiness, was better than this. *Life does go on*, Trixie thought.

Mrs. Darcy smiled suddenly, a beatific smile that traveled the room like a searchlight, directed at no one in particular.

"She seems a little better, don't you think?" Mrs. Reynolds said to Trixie from the kitchen door. Mrs. Reynolds brought in the plate of scrambled eggs and toast.

"Oh, I don't know," Trixie said. "I've been so worried, I just can't tell."

"Well, I think she looks just fine," Mrs. Reynolds said. "I'll go on back now. Call me if you need me, honey."

Mrs. Darcy sat up and began to eat. Maria, book in hand, watched her silently from the wicker armchair. Morning sun came in the glass doors, and a cross breeze ruffled the pages of the magazines on the table. Bill came back for his flippers and mask. The volume of the children rose from the beach. "How do you feel now?" Maria asked carefully.

Mrs. Darcy's watery blue eyes seemed to darken in color as she looked at her middle daughter. "When I saw the rainbow," she said in her soft southern voice, "why, it was the strangest thing!

All of a sudden I felt this, this *presence*, I can't tell you what it was like, it just filled me up until I was floating. Then I saw him."

"Saw *who*?" Maria put down the book and leaned forward in her chair. In the kitchen, Trixie dropped a coffee cup with a clatter and came to sit at the end of the daybed.

"Why, I don't know!" Mrs. Darcy said in a wondering sort of way. "I just don't know!" She began to eat heartily.

"Mother, I don't believe I quite understand," Maria said calmly. "Do you mean that you saw a stranger, some strange man, on the deck? Or did he come into the house from the front?"

"Oh, no," Mrs. Darcy said airily, waving her fork. "Oh, no, nothing like that. I went out on the porch, I was looking at the rainbow, I felt this overwhelming presence everywhere, oh, I just can't tell you what it was like! Then I saw him." She beamed at them. "Trixie, honey, could you bring me some salt?" she asked.

Trixie rose automatically, but was stopped by the sight of her son Bill standing in the kitchen door, flippers and mask in hand, staring at his grandmother. "Go on down to the beach," Trixie said to him. "Go!" He went. Trixie got the salt, came back and gave it to her mother who sat placidly munching toast and dropping crumbs all down the front of her housecoat.

"Could you be a little clearer, Mother?" Maria asked. "I'm still not sure who this man was."

"But I don't *know*!" Mrs. Darcy said. "Thank you, dear," she said to Trixie, and sprinkled salt liberally on her eggs. "He had long hair, he wore a long white thing, sort of like Margaret's dress as a matter of fact, you know the one I mean, and he had the most beautiful blue eyes. He looked at me and stretched out his arms and said, 'Lolly.' Just like that, just my name."

"Then what?" Maria said.

"Then I went to him, of course." Mrs. Darcy finished her breakfast and stood up. "I may have a swim," she said.

"Oh, I wouldn't," Trixie said quickly.

Mrs. Darcy seemed not to hear. Training her new smile upon each of them in turn, she went into her bedroom and softly closed the door. The sisters stared at each other.

"That beats everything I've ever heard!" Trixie said. "You see why I brought up the nursing home?" Under the brown thatch of hair, Trixie's face looked nearly triumphant, causing Maria to reflect fleetingly upon the strange accident of birth, the fact that if the woman facing her had not happened to be her sister, they would have had nothing in common at all. *Nothing!* Maria thought.

"I think we have to proceed very carefully here," she told Trixie. "Let me go and discuss this with Mark."

Trixie went upstairs to lie down, thinking, as she climbed the stairs, that Caswell had been right after all. They should have gone to Sea Island by themselves.

Ginny had joined the others on the beach, standing with Mark at the water's edge to watch the children swim.

"Let me put some of this on your back," Mark said, holding up a bottle of suntan oil.

"No, thanks," Ginny said. "Please. Not any more."

Mark put the top back on the bottle. "Well, what happened with Don, then?" he asked. "You want to talk about it?"

"No," Ginny said. "I don't."

"Mark, Mark!" Maria came running toward them. She arrived; she told them everything. Ginny began to laugh.

Bill came dripping up out of the water, followed by the girls. "There's a real strong undertow," he yelled to everybody. When they didn't answer he came closer, pushing the face mask up. "Grandma's going batty, isn't she?" he said to his uncle and aunts.

"Is that true?" the girls demanded. "Is she going to go in a nuthouse?"

"Of course not," Ginny said.

"What's a nuthouse?" Christy asked.

Ginny was laughing and laughing.

"This will take some thought," Mark said, pulling at his beard.

Slowly and daintily, Mrs. Darcy made her way past the whole group of them and stood at the edge of the ocean to adjust her red rubber bathing cap. Her skin was so white that she looked startling among the sun-browned children in the surf. She turned once, waved, before she walked straight out into the waves until they were hip high. Then she raised her hands and dove.

"You know I don't believe I've ever seen your mother swim before," Mark said to Maria.

Maria stood open-mouthed. "She doesn't," she finally said. In years past, her mother's beach routine had never varied: up around nine, a walk perhaps, some shopping, drinks with friends, but never — never — had she actually gone for a swim. Maria burst into tears. "She needs help," Maria said.

"Oh, come on," Ginny said. "We all do. Look, I'll drive all the kids up to the trampoline for a while, okay?"

Before them, just beyond the breakers, Mrs. Darcy's red bathing cap bobbed like a cork in the rise and fall of the waves.

THREE DAYS PASSED, ALL of them sunny and blue, calm and idyllic. Caswell arrived. The Lollipop settled into the old routine of summers past. Plans were made and carried out, menus planned, groceries were bought and cooked. Caswell and Mark chartered a boat out of Murrell's Inlet and took Bill fishing. Maria was always amazed at how well Caswell and Mark got along; she couldn't imagine what they had to say to each other. Trixie's girls found some nice boys from Charleston to date. Old friends came and went. Margaret took Mrs. Darcy to lunch at Litchfield Plantation. Pop was mentioned often, casually and affectionately, and Mrs. Darcy seemed not to mind. She did not mention the "presence" or the blue-eyed stranger again. She continued to pad about the house in her flip-flops and housecoat, but she showed some interest in the cooking and she played checkers with Christy and Andrew.

By Thursday morning, Trixie had begun to relax. She thought it was time to interest her mother in Shrink Art. Trixie had brought all the materials with her, and now she unpacked them and brought them into the kitchen and spread them out. The others had gone crabbing up at Huntington Beach State Park. "Now Mother," Trixie said, "let's do a little bit of this. It's really fun, really easy, and you'll just be amazed at what you can make."

"Maybe a little later, dear," Mrs. Darcy said. Mrs. Darcy sat in a wicker armchair, looking out at the beach.

"No," said Trixie said firmly. "Now is the time. They'll be back before long, then we'll have to make sandwiches. Now look, Mother, all you do is trace designs onto this clear plastic, using these permanent markers. Or you can make your own designs, of course. Then you cut them out and bake them for three minutes and — "

"*Bake* them?" Mrs. Darcy echoed faintly.

"Sure!" Trixie said. "Then they turn into something exactly like stained glass. They're really lovely. You can make jewelry,

Christmas ornaments, whatever. They make lovely Christmas ornaments."

"But how would you hang them up?" Mrs. Darcy came to stand beside her daughter at the table.

"Oh, you punch a little hole before you put them in the oven," she said. "I've got the hole puncher right here."

Trixie spread out the plastic sheets, the designs, the permanent pens. She turned the oven on to three hundred degrees. "Okay," she said. "All set. Which one do you want to try?"

"Maybe this," Mrs. Darcy said. She placed a sheet of the clear plastic over a design involving a bunch of tulips stuck into a wooden shoe. Trixie was mildly surprised by the choice, more surprised by her mother's easy acquiescence. Everything seemed so much better since the weather had cleared. Perhaps things were not so complicated, so serious as they had thought. Still, it was reassuring that Mark and Maria had arranged treatment for Mother, back in Raleigh. A most competent doctor by all accounts, highly recommended. Trixie felt sure that Mother would agree to see him. The teakettle began to whistle. Trixie got up to make the iced tea. This pitcher, old heavy brown pottery, had been at the beach house ever since she could remember. Out of the corner of her eye, Trixie watched Mother biting her tongue a bit and gripping her marker tightly, like a small, pudgy, dutiful child. Trixie added lemon and sugar to the tea.

"There now," Mrs. Darcy said, sitting back in the chair, her round wrinkled face rather flushed. She looked at Trixie hopefully. "Now what?"

"Now you cut it out," Trixie said, "and punch a hole, and we put it in the oven for three minutes."

Mrs. Darcy cut the design out carefully, using some old round-tipped scissors that Trixie had found way back in a kitchen drawer. Trixie took the design from her, somewhat distressed to find that Mother had colored the tulips blue. Still, it would not do to appear disparaging. "This is so pretty, Mother," Trixie said. "Now you can watch it shrink if you want to." Mrs. Darcy turned her chair, so that she could peer through the oven's glass door.

The kitchen door burst open at that moment and there they were suddenly, all of the rest of them, with two coolers full of scrambling crabs and the children all talking at once.

"Just leave those on the porch," Trixie directed. "Go on, take them right back out this instant. Right now. Go on. Bill, what do you mean tracking in here this way? Go take off those shoes on the porch."

"Bill fell in, Bill fell in!" Andrew danced up and down, still holding his piece of twine with the rock and the chicken neck tied to the end.

"You're so excited, darling," Maria said.

"Well, I'm starving." Still wearing her black bikini, Ginny came barefooted into the kitchen, so that she was the closest one to her mother, the only one who actually saw Mrs. Darcy's face as she watched her tulips shrink, and shrink, and shrink before her eyes. Ginny stopped, caught in the oddest sensation: it might have been her own face before her, it might have been her own voice that began to scream.

A FINE DRIZZLE FELL all day Sunday, jeweling the surface of things. They left for hours, it seemed, and their leave-taking took up most of the day. Lolly knew that they had been up far into the night, deciding what to do about her. She realized that she had created a problem by her refusal to leave. But she did not *want* to leave yet, and she had never created a problem before — not ever, for anyone. So. She remained stubborn and went to bed early, leaving them to deal with her as best they could.

As they told themselves over and over, the others had to go. There was no question. Caswell had to fly straight up to Washington for a conference. The children's schools were beginning again, and Trixie had to buy school clothes for the girls. Maria and Mark had faculty meetings, workshops, classes. It was hard to believe that Christy would be in the first grade.

"Look," Ginny had surprised them all by saying. "Look, I'll stick around for a week or so. Okay? You all go on. I'll bring her back to Raleigh before long." It was so unlike Ginny to be responsible that Maria had stared at her with considerable interest.

"I'd like to know why you're doing this," Maria said.

"Why not?" Ginny had answered.

And they had left, Trixie and Caswell and their large children in the long sleek car, Maria and Mark in their van. Christy and Andrew waved madly from the rear window as long as they stayed in sight. Lolly stood on the rainswept back porch, looking across the road to see the rising mist over the marsh. She traced designs in the drops of water that clung to the sides of the water heater. Each little drop seemed singular and profound, seemed to hold some iridescence of its own, or perhaps it was just the reflection from passing cars.

"Mama," Ginny said for the third time. Ginny stood in the kitchen door wearing white slacks, a windbreaker. She looked Lolly in the eye. "Listen, Mama, I'm driving up to Long Beach to have dinner with a friend, okay? The number is by the telephone. I might be back tonight, or I might be back tomorrow. There's a pizza in the freezer. Okay?"

"Okay." Lolly smiled at Ginny and watched her leave too, running lightly down the steps, slamming into her little car.

Lolly went back in the house. The silence wrapped her up like soft cotton. She got a Coke from the refrigerator, poured it, and sucked off the foam. She smiled to herself, turned on some lights. After a while she went to the telephone and called Margaret and in a little while Margaret came, bringing the friend she'd told Lolly about.

This friend was a wealthy widow of their own age, from Norfolk. "The doctor can't seem to find any explanation for it," she said. "Some sort of damaged nerve. It's just this intense pain, right here." She lifted her forearm so that the heavy bracelets jangled like wind chimes. "Sometimes the pain is so intense I just can't seem to go out at all. I can't even get out of bed."

"I know," said Lolly. Her pale eyes darkened and focused; she smiled. "Lie down," Lolly said, indicating the daybed, and she took the stringy manicured hand of Margaret's friend in her own soft white ringless fingers.

"That's right, dear," Margaret rasped from the wicker armchair. "Don't be nervous, dear. This is exactly the way she fixed my shoulder. I was lying just like that on my own chaise longue. The green one. Remarkable. Now just do exactly what Lolly says. Close your eyes, dear. Relax. That's right. Relax."

Later, healed and radiant, Margaret's friend wanted to pay Lolly, to make some contribution at least to the charity of her choice. Lolly declined, and they all had a glass of sherry.

"Really, how do you do it?" Margaret's friend asked. "Really, if you only knew how much money I've spent on doctors. Why, I even tried a chiropractor at Virginia Beach."

"It's nothing," Lolly said.

"Listen to that!" Margaret hooted. "Ha!" Margaret blew out a great puff of smoke that hung blue in the comfortable glow of the lamps.

"It's not me at all," Lolly told them. "I'm just an agent, you might say. An intermediary."

"Do you do much work with arthritis?" Margaret's friend asked. "I have a friend who's in the most terrible pain."

"I could give it a try," Lolly said.

When they had gone, she heated up the pizza and drank a glass of milk, leaving all her dishes in the sink. She took a bath. She put on a faded terry housecoat. Opening the doors to the ocean, Lolly went out on the deck. Out here everything was cold and clean-smelling and a sharpness bit through the air, signaling summer's end. There were few lights along the beach; most of the summer people and renters had gone. Beyond Lolly, out in the darkness, waves crashed onto the sand. She could taste their salt on her lips. Lolly was not even cold. She seated herself in a damp deck chair, and leaned back. "Now," she said into the night.

Acknowledgments

VERY SPECIAL THANKS TO these good friends: my wonderful editor, Shannon Ravenel; my invaluable agent, Liz Darhansoff; Louis D. Rubin, Jr., beloved teacher back when all the stories started; my publisher, Elisabeth Scharlatt; Craig Popelars, Michael Taeckens, Courtney Wilson, Christina Gates, and all the terrific people at Algonquin Books of Chapel Hill who have made this book possible; Mona Sinquefield, for her help in preparing this manuscript; and to the memory of Faith Sale, great spirit. I am indebted to Mike Troy and Annie Dillard for the jokes in "Toastmaster," and to Cy Hogue for his legal expertise on embezzlement in "Big Girl." Maggie Powell is still my best reader ever. Most thanks of all go to our children, Page Seay and Amity Crowther, who have put up with such a scribbling mother all these years.